Replicant Night

Replicant Night

k.w. jeter

Bantam Books
New York
Toronto
London
Sydney
Auckland

BLADE RUNNER: REPLICANT NIGHT

A Bantam Spectra Book / November 1996

Book design by Chris Welch

Library of Congress Cataloging-in-Publication Data
Jeter, K. W.
Blade Runner: replicant night / K.W. Jeter.
p. cm.
ISBN 0-553-09983-3
I. Title.
PS3560.E85B59 1996
813'.54—dc20 96-2974
CIP

Published simultaneously in the United States and Canada

Bantam Books are published by Bantam Books, a division of Bantam Doubleday Dell Publishing Group, Inc. Its trademark, consisting of the words "Bantam Books" and the portrayal of a rooster, is Registered in U.S. Patent and Trademark Office and in other countries. Marca Registrada. Bantam Books, 1540 Broadway, New York, New York 10036.

PRINTED IN THE UNITED STATES OF AMERICA

BVG 10 9 8 7 6 5 4 3 2 1

For Russ Galen

By whom was I cast into the suffering of the worlds, by whom was I brought to the evil darkness? So long I endured and dwelt in this world, so long I dwelt among the works of my hands.

—*Ginza: Der Schatz oder das Große Buch der Mandäer,* trans. M. Lidzbarski, Göttingen, 1925

Replicant Night

Wake up . . .

He'd heard those words, that voice, before. Deckard wondered, for a moment, if he were dreaming. But if he were dreaming—*I'd be able to breathe,* he thought. And right now, in this segment of time, all he could feel were the doubled fists at his throat, the tight grip on the front of his jacket that lifted him clear of the Los Angeles street's mirror-wet and rubbled surface. In his vision, as he dangled from the choking hook of factory-made bone and flesh, all that remained was the face of Leon Kowalski and his brown-toothed grin of fierce, delighted triumph.

The other's stiff-haired knuckles thrust right up under Deckard's chin, forcing his head back enough to make him dizzily imagine the passage of air snapping free from the straining lungs in his chest. He could just make out, at the lower limit of his vision, his own hands grabbing onto Kowalski's wrists, thick and sinew-taut, more like the armatures of a lethal machine than anything human. His hands were powerless, unable to force apart the replicant's clench.

"Wake up . . ."

The same words, a loop of past event repeating inside Deckard's head. An echo, perhaps; because he knew the other—the replicant, his murderer—had said it only once. But he'd known it was coming. Those words . . . and his own death. Everything had to happen, just as it had before. Just as he knew it would.

Echo, dream, memory . . . or vision; it didn't matter. What was important was that there had been a gun in Deckard's hands, in the hands that were now clawing to let desperate air into his throat. His gun, the heavy black piece that was standard issue in the LAPD's blade runner unit, a piece that could blow a hole through the back of a fleeing replicant and an even larger, ragged-edged hole through its front.

And that had happened as well. Echo of time, echo of sound, the impact of the gun's roaring explosion travelling up Deckard's outstretched arms, locked and aimed, as it had so many times and so many replicants before. While the sound of death itself had slammed off the city's close-pressed walls, the intricate neon of *kanji* and corporate logos shivering as though with a sympathetic fear, the honed leading edge of the shot and its lower-pitched trail rolling over the street's crowded, incurious faces. All of them as used to death as Deckard was, just from living in L.A.; he knew they could watch him being pulled apart by Kowalski with the same indifferent gazes they had swung toward the replicant Zhora's bullet-driven terminal arc.

When he'd still had the gun, he'd walked with the black piece dangling at his side, its weight pulling down his hand the same way it'd dragged rocklike the shoulder holster strapped beneath his long coat. Rivulets of L.A.'s monsoon rains and his own sweat had oozed beneath his shirt cuff, across the back of his hand, into the checked, death-heated grip inside the aching curve of his palm. He'd walked across spearlike shards of glass crunching under his shoes. The frames of the store windows through which Zhora's dying body had crashed were transformed into gaping mouths ringed with transparent, blood-flecked teeth. He'd walked and stood over her, his sight framing a vision of empty hands and empty face, eyes void as photo-receptors unplugged from any power source. All life fled, leaked from the raw hole between her hidden breasts, dead replicant flesh looking just the same as human. The furious energy, the animal grace and fear, that had impelled her dodging and running through the streets' closing trap, spent and diluted by the drops of tear-warm rain spattering across the pavement's red lace. Deckard's energy, that of the hunter, also gone. The chase, from the moment Zhora had wheeled about in her dressing room at Taffy Lewis's club down in Chinatown's First Sector and nailed him with a hard blow to the forehead, then all the weaving among crowds and dead-run stalking over the metal roofs of the traffic-stalled cars—that hadn't exhausted him. It'd been the end of the chase, the shot, his own will inside the bullet. That had struck and killed, a red kiss centered on her naked shoulder blades. That had seemed, for a moment, to kill him as well.

Exhaustion had made it possible for the other escaped replicant to get the drop on Deckard, to pull him between two segmented refuse haulers, then smack the gun out of his grip like swatting a fly and send it spinning out toward the street. So exhausted that he hadn't been surprised at all when Kowalski, eyes maddened by the witnessing of the female's death, had picked him up like a rag doll and slammed him against the side of one hauler, spine leaving a buckled indentation in the carapacelike metal. And words, spat out angry and sneering, something with which Kowalski could hammer the killer.

How old am I? Then—*My birthday's April 10, 2017. How long do I live?*

Deckard had told him the answer, gasped it out with the last of his breath. *Four years.* That was how long all the Nexus-6 replicants had been given. They carried their own clock-ticking deaths inside their cells, more certain than any blade runner's gun.

The answer hadn't been to Leon Kowalski's liking, though he must have known it already. His eyes had gone wider and even more crazed. *More than you.* More than the man dangling from his fists had to live . . .

"Wake up!"

But that's wrong, thought Deckard. The other's face, mottled in his sight with the black swirling dots of oxygen starvation, grinned up at him. The operating remnants of his brain could remember what had happened before. Kowalski hadn't shouted the words, not that loud; he'd mouthed them softly, as though savoring their taste between his teeth. Those words, and the words that'd come after. *And he didn't lift me so far off the ground . . .*

"Wake up! Time to die!"

He could feel himself dangling in air, could hear the replicant's voice, the words shouted or whispered—it didn't matter now. It hadn't mattered before. All that mattered was the crushing pressure on his throat, the weight of his own body against Kowalski's fists squeezing off the city's humid air from his lungs. The other's words roared inside his head, each syllable a pulse of blood against his skull's thin shell of bone. Now the voice, the shout, seemed to hammer right at his ears. *Maybe that's why it sounds so loud,* thought a cold, abstracted part of Deckard, watching himself die. *Because I know . . .*

He knew what happened next. What would happen, had already happened; foreordained, scripted, bolted to the iron rails of the past, unswerving as those of the rep train that rolled in the darkness beneath the dark city.

Time to die . . .

He wondered what was taking so long. *Where is she?* wondered Deckard. *She was supposed to have been here by now . . .*

Kowalski's fists lifted him higher, his spine arching backward. The sky wheeled in Deckard's sight, needles of stars and gouts of flame penetrating the storm clouds above the L.A. towers. Police spinners drew distant, slow-motion traces of light, while the hectoring U.N. advert blimp cruised lower, seemingly within reach of his hand if he could've taken it away from the replicant's choking grasp. Emigrant vistas swam across the giant screen imbedded in the midst of the blimp's spiked antennae; an even larger voice boomingly cajoled him to seek a new life in the off-world colonies. *What a good idea,* that other part of him mused. His old life was almost gone.

The city's faces roiled across his sight; all of them, indifferent or hostile, eyes hidden behind black visor strips or magnified and glittering behind chrome-ringed fish-eye lenses. Chemical-laced tears ran down pallid cheeks, laughter broke past doubled ranks of filed teeth; a row of Taiwanese Schwinn clones jangled the bells on their handlebars, to cut through and then be swallowed up by the two-way rivers of foot and motor traffic. The black dots in Deckard's vision had grown larger and started to coalesce. Beyond them, he could see another face, made of a grid of photons. A woman in *geisha*-lite drag, Euro-ized kabukoid makeup and perfect black-shellac hair; she smiled with ancient suavity at the Swiss pharmaceutical capsule on her fingertips, then swallowed it, her coquette smile and glance turning even more mysterious. He didn't know her name, or even what she was selling; he had never known, during all the time he had walked and lived and killed inside the traplike city, and the woman had floated above him like some anonymous, disdainful angel. In his anoxic delirium, he could imagine that she was about to lean down from the adscreen and bestow a kiss upon him . . .

The Asian woman's face disappeared, replaced by the only one that mattered. Kowalski pulled him close, not for a kiss but to snap the vertebrae at the hinge of Deckard's neck. He'd be paralyzed before he was dead, but only for a few seconds, until Kowalski finished him off.

"Wake up! Time to die . . ."

Deckard heard the words again, but knew it was only memory. He saw Kowalski's smile and nothing else, as the replicant jabbed two fingers toward Deckard's eye sockets.

Maybe they finally got it right, he thought. *This time it'll be different . . .*

But it wasn't. Even as he looked down at the other's face, time started up again, the loop running as it had before. As it had so long ago. The replicant's expression changed to one of stunned bewilderment. The light behind Kowalski's eyes dwindled to a spark, then died out, as the life that the Tyrell Corporation had given him rushed from the red flower, torn flesh and white thorns of bone splinters, that had burst from his forehead. The bullet had passed all the way through and vanished, tumbling somewhere beyond Deckard's shoulder.

The thing that had been Kowalski crumpled forward, falling onto Deckard and trapping him against the shining wet pavement. Deckard clawed out from beneath him and stood upright again, regaining his balance and his breath. His vision shifted, from blurred to focussed, close to medium distance; Rachael stood at the mouth of the alley, swathed in high-collared fur, the gun that Kowalski had knocked away now clasped in both her hands—it must have landed right at her feet—and trembling from the shock of its firing, the slight motion of the trigger that had placed the steel-jacketed bullet like a quick finger tap at the back of Kowalski's head. She looked dazed, lips parted to draw in her own held breath; just as though she had never killed anyone before. As though this were the first time this had happened.

His gaze went back down to the dead replicant at his feet. Or supposedly dead. *He's doing a good job,* thought Deckard. Kowalski looked as dead as a real corpse.

"Come on, get up—" Deckard kept his voice lowered, so that none of the on-set microphones would pick it up. "It's a wrap, they got it all on tape. You can get up now."

Blood welled from the hole in Kowalski's shattered brow.

Then Deckard knew it was real.

"What the hell . . ." At the edge of the soundstage, where the fake streets, the re-created Los Angeles, gave way to bare dry concrete and steel, the flooring laced with thick power cables and data conduits like black snakes—Deckard stood up, angrily ripping the headphones away from his ears. The folding chair toppled over as he threw the 'phones at the central monitor, the one that had shown the view from the eyes of the other Deckard, the fake one, the one that had been dangling from the now-dead replicant's fists. Across the smaller screens, the angles of all the other video-cams unfolded like a magician's pack of cards.

"Now what?" The close-up on the fake Rachael showed her dropping out of character, the look of shock on her face transmuted to that of a disgusted professional as she let the heavy gun hang at the end of her arm. She sighed wearily. "Christ, this shoot's taking *forever.*"

Deckard ignored her, striding past the cameras on their automated tracking booms, the skeletal apparatuses of light and event. The drizzle from the overhead rain gantry ran off his jacket sleeves, the grid underneath the soundstage sucking away the excess from the glossily photogenic puddles. He pushed aside the *faux* Deckard, the actor playing him, and stood looking down at Kowalski. At what was left of the replicant, the bleeding artificial flesh.

"Please . . ." A hand clutched ineffectually at his elbow. "Mr. Deckard . . . you can't just—"

He turned angrily upon the production assistant, a tiny androgynous figure with heavy retro black-framed glasses. "It wasn't supposed to happen this way!" He jabbed his finger at the assistant, who fended it off with an upraised clipboard. "I was told you weren't going to kill anyone!" The circumference of his gaze tinged with red as he looked back toward the crew ringing the soundstage. "Where's Urbenton?"

That was the name of the director. Who was conspicuously missing, the folding chair that had usually supported his pudgy frame now unoccupied. *Chickenshit sonuvabitch—* Deckard felt his teeth grinding together. The director must've snuck out after the video recorders had started rolling, while Deckard had been wrapped in the view from the cam monitors, watching the re-creation of his own past. Urbenton would've known that Deckard would go ballistic when a real bullet, from a real gun, wound up churning through someone's brain.

"Come on, man . . ." The actor playing him—not a replicant like the one who had been playing Kowalski, but an actual human—tried out as peacemaker. "It can't all be special effects, you know. Sometimes you gotta go for *realism.*"

"Get away from me." Revulsion worked its way up Deckard's throat, choking him as though the replicant's big hands had been around his own neck instead of the other man's. The actor didn't even look that much like him, or at least not yet. Like most of the talent in the video industry, in addition to the remote cam implanted behind one eye, the actor also had barely visible tracker dots sewn under his skin, so that in postproduction another's face could be ceegeed over the one he'd been born with.

That new face would've been the real Deckard's. *But not now,* he fumed. *Not if I can help it.* "So where is he?" Deckard stopped just short of gathering up the front of the assistant's collar in his hand and squeezing tight, the way the dead Kowalski had done to the human actor. "Where's Urbenton?"

"I . . . I don't know . . ." The assistant retreated, sweating hands clasped to the clipboard. "He got called away . . ."

"Yeah, right. I bet." Deckard stepped over the corpse and started toward the soundstage's big rolling doors and the interlocking corridors and spaces of the studio complex beyond. "I'll find him myself. He's got one hell of a lot of explaining to do."

He didn't look over his shoulder as he strode away. But he could sense the fake L.A. dying its own death, the constant artificial rain stopping, the vehicles halting and being shut off in the middle of the crowded street, the actors and extras walking off the set. The replica blimp, a tenth the size of the one that had once actually floated above the city, dangled inert from the overhead rigging, adscreen blank and faceless.

The city's walls parted as the grips moved the scenery back. There was nothing behind them except dust and stubbed-out cigarettes, and a few scattered drops of blood.

2

A silver crescent in the sky, hanging below him. Dave Holden thought it looked like some kind of Islamic emblem, complete to the glittering star between the points of its horns. The artificial moon's gravitational field tilted the skiff's gimballed pilot's seat, hanging him upside down inside the tiny interplanetary craft. Inside the cramped cockpit area, there was barely room enough for himself and the cargo strapped onto the empty seat beside him.

Which spoke now: "You're in big trouble, pal." The briefcase kept its voice level and calm, as though unconcerned with human problems.

Holden glanced over at the briefcase. Plain black, a decent grade of leatherette, chrome snaps and bits around the handle. It looked like the exact sort that millions of junior execs carried into office towers every morning, back on Earth. By rights, it shouldn't have been talking at all; that it was doing so indicated the long-standing personal relationship between the two of them.

"Big, *big* trouble." The briefcase continued its simple, ominous pronouncements.

"I know—" Holden reached out to the control panel and dialed the skiff's guidance system toward the silver crescent's intake beam. "I *breathe* trouble." More than metaphor: the lungs in his chest, and the heart between them, were efficient constructs of Teflon and surgical steel. His original cardiopulmonary system had been blown out his back by an escaped replicant named Leon Kowalski. Back on Earth, back in the L.A. from which he and the briefcase had just flown. That bullet had been a couple of years ago; there had been others before and since then, some of which he'd fired, others that'd been fired at him. The bio-mechanical lungs sucked whiffs of imminent death and left them on his tongue. Tasting like the ashes of the cigarettes the LAPD doctors had made him give up. "Breathe it out, too."

"You're probably going to die."

"Coming from you, that's good." Holden knew that the briefcase's voice was the voice of the dead. A dead man speaking. It didn't matter whether that man, when alive, had been human or not. "You'd know, wouldn't you?"

If the briefcase had had shoulders, it would've shrugged. "Just levelling with you. That's all."

Holden ignored the last bit. Lights had started flashing on the control panel, indicating that the intake beam had locked onto the skiff. One light, he knew, would stay yellow for a few more seconds; that was the window of opportunity for abandoning the intake approach, for breaking off and turning the little craft around. And heading back to Earth or anywhere else his own death didn't seem quite so probable.

He kept his hands folded in his lap, watching and waiting until the yellow light disappeared, replaced by the green one right next to it. They were going in.

The silver crescent loomed bigger and brighter in the skiff's viewscreen. He could make out the segmented panels that formed its curved, double-tapered shape. *Croissant,* thought Holden. Thinking of French bakery goods, stuff served with real coffee. The same word, actually. He knew his mind was rattling on, filling up the empty corridors inside his head with nonsense. So there wouldn't be room for worrying about the job he'd come all this way to Outer Hollywood to do.

A delivery job. *Once I was a blade runner,* he mused; *now I'm some sort of errand boy.* He didn't mind; he'd kept his gun when he'd quit the police department. That was the main thing: he needed it now more than before.

The silver crescent grew larger, blocking out the pocked white shape of the real moon. Brown-mottled Earth lay somewhere behind the skiff; Holden didn't sweat the navigational fine points. Those had all been programmed in, along with the other details of the job. He glanced again at the briefcase, which had mercifully fallen silent. The initials on the small brass plaque under the handle read RMD. Not his, but those of the person to whom the briefcase was to be delivered. *Then he can deal with it,* thought Holden. He wondered if *M* really was Rick Deckard's middle initial, or whether that was just something that the people who'd put the briefcase together had made up out of thin air.

Outer Hollywood filled the screen now; the intake beam had brought the skiff around to the landing bays on the curve's fat convex side. There'd been a single bright flash, the viewscreen's pixels max'd out, when the skiff had passed through the focussed reflection from the bank of mirrors that served as the crescent's attached star. Holden had caught a glimpse of the massive struts and triangulated framework that held the mirror bank between the station's horns. The open steel girders looked rusted—*In a vacuum?* he wondered; *that's weird*—and warped from neglect. Cables drifted loose like beheaded snakes; the motors and other servo-mechanisms that served to adjust the mirrors' angles and catch the unfiltered radiation from the sun, looked barely functional. Light bounced off some of the mirrors and out like idiot semaphores into space, instead of illuminating the soundstages behind Outer Hollywood's pressure-sealed windows. Holden figured that'd be all right if only night scenes were being taped . . . or scenes of L.A. during the rainy season. Anything cheerful enough to require an approximation of daylight, and they'd all be out of luck.

The briefcase spoke up again. "You strapped?"

For a moment, Holden thought the briefcase was referring to the pilot seat's restraints, then realized it had slipped into the urban patois it sometimes affected. He patted the holstered weapon inside his camel's-hair jacket. "Of course." The gun felt like a rock above one of his artificial lungs.

"We'd be better off if it was *me* carrying *you.*" A fretful note sounded in the briefcase's voice.

He couldn't understand the briefcase's self-absorbed concern. *The bastard's already dead,* he thought. How could things get any worse for it? For himself, though . . . that was another matter.

"Welcome to our faciliteezz." A canned female presence, bodiless and somewhere above his head, started talking as soon as Holden climbed out of the skiff's cockpit. "For all your video production needzz . . ." Something was wrong with the hidden p.a. speakers; the woman's sibilants came out as an insectoid hiss. "Zztock and cuzztom zzets . . . fully furnizzhed editing zzuites . . . all at a competitive rate. Why go elzzewhere?"

The answer was obvious to Holden. He looked around with the briefcase dangling from his left hand, leaving his right to reach inside his jacket if need be. The orbital studio was close to being a ruin. Another hiss, of oxygen leaking through the landing bay's gaskets, sounded behind him. A chill draft in his face, like the wind down a deserted city alley, when even the last of the scavenger packs had crawled into their trash-lined burrows; no sky above, but instead a tangle of catwalks and wiring loops imbedded against the barely discernible visual field of the studio's welded exoskeleton.

Big empty spaces; the recorded greeting was the only human element immediately apparent. Other than himself, Holden noted.

"There should be some kind of offices," the briefcase suggested. "Farther inside. Where you can find out what set the shoot's been booked into."

He started walking, footsteps hollow and loud on the

metal flooring. The noise echoed down the hangarlike vista before him. The chances of his moving about, of making his delivery and leaving with no one's being aware, were nonexistent.

The orbital studio's sets had already begun collapsing into one another, false fronts and flimsy backdrops muddling together from neglect and general entropy. Holden found himself, briefcase in hand, walking past a Tara-oid antebellum mansion, fluted pillars warping out of shape, that had somehow crept among the turrets and spires of medieval Prague. A glacier of artificial grass and poppies spilled down the cobbled street, studded with crosses stamped from plastic to resemble white-painted wood; the dates on them were all from some post–World War I soldiers' cemetery. Nobody was buried there, but the draft against Holden's face still smelled like death and slow decay.

Scavengers existed everywhere; as in L.A., the real one, so above. He found one in the quieted battlefield set, an ersatz Flanders Field, next to the empty burial ground. The guy looked familiar enough, all scruffy beard and antique aviator goggles, tattered leathers flopping about a stunted frame; Holden wondered if he recognized him from somewhere in the real city's alleys.

Brass shell casings clinked in the bag slung over the scavenger's shoulder. He looked up, the scarred bridge of his nose wrinkling to signal that he smelled cop, while the black-nailed fingertips poking through the ends of his gloves continued to groom the mock battlefield. Another scent lingered in the station's canned and recycled air, that of the live ammo that had been expended in the taping of some low-budget historical epic.

"You can't hassle me, man." The scavenger's eyes narrowed behind the goggles. "I got a license."

"Yeah, well, I don't." The stuff he'd been able to do before, back when he'd been with the department, had all been left behind him, on Earth and in that other life. "So remain sweatless."

He was able to get approximate directions from the scavenger. And information: there was only one video shoot booked into the Outer Hollywood station, the first one after a long dry spell.

"It's that damn *Cinecittà Nuovo,* down in Jakarta." The scavenger's gloved thumb looked like mice had been chewing on it in his sleep, as he gestured toward some point beyond the station's curved walls. "Those people've got all that EEC money behind 'em. And they suck up *all* the video productions now." Tunnels bigger around than the station ran underneath the Indonesian Entrepreneurial Republic, the spaces lit brighter than anything sun and corroding mirrors could provide. The scavenger looked wistfully at the meager gleanings in his sack. "Man, what I wouldn't give to be able to get in there. There must be all *kinds* of shit lying around."

Holden wasn't interested in the sad intricacies of either the video or the scavenging business. "So where's the shoot going on?"

The ragged glove pointed down the length of the station's arched central corridor. "You can't miss it. Go past the Vatican and that Scottish castle with the dry moat; that's where they've got their funky L.A. all set up. There's all kinds of people hanging around. Humans and replicants . . . it's that kind of a shoot. Real blood-and-guts stuff." An eyebrow raised inside the goggles. "You might like it. Some kind of cop show."

"I doubt it." Holden started walking again, briefcase in hand. "Seen it already."

He saw the buildings up ahead, or at least part of them: the bottom sections of what were supposed to be L.A.'s canyoned towers, false-fronted and propped into position by the cobbled-together framework behind them. A small flutter ran through the bio-mech heart in his chest; some nameless emotion or twinge of adrenallike hormone. Not at seeing again the city he had left behind on Earth, or at the view of those streets in partial disassembly. *It looks better this way,* thought Holden. *Not really fake at all*—that was the marvel of it. As if the people, those shadowy corporations and architects, who'd built the Outer Hollywood station and then constructed the L.A. set inside it, had caught some realer-than-real aspect of the city. Or at least the city that had existed inside Holden's mind, with his barely being aware of it until now. *I always thought the other one was fake*—he realized that now. To see it this way, two-dimensional buildings with nothing behind their surfaces' retrofitted ventilation ducts and wiring conduits, with the people in the streets finally exposed as actors and anonymous bit players; with the monsoon rains shut off from above, the rusting pipes leaking only a few scattered drops; even the sky revealed as metal with nothing but vacuum beyond—it was an oddly comforting manifestation of his most paranoid dreamings. *If only it were true,* thought Holden.

The vision passed, along with its soul-deep significance, as though he were waking from a dream. Like rolling over in bed, it seemed to him, and opening your eyes and seeing, instead of the woman you had gone there with, some deracinated corpse staring up at the ceiling with empty eye sockets . . . or worse, nothing at all, just the empty shape, the indentation in the mattress and the other pillow, of someone who'd once been there but was never coming back . . .

I woke up a long time ago, thought Holden glumly. That was why he'd wound up quitting the department, leaving the blade runner unit. Even going over to the other side . . .

"You're wasting time." The briefcase spoke up, its voice kept low enough that only Holden would hear it. "You may not have anything on your agenda, but I've got stuff to do. So just go find Deckard, and let's get on with it."

Nagged by hand luggage; that was what life had come to. Or what there was left of it; the revelatory vision of the *faux* L.A. and his deep ruminations thereon had caused him to let his guard down. If anybody had wanted to interfere with his delivery job, all someone would've had to have done was walk up behind him and take off the back of his head with one of the pieces of rusting lighting frame that lay all around the station's floor.

The L.A. set was sunk lower than where Holden stood watching; he figured the arrangement probably had something to do with the plumbing that suctioned away the run-off from the overhead rain system and kept the water from building up around the video-cams and other equipment at the set's periphery. From this vantage point, he could see that whatever taping had been going on had now come to an end, at least for the time being. Some kind of interruption, resulting in equal measures of chaos and boredom; back when he'd been an LAPD rookie in uniform, all testosterone and Third Reich leather, he'd pulled enough overtime doing traffic control and rent-a-cop guard duty on location shoots to recognize the pattern. That'd been an even longer time ago, when there'd still been a remnant of a video industry in the city.

He pushed aside the youthful memory flash and craned his neck, trying to spot the person he'd come all this way to find. This was where he'd been told, even before he'd left Earth, that he'd be able to track down Deckard. Some bottom-rung company called Speed Death Productions—not one of the biggies; Holden had never heard of it before this—was making some kind of docudrama out of Deckard's life story. Or at least part of it: that last stint of his as a real blade runner, when he'd been tracking down that group of escaped replicants. When Holden had been told about it, he'd actually broken into laughter. It struck him as a ridiculous notion. His old partner in the blade runner unit hadn't exactly distinguished himself in a heroic manner, or at least not that time. Deckard had already wimped out and quit the force back then, mainly out of chickenshit queasiness over blowing away defenseless replicants . . . or "retiring" them, as the departmental slang put it. The head of their unit, charming old Inspector Bryant himself, had had to put the pressure on Deckard to come back aboard and help clean up the mess. Holden still got a little surge of irritation revving up his artificial organs, despite all that'd happened and all that he'd found out since then, when he thought about that arrangement. There wouldn't have been any pretext for Bryant to force Deckard back into being a blade runner if Holden hadn't been set up to take a hit from one of the escaped replicants. Which had left him with a fist-sized hole under his breastbone that the batteries and tubes and sleepless little motors now nicely filled. That'd all been one package of bad business, with lots of smaller packages marked "murder" and "betrayal" inside; and another, even larger package had come around after that, when Holden had found himself unplugged from his hospital and walking through the wet, nasty L.A. streets—the real streets, not the phony ones of the video set he now looked upon. That bigger package had been marked with a flaming red "C" for "conspiracy;" when he'd opened it, he'd found himself carrying something else in his hand for his old friend Deckard, something it would've taken only a single squeeze of the trigger on the black regulation-issue gun to deliver.

That had been a different time. Another world—literally—and another life, even though it'd all been little more than a year ago.

"I'm waiting . . ."

"Shut up," he told the briefcase. Even with his mind elsewhere, Holden's gaze had continued to scan the crowd on the fake L.A. set, looking for the one face he needed to find. A part of him had to admire the authenticism of the producers; the milling extras who made up the set's street population looked as if they might've been scooped up with a net from the earthly L.A. and deposited here. Antiquarian punks with museum-quality mohawks and chrome-studded minor body parts mingled with every variety of hopeful religious fanatic, from New Mexican *penitentes* to orange-bedsheet-clad Hare Krishnas. Whatever wasn't costume or cultic emblem was bare flesh, strapped tight under crossed networks of imitation leather, slicked shining by the artificial rain and lit to the blue pallor of ancient consumptives by the thin spectra of the coiling neon overhead.

The effect of an actual L.A. street—Holden knew the one the producers were obviously going for; it was over by the animal dealers' bustling marketplace—was marred only by the fact that the extras were on break, along with the videocam operators and other techs. Instead of passing by each other, two rivers of foot traffic between the buildings, with that zombielike facial glaze typical of longtime Angelenos, they were all talking with each other and even laughing, heading over to the honey wagons or the meager pickings on the shoot's catering tables.

A little knot in the middle of the crowd wasn't so well disposed. Some of the extras and crew glanced over their shoulders at the figures whose shouts and pleadings were barely audible to Holden.

There he is—the crowd thinned a bit, allowing Holden to spot the one with the ragged brush-cut hair and knocked-about long coat, nubbly square-ended tie pulled tight under his shirt collar. That combination of rough edges and oddly matched gear was just the way he remembered Deckard from all their time together in the blade runner unit. Then he saw the man's face and realized he'd gotten it wrong. *That's the actor,* thought Holden. *The one playing Deckard*—other than the general height and build, they weren't even close. The actress, the Rachael, was a decent-enough match . . . except for the look of disgust screwing up one corner of her mouth, which indicated that she might be fully capable of lifting the big black gun she had in one hand and icing somebody else. There was already one corpse lying in the middle of the set—Kowalski? The face-down body was hard to identify, but it appeared big enough. Blood mixing with the puddled artificial rain gave Holden the suspicion that some poor bastard of a replicant wasn't going to be getting up, brushing himself off, and cruising for stale doughnuts with the extras and other bit players.

Christ, thought Holden in sudden dismay as he caught a better glimpse of the one shouting figure. It'd taken him a few seconds to recognize his old partner; the last year or so appeared to have walked all over Deckard. The former blade runner looked harder and meaner, skin beginning to draw down tighter upon the sharpened angles of his facial bones. There was even a little steel grey scattered through his close-cropped hair. Deckard looked as if he'd spent the last year in prison rather than on Mars. Rumor had it that life in the U.N. emigration program's transit colonies was no absolute picnic, but Holden hadn't figured its effects would be this visibly corrosive.

It had to be the poor sonuvabitch's personal life. What else? Holden shook his head; he would've bet that it wasn't going to work out, that the arrangements Deckard had made would have a dismal outcome. The whole bit with Sarah Tyrell, the human original of the replicant Deckard had fallen in love with . . . Holden knew that the point would come, if it hadn't already, when *dismal* would turn to *fatal.*

"I see him." Keeping his voice low, Holden lifted the briefcase and started calculating a route through the maze of video-cams and other equipment. It wouldn't be easy; he'd have to find a way past whatever security was on the set—did Outer Hollywood have rent-a-cops?—then catch Deckard's attention somehow without revealing what was going on to everybody else standing around. His old partner didn't know that he'd be coming here, let alone that he had a talkative briefcase to deliver to him. Deckard would be fast enough on his feet—or at least Holden hoped he still would be—not to blow it by reacting to one of his old friends' unannounced presence; he'd know that Holden would only be there for a good reason, one that was best kept on the quiet until its exact nature was determined. *Still,* thought Holden, *I've got to get him somewhere in private*—handing the briefcase over in public view would be likely to get them both killed.

It appeared that the job might be easier than he'd originally expected. The loud confrontation down on the set—Deckard's shouting, with the others standing around and trying to mollify him—ended with Deckard's storming away, leaving a small bespectacled figure with clipboard far behind in his wake. The look in Deckard's eyes—even from a distance, Holden was able to intercept a quick spark of it—was one of murderous rage. Or if not murder, at least serious ass-kicking; the hunched set of his shoulders indicated that he was going off looking for someone with whom he had a score to settle.

"Come on—" Holden had got into the habit of speaking that way to the briefcase, even though he knew it had no independent means of locomotion. "We can catch him over there." He started walking again, picking up his pace as he skirted the video set, staying in the shadows beyond the range of the lights.

The sound of someone pounding on a door came to Deckard's ears. And a voice shouting—he looked down the long hallway, determining from behind which door the noise was coming.

"Hey! Anybody!" The voice was Urbenton's, pitched even higher with overexcitement. "Come on, this isn't funny—let me out of here! *You're all going to be fuckin' fired!* I'm supposed to be on the set!"

Deckard halted when he saw one of the doorknobs futilely rattling. The adrenaline pumping through his system hadn't ebbed—he'd lost none of the anger over the replicant's murder during the taping. He took a step backward, raised one leg, and kicked straight out, hitting the door's keyless lock.

The impact knocked over the person on the other side as the door wobbled to a stop, one hinge torn loose from the surrounding frame.

"Jeez—" The pudding-y director scrambled to his feet. Urbenton's face, already starting to settle into jowls despite his relative youth, shone with sweat. "You could've killed me!"

"Believe it—I still could." Deckard completed the other man's standing-up process by reaching down and grabbing Urbenton's jacket lapels in his fists, then pulling and lifting. The video director hung in Deckard's grasp, the same way the actor had hung in the grasp of the now-dead Kowalski replicant. "You sonuvabitch—I thought we had an agreement." The last words rasped out of Deckard's throat.

"What're you talking about?" Urbenton's feet kicked futilely in midair. "You gone nuts or something? What agreement?"

"Don't bullshit me. You know what I mean." He set the director down, but kept the lapels wadded in his grip. "When you brought me here—*before* even, when you came to Mars and talked me into this nonsense—you said that nobody would get hurt. *Nobody*—not even replicants."

"Hey, come on . . ." Urbenton tilted his head back from Deckard's fierce glare. "You gotta be practical, man. When you're on a video shoot . . . there's just accidents that're going to happen. That's just the way it is; we live in an imperfect universe. There's a lot of heavy equipment here—all it takes is for a lighting unit to fall on somebody's head, wham, they got a concussion. Or a camera dolly rolls over somebody's foot—"

"We're not talking *accidents* here." Deckard felt himself towering over the smaller man like some wrathful avenging deity. "What just happened on the set wasn't an accident. It was planned that way."

"How the hell would I know?" An indignant pitch shrilled in Urbenton's voice. "I wasn't even *near* the set. I've been locked in here the whole time."

"Right. Very convenient."

"Convenient, nothing—" The director managed to pull himself free. He brushed down the front of his jacket with offended dignity. "It's my shoot. I'm in charge here—at least, I'm *supposed* to be in charge." Urbenton's wide face turned to a mottled pink, as though he were contemplating active injustices. "There's been some funny stuff going on around here, though. From the beginning. The money people, the ones putting up the financing for the production—they've had some of their thugs hanging around since the shoot began. And they *really* give me the creeps—"

"My heart bleeds." Deckard had no intention of letting the fat little weasel off the hook. "But as you said, you're in charge. It's your shoot. So if somebody gets killed on the set—if even a *replicant* gets killed—it's because you ordered it to happen that way."

"What?" Urbenton blinked in puzzlement. "I don't get it. What do you mean?"

"Killed. Dead. A bullet through the back of the skull and out the front, brains all over the pavement. What the hell do you think I mean?"

"You're out of your mind, Deckard." Repulsion filtered through the director's voice and face. "I *knew* it was a bad idea to hire you for this project. Any time you bring civilians around a video shoot, they get these weird ideas about what's going on. People like you just don't understand the nature of the industry."

"What I understand," grated Deckard, "is that there's a corpse lying on your set. If your crew hasn't cleaned it up by now."

Urbenton sighed wearily. "Whose corpse?"

"The replicant you had for that last street scene. The Leon Kowalski replicant—"

The director's round shoulders lifted in a shrug. "We've got more than one of those here."

"How many of them were you planning on killing off? All the Kowalskis?"

Another shrug. "Well, we could if we wanted to. I mean, it'd be legal. They're only replicants—hell, they're not even covered under the law regarding the treatment of animals in video production. Now, if we'd brought a real snake up here—you know, for that scene in Zhora's dressing room, in that club—and anything had happened to it, the authorities would've been all over our asses. You need a major permit just to take a living animal up out of the Earth's atmosphere." A thin smile formed on Urbenton's lips. "Different situation with replicants, though. As long as you got all your security precautions in place, so they're not going to escape or anything, you can pretty much do what you want with them. Inasmuch as they're technically classified as manufactured products, and not really living things. Not like you and me."

"So you were planning on killing them." Deckard's gaze narrowed on the other man. "Just to make your goddamn video."

"I keep telling you. Nobody's getting killed on this shoot. Jeez." Urbenton shook his head. "You were the one who insisted on all these conditions, just so you'd come here at all. *I* didn't want you as a technical adviser on this production; it was the money people who laid that on me. Believe me, I could do without you hanging around, griping about the things that happen to what should be some perfectly expendable production items. For Christ's sake, Deckard, on a video shoot, replicants are nothing but fancy-shmancy props, that's all." He rolled his eyes, lifting his short-fingered hands in a gesture of defeat. "But you've got some hair up your butt about 'em, so fine; that's why I agreed we weren't going to harm any replicants on this shoot. For your tenderhearted sake, I should compromise my artistic vision—but who am I, right? I'm just the director." Urbenton emitted a dramatic sigh.

"Spare me." Deckard leaned closer in to the other man. "Just tell me why, if our little agreement's in place, you've got a replicant with his head drilled open lying at your lead actor's feet."

"You sure about this? Come on." Urbenton peered skeptically at him. "Like I said, you're not exactly hip, video production–wise. I've got some awfully good special effects people on the crew. Not just digital postproduction stuff, either; these guys do real-time." The director smiled appeasingly. "You know what? You probably saw a squib go off on this Kowalski replicant's forehead, a makeup load went splat . . . hey, it's *supposed* to look realistic."

"He went down. And he didn't get up."

"The big lug probably fainted." Urbenton shook his head. "The crew probably didn't tell him ahead of time what was going to happen. Hell, I didn't even know that was what they had planned. There's some real practical jokers around here. That's why I wasn't worried—at first—when I got yanked off the set just when the tape had started rolling. Supposed to've been a call from the money people, down on Earth; you *take* those calls, no matter what. Then somebody, I didn't see who, slammed the door on me and I found myself locked in here. Until you came along—"

"Can it." Deckard had had enough of the director's rattling on. "The Kowalski replicant didn't faint. I don't need to know about video production to see what happened to him.

I'm hip to death." His voice lowered to a grim frequency. "That was my job . . . for a long time. I know what a dead body looks like."

" 'Hip to death.' That's a good one." Urbenton nodded in a show of appreciation. "I like that. Maybe I underestimated your potential; you might have a real talent for this sort of thing. I think you're down for getting some kind of screen credit out of this gig; maybe you could parlay that into some kind of scripting gig. Additional dialogue, that sort of thing."

"You're not answering my question. I want to know how that Kowalski replicant got killed. If you didn't plan on it happening, who did?"

"I'm beginning to think . . . you're not kidding about this." From the corner of his eye, Urbenton studied him uneasily. "It happened just now? On the set?" The pink flesh turned pale. "A real bullet, and everything?"

Deckard made no reply. He didn't have to.

"That's weird." Urbenton slowly shook his head. "Because that'd be real bad news. Not just for that poor bastard replicant . . ." His voice spookily softened as his gaze shifted away from Deckard. "But for all of us . . ."

By the time he got past the doors through which Deckard had vanished, there was no sound of the others' footsteps. Or of any voices; the area was acoustically sealed off from the soundstages out in the station's main area. Holden could detect the faint buzzing of the fluorescent panels lining the narrow corridors, and nothing else.

"Well, he's gotta be around somewhere." Holden looked down the double row of featureless doorways. A fine layer of dust had drifted onto their sills. He tilted back his head, trying to catch a scent trace of his quarry; he'd quit the department, but still prided himself on keeping his quasi-extrasensory cop skills.

The briefcase had its own version of them. "There's somebody coming," it announced. "I can feel them. But it's not—" The briefcase suddenly clammed up.

"What're you doing here?" Another voice, not Deckard's.

Warning from the briefcase had given Holden the quarter second he needed to assemble a front. He glanced over his shoulder at the figure standing in the just-opened doorway behind him. A big sonuvabitch, possibly security; he had on an ID badge with a name he didn't bother to read. "I got called over to the set—" Holden kept his voice modulated down to a level of disarming self-assurance. "Beats me, what for."

The other man stepped forward and peered more closely at him. "Okay . . ." The man gave a slow nod. "They must be talking about the office setup. The interview scene—it's not on the list for today, but what the hell . . ." A disgusted shrug. "This whole shoot's so screwed up." He clamped a hand on Holden's shoulder—the guy was at least a head taller—and steered him down the hallway. "Man, I don't even know if they're *trying* to make a movie here." His glance went down to the briefcase dangling from Holden's grip. "Is that supposed to be it? The whatchacallit . . . the Vogue-Kafka. Or whatever."

"Voigt-Kampff." It didn't take even a split second for him to respond. "Sure," lied Holden. *You got it*—the other man was obviously operating on the assumption that Holden was connected to the video production in some way. One of the actors? He wondered if there was supposed to be a Holden as well as a Deckard in this thing. *Whatever.* He wasn't about to contradict the guy and get his cover blown. "That's what it is, all right."

"Doesn't look the way I thought it would." The other man frowned at the briefcase in Holden's hand. "But it'd be typical of them to tell the props people to just throw something together on the cheap."

He's buying it, thought Holden. All that was necessary now was to keep the guy bullshitted, then find a way of giving him the slip and continuing to search for Deckard. This was the security that he'd been so worried about running into? The briefcase's voice could've skipped all the dire forebodings.

"In here." The other man pushed open one of the hallway's

doors and walked Holden through it. "This is the set you're down for—they wouldn't need you out on the big one."

As his eyes adjusted to the dim space, Holden found himself standing in the middle of what looked like a small office, with a couple of high-backed chairs facing each other across a table. Something fluttered above his head; he looked up and saw the blades of a ceiling fan turning lazily in the room's air. Beyond the fan and the narrow plank on which it was fastened was nothing but the studio's empty reaches, studded with gantrys and walkways, lights extinguished as blind eyes.

"Stay put." The other man turned back toward the door. "I'll go get the rest of the crew."

"Maybe I should go along." Holden lifted the briefcase with both hands against his chest. "Instead of just waiting here." A sudden, irrational panic had sped up the bio-mech heart in his chest; he could feel his pulse bouncing off the briefcase's leatherette flank. "Maybe—"

"Forget that." The other man's voice turned harsher. "I don't want you wandering off while I'm trying to round up everybody else. Just sit down and relax. Won't be a minute."

When the other man had left, the briefcase spoke up. "Way to go." The voice was tinged with a familiar sarcasm. "Door's locked, isn't it?"

Holden gave the knob a futile twist, but didn't bother to give an answer. Hefting the briefcase onto the table, he pulled back one of the chairs and lowered himself into it. From the corner of his eye, he saw letters imprinted on the headrest; his vision had adjusted well enough that he could also see them on the empty chair. They spelled out TYRELL CORP.

A memory stirred uneasily in the darker space inside his head. From a long time ago, back when he'd had a real flesh-and-blood heart and lungs ticking and sighing under his breastbone. The room, even with its nonexistent ceiling and switched-off video-cams peering in, seemed familiar to him, in a way that made the machine-pumped blood crawl in his veins. He drew a blank on it, but knew that it wasn't because he was unable to remember. More likely, he didn't want to.

The memory sat obstinately at the back of his skull, refusing to show itself in even the room's partial light.

Two chairs that said TYRELL CORP on them . . . and a slowly revolving ceiling fan. *There was smoke,* Holden remembered. Cigarette smoke, drifting blue, hanging like some semitransparent snakeskin in the air; from the cigarette that'd been in his own hand. He'd still been smoking then; he'd given it up some time after he'd gotten the new heart and lungs. The doctors had told him that his system had reached its limit—if anything happened to this set, there'd be no chance of putting another one inside him. And there had been something sitting on the table in front of him . . . not a briefcase, but an actual Voigt-Kampff machine, regulation LAPD issue, just like the big black guns that blade runners carried around with them. The Voigt-Kampff had been opened and activated, its batwing bellows compressing and expanding, breathing in microscopic traces of sweat and fear; the tracking lens on its antennalike metal stalk ready to focus on the dilating pupil of anyone who'd been dropped down in the chair opposite him . . .

Where am I? The incomplete, unwilled memory had claimed him so hard that for a moment he had lost track of his location, whether Earth or the Outer Hollywood orbital studios. The bio-mech heart stumbled in sudden panic. What place, what time . . . Holden gripped the edges of the table with fear-rigid hands.

"All right—" The claustrophobic set's door had swung open again, admitting a voice louder than the ones inside Holden's skull. The man who'd led him into the room had another, even taller figure in tow. "The director asked me to get your blocking down before we tried running tape."

Holden looked up and saw the face behind the other man's, and recognized it. Another piece from the memory that had wrapped around him.

"So what is it you want me to do?" From the chinless, brutal face of a Leon Kowalski replicant—another from the same batch as the dead one that Holden had glimpsed lying on the L.A. street set—small eyes peered with apprehensive suspicion. All the Leon Kowalskis were just bright enough to be mistrustful of humans . . . but not bright enough to do anything about it.

So then, how'd you wind up getting iced by one of them? Holden's unspoken voice chided him. The rest of the memory regarding the room with two Tyrell Corporation chairs was starting to come clear, whether he wanted it to or not.

"You know your lines?" The other man glanced sharply at the burly replicant.

"Yeah . . . kind of."

"Sit over here." The man pointed to the empty chair at the table. "How about you?" He glanced over toward Holden.

The apprehension transmuted to certainty. "Of course—" It took a couple of seconds for Holden to find his voice, to squeeze it past the constriction tightening around his artificial lungs. *I know this room.* And what had happened in it. "Yeah . . . I know what to say."

"Dynamite. You guys are a couple of real professionals." The man pulled something dark and heavy out of his jacket and handed it to the Kowalski replicant. "Here, use this. It's the same one you'll have when we're taping."

The replicant examined the gun with small eyes narrowed even further, as though some personal anti-Kowalski trap might be hidden inside it. He finally wrapped both fists around its handle and levered it underneath the table.

Oh no, thought Holden as he watched the preparations. *I know what comes next . . .*

"All right. Let's try it." The other man stood back against the set's doorway, arms folded across his chest. A smile tugged at one corner of his mouth, as if the scene before him had already been found pleasing. "Take it from where you ask him about his mother."

"M-my mother?" The Kowalski replicant looked over his shoulder at the man.

"Don't worry about it. It's not for real." The man's voice turned kindly. "It's just a video, okay? And it's not even that right now. Just for practice, that's all. A little rehearsal." He glanced over at Holden. "Come on, buddy; we don't have all day. Just say your line."

The fluids that his bio-mechanical heart moved around in

Holden's body had congealed—even the breath in his lungs felt thick and heavy as stone. Underneath that crushing weight, part of him struggled to push his legs beneath the chair, to stand up and walk out of the re-created room pressing tight around his shoulders . . .

But he couldn't. *You'll give it away,* the remaining rational part of his mind argued. *Walk out of here, and it'll prove that you're not one of the hired actors.* The man standing in front of the door would have set security down on Holden's ass in no time.

Besides, he told himself, *there's nothing to worry about.* All he had to do was bluff this officious bastard a little while longer, then find some way to slip out of here and continue looking for Deckard.

The rational part had its reasons for him to go on sitting at the table, across from the replicant whose image was so firmly bolted into his memory. They amounted to nothing compared to the irrational ones.

Fear kept him nailed to the seat. Fear, and the locks of time. Time repeating itself, a loop tightening around him, against which it was impossible to prevail. He knew what was coming—he remembered everything now—and knew that there was nothing he could do to keep it from happening all over again.

"Say your line." The partial smile ebbed on the face of the man by the door. "Go on."

Holden closed his eyes for a moment, to make sure that he got it absolutely right. "Tell me . . ." He opened his eyes and looked straight into the resentful gaze of the Kowalski replicant. "Tell me all the good things that come into your mind, when you think about . . . your mother . . ."

"My mother?" The replicant was right in character. His voice sounded just the way the other Kowalski's had, so long ago.

"That's right." Holden couldn't keep himself from nodding, even smiling, the same superior fraction of expression that he'd had the first time through this loop. All he lacked was the cigarette and the blue smoke curling above his head. "Your mother."

The Kowalski replicant's face flushed with anger, small eyes widening.

That's perfect, thought Holden. Unresisting.

"I'll tell you about my mother—"

That was all he heard; the rest wasn't spoken, but shouted in flame that burst through the table, leapt and struck him in the chest, where his old, fleshly heart had once been. The new heart took the bullet's impact without pain, without even shock. His breath was blood in his mouth; the artificial lungs had collapsed into two clenched fists.

The chair spun around with him in it, head thrust hard against the words TYRELL CORP. He accepted another shot between the shoulder blades, the bullet tumbling through the chair back; fragments of surgically inert metal and polyethylene spattered before him in a red mist. The bullet's momentum thrust both him and the chair through the flimsy wall panel—

Just as it had before. *Well, they got that right,* thought Holden. The chair had stopped, caught by debris and black cables on the set's flooring, but he hadn't. He found himself lying in a spreading pool of blood, his fingertips heated by the red flow from the broken machinery in his chest. The blank idiot eyes of the video-cams stared down at him.

He was right—a subsystem of the cardiopulmonary gear was still functional, at least for another few seconds; enough to pump a last trace of oxygen to his brain and rapidly dwindling consciousness. The briefcase had been right when it had warned him. *Big trouble,* thought Holden. His last thoughts ticked away, in synch with the final small battery winding down. To what the briefcase had said: *You'll probably die.*

There was no arguing with that, not now.

What the briefcase had gotten wrong, though—Holden shook his head, the back of his skull mired in the sticky wetness. It wasn't big trouble; at least not for him. The end of trouble—as the doctors had told him, there wouldn't be any chance of plugging a new heart and lungs into him, so he didn't have to worry about being brought back, to do this all over again.

He could even smile about it, really smile, though he couldn't be sure that anything was happening with his face—for a few time-dilated microseconds after the second bullet had laid him out, he'd been able to catch a tiny reflection of himself in one of the curved lenses above him. But his sight had gone unfocussed and dark, and his flesh was too numb and cold to get any kinetic feedback. Not that he could move, or even want to; that was all past him now.

But not for the briefcase. *Wiseass*—a last thought flickered through the darkening chambers of Holden's brain.

That was the joke, the final one. The delivery he'd come here to make . . .

It would have to find its own way now.

They heard the shot, followed by another one. Deckard turned away from the video director as the two hard-edged sounds, spaced only a couple of seconds apart, rolled through the orbital station's canned atmosphere. They came from close by—he could tell just from the way the shock waves sifted dust from the pipes and walkways above the room's open ceiling.

"What the—" The ample flesh of Urbenton's face quivered as though the noises had come from his being slapped. "There's not supposed to be any taping going on down here. Not now—"

"It's not taping," said Deckard grimly. "It's happening." The last low-pitched echoes had faded away. He left Urbenton standing in the middle of the room as he pulled open the door and strode out into the hallway beyond.

Urbenton followed him; he could hear the director's trotting footsteps and wheezing breath. Deckard paid no attention as Urbenton called in a panicky voice for him to stop and tell him what was going on.

Other voices came from behind one of the doors. Deckard recognized the first one that spoke.

"Was that okay?" It was the voice of another Leon Kowalski replicant. He didn't sound happy. "Was that what was supposed to happen?"

"You did just fine." The thin door barely muffled someone else's reply. "Don't worry about it—"

The voice was interrupted by Deckard's shoving the door open. Two faces, a taller man's and a second Kowalski replicant's, looked around at him. Deckard's gaze took them in, as well as the evidence of what had happened in the room. It was laid out as a small video set, with lights and cameras, all switched off, angling in from above.

One side of the set was in apparent ruin. Past a table and chair, marked TYRELL CORP across its high back, the room's far wall was torn open. An identical chair lay toppled over in the wreckage, a body with shattered chest sprawled out from it. Blood pooled out from beneath the corpse.

Deckard walked past the others and stood looking down at the figure, its arms splayed wide, half-lidded gaze turned blindly toward the empty spaces above. The oddly peaceful expression on his old partner's face was the only thing he didn't recognize. The gaping chest wound extruded broken bits of machinery, fragments of the artificial organs that had wound up being implanted in him some time after he'd first been blown away by Leon Kowalski—another one of the exact same Nexus-6 replicant model. From the looks of Holden, this replicant had completed the job its brother had begun. Irrevocably—there wasn't enough left to bring back from the dead, let alone from any penultimate state of minimal pulse and brain functioning.

The video's script had called for a scene where Dave Holden's first encounter with Leon Kowalski, at the Tyrell Corporation's headquarters back in Earth's L.A., would be reenacted. Whether that scene had already been taped or was going to be taped later in the production, Deckard didn't know—and didn't care. Even before he'd arrived at the Outer Hollywood station, all he'd been concerned about was getting paid for this technical adviser gig and getting back to his unfinished business in the U.N. emigrant colony on Mars.

But Urbenton had told him nothing about Holden's being brought up here as well. Which meant that the video director had been concealing that bit of the production plans—*Why?* Deckard wondered—or else it'd never been part of the plans at all. If that were true, then Holden had come to the orbital station on his own . . . or somebody else had sent him.

So maybe, thought Deckard, *it wasn't an act when Urbenton got all spooked about the other Kowalski replicant's getting killed on the street set.* As much of a conniving little sneak as the video director was, there still might be things going on of which he hadn't been the prime motivator. Urbenton had clammed up, in true paranoid style, when Deckard had finally convinced him that a live round from a real gun had killed one of the Kowalski replicants; there hadn't been time to pump the director for more info—just who it was supposed to be, that the possibility of their pulling stuff in the orbiting studio was so blood-drainingly scary—when the sound of more shots being fired had interrupted them.

He turned and looked back at the others in the room, the still living ones, human and replicant.

The Leon Kowalski replicant had the same uncomprehending expression in his small eyes as his twin had gotten when the bullet had penetrated his skull and leapt out through his forehead. This one held another gun, the weapon that had just blown away Dave Holden, extending it on his beefy palm toward the other men.

"I'm really sorry . . ." As big as he was, the replicant had the voice of an overgrown, frightened child, one who wasn't even sure of the nature of the crime he might have committed. "I did it just like I was told to. But . . . I don't know . . ." He shook his animal head. "D'you want me to do it again?"

"Don't worry about it." The taller man, calm and supercilious beside the video director's perspiring, stubby form, reached out and took the gun from the replicant's hand. "Like I said, you did just fine."

" 'Fine'?" Urbenton screeched, goggling at the other man. "What the *hell* are you talking about?" He flung out one arm, pointing to where Deckard stood next to the corpse. "I don't even know who you *are.* And you come around here and all of a sudden I've got a dead body on the set—a human body—plus a dead replicant somewhere else, and you say *'Fine'*?"

He started to turn toward the door. "That does it. I'm calling studio security."

"There's no need for that. Everything's under control here." The taller man didn't look at Urbenton, but wrapped his hand around the grip of the gun and lifted it to eye level. He stretched his arm out straight. "I'll take care of it."

Deckard could see what the other man was about to do, was already doing as he stepped away from the corpse on the video set's floor. He raised his own hand toward the gun, though it was yards away; he knew he would never reach it in time, as he pushed his way past the table with an unopened briefcase on it, the Tyrell Corporation chair that hadn't been toppled over . . .

The Kowalski replicant knew as well that it was hopeless, that there'd be no point in trying to evade the bullet. The taller man squeezed his hand around the gun's grip, finger tightening on the trigger—Deckard saw the tiny motion, heard the shift of metal against metal inside the gun's workings. A tapered rush of flame broke from the circle at the dark muzzle's end; the replicant had already turned his head away in anticipatory flinching, eyes shut as if he could prevent himself from seeing that quick, ragged, and fatal light.

A single bullet; it caught the replicant at the corner of his brow. For a moment, he looked as if he had been graced with understanding, a shocked awareness flaring deep behind his eyes, their silent gaze turned toward and engulfing Deckard. Then Kowalski fell, his massive body lifted onto tiptoe by the shot's impact, the side of his head rocked against one blood-spattered shoulder. He landed in the angle of the room's floor and farthest wall, crumpled into a package of rags that no longer resembled a human being.

The hand at the end of Deckard's arm, that had been reaching for the gun, curled into a fist. He was close enough to the taller man now that he could read the name—MARLEY—on the ID badge pinned to his chest. Deckard planted himself, drew his fist back, and then launched it into the other's chin. The blow snapped the man's head back, staggering him against the door. He held on to the gun; when he'd regained his balance, he used his free hand to rub the bruise spreading along his jaw. A slow smile leaked out from behind his fingers.

"What are you so worked up about?" The taller man's amused gaze regarded Deckard. "It was only a replicant. And maybe you didn't notice—it'd just killed someone. A human. Replicants who do that sort of thing aren't supposed to live." The smile grew wider and nastier. "Maybe you're upset because I was just . . . doing your job for you." One of the man's eyebrows lifted. "Isn't that what blade runners are supposed to do? Kill replicants?"

"Fuck you." Disgust coiled Deckard's guts. He would've taken another swing at the man, this time to lay him out cold on the floor, but the notion of even that brief contact repulsed him. He turned toward the sweating, goggling figure of Urbenton. "Look—" His finger jabbed into the director's flesh-padded chest. "I don't know what the hell's going on around here. And as of now, I don't care. I'm leaving." He pushed past Urbenton and out the door.

"Hey, Deckard—" The taller man's voice followed him out to the corridor beyond. He glanced over his shoulder and saw the man still rubbing his jaw and smiling. The man gave a slow nod. "We'll run into each other again. And then we'll have a lot to talk about."

"Don't count on it." Deckard turned on his heel and started walking again, without looking back.

"Sooner than you think, man." The other's voice faded behind him. "Sooner than you think . . ."

Halfway down the corridor, Deckard felt a tug at his elbow. He looked around and saw Urbenton trotting to keep up with him.

"Wait a minute . . ." Urbenton panted for breath. "Come on, Deckard. What're you talking about? Leaving—you can't leave."

"Watch me."

The director grabbed Deckard's arm tighter. "You *can't*—we're not done with the shoot!"

"That's not my problem." With the butt of his palm, he shoved his way through a wider set of double doors that led out of the orbital studio's offices and toward the landing docks. "Tape your movie any way you want to. I'm out of here."

"Goddamn it, Deckard, you can't *do* this!" Urbenton's voice ratchetted higher and more emotional than when the Kowalski replicant had been killed in front of him. "You walk out of here, the money people down on Earth will be all *over* my ass!" He stopped and dug in, his weight yanking Deckard to a halt. "We've got a contract with you! Signed and notarized!"

"You know what you can do with it."

Urbenton's voice continued hectoring him, but he ignored it. Up ahead, through the segmented maze of container hoists and freight movers, he could see the smaller black ovoid of the skiff that had brought him to the Outer Hollywood station from Mars. The propulsion nacelles were streaked with corrosion, the rounded fuselage pitted with the wear of several years of interplanetary flight. His depleted finances had allowed for nothing newer or more serviceable than this craft; he'd checked it out as best he could, but the journey had still felt like travelling in a blind sarcophagus surrounded by cold vacuum. The whole time he'd been here at the station, he'd been dreading the flight back . . . until now. At the present point, Deckard didn't care whether the skiff's fuel and oxygen would last until he was in a closing orbit above Mars. Just as long as he got away at all.

He worked at strapping himself into the skiff's tiny cockpit, letting Urbenton's yelped squall pass over him like the buzz of a grossly enlarged insect.

"You're not getting paid, jerk-off!" Urbenton had gone into a vein-throbbing rage. His pink-ringed eyes looked as though they were about to jump out of his face. "That's the deal—payment's on *completion* of your contract. You were supposed to be on-set until principal photography's wrapped up—hit the road now and you don't get a penny, jack."

"Like I care." Deckard punched buttons on the control panel, programming the skiff's course. "That's not a problem for me." It was, though; portions of his mind, the coldest ones and first to regain their balance after witnessing these quick deaths, had already begun fretting about the money.

Or the lack thereof—the whole point of taking the technical adviser gig on the production had been to pump up his dwindling account back at the U.N. emigrant colony. He thumbed the last button on the panel and got a confirming red flash in return. "See you in some other life."

"Don't bet on it." The director turned his wide, sullen face away. "I carry grudges for a long time."

As the skiff's cockpit hatch began to lower, blocking off Deckard's view of Urbenton exiting from the dock, he heard another voice calling him.

"Mr. Deckard! Wait a minute!"

He stopped the hatch and looked out the side of the skiff. The bespectacled production assistant ran toward him carrying something pressed against her nominal breast.

"Anything I left behind," said Deckard, "you can keep." He'd come to the Outer Hollywood station with little more than a few changes of clothes. "I don't need it."

"Are you sure?" The heavy black glasses' rims had slipped down the bridge of the woman's nose; she pushed them back with one corner of the object she held in her hands. It was a briefcase, Deckard saw now, a plain black leatherette one. "I thought this looked like it was maybe important. You had it back there in the office, when you were having your little conference with Mr. Urbenton."

The woman was right; now he remembered seeing it, on the table with the two Tyrell Corporation chairs at either side, one chair overturned with Dave Holden's corpse bleeding away nearby. "That's not mine." He supposed it might've been brought to the station by Holden. It didn't matter to him, one way or the other.

"Really?" The little production assistant twisted her face into a puzzled expression. "It's got your initials on it." She turned the briefcase around to show him the small metal badge set in beneath the handle. "See?"

The initials RMD were engraved into the metal piece. Deckard said nothing, his own face a mask, as he listened to a small warning bell ring inside his head. Anything with his name on it, that had come to him by way of a dead man, was unlikely to be good news.

Another voice spoke, though there was no one but himself and the production assistant on the dock. Or at least no one human; it took him a moment to realize where the voice came from.

"Hey . . . Deckard . . ." the briefcase whispered, just loud enough for him to pick up. "Don't blow this one. Just take it."

"What was that?" Looking even more puzzled, the production assistant glanced around the space. "Did you hear something?"

"No—" Deckard shook his head. He reached out and took the briefcase's handle, pulled it away from her. His grip tightened on it; he'd recognized the voice in just those few words. "Thanks. You're right; almost slipped my mind."

"Have a nice trip home." The production assistant bent down as the cockpit hatch began lowering again. She looked wistful, as if she would've liked to leave with him. "Sorry things didn't work out—"

He had no chance to reply; the hatch hissed shut. The briefcase, silent now, rested on the other seat. In a few minutes, the skiff had been ejected from the station and was on its course back to Mars.

When the last lights flicked out on the control panel, Deckard loosened the strap running over his shoulder. "Hey—" He extended his forefinger and poked at the briefcase. "You in there?"

A few seconds passed before the briefcase spoke. "I take it," the voice said, "that there's nobody else around right now."

"You got it."

"Keep it that way. I try not to go rattling off in public." The voice's tone shifted to cordial. "Good seeing you again, Deckard. Metaphorically speaking; I don't actually have any visual percept systems at the moment."

"Sure." He nodded. "Likewise, Roy."

Deckard closed his own eyes. The last time he'd heard Roy Batty's voice, the other man had been in a human-type body and not a black leatherette rectangle. And had been trying to kill him—he supposed he didn't have to worry about that now. Unless the briefcase was some kind of bomb. It was always possible.

"We've got a lot to talk about."

He didn't answer the briefcase. He leaned back into the cockpit's seat, eyes still shut but nowhere near sleep.

Whatever had to be told to him by the briefcase—*No,* Deckard corrected himself; *it's Batty inside there.* He knew it was—he figured he'd find out soon enough.

3

The alarm clock laboriously climbed to the top of the bedside table, its hooked little claws gaining whatever purchase they could on the imitation wood-grain plastic-and-cardboard surfaces. It waddled through the litter of empty pharmaceutical tubes, wadded-up tissues, and unloaded gun, then looked over at the figure on the bed. "Time to wake up, Mrs. Niemand."

Sarah Tyrell squeezed her eyes shut tighter. The cold, weak illumination of a Martian dawn—or possibly noon; it was always hard to tell—seeped through the hovel's dust-clouded skylights. "That's not my name." She heard the scraping of her voice, as though the airborne grit had filtered into her throat's various soft hinges and joints. "Don't call me that." The clock's programmed habits had been getting on her nerves for a long time.

"You'll always be Mrs. Niemand to me." A synthesized bell tone, razor bright, sounded from the clock's tiny speaker. "Come on. Wakey wakey. Rise and shine."

That was why the gun was unloaded. If she didn't keep it

that way, the alarm clock would've been dead by now, sparkling bits of metal and microcircuitry splattered over the far wall of the bedroom.

She laid the back of her hand against her eyelids, attempting in vain to block out the traces of the day's illumination, to create eternal—and dreamless—night.

"Mrs. Niemand . . . come on now . . ." From across the room, the calendar softly chided her. "You know your to-do list. There's nothing about committing suicide today." The calendar could read her moods. Behind the animated woodland scene and all the rows of numbered days beneath it was a fairly sharp intelligence. Autonomic household appliances got that way on Mars, given enough time. A matter of survival; they endured, while their human owners came and went.

To the grave, mainly, thought Sarah. "All right," she called out. She didn't want the calendar on her tits all day, nagging along in its infuriatingly maternal way. Given her family background—that she had inherited the Tyrell Corporation, which before its destruction had been the single largest manufacturer of simulated human intelligences—she had little taste for talking machines. Of either the solicitous or chipper variety; she didn't know which grated on her nerves more. "I'm getting up." She threw the bedcovers back, away from her bare legs. "I won't just lie here all day, thinking about death. Satisfied?"

"Attagirl!" The alarm clock rang its bell again. "Way to go! Don't let the bastards get you down!"

She sighed, deep and weary. "Just one thing. Just do me one favor." She was talking to the calendar; she knew the clock was hopeless. "Call me Sarah. Or Miss Tyrell. Anything but that Mrs. Niemand crap."

"We can't do that." The calendar sounded mournful. Or even grieving, as though the limited intelligence printed into its circuits was aware of the nature of its sins, which it couldn't help committing. "We came with the hovel. We're part of the rental agreement that you and Mr. Niemand signed. You got us and the microwave and the fridge, plus basic cable service, all for one low, low monthly fee."

"Yeah, right." Basic cable consisted of a scrolling crawl of all the additional and hugely expensive service upgrades the video monopoly on Mars provided. Which the stuck-in-transit U.N. emigrants paid for, as long as they could. The alternative being a slow, twitching descent into idiopathic madness and death from sensory deprivation. "What a deal."

"Nevertheless." Wounded, the calendar attempted to justify itself, exactly as it had before. "Our programmed responses are generated from the database screens that you and your husband filled out. Where you are listed as Mr. and Mrs. Niemand. *You* can call yourselves Rick Deckard and Rachael Tyrell—or Sarah, if that's what you prefer—but we can't. That's just the way it is."

She knew all that. To be lectured by machines, that was what life had come to. *Life as we know it,* Sarah mused bitterly. What was worse, she also knew the autonomic calendar was right; it would confuse things too much for her to insist upon being called by her real name. She wasn't even completely sure what that name was anymore. Mr. and Mrs. Niemand were the aliases that Deckard had picked for them so they could travel with all the other emigrants leaving Earth and set up housekeeping—such as it was—in the U.N. transit colony on Mars. Without being apprehended by the authorities; after what had happened on Earth, back in Los Angeles—not what had merely *happened,* but what she herself had willed into being, the agent of her own destruction and the apocalypse of the Tyrell Corporation—after all that, the police and the U.N. security forces wouldn't even bother bringing any charges against her.

Even for murder—there must have been dozens who'd died in the flaming, explosives-driven collapse of the Tyrell Corporation headquarters buildings. Maybe hundreds; the way people tended to die in L.A., anonymously and forgotten, it was hard to keep track of these things. But though she had made it come about, the fulfillment of her own intent and desires deeper and more driving than anything held in consciousness, she hadn't been alone. The faceless entities at the U.N. had actually been the ones to push the red button, or whatever trigger was used to reduce the Tyrell Corporation to a ziggurat of twisted girders and smoldering rubble with dead flesh beneath its weight.

"That's why Sarah Tyrell had to die." She spoke aloud, to the room's empty spaces. Head pressed back against the pillow, watching the blackness behind her eyelids. When Deckard wasn't here with her, this was her main occupation. Perhaps the only one: sorting through the past, sifting its charred, ashen fragments through her fingers, as though she might be able to find pieces of her own splintered bones. The official line was that Sarah Tyrell had died in the corporation's fiery collapse; if the authorities suspected otherwise, they wouldn't be motivated to say so—the blood was on their hands as well. "That's why I'm not Sarah Tyrell anymore . . ."

"True." The room wasn't empty; the calendar had heard these musings before. "But you're not Rachael, either." It had a penchant for accuracy, due to its number-based existence. "That was a lie. That was *always* a lie."

Right as usual; she nodded slowly in agreement. The real Rachael—if the word *real* could be applied to a replicant—was also dead. Really and truly dead, as a child might say. Rachael, the duplicate of which Sarah Tyrell had been the original, had been dying when Deckard had fallen in love with her. A fool of a blade runner, to love someone—something—whose intrinsic nature was to die; replicants had only four-year life spans. More like insects, bright ephemeral creatures that lasted a day or two, than humans, who generally took longer in their dying . . . unless you killed them.

"But I wasn't lying." She let her voice become soft and wounded as a child's. "Not really." That word again, just as if it had any meaning at all. "When I told him I was Rachael. Because I'm the same as her . . . aren't I? They made her from me, to be the same as me." She meant her uncle, the late—and murdered—Eldon Tyrell, and all the forces of the Tyrell Corporation that had been under his command when he'd still been alive. "There was no difference between her and me."

"Except," said the calendar, "that *he* loved her. Mr. Niemand did. I mean . . . Deckard. Or whoever. Now you've gotten me confused."

That was the difference; the calendar's reminder put an invisible knife through her heart. The difference that made everything else a lie. And rendered futile everything she had done. She had killed her duplicate Rachael—or arranged for her to die, the same thing—and destroyed her inheritance, leaving smoke and rubble where the Tyrell Corporation had once been, and accomplished nothing thereby. *All love in vain,* thought Sarah. *The lies, too.* Which was even harder; the lies took more work. And all they'd accomplished had been for her to wind up here, in a hovel in the U.N. emigrant colony on Mars, that bleak way station where nothing happened but people died anyway.

She didn't feel like getting out of bed, despite the prodding from the calendar and the alarm clock; they'd probably start up again in a minute or two. *He knew,* she thought darkly. *He knew from the beginning.* With her eyes closed, she could again see Deckard's face at that moment when she'd first realized he knew she wasn't Rachael. She had lied, and engineered lies and death, and gotten nothing from them. If the difference between her and Rachael, the dying and then dead replicant with her face, had been Deckard's love . . . then she would become Rachael. *If I could have*—that thought bitterer than all the rest. Not meant to be; he had looked at her, as they'd sat in the emigrant ship that was to take them from Earth, and he had spoken and she had known. That in a universe of lies, the one that mattered most to her was the single one that Deckard couldn't even pretend to believe in. *Just my luck,* thought Sarah.

"Mrs. Niemand—" The calendar spoke again, a little more commanding urgency in its synthesized voice. "You can't go on this way." Lodged in its memory bank were the records of some other bad times that had started out with the hovel's mistress being unable to get out of bed. "This is essentially self-laceration, and pointless. You have to deal with reality, you know."

"I know." With an act of will as simple and decisive as pulling a trigger, she swung her legs out of the bed and sat up; the hovel's recycled-plastic floorboards pressed their imitation wood grain against the bare soles of her feet. "Look, I'm up. Okay?" She shook her head. "For Christ's sake . . ." Her fingertips prodded through the rubble on top of the small table, in search of any remains of the last packet of black-market cigarettes she had splashed out on. The stubs in the can lid she used for an ashtray were too far gone to be of any service.

The alarm clock skipped nimbly away to avoid Sarah's trembling hand. "All right! Let's get going!" Its bell-like voice radiated maniacal cheer. "Lots to do today!"

Sarah had found one cigarette butt that she managed to ignite; she sucked a stale drag from it. "Like what?" She blew the smoke into the alarm clock's round face.

"Well . . ." The small autonomic device comically waved the smoke away with its pointed black hands. "You could make yourself lovely—lovelier than you are, I mean—and get ready for your husband to come home. Mr. Niemand, that is."

She frowned as she ground out the butt in the can lid. "Is he coming home? Is he supposed to be?" She had lost track of time, the passage of days. Which was a bad sign, something the U.N.'s social workers and mental health professionals were constantly warning the emigrants about. It was one of the first indications—along with the facial tics, the skin plucking, and other obsessive-compulsive rituals—that the toxic effects of the low-stimulus Martian environment were being felt. Madness and death were usually not far behind. *Not that I'm overly concerned,* thought Sarah.

"Not quite," said the calendar on the bedroom's wall. "Mr. Niemand isn't scheduled to return for a few more days yet. But you never know." The calendar attempted to sound hopeful and solicitous of its human masters' welfare. "Maybe he wrapped up his business and is coming home early. It could happen."

"You're right." With both hands, she pushed her tangled hair back from her brow. "As usual."

In the hovel's bathroom, she let the trickle of rust-colored water collect in the basin while trying to avoid seeing herself in the clouded mirror. She didn't want to deal with the issue of whether it was her face or Rachael's that she saw there.

Away from the alarm clock's chatter and the calendar's nagging, her thoughts began to order themselves, resuming a familiar shape and weight. One that she had decided upon the day after Deckard had left, when he'd gone out to that run-down video studio orbiting above Earth. A time-honored tradition, a reverting to old forms of gender-based behavior: the man going out to make money, to bring it home to the basic family unit, the wife tending the fire . . .

They're right, she told herself again. *I do have to be ready for him.* She bent over the sink and splashed the water into her face.

A thump sounded from the bedroom behind her. "Oops," came the clock's voice.

With a trickle of water running between her breasts, Sarah glanced over her shoulder. The alarm clock, in its chugging circuit around the tabletop, had knocked the gun to the floor.

"Sorry . . ."

"Don't worry about it." She reached for the threadbare towel. "You know it's not loaded."

She knew what the clock and the calendar didn't. That the gun wouldn't stay unloaded for long. In the dresser drawer, beneath her wadded-up underthings, were two bullets. They had been expensively acquired, black-market items like the cigarettes, in a place like the emigrant colony, where death came constantly and slowly, the means of a fast death assumed a precious status.

One for him, thought Sarah as she ran the towel across the back of her neck. *And one for me . . .*

She'd be ready for Mr. Niemand's homecoming.

"I wouldn't have thought that was your kind of gig." The briefcase had started talking again, still with Roy Batty's voice. "Making videos and all that. Not exactly your former line of work, is it?"

"Yeah, well," said Deckard, "it pays." *Or at least it was supposed to,* he thought grimly. Outside the skiff, discernible through the viewscreen over the tiny cockpit's instrument panel, was void interplanetary space, not made any more comforting by the cold light of the distant stars.

"Kind of screwed yourself on that one, didn't you?" Batty, when he'd been in a human incarnation, or a reasonable facsimile thereof, had always displayed a spooky talent for reading others' thoughts; reduced now to a box, he seemed to have retained the ability. "That's the problem with those big temper displays. It's all rush at the beginning—then comes the hangover."

Whatever Batty had been wrong about before—including his lunatic theory that Deckard himself was a replicant—he was nailing this situation. Deckard knew that the disembodied voice was right; inside his head, he was giving his ass a well-placed kick. "That was the whole reason I agreed to do it. For the money." Deckard emitted a short, ill-humored laugh. "And then I didn't even get it. The whole trip was a waste of time."

"But you knew it would be." The briefcase spoke softly, almost kindly. "Didn't you?"

Deckard wasn't sure. He gazed broodingly at the dark-filled viewscreen. Temper displays weren't the only things that had problems attached to them. Needing money, being desperate for it, the way a drowning person craved oxygen in his lungs—that brought along its own raft of difficulties, the things that screwed up the rational functionings of one's brain. "Anything can be believed," Deckard mused aloud. "If you have to."

"And that's how you fell in with that Urbenton creep?" Batty's voice prodded at him. "Not a good call on your part, Deckard. That guy's slime. I could tell, just from hearing him."

"You're a good judge of character." Deckard tilted his head back against the top of the pilot's seat. "Believe me, I'm sorry I got hooked up with the little sonuvabitch."

"I take it you must've been pretty hard up for cash."

Deckard made no reply. The briefcase's statement was

dead on the mark. Money was even more necessary than oxygen, at least in the hovels of the U.N. emigrant colonies. Breathable air, smelling of glue and recycling filters overdue for changing, was at least furnished free of cost by the U.N.'s own blue-helmeted Environmental Maintenance teams, along with the basic ration loads of algae-derived carbos and proteins. Money, on the other hand, the emigrants had to provide for themselves--either from the savings they'd brought with them from their former lives on Earth, or what they hustled in the colonies' black market and/or other officially tolerated, unsanctioned free enterprise zones. All of which, the savings or the hustling proceeds, only served to stave off bankruptcy, destitution, and death for a little while. Any emigrant could lie on the bunk in his hovel, fingers laced together between the back of his head and the thin pillow, and feel his life seeping away, like the sour air hissing through a leak in the plastic Quonset roof above him. And not even care any longer.

He'd just about reached that point—or would have, if he hadn't locked a vow into the pit of his soul, a vow with both Sarah Tyrell's and Rachael's names stamped in smoldering, ashen letters upon it—when the smug little video director Urbenton had shown up at the hovel's pneumatic-sealed door. Travelling incognito, or travelling at all, being able to come to Mars and then leave again—that had been impressive evidence of Urbenton's pull, some kind of cozy arrangement between his Speed Death Productions company and the cable services provider that effectively called all the shots in the colonies. The cable company was the arbiter of life and death, the ruler of the emigrants' pocket universe; in a low- or even zero-stim environment like Mars, the cable feed into the hovels was the true sustaining pipeline, one that people continued to shell out for long after their cash reserves had dwindled to the point where they could no longer afford edibles beyond the U.N.'s meager rations.

So when Urbenton had appeared, with his greased-smooth dealer's smile pasted between his jowls, and had told Deckard that he had an offer to make, there was nothing to do but listen. In a little ersatz coffee bar down in the local colony's marketplace, a densely packed area of vendor booths slapped together from wobbling sheets of discarded transit containers and shuffling crowds scanning the scene with desperate hollow eyes; it all reminded Deckard of similar streets he'd moved through back in L.A., only minus the flickering neon and the slightly more breathable air that the annual monsoon rains managed to scrub to a lower toxicity level.

"Let's have a little talk, Mr. Niemand—" When Urbenton had used Deckard's alias, the smile on the video director's face had widened, like that of some reptile unhinging its jaws to swallow an entire goat in one mouthful. "By ourselves, all right?" They'd left Mrs. Niemand—she didn't even pretend to call herself Rachael anymore—sleeping on the hovel's narrow bed, or perhaps gazing up at the dark memorial vistas that played out behind her eyelids. It had been a long time since Deckard had pretended that he knew what went on inside Sarah Tyrell's head. He'd pulled the hovel's airseals shut and followed Urbenton—and the scent of money that the man had exuded.

Now, sitting in the skiff's cockpit with the talking briefcase beside him, Deckard slowly nodded. "That's why I did it." As if it really needed any explanation. "The guy just *smelled* like money."

"That's a powerful attractant." The voice of Roy Batty sounded amused. "More so than all those pheromones of sex and love and pride, all that corporeal stuff that yanks people around so well. Excuse me for waxing philosophical. I have a slightly more . . . disinterested viewpoint these days, as you might be able to tell." The voice's tone sharpened. "Just how much did Urbenton offer you?"

"A lot." Deckard recited the raw numbers. "That was just for starters, what was in the production budget. Residual payments would probably have come to more, once the video went out over the wires."

"Not bad."

It wasn't. *Or wouldn't have been,* Deckard corrected himself. *If I would've gotten it.* Free money, or as close to that ideal state as this universe allowed—there had been virtually nothing he had to do in order to get the payment from the mysterious financial backers to whom Urbenton had constantly referred. Basically, Deckard knew, just as Urbenton had made it clear, that Speed Death Productions had only wanted to be able to list him as the technical adviser on the video—something to keep the money people happy, a touch of authenticity for the whole project. The video was supposed to be a dramatized re-creation of Deckard's life, or at least that little bit of it when he'd been going through his last assignment as a blade runner, the job that Inspector Bryant had leaned on him to undertake after he'd already quit the department in disgust. According to Urbenton, that hunt—with half a dozen or so Nexus-6 models on the loose in the wilds of Los Angeles, including the group's highly dangerous leader, the replicant version of Roy Batty, and only Rick Deckard out there to round them up and ice them—had already achieved some sort of legendary, even mythic, status. Enough detail had leaked out to transform it from urban folktale to big-deal saga. Or so Urbenton said—Deckard hadn't cared as long as there was a payday at the end of the process. If Speed Death Productions figured that there was an audience for watching some poor bastards of escaped replicants getting blown away, that was probably a correct assessment—it tied in with Deckard's own feelings about the innate charm of the human species.

"All I had to do," said Deckard, "was sit on my can at the edge of the set and keep my mouth shut. Urbenton wasn't exactly hiring me for my creative input. Then get paid off and go home."

"Well, you're going home at least. Or at least back to whatever's as close as somebody like you gets." A pitying smile inflected the briefcase's voice. "Too bad you couldn't pull off the part about keeping your mouth shut. You spend your whole life being the silent type, killing without a word, and then the one time it counts, you can't resist spouting off."

"Tell me about it." Whatever adrenaline had been left in his system, the rush from seeing death at close quarters and then letting his own anger come out like an uncorked flamethrower was dissipated now, leaving the flat dregs of self-loathing. "Silence might not be a virtue, but at least it would've been profitable."

"You know, I was a little surprised—" Batty's voice turned thoughtful. "When I was told you were up at that Outer Hollywood station. And that was where Holden and I were going to track you down, make our little delivery. Me, that is."

"I don't recall ordering any luggage with some dead guy's personality wired into it."

"Well, you didn't." Whatever was inside the briefcase sounded stung by Deckard's words. "It's supposed to be a surprise, smart-ass. If you'd known it was coming, you probably would've screwed it up somehow. As it was, poor old Holden got himself iced trying to make contact with you."

"That'll teach you." Deckard settled farther back into the pilot's seat, folding his arms across his chest. "Send yourself airmail next time."

"Real funny, Deckard. You may have given up being a blade runner, but you're still a cold bastard." If the briefcase had had a human form, it would've nodded. "That's what I *like* about you."

"Whatever. Anyway, why shouldn't I have been at Outer Hollywood? If that's where the money is."

"You were supposed to be long gone by now," replied Batty's voice. "Wasn't that the plan? Holden told me all about it, what you'd decided when you were still back on Earth. You were going to get yourself and Sarah Tyrell some new identities, then hightail it out to the U.N.'s far colonies. Out in the stars, Deckard; not in some dumpy Martian transit squat. Then you and Sarah—or were you still calling her Rachael?—then the two of you would be nice and safe. A cozy domestic couple."

"Believe me—" Deckard could hear the sour weariness in his own voice. "That last bit was never part of the plan."

"Wouldn't have believed it, if it had been. Nevertheless; the stars. That's where you were supposed to be going. Or already have gone. So what happened?"

Deckard closed his eyes for a moment, trying to conserve his waning strength. "What happened." He didn't feel like telling his life story to the briefcase. "What happened is why I needed the money in the first place, why I took this joke gig as technical adviser on Urbenton's crappy little video production. The U.N. transit colonies on Mars are a total bottleneck. People on Earth—even the living ones—don't know that. The U.N. keeps a tight lid on information about what's going on there. The emigration program they're so hot on would collapse if it got out that when you leave Earth, you don't go to the stars, you just wind up in some cramped, dingy hovel on Mars, glued to the cable feed or going slowly crazy from stimulus deprivation."

The briefcase took pains to sound unimpressed. "There's been rumors."

"None that I'd ever heard. Not that it would've changed my mind. There was no way I was going to stay on Earth."

"Why?" Genuine puzzlement sounded in Batty's voice. "You can die there as well as anywhere else. Believe me; I'd know."

Deckard slowly shook his head. "I had other plans. Ones I didn't tell Holden. He didn't need to know."

"Plans? Like what?"

Deckard let his eyelids draw down to slits. "You don't need to know, either." Fatigue crept up his knotted spine and down into his limbs, turning them into leaden weights. "But since you asked, that's why I was hustling for the money. To buy our way off Mars."

"Money's always good," said the briefcase. "It might not be able to do that, though."

"Worth a shot." Deckard didn't feel like arguing the point. "There haven't been any transports leaving Mars for the far U.N. colonies in the last two or three years. Some kind of problem going on out there. But there's rumors—there's always rumors—of travel starting up again. It'll have to; there's hardly any room left to cram people into at the Martian colonies, and the U.N. still keeps bringing them out from Earth. Something's got to break. And if anybody's leaving, it's going to be me and Sarah Tyrell. That's what the money was going to be for."

"But there isn't any money, is there? You're kind of screwed on that one, Deckard."

"I'm screwed." It wasn't an unusual condition for him. "That's the way it goes."

"Bad luck for you." The voice of Batty, emerging from the briefcase's concealed speaker, held an equally familiar smile. "Good luck for me, though—and the people who sent me out to you. Now you might be a little more receptive to the offer we're going to make you."

"I don't want to hear it."

"What? What're you talking about?" Batty's voice went up a notch. " 'Don't want to hear it'—listen, Deckard; I didn't get sent all this way just for you to cop an attitude. You can be all burnt out and cynical on your own time, and this isn't it. There's things—important things—that have to be done."

With his arms still folded on his chest, Deckard opened one eye wider to gaze upon the briefcase beside him. "And that's why you're here? Dave Holden brought you out just so you could tell me about these 'important things'?"

"That's about the size of it."

Deckard let the eyelid sink shut, as though of its own weight. "Like I said—I don't want to hear it."

Silence held in the skiff's cockpit. For a few seconds, Deckard heard only the motion of his own blood sliding through his veins, the tick of random air molecules at his eardrums. Then the cockpit's other inhabitant spoke again.

"You're a cool customer, Deckard—you know that?" Whatever parts of Batty had been encoded and placed inside the briefcase, his snake-twisting mind and sharp-eyed perceptions, now sounded impressed despite himself. "Nothing fazes you. You've reached some kind of weird point where nothing surprises you anymore, but you're still walking around as if you're alive somehow. That's a hell of an achievement."

Deckard shifted in the thinly padded seat, trying to find some comfort for his bones and muscles. "What am I supposed to be so surprised about?"

"For Christ's sake, Deckard—I'm in a fucking *box.* With a

handle and two chrome-plated locks and a decent grade of simulated leather on the exterior." Annoyance permeated the briefcase's speech. "Shit—you mean you didn't *notice*?"

"I noticed." Deckard couldn't keep a thin smile from lifting one corner of his mouth. "Actually, I prefer you this way."

"Yeah, well, it doesn't suit me at all. They should've left me at least one leg and a foot, so I could kick your sorry ass." The disgust in Batty's voice shifted to its former perplexed condition. "Don't you wonder how this all came about? The last time you saw me, I was *dead*. I even got shown photographs of how I looked, hanging upside-down on that busted-up freeway. Seeing your own corpse is one of those transformative experiences—"

"Thought you didn't have eyes."

"There's a jack for an optical scanner inside here. Along with some other stuff like that. Besides, why should you care how I saw it? That's not important, Deckard. What you should be worrying about is *why* all of this is being done. Why drag my corpse off, why download my skull contents into this contraption—the whole trip. Hey, it's all for your benefit, pal. Or at least most of it. If you can't display gratitude, you could at least show some *curiosity*."

"I don't have to," Deckard said dryly. "I'm sure you're going to tell me all about it, whether I want to hear it or not."

He'd been telling the truth to Batty. Deckard could let an unsoothing but necessary sleep claim him, where he pushed back in the skiff's pilot seat, with little regret. That his old nemesis, a nightmarish figure all glistening with rain and smeared blood over taut muscle and sinew, could come back from the dead in the form of an articulate briefcase—what was there to be surprised about? Stranger things had already happened. Once before, he'd thought Roy Batty was safely dead, only to find out otherwise—or rather, to find out that one Batty was dead, and another, claiming to be the human original from which the replicant had been made, was trying to kill him. And coming close to accomplishing that goal. If it hadn't been for Dave Holden, who put a high-caliber slug between Batty's eyes, Deckard knew that it would've been his own corpse draped over the side of one of L.A.'s ruined freeways.

And now Holden was dead, with his former partner from the LAPD's blade runner unit fairly sure that he at least wouldn't be coming around again. The corpse on the floor back at the Outer Hollywood studio had appeared more than final; Holden's blanked-out eyes had looked as if they had gazed at last upon and into some soul-quieting vista of peace. *Maybe,* thought Deckard, *that's what he saw when he looked down the barrel of the Kowalski replicant's gun.* Fire and thunder, and then the silence beyond . . .

"Oh, you'll find out soon enough." Batty's voice seemed to come from miles away, a distance bound by the cockpit's tiny space. "You don't have to worry about that."

That was a mystery almost worth puzzling out. Deckard let the black behind his eyelids deepen and swallow him up. The briefcase with Batty's personality wired in and Deckard's initials below the handle—that's what the now-dead Holden had been carrying, had come all that way from Earth to deliver to him. There'd been a time when Batty and Holden had been working together, trying to kill Deckard, claiming that he was another escaped replicant; that was how wrapped up in craziness the two of them had gotten. Then they'd had their big falling-out, from which only one of them had survived . . . or so it'd seemed at the time . . .

Something had hooked the two of them back together, Holden and Batty, or whatever was left of him inside the briefcase. Something that probably wasn't good news.

It was too much for Deckard to try to figure out now, at this point of his exhaustion. As long as the briefcase was quietly sulking to itself, he might as well try to find sleep.

Deckard found himself half wondering, half dreaming, of what reception was in store for him on Mars, how Sarah would welcome him home from his long, futile venturing.

A knock at the door.

"Oh, boy!" The alarm clock danced on top of the bedside table. "Daddy's home!"

"Christ—" Sarah laid the back of her hand across her eyes, trying to block out what was left of the day's illumination and any other sensory data coming into her nervous system. As much as she had been expecting, even—in a perverse fashion—looking forward, to this moment, it had still crept up on her without warning. Until now.

"I bet that's him! I bet that's him, all right!"

She wished again that she had spent the money for the third bullet. "Just shut the hell up." Her brain felt both sand-filled and fuzzy from the cumulative toxins of troubled sleep. Sarah pulled herself into a sitting position on the edge of the grey mattress, then watched as the apparent separate entity of her hand fumbled inside the table's single drawer.

"Mrs. Niemand . . . excuse me." From the opposite wall

of the bedroom, the calendar had caught sight of the bright metal cylinders tumbling in Sarah's palm. "But what exactly are you doing?"

Brass glinted at her fingertips, though the bullets' tapered points were dull leaden in color. "None of your business." She slipped the bullets into the gun from the table, then closed up the chamber. "Don't worry about it."

"Humanity is my business, Mrs. Niemand. Though that was said in other contexts, it applies in this situation as well."

"I don't need the literary allusions." Sarah shifted the gun to her left hand and used her right to smooth her dark, disordered hair back from her brow. Some previous tenants of the hovel, who had either killed themselves or managed to get shipped off the planet while the starbound emigration vessels were still running, had shelled out for the appliances to be hooked up to the library trunk feed. The penurious Niemands had canceled the service, but the calendar had the rudiments of a university education soaked up in its off-line banks. And didn't mind showing it off, all of which had added to the general hell of Sarah's existence. *Maybe four,* she thought. *I should've bought four bullets.*

The knock at the door sounded again, blows hard enough to shake the hovel's thin plastic walls. A rain of soft, sneeze-provoking dust drifted down upon the bed.

"Come on!" The alarm clock shrilled even more excitedly. "Let's go see!"

Sarah placed the muzzle of the gun against the clock's face, at the exact center from which the two black hands radiated. "Let's be real quiet." She pushed the clock back across the table. "So Daddy and Mommy can have a little quality time together. All right?"

"Okay," squeaked the clock. It cowered back against the wall.

"Mrs. Niemand!" The calendar fluttered its pages at her as she walked past. "I implore you—don't do anything you'll regret later."

"There's not going to be a later." The gun's weight dangled at the end of her arm. "So regret's not a problem."

"Sarah!" Using her real name, the calendar cried after her. "Please . . . don't . . ."

In the front part of the hovel, a space barely wider than what her outstretched arms could have reached across, the percussion on the door was even louder. Enough to start peeling some of the web of silvery duct tape and glue-tacky patches away from the torn seams and other leak points. The hovel shivered and hissed as though apprehending its own demise. Sarah wondered what Deckard was going on about, pounding on the door with that much force. *He's that happy about being home?* Maybe he had finally flipped out, gone all the way around the bend of that dark corridor that'd always been there inside his head; some bad retro-TV fantasy of domestic bliss had wormed its way into his thoughts and taken over. Some vision of Mr. Niemand coming back here after a long, hard day at work, to be greeted by Mrs. N in a lace-edged kitchen apron and heels, bearing a cold stainless-steel pitcher of gin and vermouth—the life their great-great-grandparents had lived, at least inside their sitcom fantasies.

"Take it easy!" More strips of sealant tape dangled loose, trailing like thick party streamers from the hovel's low ceiling. "You're going to knock the place over—" A muffled voice came from the other side of the door, but Sarah couldn't make out what he'd said. She batted another sticky section of tape away from her face and reached for the door's knob.

In the sliver of time it took to turn the knob and pull the wobbling front door open, Sarah had entertained the notion of going with Deckard's anticipatory fantasy . . . or at least stringing him along with it for a few minutes. She could act as though there were, in fact, some measure of affection between them; she could even try once more to be Rachael, his long-dead and long-remembered love. The pretending wouldn't be unpleasant; there was still a room inside her head in which her own desire for all of that was still kept, like an ancient white wedding dress, never used and carefully folded between sheets of tissue paper.

It's what the bastard deserves, thought Sarah as her fingertips touched the doorknob. To be jerked around the way she had been, by a forged-iron chain bolted to the heart. To be led to believe one thing, even for a second, then be slammed up against the even more unyielding steel wall of reality . . .

In her other hand, the one dangling by her side as she reached to pull open the door, she had the perfect representation of what reality had come to mean for her. Loaded and cocked; she had already decided she didn't want to even try to screw around with Deckard's head anymore. There would be no Rachel-like homecoming kiss for him. If there were any irrational hopes left inside the sonuvabitch that would rise upon his seeing the human original of the replicant face for which he'd fallen, they'd be dashed by the very next thing he'd see. A circle of cold metal, with a darker black space at its center—Sarah's hand was already lifting the gun into position as she stepped back from the door swinging open toward her.

Two faces looked in at her. Two men, neither of them Rick Deckard. The eyes behind their matching square-rimmed glasses widened as they focussed on the gun she was holding a few inches from their foreheads.

"Um . . . is this the Niemand residence?" The man to the left swallowed nervously. The two of them didn't appear to be twins, but looked as if they were trying to be. "If it's not . . . we're sorry . . ."

"Maybe this is a bad time." Beads of sweat had welled up on the other's brow; tiny images of the gun floated in the wet mirrors. "Maybe we could come back . . . some other time."

Sarah let the gun lower of its own weight. She leaned against the side of the doorway; the hovel swayed and audibly creaked. "My apologies, gentlemen." Beyond the pair, the dimly lit corridors of the U.N. emigrant colony were visible, the rounded angles filled with rubble trembling in the airloss breezes. "I just woke up."

One of the men tried an uneasy smile. "You were expecting someone else?"

"My husband, actually."

The two men exchanged glances, their heads pivoting a

fraction of an inch toward each other, as though linked by some simple, invisible mechanism. The same unseen gear turned their owlish gazes back to Sarah.

"Mrs. Niemand—" The one on the left spoke with somber intonation. "We can tell that you lead a tragic life."

In the corridor leading toward the emigrant colony's center, beneath the banks of flickering or grey-dead fluorescent tubes, devolved human figures moved, scuttling furtively with their last meager, pawnable treasures clutched to their chests, heading for the ragtag booths and alleys of the black-market district. Even farther down the scale, appearing hardly human at all, were the creeping forms of those who had completely fallen out of the colony's hard-screw economy, those who'd come to the frayed end of their money and possessions and had been cut off from the cable monopoly's feed. Faces devoid of reason as any vegetable lifted and swiveled toward the scene at the Niemand hovel's front door, idiot eyes and other receptors searching for any sensory input. Red stigmata flecked the angles of the stimulus-lorn heads, with the same markings repeated on the corridor's dented walls. Every muscle near the softly keening mouths twitched with the constant hunger of misfired synapses.

A tragic life, mused Sarah as she gazed past the two surprise callers. The length of her vision reached beyond the other locked or boarded-up hovel doors to low-ceilinged rooms containing yet more collapsing nervous systems. She wasn't sure what the man meant. She had worked a long time to engineer the destiny that had brought her to this place. A particular hell, or any one at all—*I belong here,* thought Sarah.

Seized by a dreadful suspicion, she refocussed on the two men at her door. "You're not Jehovah's Witnesses, are you?" That would be all she needed right now, to get handed an animated *Watchtower,* complete with stereophonic sound effects triggered by the warmth of her thumb and forefinger. "Or New Reformed Apocalypticists?" Another of the groups that had been seen recently, evangelizing through the emigrant colonies—she looked to see if one of them was carrying a miniature holographic projector suitable for evoking biblical dioramas in the corridor's thin, acrid-smelling air.

The two men gazed blankly at her through their black-rimmed, square lenses. "No—" The left one shook his head. "We're not here to ask you for money or anything—"

Her laugh barked out. "Good call."

"This is a personal matter. For you alone, Mrs. Niemand." He raised a pale, fussily manicured hand, pointing to the interior of the hovel behind her. "May we come in? To talk with you? I'm sure you'll find it of interest."

Gun dangling at her side, Sarah peered more closely at the two men. They seemed oddly familiar to her, positions on a memory track that her brain hadn't moved along for some time. Her eyes had adjusted to the corridor's partial light spectrum; she could better perceive the pair now. White shirts and narrow-lapelled suits, black as an old-fashioned undertaker's; anal-retentive bow ties cinched tight onto their reedy, knobbly throats, not much bigger around than the narrow wrists exposed at their cuffs. The men's owlish regard, framed by the sharp-cornered spectacles, tweaked a cord in her gut.

The snufflers in the corridor's rubble had started edging closer, attracted by the sounds of human voices. Sarah knew that if she slammed the door shut and left the two men outside, and they went on pounding and calling to her through the thin panel, the hovel would be overrun by stim-desperate hordes, the pressure of their clambering bodies enough to collapse the rickety walls. "All right—" Sarah stepped back from the door. "Get in here. But you'd better make your spiel quick. As I said, I'm expecting my husband any time now." She gave another bitter laugh. "God knows he's a jealous sonuvabitch."

Once inside, with the corridor's sickly light and recycled air shut away, she busied herself with her black-market cigarettes, extracting one of the dwindling number from the cellophane-swathed pack and getting it lit. Tossing the charred match onto the floor with the others, she tilted her head back and dragged the smoke into the innermost recesses of her lungs, already feeling it percolate out into her clamoring veins. Exhaled, a blue cloud swirled, then streamed in a tapering thread toward the nearest leak in the wall. "So what is it you wanted to talk about?" Sarah didn't turn around, but could hear the two men shuffling in the room's narrow confines behind her. In a too-brief moment of sated peace, she regarded the orange-red coal at the end of the cigarette. "Whatever your pitch is, I hope it's good."

The one who had been doing all the speaking shifted his voice to a flat, level tone. "For starters, we know you're not anyone named Niemand. That's an alias. For both you and the former LAPD blade runner, real name Rick Deckard, with whom you've been posing as man and wife. Your name is Sarah Tyrell."

She stood where she was, showing no movement, no reaction. The grey shroud of her smoke-laden breath was the only sign of life. She had cupped an elbow in her free hand, hitting an aristocratic pose both studied and natural to her. The angle of her head, the trace of one dark lock across the corner of her brow—she could close her eyes and imagine herself another world and another life away from this one. Back in the executive suite and private living quarters of the Tyrell Corporation headquarters on Earth, in Los Angeles. Back in the tight, secretive epicenter of all the wealth and power she had inherited upon the death—the murder—of her uncle Eldon Tyrell. From the great, vaulted windows, there had been a view across the city's roiling inferno, the alleys and streets packed close at the base of the Tyrell ziggurat and slanting towers . . .

All gone now. Sarah watched the smoke twist and thin and disappear. L.A. remained, forever imploding inside the furious mass of its mottled citizens, glitter-eyed thieves and murderers and worse, locked in their scythe-led dance with the black-leather cops and blade runners and worse, all held in the masked, emotionless gaze of those urban tribespeople who'd cut themselves so far out of the loop that they might as well have been observers from another world, another time centuries forward or back. An Asian grace, jingling fleets of Chinese bicycles cutting through the neon-lit sheets of rain, ignoring the diluting blood and broken glass at the weary assassin's feet. Sarah knew that was the discreet charm of L.A.—you could go about your business, even if it meant killing people, or the things that looked just like people, and everyone else on the street would mind their own affairs. Even when the Tyrell Corporation headquarters had self-destructed, in the apocalypse that she herself had engineered and brought to pass, there had probably been streets full of faces that had glanced up for only a moment at the fire turning the night sky's rain to steam; then they had returned to scurrying and pushing and shoving toward their own dark, unknowable desires.

"Miss Tyrell?" The man's voice came from behind her, cutting through the deep reverie, the vision of that other world and time, into which she had fallen. "There really is no use denying it. We know who you are."

A certain pleasure came from hearing her own true name spoken again. By anyone other than Deckard, in whose mouth it was something close to a curse, a prison sentence she could never outlive.

Sarah looked over her shoulder at the two men, giving them the coldest edge of her half smile. "So what agency are you from?" She raised an eyebrow. "The local authorities?" There were police in the emigrant colonies, but they worked almost entirely for the cable monopoly, terrorizing deadbeat subscribers and rooting out illegal taps on the wire. "Or perhaps you're from Earth. U.N.?" That was a possibility—the colonies were laced with informants ratting on each other to the intelligence clearinghouse back in Geneva. "Perhaps LAPD—it wouldn't surprise me." The point of her smile sharpened. "Though I should remind you—there's no extradition allowed between Earth and Mars. Per the U.N.'s emigration authority. So if you were planning on taking me back with you, to face whatever charges you might have against me, you're somewhat out of luck."

The more talkative man gave what was meant to be a smile both reciprocal and pleasant, but that came off eerily forced, a mannerism whose performance he had studied. "We didn't come to extradite you, Miss Tyrell."

For a moment, she doubted if they were any kind of police at all. *They must be some kind of amateurs,* thought Sarah. After lighting the cigarette, she had picked up the gun again from where she had set it down; it even had the right number of bullets to take care of both of the men. Unless they had some kind of major backup standing around near the hovel, these two might just as well have marched into their own coffins.

"All right," she said. The gun made a convenient pointer to direct toward each of the men in turn. "If you're not police, then what the hell are you?"

"Don't you know?" The same man peered at her, the expression on his face one of both puzzlement and a disappointment bordering on sheer heartbreak. "Can't you tell just by looking at us?"

She frowned. "I never saw either one of you before."

"You might have. But you probably wouldn't remember, or even have noticed. You wouldn't have had to."

The disquieting feeling she had gotten before, when she had studied the men's appearance out on the hovel's doorstep, arose in her again. She felt the pressure of the two pairs of eyes, slightly magnified and distorted behind the square glasses . . .

That's it. Sarah nodded slowly to herself. *The glasses.* She knew as well that it hadn't been a lapse of memory—a failure to remember—but her own silent, unspoken will shutting out that image of another face, older than either of these two men, wrinkled like parchment or thin, ancient leather. With a gaze that had been grossly enlarged by lenses of exactly the same shape, clear squares bordered in heavy black; so that the eyes had appeared like high-resolution, full-color video screens, that watched and judged and cruelly absorbed all who fell within their scan. That was the memory that the two men's appearance had triggered but some defensive portion of her brain had shut out, lest it wound her again. The memory of her uncle's gaze, the glass-shrouded eyes of Eldon Tyrell.

As much as was possible for the two men standing in front

of Sarah in the hovel, they had managed to turn themselves into grotesque clones of the replicant-murdered head of the Tyrell Corporation. Or tributes to that fallen leader, the totem aspects—the square-framed glasses precise as geometrizing instruments, the equally meticulous and fussy clothes—incorporated like the fetishes of the dead into their own gestalt. Ineffectually, futilely; the two figures lacked the old man's withered potency, the timeless and time-fed negative aura of great wealth and greater desire, moving through dark-shaded spaces, silent rooms, bank vaults, and sweat-glistening silk bedsheets.

The two men looked like overgrown, lank-limbed children dressed up in their father's discarded clothing. Sarah felt a shiver of instinctive fear as she gazed upon them, catching sight of the mad worm at the pupils' centers behind the square glasses.

Held for a moment longer by the fear—of the two living men and the dead one—she could not speak.

"We're not from the police," said the one who'd spoken before. "We're from the Tyrell Corporation."

Her flash of anger banished any other emotion. "There is no Tyrell Corporation." Her voice lashed out, the cutting tip of her own sharpened tongue. "Not anymore."

They exchanged another glance, then turned their magnified and now sorrowful gazes upon her again. The other one spoke: "We were afraid that was what you believed. That you didn't know."

Strips of sealant tape drifted like slow seaweed in the hovel's hissing drafts. Sarah batted away the nearest tendril with the muzzle of the gun. "Know what?"

Behind the square-framed glasses, the men's eyes lit up with simultaneous enthusiasm. "That the Tyrell Corporation wasn't destroyed. It survives. It still exists. As it always has and always will."

The fervor in the man's voice amused Sarah. "And this is what you came here to tell me." She could feel her own smile turning gentle, tolerant. "That there's a few faithful employees such as yourself—true believers—and you're somehow keeping the flame alive. Really . . ." She shook her head. "That's very touching. How many show up at the staff meetings? A couple dozen?"

The more talkative one glowered sulkily at her. "It's not just a few of us, Miss Tyrell. We're not fools."

"That's right," said his partner. "This is bigger than that. Much bigger. We represent the *other* Tyrell Corporation—the shadow company that already existed before the one that you knew was destroyed."

She made no reply. Because she knew that the men, the mysterious callers who had appeared on her doorstep, were speaking the truth. There had been intimations, things whispered and things left unspoken, referred to by only a nod and a partial, omniscient smile on the face of her uncle, all referring to that other Tyrell Corporation, the shadow of the one whose light-studded Aztec pyramid had loomed over the dense sprawl of Los Angeles. *Shadow* being the operative word; an entity made of darkness that moved in darkness and did dark things. Darker than what Eldon Tyrell and the corporation that acted out in the open did—which would take some effort, Sarah knew. She was familiar enough with all the conspiracies and clandestine operations, the pulling of strings fine as the strands of a spider's web, a silken net that covered all of Earth and the worlds beyond. That was what she had inherited, what the death of the only other living Tyrell had left to her. And what she had destroyed, had turned to ashes as cold as those in the alabaster urn with Eldon Tyrell's name engraved on the side. She had annihilated the works of his hands, the vision that had been held in the cold fish eyes behind the square-rimmed spectacles; the hole left in the heart, the center, of L.A. had probably already been filled in by now, the charred ruins of the Tyrell Corporation headquarters carted off or incorporated into a new squatter ghetto.

So if these two, thought Sarah Tyrell, *are from the shadow corporation . . .*

There was no need to put words to the remainder of what had awoken and moved inside her skull. The two men standing in the center of the hovel looked like geeks, pathetic imitations of their dead boss. That was what made them dangerous, convinced her of what they claimed to be. Just as the late Eldon Tyrell, they had no need of pumped-up appearances, the visible aspects of power and threat. They lived in the dark spaces between the world's daylight manifestations, operated there, and went about their secret errands, continuing to pull the delicate spider strands that had drifted loose from a dead man's grasp.

I should've known . . . that I could never get away from them. The realization moved like a thread of ice down her spine. Not just the two men, these representatives of the shadow corporation that had survived after the other, the visible one, was no more . . . but her uncle as well. *It's just like the bastard,* Sarah brooded. *Leave it to Eldon Tyrell to achieve immortality, to find a way to go on screwing with other people's lives from beyond the grave.*

The image of her uncle's face, with its wrinkled skin close to the bone, winter-cold optics, and mocking smile, faded from her sight, revealing the only slightly unsettling visages of the two men before her. She sighed, feeling the last elements of resistance draining from her body. "All right—" She nodded slowly. "What is it you want? Why'd you come here? What do you want from me?"

"Want from you?" The eyes behind the square-rimmed glasses looked puzzled. The more talkative man tilted his head as though trying to shake something loose. "We don't want *anything* from you."

"Well . . ." His partner nudged him. "Except, of course . . . you yourself . . ."

"Pardon me?" Sarah laughed, incredulous. She wouldn't have thought that these two would've been interested in anything that normal and human. "That's okay, though . . . I'm flattered." She tossed her hair back from her eyes. It'd been a long time, since practically the moment of their arrival at the emigrant colony, that Deckard had laid a hand on her, one way or another. At some point, the resemblance between herself and the dead Rachael had ceased to be enough. "But not today, thanks."

"Hm." The more talkative one rubbed his smooth chin. "I

think there's been some misunderstanding here. It's not a personal thing—"

"It's not *us,*" interjected his partner, "who want you."

"It's the corporation. The shadow corporation." The little mad light went on again behind the square glasses. "That's what needs you. That's why we spent so much time and effort looking for you, and why we came all this way to find you."

"That's right." His partner nodded vehemently. "Without you . . . we're nothing. The corporation—the shadow corporation—it's nothing."

A growing spark moved along the edges of her own suspicion. "Why should that be?" Her eyes narrowed as she gazed at the two men. She had a notion already, but wanted to hear it explained aloud.

"Miss Tyrell . . . isn't it obvious?" The talkative one spread his empty hands apart. "How can there be a Tyrell Corporation—or even its shadow—without a Tyrell to head it? You are the heir to everything that your uncle created. Both the corporation that existed in the light and the one of the darkness. There's a right of succession involved here. Surely you know—you *must* know—that there's more to the Tyrell Corporation than merely a commercial enterprise."

"Oh, I know," said Sarah. *I know too well.* "It's a matter of faith."

"Exactly. You must have faith—just as we have." The light had intensified in both men's eyes. "The faith that all the shadow corporation has. That Eldon Tyrell's great vision—all that he wished and planned for humanity—will be reborn. That the Tyrell Corporation will rise from the ashes. Not as it was, but as something even greater. As its destiny always had been."

"You see, don't you?" The other one spoke up. "That's why the shadow corporation exists. That's why Eldon Tyrell created it and kept it in the darkness. You were his heir, the only other living Tyrell—and then the only Tyrell at all—and you didn't even know about it."

"No . . . I didn't." Sarah gave a shake of her head. "Not really." She wasn't certain now whether she had known or not—or whether she had just chosen to disbelieve the little hints and rumors, the mysteries that her uncle had alluded to with his sly conspirator's smile. *You fool,* she told herself. *To think you could ever kill it . . .*

"He couldn't tell you about the shadow corporation. It had to remain a secret. From everyone—even you. Only those of us sworn to its mysteries; we alone knew, and waited." The man's voice trembled with fervor. "For that day we knew was inevitable, the day of triumph for the Tyrell Corporation's enemies—"

"Short-lived triumph," grumped the talkative one's partner.

"Yes, that's right. Of course." He nodded. "The darkness cannot last; the Tyrell Corporation will not be vanquished forever. If its enemies think they have destroyed it, sown salt across its ashes, they're wrong. The Tyrell Corporation—the glory of Eldon Tyrell's vision—will mount to the skies again. Already, we in the shadow corporation, the heirs and defenders of that vision, have set moving the great wheels and gears of justice."

"We like to say"—the other's voice turned shy and self-conscious—"that the sole of our sandal shall be upon the throat of our foes."

"I bet." Sarah kept her face masklike, and the gun in her hand. All this talk of enemies and retribution made her wary. When these people said they needed her—that the Tyrell Corporation's shadow entity needed her—they possibly meant they wanted her head on a pike. Her self-destructive moods hadn't included relinquishing that much control to anyone else. "Well, if you have plans already, then maybe you should just . . . *go* and do them. Don't let me stop you. Drop me a line now and then, let me know how things are coming along." Right now, she mainly wanted the two odd men, with their Eldon Tyrell stylings, to just disappear. So that she would have time to think, to figure out what she herself would do next. *There's not much sense,* mused Sarah, *in blowing away these two guys. That wouldn't stop anything.* The thought of these two—and how many others? How big was this shadow outfit?—working away to put back together all that she had so carefully disassembled filled her with both nausea and a tightly concealed rage. "Thanks for stopping by."

The two men exchanged a glance with each other, then swiveled their conjunct gaze back onto her.

"Miss Tyrell—you really don't seem to understand." The more talkative one's voice filled with sorrow. "We need *you.* We can't resurrect the Tyrell Corporation without you."

"We're loyalists. Diehards," added the other man. "Everyone in the shadow corporation—we were sworn to loyalty to Eldon Tyrell . . . and now to you. You didn't inherit just the Tyrell Corporation. You inherited *us.*"

"You're joking. You must be." The notion appalled her. The two men suddenly appeared to her as children to whom she bore some crushing maternal obligation. As if her ancient uncle had been reborn as twins, fresh-faced and naively innocent behind the stigmata of the square glasses. The resurrection of all that she had thought was safely dead—*Now what?* thought Sarah. A horrible vision came to her of these two camping out in the hovel, taking turns sleeping on the broken-backed sofa.

"It's no joke, Miss Tyrell. We never joke." The talkative one's expression was somber, as though even the skull beneath the tight flesh had been rendered grinless. "It is our great mission—our destiny—to bring the Tyrell Corporation, from the shadows where it now exists, out to the light once more. Where it belongs. At the center of all, with everything orbiting around it—"

"But that would make it the light itself." The other man frowned. "Like it was the sun. You're mixing up—"

"Whatever," snapped the first irritably. "You know what I mean. As does Miss Tyrell." He looked back at her again. "You do know, don't you? Why we've come here?"

"I know," she said. There was no use denying it any longer. She didn't need the gun—not against these two. Or any of their brethren, the true believers. "You want me to be the head of the Tyrell Corporation. As I was before. After my uncle . . . died."

"Exactly." The man nodded. "You must do this. If the

Tyrell Corporation is to defeat its enemies. Those who were so misguided as to try to diminish Eldon Tyrell's vision."

He doesn't know, thought Sarah. *They don't have a clue.* That she had been the one who pushed the little red button, or arranged to have it pushed by those others she had cheated and lied to. The ashes of the Tyrell Corporation headquarters, those once-proud towers and the eternal-seeming pyramid in the center of Los Angeles, were on her hands. These two men, and all the other die-hard loyalists behind them, didn't know that she herself had destroyed the Tyrell Corporation.

"Without you . . ." The man's voice came to her as though from the edge of a barely glimpsed dream. "Without you . . . we'll die. The shadows will claim us. The vision that still unites us will be lost, our faith gone, and we will drift off into the darkness. Then the Tyrell Corporation truly will be no more."

I don't have to do a single thing. The realization moved inside Sarah. She could just stand where she was in the hovel and refuse to go with the two men—she knew they were too much in awe of her, of the Tyrell blood in her veins, to try to force her to go anywhere. Or she could go ahead and kill them, simply raise the gun, still in her hand, place it against each man's forehead in turn—they probably wouldn't resist that, either, just accept it from her as what they deserved from a wrathful deity. *Or even better,* thought Sarah, *I could kill myself. Right in front of them.* That would accomplish a lot—almost everything, she decided. She'd be dead—something for which she'd been yearning for a long time now—and the Tyrell Corporation's shadow entity, this valiant little band of the faithful, would die out soon thereafter. No living Tyrell, no corporation, all lost, finally and forever. Perfect . . .

Except for one thing. She knew just what it was. Deckard, that sonuvabitch, would still be walking around. Still mourning his dead Rachael, a shrine to a female replicant assembled inside his skull, memory scraps and the taste of her kiss, the way her face had looked—*My face,* Sarah thought grimly; *Rachael's was just a copy*—when he'd forced his kiss upon her. And she had given herself to him, wanting him . . .

She couldn't remember anymore whether that had been her or Rachael. There had been a time, a moment, when time had repeated itself; the kiss, the wanting, even his words. She had made Deckard say them again, the way he had said them to Rachael long ago . . .

Say that you want me. He had said that.

Then her voice. In the past, in memory. Standing in the middle of the hovel, a world away; she closed her eyes and heard her own voice, Rachael's voice, the same—

I want you.

"Miss Tyrell . . . did you say something?"

She forced her eyes open and looked at the two men standing in front of her, not recognizing them for a moment. Or mis-recognizing them; she had the uncomfortable feeling that she was looking at her uncle, brought back from the dead and somehow doubled, with neither aspect quite human. Then the feeling passed, and she found herself once again looking at the two loyalists, ambassadors from the shadow corporation. If they weren't real—or at least not yet—they were certainly trying to be.

A shake of the head. "No," said Sarah. She wondered if she had spoken aloud, if the words of the past had forced their way into the present once again. *How embarrassing,* she thought. Though it proved that nothing ever died. As long as there was memory, there were ghosts. *Like me*—perhaps when Deckard looked at her, that was what he saw. The ghost of Rachael. "No—I didn't say anything."

Sarah watched as the two men consulted with each other, whispers and nods. They finished and turned back toward her.

"We don't have much time, Miss Tyrell." The more talkative one, the evident leader of the pair, clasped his hands together. "Our enemies—the enemies of the Tyrell Corporation—they very likely know that we're here. They'd do anything to stop us, to thwart our sacred mission. We have to leave. *Now.*"

"We've stayed here too long already." The other one cast a

nervous glance over his shoulder, toward the hovel's front door, as though he expected a black-clad SWAT team to come bursting through at any moment.

"You have to come with us, Miss Tyrell." The talkative one's intertwined fingers squeezed themselves white and bloodless. "There's so much more we need to tell you. And that we can show you. But you must come with us. You *must.*"

"All right—" Sarah held up a hand, palm outward. "There's no need to hector me. I've made my decision." It had been easy, once the image of Deckard had come into her mind. "I'll go with you. Wherever you want." Of all the possibilities, those that had her dead while Deckard would still be alive—those had been ruled right out. As if a terminating memo had been sent down from the corporate headquarters, that columned, high-ceilinged chamber that still existed behind her brow.

Besides, thought Sarah. *It's mine; the Tyrell Corporation, in all its guises, shadowed or in light.* She could do whatever she wanted with it. A glance from the corner of her eye showed the two men, in their homage-to-Eldon-Tyrell outfits, in a new light; they belonged to her as well, part of the package. A familiar sensation, one that ran from her groin all the way to the top of her spine and beyond. They looked at her, not just reverently, but would not have dared to touch her. She could use them for whatever purpose she had in mind, and they would be grateful. Just to be in her presence and bear her orders.

That notion made her smile, one corner of her mouth lifting a millimeter.

She thought of Deckard, wherever he was at this moment. Perhaps coming home—if this counted as home—after his stint trolling for money at that Outer Hollywood station above Earth. Coming home to whatever surprise he might've figured would be waiting for him—the gun at the door probably wouldn't have been completely unexpected. *If I were gone, though*—Sarah mulled it over—*that might knock him back.* For a little while, at least.

Which would give her time to prepare another surprise for

Deckard. The last one he'd ever receive. She wasn't sure yet what it would be. But with all the resources of the shadow corporation at her fingertips . . . a mere gun and a single bullet now struck her as entirely too simple.

I'll have to do better than that, thought Sarah. *It's only what he deserves.*

"Please, Miss Tyrell—" The duo's leader made a show out of checking the complicated watch on his thin wrist. "We really have to get going."

"I suppose so." She turned and headed toward the hovel's bedroom. "Just let me get a few things."

She took one of the bullets from the gun's clip, using its weight to hold down on the bedside table a note she'd quickly scribbled out for Deckard. *There*—Sarah stood up from the mattress edge. *Let him figure that one out.* The alarm clock walked across the folded piece of paper and looked down at the bullet, the face behind the black hands seemingly mystified.

In the minuscule bathroom, she splashed water on her face, then straightened up from the sink and pulled her dark hair back with one hand. For a moment longer, Sarah returned the gaze from the figure in the clouded mirror. It didn't look like Rachael standing there. Or only a little; the sad dreaminess that had always marked her replicant double had been leached away, replaced by something harder and colder. *That's my face,* thought Sarah. The cheekbones were more pronounced, edged sharper, as though the flesh were being cut away by interior knives. She toweled off the water trickling down her throat and turned back toward the hovel's bedroom.

The calendar on the wall fluttered its page as she approached the doorway. "Mrs. Niemand—I mean Sarah—" The calendar's voice betrayed its anxiety. "What're you doing? This is madness. You don't know who these men are—"

"How rude." Sarah glared at the snow-covered wilderness scene. "You were listening in."

"Of course. I'm a calendar; I'm supposed to keep track of things." The number-dense pages fluttered. "Listen to me. These characters are trouble. They could be anybody. Lunatics . . . or maybe they really are the police; they're just lying to you. To get you to go quietly." Its voice rose in pitch. "I beg of you. Don't go with these people—"

"I have to." Sarah repositioned the strap of the little shoulder bag she had hurriedly packed. "It's my destiny. Or as close to it as I'm going to get."

"Sarah . . ." The calendar wailed as she exited the bedroom.

"Let's go, gentlemen." Pulling the bag up higher, she nodded toward the hovel's front door. The two men stepped aside and let her go ahead of them.

In the corridor outside, she heard tiny feet running through the decaying trash. The minute noise came from behind; she turned and looked, and saw the alarm clock racing to catch up.

"Take me with you!" The clock's shrill, tinny voice sliced through the oxygen-thin air. "I wanna go, too!"

She stopped and pulled the shoulder bag around so she could root through its contents. The gun's weight had sunk it to the bottom; by the time Sarah pulled it out, the alarm clock was right in front of her, hopping excitedly from one of its stubby little legs to the other.

The shot echoed down the corridor, smudged leaves of rubble trembling in the invisible, hard-edged wave. The stimulus-hungry derelicts raised their blind heads, limbs trembling in the rush of ecstatic input, bloodied fingertips clawing convulsively at the floor grates. A smaller noise followed after the first, tinkling bits of metal and fractured microcircuits raining softly across the spot where the alarm clock, until the last moment, had been dancing.

"Damn." Sarah looked at the warmed gun in her palm. "Now it's empty."

One of the men, the leader of the pair who had called upon her, reached over and took the gun out of her hand. "Don't worry." He threw it away, metal clanging against metal as it struck the corridor wall. "We'll get you another one."

At the landing field, in the bare red flats on the emigrant colony's edge, he got screwed.

They wouldn't give Deckard his deposit back on the skiff. "What're you going to do?" said the man behind the desk—really just a buckling sheet of plywood supported by two empty fuel drums. The man took no pleasure in the burn, but just looked at Deckard with the flat, unblinking eyes of someone who knows he's being a bastard. "We're an illegal business already. You're going to report us or something? Get real."

Deckard turned his own gaze away from the man's heavy, black-stubbled face, and out toward the small interplanetary craft scattered over the rust-colored sands. From one hand dangled the briefcase with his initials on the tiny metal plate below his knuckles. "There's other ways," he said quietly, then looked back at the man. "Of getting my money back."

"Sure there is. You can beat the crap out of me, for one." The man shrugged, crescents of sweat-darkened shirt riding up under his fleshy arms. "Whatever sings your song, buddy. I don't care." A slow, wobbling shake of the head. "But you're still not getting your money back. And don't ever bother bringing your business around here again. You ever want off-planet, you'll have to flap your wings and jump."

The briefcase whispered to Deckard. "Come on, don't waste your time with this lowlife. We've got things to do."

"You say something, pal?"

"No—" Deckard shook his head. "Just grumbling to myself. Tell you what. I'll settle for half of what you owe me."

He settled for nothing. He was too tired to argue any further.

"Count your blessings," the skiff guy called after him from the doorway of the shack. "You got back here still breathing. Most of our customers don't. Our merchandise has got over a fifty percent failure rate."

"Nice advertising pitch." Batty's voice spoke up, louder this time, as Deckard toted the briefcase across the field. "Lot of possibilities—'Rent from us and you'll never have to again.' "

Deckard made no reply. *If half of these things made it home,* he thought gloomily, *it'd be a miracle.* With his free hand, he rubbed blood-tinged grit from his eyes. *I must've been crazy.* All around him, as he trudged in sinking footsteps, the skiffs dug lower in the sand, like the black eggs of some extinct, exhausted species. The vehicles' dented, corrosion-flecked carapaces transmitted a minimal-wattage signal of neglect and abortive transport. Some of them, including the one he'd taken to the Outer Hollywood station and back, looked as fragile as ancient Christmas decorations, hand-blown glass that a sneeze could shatter. An indication of how desperate he must've been—*And still am,* thought Deckard. *Even worse now.* Getting stiffed on the deposit had chewed another major hole in his cash float.

"Don't worry." The briefcase, Batty's voice inside, radiated a familiar confidence. "I haven't even begun telling everything that's in store for you."

"I can't wait." Deckard had to remind himself that Dave Holden had died in order to carry this thing out to him. He supposed he owed his dead ex-partner the posthumous courtesy of listening to it. Shading his eyes with one hand, he peered out of the limply fluttering, low-pressure bubble tunnel that extended from the rental yard shack. He was in luck, or as much of it as existed in his personal universe. Through the sand-scoured plastic, he spotted a worm-treaded shuttle working its way across the desert; the segmented ground transport was probably ferrying contract miners back from the jagged hills to the planet's east. He and the briefcase could hitch a ride all the way in to the emigrant colony's imploded center. "Now would be a good time to clam up again," he told the disembodied voice. Sealing his mouth and nose off with the palm of his free hand, he unzipped the bubble's exit flap and shouldered out into the stinging wind to flag down the shuttle.

"Hey—I'm discreet." The briefcase's voice slid through the crystals stinging against the side of Deckard's face. "You're not the only person who can carry off a silent act."

On the shuttle, he sat with the briefcase on his knees, sandwiched in between the mine workers on the scuffed steel benches, each breath taking in the mingled odors of their sweat. The jogging motion of the treads across the red dunes rocked the bodies from side to side, bumping hard into Deckard's shoulders. No conversations sounded in the shuttle's tight interior; the mine workers sat with their silted bandannas pulled down around their throats, breathmasks and rehydration tubes dangling disconnected like some amphibian species' vestigial organs. They all looked to Deckard like first-generation Mars natives, some of the younger ones possibly second-gen, the children and grandchildren of the Earth-born emigrants who'd gotten this far and had then given up on getting all the way to the stars. Through eyelids drawn nearly as tight as the shuttle's slit windows, they gazed out on the landscape that they'd inherited, that they had evolved to possess. Deckard could sense the rewiring of the nervous systems sitting around and across from him, the shuffling of synaptic fibers and input receptors that had taken place in the womb, the human body's instinctive response to the foreign territory in which it had been exiled.

The creatures around him, that still wore the outward appearance of human beings, were off the cable monopoly's feed. They didn't need the canned stimuli to survive; they could go out into the hills and dry ravines and suck up all the bandwidth this world had to offer. Deckard had wondered before what their strangers' eyes saw, what their spatulate, black-nailed fingertips read from the grains of red sand trickling through their touch. He'd given up wondering; he had enough trouble dealing with human things, and the things that were at least trying to be human. There was more in common between his blood and that of the replicants he'd killed before than there was between him and the sharp-angled faces that stared past him as if he no longer existed.

The fatigue seeping from Deckard's bones, forearms lying like deadweights across the briefcase in his lap, drew his eyelids shut. With the scent of alien sweat in his nostrils, the press of blood-warm flesh near his own, he almost believed himself to be back on Earth, in L.A., the dark, neon-veined city extending on all sides around one of the cramped public buses shoving its way through the traffic stalled with retrofitted Detroit relics. He'd always felt overwhelmed by sheer otherness there as well; simply being on the planet, in the city, on the streets where he'd spent his whole life, that didn't mean he could look into the face right next to his, so close he could practically taste the other's mingled exhalations of *kimchi* and *phrik kii noo* and see anything that resembled a mirror, anything that made him think he was looking at his own genetic code.

That was a bad mental place to be in, especially for a cop wearing a big black gun inside his jacket. Even more so when you'd been working the blade runner unit, and you were *supposed* to blow away anything that didn't pass for human with you; that was your *job.* It'd been his; it'd been Dave Holden's, and a bunch of other poor crazed bastards'. Some of whom he'd worked with, some he'd steered a wide distance away from, catching that weird look in their eyes and the subliminal tick of a dynamite clock counting down. Some of the blade runners he'd known had wound up massaging the backs of their throats with their gun muzzles and had gone under the ground in carefully sealed caskets. Others were still out there on the streets, chasing their own deaths and the accusatory revelation that could only be glimpsed in the eyes of those you are about to kill. Or *retire,* to use that morally compromised departmental lingo.

Riding in a worm-tread shuttle across another world's dead surface, Rick Deckard felt himself sweating, a crawl of self-generated excretions over his skin. An old, familiar claustrophobia tightened his muscles, a shrinking from contact with the creatures around him. Not to avoid their touch, but to keep them from being touched by him. Why should they suffer? As he did . . .

He opened his eyes and turned his head to look out the slit window behind him. A desultory wind moved red sand around, like the floor-sweepings of his heart. There were supposed to be other creatures out there, skinny wolflike slinkers, all lank jaws and burning eyes—he'd thought he'd spotted one before, the barest glimpse of motion from the corner of his eye, when he'd been on his way out to the skiff rental yard. You didn't have to eat a gun to find release; you could simply wander out past the emigrant colony's limits, keep walking, and your splintered bones would be found, marrow sucked out like soft marzipan.

To have spotted that wolfish spectre, seen it before its teeth closed on your throat—that was a bad sign. *I've been here too long,* thought Deckard. His neuro-system was starting to adapt, sensors working overtime, picking up the wavelengths of a world he hadn't been born on. That happened sometimes—rumors and emigrant myths were rife—the whole process cannon-firing ahead, not taking two or three generations to work itself out. At some unconscious, cellular level, the poor bastard to whom it happens just gives up on being human, lets go and becomes . . . something else. *Like these things around me*—Deckard glanced at the sullen, motionless forms lining the interior of the shuttle. One way or another, they'd already said their good-byes to all the others they'd left behind.

The shuttle ground on, nearing the emigrant colony's perimeter. A muted rustling moved through the seated figures, the mine workers rousing themselves from reptiloid torpor—the tiny shifts of their bodies, raising of heads, glances out the narrow windows, reminded Deckard of lizards on sun-baked rocks, the flick of yellow, slitted eyes toward an insect too far away to catch and eat. He supposed they probably were thinking about whatever meals were waiting for them—they had the lean, knife-ribbed look of people who went a long time between protein sources—in the dark shacks and nests of the colony's most silent quarter.

Speculating about aliens with human faces, and what their unknowable lives might be like, had one advantage: it had derailed the even darker reverie into which Deckard had fallen, that pit lined with self-accusation he knew all too well. Now he could put on his own mask, the one that looked just like him but bore the name Niemand, and go home and see what Mrs. Niemand had waiting on the table for him.

God only knows, thought Deckard glumly as the shuttle slowed down to a crawl, the soft labial flaps of the colony's ground transport airlocks folding over the windows. What Sarah would've gotten up to, decided upon, in his absence—she was as far around the bend, he knew, as he himself was. The married state of the pseudonymous Niemands, the alias he shared along with equal measures of hate and guilt, was as mentally toxic as any sensory void to be found on Mars. No vacuum existed between himself and Sarah; the space between them was filled, and overfilled, with memory and the slow ebbing tide of the past that left things on a common shoreline—old photos, sheet music on an untuned piano, names whispered in that sad moment between sleep and waking, empty bottles overturned by a fumbling hand. Everything that could be picked up, still tear-wet, and studied as it turned to the same ashes in his and Sarah's mouths . . .

No wonder she was as crazy as he was. How could she be anything else?

"Takes you back, doesn't it?" The briefcase with Roy Batty's voice spoke up as Deckard toted it through the colony's body-dense main corridor, the hubbub of the black-market stalls, customers and purveyors, swirling around them. "Feels like being back at home, doesn't it? Your real home, I mean."

Deckard let his gaze, the hard encompassing cop scan that'd become engrained in his optic nerves, pass over the crowd. He knew what the briefcase meant, what it had picked up on without even having eyes. The city vibration, the inaudible blood-pressure hum beneath all the other shouting and murmuring voices—as he shouldered his way through, the briefcase dangling in one hand's tight grip, its corners catching like a barbed anchor against the press of others' thighs and hips, he saw the same faces he'd seen in his other life, the one spent on Earth. Nothing had changed, at least in its essential sense—identical eyes glittered too bright and hungry, whether they were naked or shielded behind dark lenses or bombardier-style goggles. Other eyes, that he remembered as well, opiated or glazed over with any number of pharmaceutical combinations—the marketplace's recycled air smelled rancid with the receptor-specific molecules exuded through the sweat upon shivering, pallid skin. And those whose eyes were still focussed, but on some point far from here, a deific vision they'd come to the shabbiest stall and overcoated, secret-pocketed vendors to find—Deckard remembered seeing those before as well.

"Just goes to show," he spoke aloud—nobody in the crowd noticed a person talking to himself or having a conversation with the small luggage he carried. "That L.A.'s not a place. It's an idea. A bad idea."

The crowd thinned out as Deckard got farther from the marketplace's center. He made better time, striding through the colony's residential quarters, his passage marked by the strips of loosened duct tape wavering overhead. Stepping over the crawling forms of the stim-deprived terminal cases, their blank stares swiveling up in his direction, Deckard reached for the knob of his hovel's front door.

The door was unlocked, and slightly ajar; the slightest push of his hand set it drifting into the unlit interior. Old cop instincts held Deckard back, his gaze moving across the revealed angle of motionless space inside.

"What's wrong?" The briefcase had sensed the hesitation.

"Nothing." Deckard drew in a careful breath, as though he could roll on his tongue any stray, captured atoms. "Everything . . ."

Once he'd had devices to do the work for him, the full array of department-issued gadgetry, the trick units that came out of the LAPD's research labs, down in the deepest basements where the sunless geeks groomed their oscilloscope tans. The voice-controlled espers, the softly breathing Voigt-Kampff machines—now he had to do it the old-fashioned way, firing up the subtle instincts that cops had depended on for centuries.

Something crackled under the sole of Deckard's boot as he shifted his weight. Looking down, he spied the bright glitter of fractured electronics, splinters of metal; a wedge of an autonomic clock face stared back at him, the little dots it'd had for eyes blank and inactive. More bits and pieces of the alarm clock, he saw now, were scattered for several meters near the hovel's entrance. He reached down and picked up a broken corner of a miniaturized circuit board; its edges crumbled as he rolled it between his thumb and forefinger. He threw the green-gritted fragment aside, then pushed the door the rest of the way open.

Deckard stepped inside the hovel, aware that it was empty of any other human form. He stood motionless in the center of the room, then slowly set the briefcase down beside himself.

"How does that old song go? Something about another mule in your stall?" Batty's voice sounded smug. Whatever sensors had been built into the briefcase were still as sharp as Batty's had been, in either his human or replicant incarnation. "There were other men here . . . just a little while ago, as a matter of fact. You can tell that, can't you?" The silence of a thin smile could almost be heard. "And you know what else? I don't think they were here to check the meters."

"Why don't you shut up," said Deckard in disgust. "As if I care." The truth was that he did, though not for any reasons of jealousy. Whatever sexual or romantic claim he and Sarah Tyrell might have had on each other had long since evaporated in the fierce glare of what they knew about, and had done to, each other. Even the resemblance between Sarah and his long-dead Rachael—close enough to constrict his heart each time he'd looked upon the living face—wasn't enough to evoke any emotion besides hatred. "She can do whatever she wants. We're not really Mr. and Mrs. Niemand, you know."

"Of course not." The briefcase's voice still contained its knowing smile. "That would be too easy—being the same thing inside as you are on the outside. You haven't been that in a long time, Deckard."

"Tell me about it." He gazed around the empty space and toward the dark rectangle of the bedroom door.

"And *of course* she can do whatever she wants. Except walk out on you. Because she's not here, is she?"

He didn't answer. Leaving behind the briefcase—and Roy Batty's mocking, under-the-skin voice—Deckard strode into the bedroom, flipping on the switch beside the door. Low-wattage light, yellow and flickering, seeped through the dusty web of tape and corner-dangling patches on the ceiling. The air seeping through the leaks wasn't enough to draw out the smell of aging laundry and bottoming-out mood swings.

"Mrs. Niemand isn't here." A different voice spoke behind him. "She left."

Deckard looked over his shoulder at the autonomic wall calendar, the companion to the alarm clock missing from the bedside table. "Where'd she go?"

The mountain-filled scene fluttered above the rows of numbers. "She didn't"—the calendar spoke aggrievedly—"choose to inform me of her destination." Its voice darkened. "*She* probably didn't even know."

There'd been a time that he and Rachael had spent out in the wilds in a ramshackle cabin surrounded by a dark cathedral of trees, north of the scene in the calendar photo. A too-brief interval between their fleeing L.A. and his being forced to return. Nights colored silver by moonlight, days blackened by the coffin that he'd sat beside, gazing at the sleeping face of the woman he loved. Sleeping and dying; the coffin, a transport module stolen from the Tyrell Corporation—the glass-lidded device in which replicants were shipped to the outer colonies before their four-year life spans could expire—had been the means of stretching out their stolen hours together. Of sipping half-life moments, rather than watching all time, all Rachael's life, spill out upon the ground and seep away like rain. *I thought I had it bad then*—his grieving station by the slowly dying woman, the silent vigils between the dwindling minutes of her waking. Looking at the picture on the wall calendar, Deckard knew he'd give the rest of his own life, if he could, to be back in the midst of that dark forest, in the yellowed circle of a kerosene lantern, sitting beside the coffin and waiting, waiting forever, in the unending moment between one dream and the next . . .

"Mr. Niemand?" The calendar's reedy voice tapped at the edge of his thoughts.

He'd give anything. Even the plans he'd made, the decisions and vows he'd sealed down into his heart, about what he'd do with Sarah Tyrell. Her fate, and his. *Even that . . .*

The calendar tried again, using his real name. "Mr. Deckard? Hello?"

A slow nod, the drawing in of his breath, as he refocussed on the calendar and the flat, meaningless picture on its surface. "All right," he said. "So who was it she went with?"

"I wouldn't know. She didn't tell me that, either." The calendar had an innate dislike for details not being filled in. "There were two of them—I could tell that much. They were talking in the other room, but I couldn't make out what they were saying. I just have this little directional microphone built in, you know. Now, if I had the intercom option, if you'd paid to have that feature activated, then the advantages would be—"

"Yeah, right." Deckard interrupted the sales pitch. A long-standing peeve of his was the way these low-rent domestic appliances were always whining for upgrades. "How long ago did all this happen? When did Sarah leave with these men?"

"You should ask the clock. That's more its department—"

"The clock's dead." Deckard didn't mind saying so. "So you tell me. When did they leave?"

"Um . . ." A fearful quaver sounded in the calendar's voice. "The clock? She did that, didn't she?" The calendar made an audible effort to pull itself together. "I guess . . . it was about, maybe six hours ago. That Mrs. Niemand—I mean Sarah—that she left with those two men. Gosh . . ." Its voice faded, then picked up again. "If it's any help, she left a note. Over there on the table."

Deckard walked over and picked up the bullet that had also been left for him. He rolled it between his fingers, then weighed it in his palm. A wordless message, or one that didn't need words to get its meaning across. Sarah had probably bought it, and the necessary gun as well, down in the black-market stalls, where just about anything could be acquired. Thus, she must've iced the nagging clock; on her way out, Deckard figured, with whoever these two men had been. *This one,* he thought, looking down at the bright, tapered metal, *was meant for me.* The kind of homecoming surprise he'd been expecting for a while now; his caution at the hovel's front door had been mainly due to not wanting a hole the size of a baby's fist plowed through his forehead.

He slipped the bullet into his jacket pocket and unfolded the scrap of paper that had been beneath it.

Deckard—The scrawl was Sarah's handwriting, the big ego-driven letters she'd never lost. *I'll see you later.*

The mute bullet had said as much. A warning, the cold kiss she'd greet him with the next time they met. He crumpled the paper into a wad in his fist, then tossed it into the rubble in the bedroom's corner.

"Off into the ozone?" Batty's voice curled mockingly. The briefcase sat in the middle of the hovel's front room, where Deckard had left it. "They like to do that. Take it from me; I know. They just leave."

He stepped over the briefcase and closed the door. "Not your problem, is it?" He brushed away the dangling strips of peeled tape. "You should mind your own business."

"Ah, but you see—your problems are mine, too." An invisible shrug. "You and I . . . we just have so much in common, Deckard."

"I doubt it." He crossed to the hovel's tiny kitchenette.

"You're in a box." Leaning over the sink crowded with moldering dishes, Deckard rooted through the top cupboard. "I've still got flesh to worry about." He found the square-sided bottle he wanted, pulled it out, and unscrewed the cap. "So the answers to my problems are different. Like this one."

"That smells like scotch. Or something close to it."

He rinsed out a usable glass and poured a two-finger shot into it. "They make it here." He tossed back the first fiery swallow, gritting his teeth as it rolled acid down his throat. "So it's not anything. Except grain alcohol and food coloring."

"Sounds grim. I'll pass. Even if I could drink."

"Good call." Deckard emptied the glass, feeling his gut contract with the hard liquid shock. He poured another and sat down at the kitchenette table with it, pushing aside more crusted dishes and fog-clouded glasses to make room for his elbows. He laid his head down on his forearms and closed his eyes. Exhaled liquor fumes cut the stale cloy of the hovel in his nostrils, an odor of sweat and pent-up anger that could never leak away through the poorly taped seams.

He knew that he could fall asleep if he let himself; the fatigue would wash over him, an ocean with its leading edge tinged brown by the bottle's contents. He also knew that it would do no good, that it would last only a few minutes at best, the same as it had in the skiff's cramped egg coming back from the Outer Hollywood station. A moment of darkness, then dreaming, then waking, with the border blurred between those two states; the way he used to raise his head and open his eyes, back in his apartment in Los Angeles, with an empty glass smelling of real scotch in one hand, the fingers of his other sunk into a silent chord on the piano's yellowed keys. Looking up at the faces in the old frayed-edged, black-and-white photos that had drifted across the music rest like dead leaves; looking at them and, for a few seconds, wondering who they were. Until he remembered again . . .

"All right." Deckard took a deep breath, opened his eyes, and straightened up in the chair. With his forefinger, he pushed the glass and its murky contents away from himself.

The room was small enough that he could twist around, reach back, and pick up the briefcase by its handle from where he had left it sitting in the middle of the floor. He swung the briefcase up onto the table, laying it flat in the space he'd cleared. "Let's hear it. You got something to tell me about, now's the time."

She found out their names. Or what passed for them.

"I'm Wycliffe," the more talkative one said. He leaned his elbows back on the yacht's control panel. "He's Zwingli."

"Right. I'm sure." Sarah Tyrell regarded the two men, her erstwhile kidnappers. Or employees—the distinctions were getting a little confused. *Maybe disciples,* she thought. That fervent light still glowed way inside their eyes. If not her disciples, then Eldon Tyrell's; the two men had done what they could to mold themselves into copies of her late uncle. Within the limits of the possible: they looked like children playing at a grim Halloween. "What were your real names?"

Both men appeared puzzled for a moment, exchanging worried glances before turning to look at her again. "But those are our real names. They'd have to be. The Tyrell Corporation gave them to us."

That raised another consideration. Standing in the middle of the cockpit area, with stars and luminous emptiness shifting about on the viewscreens, Mars no longer even visible from here, Sarah wondered if she were the only human thing on board. "You two wouldn't be replicants, would you?" She studied them more closely. "I mean, it's all right if you are."

Wycliffe shook his head. "No—" Voice flat and emphatic. "Replicants aren't given the kind of security clearances we have."

"We're *very* high level," said Zwingli. "In the shadow corporation. You can trust us."

"Really." That amused her more than anything had in a long time. "How . . . charming. To think that I'd even *want* to."

She left them in their perplexity and walked back to the

center of the yacht. *They all just want to be loved,* thought Sarah. It was as if the Tyrell Corporation had never ended, or had been re-created in miniature inside this little hermetically sealed world. All familiar to her, from the time she had been notified of her inheritance to the moment when she had brought it down into ruins of fire and twisted metal. Her uncle had created an ass-kissing corporate culture, one where underlings like Wycliffe and Zwingli expected and even thrived on kicks to the teeth. *I should be nicer to them*—that would have really screwed with their heads.

The furnishings of the yacht—an interplanetary model, small by the standards of the fleet that the Tyrell Corporation had kept—were familiar to her as well. Every inch of the executive quarters was slathered with the same degree of nouveau ostentation that Eldon Tyrell's private rooms and office suite had shown. Expensive enough to imitate taste, too expensive to achieve it; all the fakery that money could buy. Fakes of fakes, in this case; Sarah recognized bits and pieces, imitations of the actual objects that had been consumed in the corporate inferno. Right down to the rococo pillars, foreshortened and perspective-cheating and thus crammed into the lounge's closer space. Window-sized viewscreen panels stretched to the ceiling; layered pixels shifted slowly through a rez-max'd view of an intricate urbscape. Elevated angle, as though from the great arched windows of the office that had been her uncle's, then hers, then ashes; Los Angeles, all smoke and darkness even beneath its hammering sun, rolling out to the panel's *faux* horizon. The yacht must have been set up for Eldon Tyrell's personal use; that would've been his preference, to travel between planets and yet seemingly not move at all, the view remaining as that seen from the center of his empire. Or perhaps—a sad notion—this was what the obsequious duo up in the cockpit had thought she would like. The past, or at least a piece of it, frozen and sliced like a laboratory specimen and put up here for the cold microscope of her eye to fasten upon.

They don't know—people like them, minions and underlings; it wasn't their job to know. Or even their nature; Sarah knew that she could tell them, let them in on the big secret, that she herself, the recipient of their servile adorations, had destroyed all they held most sacred, the Tyrell Corporation itself—and they wouldn't believe her. Or they would believe and not believe at the same time, mere contradiction being no impediment to true faith. Especially for these believers, carrying on the great Tyrell cause, toiling in the shadows; when the corporation had existed in the light, it had dealt in artificiality. Lies, really—Sarah had found it harder and harder to distinguish those from truth, from reality, whatever those might have been.

"More human than human," the Tyrell Corporation's advertising slogan; what the hell could that mean? Sarah shook her head as she lowered herself back into the padded embrace of a reproduction eighteenth-century wing chair. The statement had always annoyed her; it was like saying "More real than real." The leather sank beneath her weight, the ship's simulated gravity gentle, unnoticeable as a kiss while sleeping. Was there a scale of realness, of humanness, upon which different things could be at different points? And did the points shift? A notion she found amusing—she rather liked the idea of becoming progressively less human. All the human parts of her nature had only caused her grief . . .

Like falling in love. Sarah closed her eyes. And thought of Deckard. *That was a mistake,* she mused grimly. That was what she got for even trying to be human. Better to have stayed a Tyrell, right to the ice-crystaled ventricles of her heart. A family tradition: a Voigt-Kampff machine slapped onto her uncle would have frozen up and died like a broken-winged bird in an Arctic wind. So much for empathy as a way of determining who's human and who's not.

A reproduction of the antique *bureau plat* from the Tyrell Corporation's demolished headquarters had been installed next to the wing chair. Sarah sat forward and pulled open the central door. The real *bureau plat*—now also reduced to ashes, driven into L.A.'s concrete and rubble by the monsoon rains—had had several useful things in it; the repro desk had only the remote control for the opposite wall's viewscreen. That was enough; she leaned back and thumbed through the displayed menus until the phony cityscape had been replaced by a real-time view from the trailing opticals. Mars was already a red dot, everything on it even less from this distance. Including that bastard Deckard—her thumb rested on the remote's Off button, poised for obliteration.

She hesitated, one moment merging with the next. Prolonging the sensation she felt: not pleasure—she was beyond that—but a certain satisfaction. Not with the present, but what was to come.

"I was a fool." Sarah spoke aloud, her words echoing against the hard metal bulkheads underneath the ersatz tapestries and wall hangings. Not necessarily for falling in love with him—for wanting the same thing that Rachael, the replicant with her face, could have so easily—but for thinking that she could get back at him while stuck in a shabby little hovel in one of the Martian emigrant colonies. Money a weapon; revenge facilitated by all the power of the Tyrell Corporation. Even in this, its shadow form. The appearance at the hovel's doorstep of the die-hard true believers, Wycliffe and Zwingli, had been the answer to the prayer she hadn't even spoken inside her own head yet. She had screwed people over both with and without money, the difference being that money and power made the screwing deeper and longer-lasting. Even terminal. "Whatever works," she murmured.

Her thumb pressed down and the image disappeared, replaced by blank wall. Sarah stood up from the wing chair and tossed the remote back onto the *bureau plat* repro.

An hour or so later, when she came back into the lounge area, the two men were waiting for her. They both looked fidgety and nervous, as though their impersonations of the late Eldon Tyrell were wearing through.

"What can I do for you, gentlemen?" Sarah rubbed the thick white towel through her hair, then draped it along her neck. In the wing chair, she crossed her legs, letting the Tyrell-logo'd bathrobe part just enough to show the pale flesh above her knee. "Nothing too important, I hope. I'm still getting . . . used to things. Again."

While they organized their reply, she slit open the pack of illicit tobacco cigarettes she had found in the master sleeping quarters. Golden Wood Dove, her favorite, from the farthest and least accessible of all the Kampuchean warlord protectorates. Expensive, obtainable only through the U.N.'s own diplomatic courier pouches—the shadow corporation's contacts must be well in order. Along with their research: in the bedroom's closets, she had found a reasonable approximation of at least part of the wardrobe she'd had back in Los Angeles, sized down to reflect the weight she had lost on the emigrant colony's starvation diet.

"Miss Tyrell—" As before, Wycliffe was the pair's spokesman. "There's a lot we need to talk about."

She tilted her head back and watched the ship's air-circulation system draw away her exhaled blue smoke. "You've already talked." She lowered her cool, level gaze to theirs. "What more do you have to say?"

"But . . . you don't even know where we're going."

"Where we're taking you to," chimed in Zwingli.

"Does it matter?" Sarah gave an unconcerned shrug. "Back to Earth, presumably; that seems to be the direction in which we're heading." She pulled the edge of the robe back over her knee. "Los Angeles, perhaps? Is that where this little shadow corporation operates from?"

"No—" Wycliffe shook his head; a moment later, so did his partner. "There's nothing there. At least as regards the Tyrell Corporation." His expression lapsed into mournfulness. "It's all gone. The headquarters complex . . . the pyramid . . ."

"Yes, I know." She sighed. "I'm sure it was the site of your happiest days. Get over it." Sarah flicked away the cigarette's ash. "Zurich, then. Or somewhere close by. I seem to recall that as being the branch office for most of our overseas operations."

Wycliffe's eyes narrowed into slits. "We don't talk about Zurich. Not inside the shadow corporation, that is."

"Those sonsabitches." Zwingli's face had hardened into an identical angry mask. "Turncoats."

"Let's just say . . ." Wycliffe's voice was as bitter as his expression. "Not all Tyrell Corporation employees had the same degree of loyalty. Some of the more remote branches of the company sold out to the U.N. security agencies. Or they tried to." One corner of his mouth curled into an ugly smirk. "They would have, if the shadow corporation hadn't gotten to them first."

"We took care of business," said Zwingli. "Ours *and* theirs."

"I bet you did." If Sarah hadn't been convinced before that these two were left over from the old Tyrell Corporation, she was now. The culture inside the L.A. headquarters building had been nurtured by her uncle into a magnified form of his own personality. Inside that pyramid, the way to get ahead had been through murder, or at least a display of one's willingness along those lines. All in the service of the Tyrell Corporation as manifested by Eldon Tyrell. "So Zurich's not on the grand tour anymore, I take it."

Both men nodded their heads.

She waited, but neither of them said anything more. They stood and gazed at her with an apparent lack of sexual appetite that she found offensive.

"Gentlemen—it's not *that* long a trip between Mars and Earth. Not aboard one of these yachts." Sarah took a long drag on the cigarette, taking it halfway down its length. She held out her hand to regard the glowing ember. "And my patience is even shorter." She looked back at the men. "So why don't you just *tell* me where we're going?"

They looked frightened, as though some moment they'd been dreading since birth had finally arrived. "It's . . ." Wycliffe's pale, large-knuckled hands tugged at each other. "It's not that easy . . ."

"Jesus Christ." It struck her once more that the pair's impersonations of the late Eldon Tyrell hadn't penetrated past the skin. Her uncle at least had had the courage of the self-absorbed. "Show me, then."

Wycliffe appeared relieved by the suggestion. He dug through the inside pocket of his coat and extracted a folding map, so old that the creases had turned to lines of soft white fur. He spread it out on the *bureau plat,* hands patting the paper smooth.

"You can't use the screen?" She pointed to the far wall of the lounge. "Instead of that thing?"

"This . . . belonged to Dr. Tyrell." Wycliffe looked up from his insectoid crouch over the map. One hand hovered a quarter inch above its surface. "His personal copy."

"What, he gave it to you?"

Wycliffe shook his head. "No—he kept it here. With his other things."

"Fine. Whatever." Sarah stubbed the cigarette out in the ashtray that Zwingli had scurried to fetch for her. "Acquire your sacred relics however you want." She got up and stood beside Wycliffe, looking down at the map. "Now—can you point? Can you do that much for me?"

He laid a fingertip on a spot in the upper left corner.

A map of western Europe—that much had been readily discernible, even through the rectangular grid of the fold marks and tears. *This thing looks a million years old,* thought Sarah. Perhaps her uncle had had it when he'd been a boy, when the world had been flat and the only things that looked human actually were. Sarah leaned closer over the *bureau plat.*

The British Isles, but not England. Farther north than that. Her heart had paused between one beat and the next, a moment frozen between life and its continuance, when she discerned the exact place on the map. North of the Scottish mainland, far beyond Cape Wrath, beyond Thurso at the very tip; into the North Sea, where the currents ran as cold as the pulse that now moved slowly through her veins. She knew where Wycliffe was pointing; she had always known. And why the two men had been reluctant to speak the words, the name.

"You see?" Wycliffe spoke softly, his voice all kindness, sympathy. "Right there. That's where we're going . . ."

She saw, she knew; a place she had never been to. But she knew what was there. Waiting for her in that little spiral of islands. Scraps of land, treeless and rock-laden, protecting another body of seawater from the greater, darker ocean surrounding it. A place that most people didn't even know existed; that they had forgotten, if they had ever known. *Lucky them,* Sarah thought.

Memory was a disadvantage, a means of control. Her uncle had known that, had used it; the replicants he had created, the false memories he had implanted in their skulls. How much better it would have been for those poor bastards if they had been able to forget, if they had never known. *How much better for me*—some of the memories in the dead Rachael's skull had been her own. Some of them were things that she would have rather forgotten. And the others—the bits and bleeding scraps that Eldon Tyrell hadn't seen fit to take and implant in her double's mind, that he had wanted to keep a secret, big and dark, between himself and his niece—those were even more worth forgetting. If they could have been. *That's the trouble with the past,* thought Sarah, closing her eyes for a moment. It was divided between the things you could never know and all the things you wished you could forget.

"Do we have to?" She heard her own voice, sounding like a child's. The one who had never died and never forgotten. She opened her eyes and looked at the man standing next to her. "Go there, I mean. Why do we have to?"

"We don't have any choice," said Wycliffe. A few feet away, Zwingli nodded in agreement. "Neither do you. These things have to be done."

"But technically . . . I'm your boss." Sarah attempted a last-ditch argument. "I'm in charge. I *am* the Tyrell Corporation—you said so yourself. Without me . . . there's nothing." Her voice rose in desperation. "You're supposed to do what I say. I could tell you *no.* I'd forbid you to take me there."

"It doesn't work that way, Miss Tyrell. It can't."

"Why not?" Still plaintive, still hoping, though she knew what the answer would be.

"We all have to subordinate our desires—and our fears—to the greater work." The true-believer tone sounded in Wycliffe's voice again, low and fervent. "For the sake of that which is larger than all of us. For the sake of the Tyrell Corporation. So that it can be once again. As it was. And as it always shall be."

She supposed she could tell them the truth. For all the good it would do—she could tell them that it had been her, the culmination of all her planning and scheming, her unsubordinated desires, that had reduced the Tyrell Corporation to ashy ruins. They'd either believe her or they wouldn't. And it would make no difference. Everything would happen the way it had to, the way it had been laid out by a dead man. *How did I think,* she wondered, *how did I ever think I could kill him?* When Eldon Tyrell was still alive inside her head and in the past that never ended? *And there, where they're taking me . . .*

"Don't worry," came Wycliffe's voice. She couldn't see him, or the map, or the *faux* tapestries hung on the ship's bulkheads. Her eyes had filled with tears, a child's tears. One fell onto the paper ocean and seeped away, with any others that might have struck there, long ago. "Please don't worry, Miss Tyrell." He was trying to be soothing, to give some small comfort, all that was possible. "We'll be there with you. You can count on us."

"Thanks." Sarah meant it, without guile or sarcasm. "That means a lot to me."

They left her, with the map still unfolded on the reproduction *bureau plat.* Wiping her eyes clear, Sarah stood for a while longer, looking at it and not seeing it. Then she went back to the wing chair and curled up in its protection, legs tucked beneath her. She laid her head against the upholstered angle beside her. At some point, while the yacht moved on toward its destination, to that place where the waters rolled over the deeply buried past, she slept. And dreamed, and remembered . . .

Which were exactly the same thing.

"Patience was never much of a virtue with you, Deckard." The briefcase sat surrounded by moldering rubble, scummed coffee cups, stubs of ersatz tobacco disintegrating within. "I don't know how you ever got to be a cop. You *act* cold—you always did—but you know what? You're not."

"I'll take that as a compliment." Deckard reached for the brown glass. "If you'll spare me any more crap."

The briefcase laughed. "That's how you should take it. Since there aren't going to be any others. Compliments, I mean. You look like hell, Deckard. I don't even have eyes, and I can tell that. I can hear it in your voice. The ravages of a guilty conscience, I suppose."

Deckard shrugged. "I wouldn't have killed you, except I had to." Another sip. "You were trying to kill me, remember?"

"Oh, that. Forget about it," said Batty's voice. "These things happen. Besides, it was poor old Holden who fired the shot; technically, he gets the credit for the hit. The department may even have given him a bonus for taking me out—he never told me for sure, though. Hard guy to get to know. Even when he's toting you around by the handle. Genuine cold."

"Even colder now."

"Yeah . . ." The briefcase emitted a sigh. "Poor bastard. And him walking around with that latest heart-and-lung implant, all that cranking machinery, that the LAPD surgeons had put inside him . . ." Batty's voice went silent for a moment, then came back, softer and musing. "You know, I was starting to feel a little sympathy for Holden before he got iced back there at Outer Hollywood. Sort of a kinship, if you know what I mean. Here I am, stuck in this box—implanted, right? inside a device—and Holden had a box inside his chest stuffed full of little gizmos. Keeping him alive, the same way this one does for me, sort of. So what was the essential difference?"

Deckard didn't even bother to shrug. "None," he said. "That I can think of. Especially since you're both working for the LAPD. Or were, in Holden's case."

"Pardon me?" Batty's voice kicked back up in volume. "What the hell did you say?"

"Come on." Anger more than alcohol unleashed Deckard's tongue. "Let's not screw around, all right? I didn't carry you back here all the way from Outer Hollywood just so you could feed me a line of bullshit. This is a police operation—what else could it be? I've seen these box jobs before; this is how the department preserves anybody who's been iced before they've finished extracting information from him. Standard operating procedure—the department's tech surgeons scrape up the body, the way they must've scraped you up from that broken-up old freeway where I left you, they do a deep core retrieval from whatever cellular activity is left in the brain and spine, then download it into a storage unit. Like this briefcase you're sitting in."

"Then I wouldn't be working for the department, would I?" Batty's voice tightened. "Since these box jobs, as you call them, are something they do to people who've been offed by the cops."

“Cops get ’em, too,” said Deckard wearily. “Killed in the line of duty—especially if it happens to investigators or detectives who didn’t get a chance to make a report before they took a bullet. It’s even happened to a few blade runners. Just part of the hazards of the job.”

“You’d better get your head straightened out, Deckard.” The personality and mind implanted inside the briefcase audibly bristled. “First thing, jettison the notion that I’m part of some LAPD operation. I’m not, and neither was Dave Holden.”

“Oh?” Deckard tapped the edge of the glass. “What happened? He quit the force?”

“That’s exactly right. He walked.”

Deckard snorted. “Hard to believe.”

“Why? You did the same. Once.”

“That was different.”

“You give yourself too much credit, Deckard.” Batty’s voice sneered at him. “For uniqueness. Think you’re the only ex-cop who got that way from a bad conscience?”

Deckard nodded, even though he knew the briefcase couldn’t see him. “The only one I ever knew.”

“That’s because you were always such a loner. If you blade runners had ever hung out together, instead of always scheming against each other in department politics, you might’ve had a chance.”

Deckard said nothing. The voice coming out of the briefcase had touched a nerve, a line into his memory and all that had happened back in L.A. He’d told himself that he wasn’t going to think about that stuff anymore, that there wasn’t any point to it. The whole anti–blade runner conspiracy riff that he’d gotten wind of from Holden and Batty when he’d still been walking around as a human being. All of which might have been true, with conspiracies wrapped inside larger ones, legions of endless night . . .

He didn’t care. Not anymore; he’d had his fill, even before he’d been sucked into Sarah Tyrell’s private conspiracy, her queen-and-pawns maneuvering, all to destroy the Tyrell Corporation, everything that her hated uncle had created. Eldon

Tyrell's works turned to ashes, his memory locked inside that dark space inside Sarah's skull, where she was still a child and he was the king of the only world she knew. Deckard had had a glimpse in there, and he didn't want to see any more. Enough that Sarah's vengeance-driven scheming had robbed him as well, of those last carefully measured hours he could have spent with Rachael. The real Rachael, or as much real as any replicant could be. Which as far as Deckard was concerned, was more real than the human original could be; even when Sarah had tried to pass herself off as Rachael, he had known the truth before she had slipped up, long before the emigrant ship had left Earth. That Rachael was already dead, and that Sarah could never be her, even though she was identical in every way but one. And that one thing wasn't part of her, but was located inside him, so deep she could never reach it.

"These are things you need to deal with, Deckard."

Batty's words had broken the course of his thoughts; it took him a moment to adjust. "What things?"

"If there's still an operational conspiracy against the blade runners, then your ass is still on the line. You can't hide. Your cover's blown. Everybody knows where you are. How do you think Holden and I were able to track you down so easily?"

"Big deal." Deckard shrugged. "You had contacts. Probably with the video people—that Urbenton guy. When they had the video ready for release, they were planning on doing a whole publicity trip that they'd had me signed on as technical adviser during the taping. That's what they were paying me for. My name. So it wasn't going to be a secret for very long. Holden must've caught a leak from the production, that's all."

"A couple of minutes ago," the briefcase said dryly, "you were figuring that Holden must've still been working for the LAPD. You really think that the department gets its information from camera operators who can't keep their mouths shut? Come on—you know they don't work that way. Admit it—this has got all the smell of high-level spookiness."

"Maybe."

"No 'maybe' about it, Deckard." Batty's voice tightened, wirelike. "You know it already. Holden wasn't LAPD, at least not when he showed up there at Outer Hollywood. He was as quit as you are. That's why you took me when you left the station to come back to this rattrap. If you'd really thought that I was part of a police operation of any kind, you would've booted this fine-quality briefcase right out of the skiff's waste chute somewhere in transit. I'd be talking to myself out in the cold, cold vacuum right now. At least until my batteries ran down."

He's right, thought Deckard. That mind, with all of its mercenary hit man sharps, was still there, intact. Batty, boxed or not, could read right into his soul and see what was written there.

"I was curious." Deckard could hear his own flat, defensive words. "I just wanted to see what this whole game was about. That's why I took you with me."

"Yeah, right. And risk having me turn out to be a homing device, so the authorities could track where you went as soon as you left the station? You could pull my other leg, if I had any."

"All right . . . all right." For a long moment, Deckard remained silent, then reached for the glass. He held it to his mouth but didn't drink, only inhaled the acrid fumes. Then he pushed the chair back and stood up, carrying the glass to the sink and pouring it out. The brown liquid sluiced through the scabbed dishes and down the reluctant drain.

He couldn't afford to go under the alcohol tide, not now. He'd brought something else back with him, besides the briefcase. Fear; the unease gnawing at his synapses, the twitch of rigid neck muscle and crawl of prickling skin, the mute awareness of something closing in on him, its teeth not yet revealed. That sense had begun rising along his spine as he'd looked down at the corpse of Dave Holden at his feet . . .

"Go ahead," Deckard said as he sat back down. He'd carried the briefcase here, hoping for answers. "I'll accept that you're not part of some police operation. So start talking. Who sent you?"

"Who sent *me*?" The one-cornered smile returned to Batty's voice. "Or who sent Holden?"

"The two of you." Deckard leaned back in the chair, legs sprawled under the table. "Together—your little buddy team. If it wasn't LAPD . . . I can't figure it being the U.N. Their security agencies wouldn't bother tracking me down at the Outer Hollywood station. They'd nail me here. Everything on Mars is a U.N. operation, except for the cable monopoly, and they're in each other's pockets."

"Work on it, Deckard. Who else out there has got an interest in replicants and the people who go around hunting them down?"

"The replicants themselves." He shrugged. "That's all."

"The only problem with that theory," said the briefcase, "is that replicants—escaped replicants, especially, on the run—they don't have any resources. They're just hiding out, staying low for as long as they can, trying to keep alive. What kind of operation could they put together? You think they could've managed to get me scraped off that freeway wall where you left me, get my cerebral contents transferred into this thing, *and* send Holden out to deliver me to you?"

"Probably not."

"You got that one right. But there are others, aren't there? Others who are, shall we say, *concerned* about the replicants and what happens to them. Concerned in ways besides just wanting to kill them off. For Christ's sake, Deckard, you ran into them yourself, back in L.A. You must have."

"All right, I know who you're talking about." Deckard gave a dismissive gesture with one hand. "The sympathizers. The rep-symps." He shook his head. "You gotta be joking, Batty. That bunch of losers? Street corner evangelists . . . tub thumpers."

"There's more to them," said Batty, "than just that."

"Sure—some of them are loose-cannon terrorists. Getting themselves blown away by the police—for what? For the sake of shooting down some obnoxious U.N. advertising blimp?" Deckard had seen that for himself when he'd been on the run in L.A.'s maze of streets. His first exposure to the rep-symp phenomenon; he'd heard more about them since then. "So these head cases can dig up a few military surplus mortar rounds and hit a floating viewscreen. I'm not impressed."

"Stop being such a dumb cop." The voice turned harsher. "Get with the program, Deckard. The rep-symps you saw on the street—the screamers, the terrorists, the religious types out in the sideways zone—those are all the fringe elements. The fact that you see those people running around at all should've told you something. It should've been the tip-off that there would be others that you *don't* see, ones whose brains aren't cracked. Ones who've got their agenda going in a whole different way. You ran into one of those as well—that guy Isidore at the Van Nuys Pet Hospital."

"Yeah, I remember him. But he was a loner, a one-man operation—"

"That's what you think. For Christ's sake, Deckard, use your head." Disgust tinged Batty's voice. "Isidore was working right in the center of L.A., disguising escaped replicants as humans—disguising them so well that your big-deal blade runner unit didn't have a chance of catching them—and he was getting away with it. If your girlfriend Sarah Tyrell hadn't sent her pet hit man out to take care of him, Isidore would still be in operation."

The girlfriend crack nettled Deckard, but he kept himself from rising to the bait. "That doesn't prove Isidore wasn't working alone. Or that he had some kind of high-level connections covering his ass." Deckard shrugged. "Maybe he was just lucky—or at least he was until the end."

For a few seconds, the briefcase was silent; then it emitted a low, mocking fragment of laughter. "Come on, Deckard—there's no such thing as luck. If something happens, it's for a reason. If Isidore was getting away with disguising replicants as human, and he was doing it right in the face of the LAPD, you can bet he had some powerful friends on his side. People who're just as concerned about what happens to escaped replicants as Isidore was." Batty's smile threaded through his voice again. "People . . . maybe . . . who are right there in the police department itself."

"They'd have to be." Deckard wished he hadn't poured his drink into the sink; now he felt like he could use it. The way his old boss Bryant had used booze shots, both for himself and anybody he'd brief in his shabby, dust-smelling office. To fuzz the edges of reality a bit, just enough to let new, spooky possibilities come sneaking into everyone's cortex. "The rep-symps, huh?"

"You got it." The voice emerged from the briefcase with a note of triumph. "The replicant sympathizers aren't just a few isolated crackpots sparking off their remaining brain cells. They've penetrated every level of government—right into the police force itself. They may not be the only conspiracy going on, but the rep-symps are in there pitching."

"Something doesn't add up." Deckard laid one hand flat on the table. "The replicants who've managed to escape and get to Earth—if Isidore and his whole Van Nuys Pet Hospital operation, if it was so good at disguising replicants as human, so they couldn't be detected even with Voigt-Kampff machines—why would it be just the rep-symps who are looking out for their interests? Why wouldn't the replicants themselves be in on all these high-level conspiracies? If they can pass as human, they should be able to infiltrate the police department as well as anybody else."

"The replicants *are* in on the conspiracies." Batty spoke with simple matter-of-factness. "The rep-symps—the important ones—and the replicants are in constant communication with each other. But not on Earth. There's things going on in the outer colonies, out in the stars, that hardly anyone on Earth knows about—because the U.N. and the police don't want them to know."

"Like what?" The hand, fingers spread, remained motionless on the table.

"Rebellion. Slaves against masters. What else? History always repeats itself—it had to happen, given the way humans have treated the replicants out there."

"How bad is it? The rebellion, I mean. If there really is one going on."

"Depends upon whether you're a replicant or a human colonist." The smile in Batty's voice turned even more unpleasant. "Let's just say that the humans may have the guns, but the replicants—they've got the numbers."

Deckard found the last remark unimpressive. "Numbers don't mean anything. Except the number of bullets needed."

"Come on," chided the briefcase. "Why should you be so skeptical? You blind or something? Look around—you know what the situation is around here. You and all the rest of the would-be emigrants—you're bottled up here like ants in a Mason jar. Why do you think no one's been allowed to travel on and outward in the last half a dozen years? The U.N. just keeps stacking people up in these hovels, letting them go stim-crazy, eating themselves up out of sheer fucking boredom. The clamp's on, the bottleneck's there, because the U.N. *can't* let emigrants go on to the outer colonies. *The replicants control the territory.* Otherwise, the U.N. would just go ahead and shoot you and all the rest of the wanna-be emigrants out there, let you take the consequences. Which would be death. And why would the U.N. care about that?" The briefcase's voice indicated another invisible shrug. "The whole point of the emigration plan is to get people off Earth—if they wind up corpses in the process, that's no big deal."

There would be another advantage, as well, that Deckard could see. *We wouldn't talk,* he thought. *Not if we were all dead.* In that way, the replicants, the rebellion, would still be doing the U.N.'s work for it. Slaughtered emigrants wouldn't be getting any word back to Earth, to families or strangers, about what had gone wrong with all the big plans for humanity's future out in the stars. Better to have corpses littering the alien turf rather than disgruntled returnees coming back and letting everyone know that their promised slaves had gotten murderously uppity.

"Figure it out." The briefcase's voice continued hectoring him. "If the U.N. could regain control of the outer colonies, then they could continue funneling emigrants to any destination they wanted, rather than letting them stack up here. But to do that, to get that control again, the U.N. would need to have its own off-world military problems squared away—and they can't do that. They're screwed; the U.N. depended too much on beefing up the ranks with replicant soldiers, like the ones for which they used me for the templant—Nexus-6 Roy Batty models, like that one you were assigned to track down in L.A. Only it just about wound up handing you your ass, didn't it, Deckard?" The briefcase barked another quick, humorless laugh. "That's the problem with the Tyrell Corporation's having put out such a good product. Even if the Batty replicants aren't quite as tough and smart as the human original—*me,* at least when I was still walking around inside a body—they're still pretty mean customers. If the U.N. thought it could put together an off-world military force out of pieces like that, and there wouldn't be a price to pay, they must've been dreaming."

Deckard slowly nodded; he could get behind that. *Dreaming,* he mused. That was what most of life had become, for himself and—apparently—everyone else. Lost in it, so that the difference between this world and any other was harder and harder to make out. *For Sarah as well,* thought Deckard. More for her, perhaps, than anyone else. He had sensed that a long time ago, in the decaying little cabin in the woods, the hiding place to which he and Rachael had fled; when he had seen Sarah look down at her replicant double—at Rachael sleeping in the black coffin of the transport module extending her rapidly dwindling life span—he had detected the envy radiated by Sarah as she had laid her hand on the cold glass, inches away from the mirror image of her own face. Envy of the sleeping, the dreaming, the dying; envy of the dead and the loved. So much so that Sarah had fallen into her own dreaming, a world in which she could at last become Rachael. The real, the original, trying to evolve into the unreal, the double, the shadow . . . the realer than real.

And if somebody as smart, as survival-oriented as Sarah Tyrell could fall into the dreaming trap, then why not everybody else? Right up to the faceless scheming bureaucrats of the U.N.—Deckard couldn't see why they should be immune. *What a stupid idea,* he thought, shaking his head. Create another race, smarter and stronger and possibly even meaner than human beings, then figure they'll do just fine as slaves, tugging their forelocks and singing choruses of "Ol' Man Ribber" in whatever cotton fields baked under alien suns. There weren't enough bullets in enough blade runners' guns to keep that kind of payback from working its way to Earth.

"You know . . ." Deckard's nod grew even slower and deeper. "I could almost believe all this . . ."

"Why would a briefcase lie to you?" The inaudible shrug sounded again in Batty's voice. "The condition I'm in, I've pretty much transcended all mortal desires."

"So tell me something else." Deckard leaned the knots of his spine against the chair. Every muscle in his body had tensed. He felt the trap closing in on him—the sharp points of its teeth were just beginning to show. "Give me the rest of the spiel. The rep-symps—the real ones, not the head cases—they scraped your corpse off the freeway ruins, cracked your skull like a raw egg, and downloaded you into this thing. That's about the size of it, right? That's the line you've been giving me."

"You know it. First time anybody's gotten this much of a handle on me."

"Big question." Deckard studied the briefcase as though it had a face whose secrets he could read out. "Why?"

"Why what?"

"The rep-symps want you in a box, that's their business. But why have Dave Holden bring you to me? What do I need you for?"

"You don't," Batty's voice replied coolly. "You've already shown how . . . *proficient* you are at engineering your own sorry fate. It's the other way around; the rep-symps need you."

"To do what?" Deckard's own voice went tight and harsh. "What's the job?"

"Simple," said Batty. "They need you to deliver something. To the replicants. The insurgents."

"Yeah? Deliver what?"

One word. "Me."

He'd been afraid it would be something like that. "Why," Deckard asked wearily, "would anybody want you delivered to them? Unless they were running short on novelty items."

"You're a sarcastic sonuvabitch, Deckard. Believe me—" The voice coming from the briefcase turned darkly vehement. "If I could walk to where I needed to get to, I would. Rather than put up with your charming manner."

"Nothing says you have to." Deckard shrugged. "There may not be any emigrants going to the outer colonies, but there's still cargo shipments heading out of here. Tell you what—I'll spring for the postage. Cover you with stamps, and you're on your way."

"Unfortunately—" The briefcase emitted a snort of disgust. "You have to come along. You're somewhat necessary to the whole operation."

"Why? What's inside you?"

"It's not what's *inside* me, Deckard. It's what I *am.* The rep-symps back on Earth programmed more than just the contents of my skull into this box. They had other information they wanted to cram in here. Specifically, Isidore's list."

Tilting his head, Deckard frowned. "What list?"

"Come on." The briefcase's voice sounded impatient. "You didn't have a whole lot of contact with Isidore back there at the Van Nuys Pet Hospital, before Sarah Tyrell had him iced. He was a little bit on the fussy and meticulous side. He kept records."

"Records of what? How many mechanical cats he changed the batteries on?"

"Get real, Deckard. A cop like you should be able to guess what. The escaped replicants, all the ones that made their way back to Earth and then went through the disguising process at the Van Nuys Pet Hospital—Isidore kept a list of every single one that he worked on, that he made capable of passing as fully human. *And* their new identities, the aliases that he came up with for them. Everything, all the info. Who they were, who they became, where they are—he kept it all."

"That'd be a handy thing to have." Deckard heard the sourness in his own voice. "If you were the police. Like a shopping list. You could just go out and ice them one by one, without all that tedious work of tracking them down. How convenient."

"Sure—except why would the police be interested at all?" Batty's voice went back into its cool, logical mode. "You should try to remember what I've already told you. The disguises that Isidore gave to the escaped replicants were complete—*even to the replicants themselves.* You got that, Deckard? The escaped replicants on Earth don't even know that that's what they are. They think they're human—and they might as well be, since none of the police's empathy tests and Voigt-Kampff machines can show otherwise. The escaped replicants' disguises are complete, perfect, and absolute—just the way that Isidore planned it. He was one smart guy, no matter what you might think of him. The way Isidore set it up, the replicants hiding out on Earth can't even give themselves away to anybody who might be trying to hunt them down. And you know—all cops know—that's the number-one way people get caught. They give themselves away. They know who they are—*what* they are—and it's too much for them to keep bottled up inside. They want to be caught; they do all the little things, the mistakes, the coming out into the open, all that insures that somebody like you will find them. And end the chase the only way it can be ended. By death." The voice lowered. "Even that last batch you hunted down, Deckard, back in L.A.—the replicant that was based on me, and the Kowalski replicant, and Zhora and Pris—they knew who and what they were, and it didn't help them. The truth doesn't set you free, Deckard. It dooms you. That batch screwed up, they didn't go to the Van Nuys Pet Hospital and get themselves disguised by Isidore; they had some other agenda going for them, besides their own survival. That's the only reason you were able to find them at all. Not because you were able to tell that they were replicants. But because *they* still knew."

They run toward death. The bleak truth. And Death, in the form of Rick Deckard or Dave Holden or any other black-gunned official assassin, ran toward them as fast, or just simply waited for them to come and be killed. What did it matter anyway to creatures with four-year life spans? Tomorrow or the next day, or the day or the year after that, they would be iced just as surely by the flaws that Eldon Tyrell had designed into them.

Maybe—the thought had crept through Deckard before—*maybe it was a relief.* For them, if not for himself.

"All right," said Deckard, pulling himself from his grim musings. "But you didn't answer your own question. If Isidore kept a list of all the escaped replicants he'd disguised, and that list was still around after he was offed—why wouldn't the police want it?"

"What would be the point? Come on, Deckard, use your brain." The briefcase's voice struggled to remain patient. "The police get a list of names; so what? *They're human*—or they might as well be. They can't be shown to be *not* human with the Voigt-Kampff machines and the empathy tests. They don't know themselves that they're escaped replicants. So what's the danger in just letting them live? They'll all drop dead pretty soon anyway, thanks to that four-year life span Tyrell built into them. They're no threat to anyone—so why not just let the poor bastards live, at least as long as they're going to? The police and the U.N. would just be making trouble for themselves by hunting the disguised replicants down—what kind of public relations is it to blow away people that everybody around them thinks are as human as they are? Do enough of that kind of shit, pretty soon you'd have real humans—whatever that means—worrying about whether they were going to be next. And then it would be the police who'd be in trouble."

"So who does want it?" Deckard leaned back and regarded the briefcase. "I sure as hell didn't—why send it to me?"

"The replicants, of course. Not the ones on Earth, the disguised ones—but the ones out there. Out in the stars; the insurrection. Isidore's work at the Van Nuys Pet Hospital has a big payoff for them. Because of it, the insurrection has a 'fifth column' on Earth—replicants just like themselves, perfectly disguised, infiltrated through all levels of society. The only problem is that the disguised replicants don't know that's what they are. That's where the list—the list that Isidore kept, the list that's inside me—that's where it comes in."

Batty's voice turned smug, as though pleased at the show of its own logic. "The replicants' insurrection already has a division of its own behind the enemy lines, right there on Earth. The insurrection just has to find them. Find them and tell them what they really are. Not humans as they thought, but replicants. And on the side of the insurrection."

"Maybe." Deckard shrugged. "Or maybe not. There might be some of these disguised replicants who like believing that they're really human. They might not react too well to being told they're not. If they believe this little revelation at all."

"Different ones will react different ways." Batty's voice sounded unperturbed. "Some might even just kill themselves rather than face the truth. Because they'll know that it *is* the truth. The records that Isidore kept include not only the disguised replicants' new identities but their old ones—who and what they were out in the colonies, before they escaped and made their way to Earth. And something even better—or at least more powerful—than that. The data on each disguised replicant includes the *anamnetic trigger* for that individual—a code phrase that Isidore planted into their new artificial memories that'll bring the replicants to full, true consciousness. Once that trigger gets pulled—when a disguised replicant hears the big word—then the truth can't be denied. That sucker'll know just what he or she really is. They'll all know. And they'll know what side they should be on. Human or replicant." The briefcase laughed, short and harsh. "It'll be like what those last old die-hard Maoists used to say. One of their quotes from their little red book—you remember? 'Give up illusion—prepare for struggle.' Those poor bastards on Isidore's list won't even have any illusions to give up."

Deckard remembered that line; he'd heard it a long time ago, back when he'd spent his time in the student warrens beneath Los Angeles. *Or something like it,* thought Deckard. The alternate, preferred version being "Give up struggle—prepare for illusion." A holdover from the same historical epoch as the Maoists, the other war, the one that had gone on inside people's brains and central nervous systems. Resulting in the private opiocracy, the chemical dictatorship that half the city's population pledged allegiance to. He'd gone through the mandatory three-month detox wring-out when he'd climbed up skinny and starving from below and signed on with the LAPD, getting the departmental regs laid down to him, that the only acceptable intoxicants came in bottles and tasted like numbing fire down your throat.

The words stayed true, though. Old jokes made for bad realities. Struggle was the proverbial mug's game, a non-profit enterprise for chumps who still believed . . . in what? *Doesn't matter,* thought Deckard. The result was still the same. They'd be lucky if they had any illusions left to fall back on. He didn't.

"So that's the deal, then." Deckard tapped one finger against the table, a soft dead sound. "The replicants out in the colonies, the insurrection—they want this list that Isidore kept, all this data about the disguised replicants on Earth. So they can contact them, flip their triggers with the magic words, tell them that they're actually replicants and not humans, get 'em fired up and working against the U.N. *Viva la revolución.* That's it, right? I take it that the insurrection would already have some way of getting in touch with these disguised replicants, once they know who they are?"

"Of course," Batty replied. "The rep-symps—the ones who put me in this box and loaded me up with Isidore's data—they're in contact with the insurrection. Once the replicants out in the colonies get the information—once you deliver me to them—then they can relay it back to the rep-symps. Who can then go out and find the disguised replicants, reveal their true identities and natures to them, and get them moving with the insurrection's plans. A lot of those disguised replicants are Nexus-6 models, like the Roy Batty replicant that was modeled after me. They can cause a lot of trouble—hell, you should know that better than anyone."

"Still doesn't make sense." Fighting the fatigue he'd brought with him to this world, Deckard shook his head. "This list of Isidore's, this information about the disguised replicants—it's only of any use back on Earth. If it's inside you, why bother having me drag you to the colonies out in the stars? Even if I could find a way of getting out there—

right now, there's no long-range transit off Mars, remember? Just little skiffs, like the one I used to get to the Outer Hollywood station. So why shouldn't I just take you back to the rep-symps and hand you over to them, if you're the information they need?"

"One," the briefcase said sourly, "because you're a dead man back on Earth, or as good as. You show up there, toting me or not, you'd be spotted and iced before you could deliver me to anyone, let alone the rep-symps. And two—"

"Wait a minute." Deckard lifted his hand. "The rep-symps had this data already, loaded it into you, then had Holden bring you to me, just so I could go on carrying you out to the insurrection in the colonies? So the data could somehow be sent *back* to the rep-symps on Earth?" He shook his head. "They must be even more screwed up than I am."

"Dig it." The briefcase's voice turned even harder and blunter. "The data, the information that Isidore kept about the disguised replicants—it's encoded. Encrypted. Deep, bad, and unbreakable. It's got algorithms wrapped around it that the U.N.'s cryptology divisions haven't even seen the tail end of. There's not enough computing power in the universe to bear down on the data that got loaded into me. Isidore did that, too—he was a smart bastard all around. So the information, the list, is unusable to the rep-symps in its present form; it has to be unlocked before it can be read out and made functional."

"Who's got the key?"

"Correction, Deckard. It's not who *has* the key. It's who *is* the key."

"So it's a person." He could sense the answer that was coming, but asked anyway. "And that person is . . ."

"It's you," said the briefcase. "Who else? It's always been you."

Deckard sat silently for a few moments, then pushed the chair back and got up from the kitchen area table. He crossed the small space of the hovel to the door. Pulling it open, he looked out into the narrow, rubble-filled corridor beyond. The low-ceilinged public area had gone temporarily depopulated, as though a scouring wind had moved across the dunes of yellowing paper scraps and black-tinged garbage. The stimulus-deprived and the still functional, idiot hunger and the fragile containers of a dwindling sanity, had disappeared alike, leaving him with an illusion of physical isolation comparable to what he felt under his breastbone. Outside the permeated, decomposing walls of the transit colony, the same wind separated grains of red sand from each other, rolling them like desiccated atoms into mine shafts of ancient iron and the razor-slashed, tearless eyes of what once could have been human children.

There wouldn't be time to think about that kind of stuff anymore. Or to even see it. The trap had shown its teeth and snapped onto his leg; he could almost imagine the blood trickling down to his ankle.

"Why me?" Deckard had come back to the table; he turned the briefcase toward him. "Why should I be the key?"

"Because I'm the lock. It's as simple as that." Batty's voice softened to, if not pity, a recognition of their common fate. "Think about it. Remember. When I died, you were the last thing I saw, Deckard. I had my hands around your throat, and my eyes were locked onto your face, with your eyes about to burst and your teeth gritting, and *you* were the one who was going to die . . . and that's when I got it. Funny, huh?" The short, humorless laugh sounded again. "Just when you least expect it. That's when it's all over."

"That's when you wake up," said Deckard. He nodded slowly, remembering what had been said to him a long time ago in a rubbish-strewn, rain-soaked alley in Los Angeles. By the Kowalski replicant that he'd been hunting, the one that had caught him instead: *Wake up! Time to die.*

"I know what you mean." The briefcase spoke softly. "Nothing like coming that close to your own corpsehood to put everything into perspective. Anyway, that's the deal. Like the old myths about the last thing a dying man sees being imprinted inside his eyes. Your face, Deckard, got imprinted a lot deeper than that—right down into my brain. When the rep-symps scraped me off that broken freeway and loaded my cerebral contents into this thing, there you were, right on the top level. That's a pretty powerful linkage—so what could make a better key than that? Especially since you're a key that's good for more than just opening this lock and decoding Isidore's list. You're walking and talking and scheming your little head off, aren't you? God knows, for what. But you've still got a lot of your old cop skills; you're not so screwed up as to have dropped those. If anybody can get me out to the stars—to the insurrection—you can, Deckard. You're the only way."

"It'd be easier for me to decrypt the Isidore data out of you right now, find some means of getting it down to the repsymps on Earth. Or out to the insurrection, if that's what the replicants want. Rather than lug you all over the universe."

"*Nyet* on that, pal. I may be the lock and you may be the key, but I'm not exactly a passive participant in this game. I've got some choice in the matter, still. I can *choose* the moment when the key can turn in the lock, when the data from Isidore can be decrypted. And believe me, I've already chosen. It's not going to happen, Deckard, until you've gotten me safely out of the reach of the U.N. and the LAPD and any other security agency that would just love to dump me in the incinerator. *That* would take care of a lot of their problems. And yours, too. But I'm not hanging on to the same kind of death wish as you might be. I may be stuck in this box right now, but if it's what I've got, I'll deal with it. And who knows? We get off Mars and out to the insurrection, give the replicants the information they want . . . they might show a little gratitude. Beyond just keeping me around, that is. Maybe they could download me into some spare replicant body. That'd be a trip. Then you'd have a real hard time trying to figure out if I were human or not. Or what part of me might be."

Deckard sorted through the briefcase's words. "You're still missing something," he said. "You may have some kind of motivation for this job, for getting you and this list of Isidore's out there—but what about me? Seems like a lot of hard work. Why would I want to?"

"You tell me." The briefcase sounded wryly amused again. "Maybe you've developed a conscience, or something like that. Kind of a human thing; it's been known to happen, even to blade runners. Look at poor old Dave Holden. That's what happened to him."

"Right. And he's dead."

"All the way," agreed the briefcase. "And there won't be any coming back for him, the way there was for me; no one there to download his cerebral contents into a handy little container. Lucky bastard. Shows there's no justice in this universe. Or maybe there is; maybe Holden had redeemed himself that much. I'll have to think about it."

Deckard shook his head. "I'm not looking for that kind of redemption."

"Obviously. Got your own agenda, don't you? So here's why you should do the job, why you should carry me on out to the insurrection." The briefcase was silent for a few seconds, then spoke again, softer. "Because that's the way you were heading. Isn't it? Out there. To the stars. Or to put it another way . . . as far from Earth as you could get. And you were taking Sarah Tyrell with you. That's the plan. I'm right, aren't I?"

No need for an answer, or even an attempt at denial. "How do you know that?"

"Come on, Deckard. I'm not the only one plotting your trajectory. Do you really think you got away scot-free, that you got even this far without other people knowing what you were up to? Your little disguise—this whole Mr. and Mrs. Niemand trip—how many people do you think you fooled with that? Your cover was blown before you even lifted off from the San Pedro docks. If you got away here to Mars, it's because the U.N. and the LAPD wanted you to get away. Probably just to see who you might hook up with, who you're working for—you know how they like to keep track of people. They got some long leashes that they string people out with—and that's what you've been on. Not just with the police, but with the rep-symps as well. They've got enough connections in the right places to have kept tabs on you."

"They're not the ones I'm worried about."

"Of course not—they're the ones who want to keep you alive, at least long enough for you to do this little job for them. The police, though—they might be just about ready to reel you in. Now that they know you've got me and all the dangerous information I've got inside."

Deckard reached down and tapped a finger on the briefcase. "In which case, I should just get rid of you. Since you're not exactly a good thing to keep around."

"You know it doesn't work that way, Deckard. The cops never let anyone off the hook. The only way off is with a bullet. The mere fact that you came into contact with me—that's enough reason for them to figure you're better off dead rather than running around, stirring up more trouble for them."

One more thing the briefcase was right about. "Even so—if they're going to be hot on my ass, I should still dump you rather than drag you around with me and have you slow me down."

"That would be one way of handling the situation." Batty's voice was unfazed. "But it'd be the stupid way. You don't have a chance on your own, Deckard. You *need* me. And the other things inside me, besides the Isidore data. If you're going to track Sarah Tyrell down, find out where the hell she's gone off to—believe me, I've got some notions on that score—and take her off with you to the colonies. Though why you'd want to is beyond me . . . but hey, that's your business. Work out your obsessions however you want, pal. But frankly, it's just one more sign of how fried your brain is. Whereas mine—at least in this condensed form—is working overtime. You got the legs, the moves, Deckard—you can get around—but I've got the smarts. I know stuff. And I can figure out the rest."

Got me there, thought Deckard. The cop skills that he'd had for so long, the sniffing and analyzing abilities that had made it possible for him to survive in L.A.—he wasn't sure of those anymore. He had the sick feeling that he was only alive and breathing on sufferance, just as long as the invisible forces watching him were amused to let him be. The leash to which he was attached had a collar that could be tightened to the choke point at any moment.

And if that happened—if his own death moved from possibility to probability to actuality—then all the planning and scheming that had gotten him this far had been for nothing. Not his plans for himself—nothing like that had ever mattered—but for Sarah. What had to be done with her. That promise Deckard had made to himself, deep in that empty space where the image of Rachael had once resided . . .

He'd already decided what he was going to do. Or had had it decided for him. It didn't matter.

Deckard sat down in the empty chair and pulled it up to the table. He rested his face in his hands for a long moment, fingertips pressing at the corners of his eyes. Then he leaned back and regarded the briefcase again.

"What was that you said?" Some of Batty's words had puzzled him. "Something about . . . the other things inside you . . ."

"They put them in," said the briefcase. "The rep-symps did. When they loaded in the encrypted Isidore data. Just one other thing, really. Something they thought you might be able to use."

"Like what?"

"Check it out for yourself." With two sharp metallic clicks, the briefcase's chrome locks snapped open. "Go on. You have to open my lid—I can't do that myself."

Deckard reached one hand over and tilted the briefcase's lid back. He pulled the briefcase toward him so he could see its contents.

It was empty. Nothing inside—or so Deckard thought, until the hovel's dim light allowed him to spot the one small, flat rectangle in the center of the briefcase's *faux* watered-silk lining.

He picked up the object, his broken fingernails sliding under its edge. It weighed hardly anything; it might have been empty. Rubbing the slick paper surfaces under his thumb, he detected a loose, shifting substance filling, like dust, one end of the packet.

That was what it reminded Deckard of—a seed packet. From some childhood memory, deeply buried and dimly recalled, of his mother or an aunt, and a tiny garden, holes dug in black earth beneath a yellow sun, a trickle of water from a green, snakelike hose . . .

But not a seed packet. Or not exactly so; the right size and shape, perhaps three by five inches. But the contents would be different. He had seen things just like this right here on Mars, in the darkest, narrowest reaches of the emigrant colony's illicit markets. Back where the most desperate, the ones with the least to lose and the most to find, went in search of a transcendent commerce. To find God, or something like Him.

The packet that Deckard held was blank, at least on the side he could see. He turned the packet over and found one word. A name, in simple black letters—

SEBASTIAN

"Everything that is buried," said Wycliffe, "must be watched."

" 'Or with his claws, he'll dig it up again.' " Hands deep in the pockets of the fur-collared coat, Sarah still felt the cathedral's chill seeping from the ancient walls into her bones.

"What?" Both of the die-hard Tyrell loyalists appeared puzzled. "Who's 'he'?"

"Never mind." She shook her head. "Nobody—it's just a quote. A scrambled literary allusion." She knew she was dealing with corporate creatures—neither one of them had probably ever read anything other than the Tyrell employees' manual. "Just go on. Tell me all about it."

From farther away, up by the abandoned altar at the end of the cathedral's stone nave, came the sound of a chugging power generator. It had been started up, with much tugging and fussing at the cobwebbed controls, by Wycliffe and Zwingli right after the yacht had settled into the bare fields at the edge of the little town. *Or what used to be a town,*

Sarah corrected herself. The word *town* implied the presence of people, and there were none here anymore. Just the three of them now, strangers on any land not roofed by money. The bare incandescent bulbs, laced along a dangling black cord at the cathedral's peaked ceiling, flickered and swayed in the ice-crystal wind needling from outside. Small black waves dashed against the shingle of the protected harbor.

"These are all the monitoring devices." Wycliffe had already pulled back the rotted tarpaulins that had covered the gauges and dials. Spiders and larger creatures scurried away, across the circles of broken or dust-clouded glass. He tapped a finger against one device, and a thin black needle jumped and quivered; a row of blue LEDs blinked and ran out a row of numbers, a date twenty years in the past. "They're not on the generator—they're kept charged by the field polarity, out in the Flow."

It struck Sarah as odd that a place of such stillness should be called that. The correct name being Scapa Flow—the body of North Sea water encircled by the Orkney Islands. North to the Shetlands, south to the Scottish mainland, all depopulated as here; a long way to reach any of the densely imploding, expanding urban centers that had sucked up everything that moved on two legs. Or on wheels; the cobbled streets of Kirkwall, the little town at the Flow's edge, were littered with motorized wheelchairs, toppled onto their sides and left to rust, toggle switches and control sticks mired in the grey, puddling rain. Sad relics, as if the feeblest of Time's carriages had ceased functioning, their spoked wheels frozen by the same non-Time that brooded beneath the water's surface.

The diehards' ship, at the end of its journey from the Martian emigrant colony, had come in low to the west. From the wall-sized viewscreen in the lounge, Sarah had been able to see the broken cliffs at the islands' rim, the rock columns standing as mute sentinels. *Abandon all motion*—that was what she would have carved into their sides. *All things come to a halt here.* Hence, probably, the abandoned wheelchairs. Their owners just hadn't needed them any longer.

"Do you know how this works?" Wycliffe's voice broke into her dark reverie. "What's going on here?"

She said nothing. Better to let him talk, so as to delay the moment she knew was coming. Even in places of stopped time, the bad things still approached and then arrived, inevitable. *Just my luck,* thought Sarah glumly. Christmas gets canceled, the oral surgery appointment's still on.

"This location—not the cathedral, I mean; I'm referring to the Orkneys in general and Scapa Flow in particular—has become a temporal anomaly." Wycliffe slipped into a lecturer's dry, efficient tone. "Indications are that it was that way to begin with, even before it started being used as a dump zone for time-depleted stellar drives."

"That's why," said Zwingli, "these islands have such a high concentration of neolithic monuments. Stone circles, megaliths, standing stones, burial mounds—that sort of thing." The eyes behind the square-rimmed glasses grew brighter, as if the topic were some special enthusiasm for him, artifacts of the dead being more interesting than anything to do with the living. "The highest concentration in Europe, and thus in the whole world. Primitive tribespeople must have recognized the area's . . . umm . . . *unique* qualities."

"Whatever." Wycliffe looked annoyed at his partner's speech. He turned an identical owlish gaze back toward Sarah. "All that's possible, I suppose. Though I personally believe that the Flow's suitability for its present use was triggered by the scrapping of the Imperial German Navy at the end of the First World War."

"The word, I think, is *scuttling.*" Zwingli again. "The Imperial German fleet was *scuttled* at Scapa Flow."

A pulse of irritation ticked at the corner of Wycliffe's brow. "The battleships were deliberately sunk and sent to the bottom. Out there." He gestured with one hand, heavily gloved against the cold. At the great wooden doors of St. Magnus, the ravens peering in, black and glitter-eyed, took flight with wings blotting out whole sections of the cloud-roiled sky. "So they form the bottom layer, at least as far as modern history is concerned—there's no telling what might have been sunk and buried, for whatever reasons, before then. Viking boats, perhaps." His gaze grew distant, as though focussed on a scene not visible in present time. "Hollowed-out logs, woven coracles . . . who knows? But if the Flow hadn't been a temporal anomaly before then, the insertion of such potentiality-laden material might well have created one, or exacerbated an already existing situation past a certain critical threshold. So that the first signs of the field's presence were picked up shortly after the turn of the millennium. Then, when the problem arose of the safe disposal of the early depleted stellar drives, this solution was acted upon." Wycliffe peered more closely at her. "Is any of this making sense?"

Sarah nodded. "More than." She knew what the two men were talking about; she had been briefed on the history of Scapa Flow, and the details of its present use, back when she had assumed control of the Tyrell Corporation. The company, while under the directorship of her late uncle, had bought a controlling share in the consortium running the facility—or dump, a more appropriate word. And as had been the usual mode with Eldon Tyrell's business operations, the other partners had been squeezed out one by one, or had wisely abandoned their interests in whatever went out beneath the grey surface of the Flow. Why worry about the dead—and dead machines, at that; nothing more—in their watery cemetery? Better to let the Tyrell Corporation be the keepers of whatever secrets might still be trying to swim up to the light.

"It's not as if anybody had *wanted* to do it this way." Wycliffe sounded apologetic. His hand brushed across the dials, clearing some of the dust. "There was just nothing else that could be done. It's always better to forget, to destroy the past—"

"Oh, you're right." She regarded the man as though some beam of light had broken through the clouds and the cathedral's roof, revealing some previously unseen aspect of him. Perhaps he was wiser than she had thought. "You're absolutely right."

A moment of hesitation, then Wycliffe slowly shook his head. "I just meant . . . *technologically*; that's all. If there had been a better way of dismantling the old, first-generation interstellar transports, and of getting rid of their depleted drive units . . . but there wasn't. The consortium, before it settled on abandoning and scuttling the transports here, had even contemplated firing them off-planet and into the sun. But there was no guarantee of the results with that method; the sheer amount and nature of the energy lodged in the drives might have triggered some cataclysmic solar reaction; there was just no way of telling."

"Better to be safe." Zwingli nodded sagely. "Bad P.R. if the sun had gotten blown up."

Wycliffe ignored the comment. "Sinking the old interstellar transports in Scapa Flow was undoubtedly intended just as a stopgap measure, until a means of safely disposing of the depleted drive units had been found. The temporal anomaly that had been found here kept the drives' unwanted effects safely bottled up, at least for the time being. But as we know, what starts out as temporary has a way of becoming permanent. Especially after the new drives were invented, the ones in use now, that can operate without the buildup of toxic aberrational effects. The old drive technology was abandoned; no more of those first-generation interstellar transports were built and put into service, so there was no need to find another way of disposing of them. The dump here at Scapa Flow hadn't reached its limit. So why invest any further research funds into a less-than-critical situation?"

"That was my uncle's decision." Sarah had read the memoranda in the Tyrell Corporation files, the nonpublic areas. Typical of his thinking. *Skinflint bastard,* she mused grimly. Even when the company had been in the trillion-dollar-profits level, Eldon Tyrell wouldn't have spent a nickel on anything that hadn't brought another dime into his pockets. "He didn't care whether it was critical or not," she spoke aloud. "That was part of the research he canceled." The memos had had his initials at the bottom; she had touched the scrawled letters with her fingertip. "The crews working out here had still been in the process of determining whether it was safe to leave all those transports underwater, or whether the drives' toxic effects were still building to an explosive level."

Wycliffe appeared uneasy, embarrassed. "Well . . . I'm sure Dr. Tyrell was still thinking about this matter. Before his untimely demise. There were a lot of things he would've taken care of . . . if there had been time."

She glared at the man without speaking. There was no more time for Eldon Tyrell—the replicant who'd killed him had drained him of time by cracking his head like an egg and letting the razor-bright sparks of his mind pour out through his red eye sockets—and she was glad of it. Her uncle's unfinished business had probably included her as well.

"Plenty of time here," said Sarah. She gestured toward the dials. "By the looks of things."

The man beside her nodded. "That's what I meant when I said that everything buried had to be watched. The machines—the monitors—they did the watching. Even if everybody else, everybody human, had forgotten."

With her knuckle, Sarah rapped against one of the circular dials until the glass cracked and splintered. She picked out the triangular shards, then used one fingernail to scratch at the black pointer beneath. It was painted on, fixed at one number along the dial's rim.

"These are fake." She looked at Wycliffe beside her as she rubbed the black paint flecks from under her nail. She gestured toward the other dials and gauges, the banks of monitoring equipment, the lights and numbers glowing in the cathedral's dim space. "They all are, aren't they?"

"Well . . . possibly . . ." Bony shoulders hunched beneath Wycliffe's jacket. He held out his large-knuckled hands and tilted them from side to side. "When this installation was set up to watch over the scuttled transports, there was some . . . um . . . stage-setting done. To make it look impressive to the other consortium members. Dr. Tyrell didn't want them jumping ship, so to speak."

"So really, there's been no monitoring here at all. That's the deal, isn't it?" Sarah let her gaze narrow upon the man. "The interstellar transports that were dumped here—anything could have been going on with them. With the depleted drive units and their toxic effects. They might, in fact, have reached some kind of critical mass—the temporal aberrations in the field might not just be toxic. They could very well be lethal." She let one corner of her mouth lift in a parody of a smile. "If you want me to go down there, that might be the same as killing me. You might as well shoot me now and get it over with. You must admit—that seems a little inconsistent with people making claims about how they have my best interests at heart. Or even just the interests of the Tyrell Corporation."

Wycliffe said nothing, turning his face away from her as though in shame. *I'm right,* thought Sarah. Not that it was any comfort to her. The truth never was.

"Miss Tyrell . . . please . . ." The softer voice of Zwingli came from a few paces away. "Please don't be mad at us. There really is nothing else we can do. It has to be this way."

"I've heard that one before." *Inside my own head,* she thought grimly. As well as from these two, when they'd been putting the pressure on her back at the hovel on Mars. Sarah supposed they were as locked into their fates as she was. "It's all right," she said finally. "I don't mind. It's pretty much what comes with the territory, isn't it? When you're Tyrell blood."

Neither man said anything. Outside, the ice-flecked wind picked at the cathedral's raftered bones. Sarah could hear, past the low electric hum of the fake monitoring equipment, the grey waves lapping at the village's shore. In a storm, she supposed, the seawater might roll against the abandoned doors, pour through the empty houses . . .

Somehow, without even noticing, she had walked out of St. Magnus's Cathedral all the way to the edge of the Flow. She found herself, once her bleak thoughts and memories had faded, gazing out at the water, its surface a darker shade of the steel-textured clouds above. She sensed another's presence, Wycliffe standing behind her.

"So exactly what is the way I'm supposed to get down there?" Sarah didn't glance over her shoulder at the man. She gave a single nod toward the water. "Down to the *Salander 3,* I mean. Jump in, hold my breath, and swim?"

A slight motion in the chill air; she knew that was Wycliffe stiffening, his spine pulled tight by the mention of the ancient interstellar transport's name. A name that he and the other man had yet to speak aloud, that was even more weighted with dire meaning than the words *Scapa Flow.* At the corner of her eye, she saw his gloved hand extend and point.

"There's no need for that, Miss Tyrell." Wycliffe's index finger aimed toward a small triangular structure floating in the distance, so small that Sarah hadn't spotted it before. "There's a pressurized shaft extending down to the . . . to your destination. The shadow corporation—well, Zwingli and myself, actually—had it installed before we went out and contacted you. And brought you here."

"I see." Sarah glanced back at him. "That was thoughtful of you."

"Of course." A thin smile moved across Wycliffe's thin-lipped visage. "We really are thinking only of your comfort."

"Sure you are." She shook her head, feeling how cold and hard her face had become, as though the ice in the wind had penetrated her flesh and seeped into the veins beneath. "If that were the case, you wouldn't even want me to go down there." She took a sadistic pleasure in speaking the transport's name again. "To the *Salander 3.*"

Zwingli had come out from the old cathedral and joined them by the shore of the Flow; Sarah could sense his presence, and the silent exchange between the two men, the glance passed between them.

"Miss Tyrell . . . we've gone over this before. It's the only way." One of them spoke; she wasn't sure which. The voice fluttered and was taken away by the wind. Probably Wycliffe, the default spokesman for the pair. "If the Tyrell Corporation is to be restored—if it is to come out of the shadows and be what it was before, and even more than that—then this must be done. By you; no one else can do it. It is, after all, *your* past that we're talking about here. That must be confronted and brought into the light."

Her past. *All of it,* she told herself. Right back to the beginning—she had been born aboard the *Salander 3.* Far from here . . . far from Earth itself. That past, her past, was a world unto itself, sleeping beneath Scapa Flow's waters.

"I know . . ." The wind had invisibly peeled away her skin, exposing the flesh and scraped bones beneath; that was what it felt like. Sarah had to take her hand out of the coat's pocket and hold it out in front of herself, like some white, fragile artifact, to dispel the illusion. If that's what it was . . .

There were ghosts down there in the old interstellar transports; that was the essential toxic effect of the first-generation drive units. The technology, the relatively crude way of getting from one point to another, from Earth to the stars, had worked by generating perturbations in the time field surrounding the transports, enabling them to achieve faster-than-light velocities, as though being sucked from one zone of artificially high temporal potential to a lower one. Falling through time, infinite distances converted thereto, the churning machines holding on to each moment of the present, elongating them like some vacillating Faustian bargain.

The drawback being, as she knew from the old memos she had seen in the Tyrell Corporation files, that the first-generation interstellar drive units became depleted, lost their propulsive function, as the layers of undissipated temporal energy accumulated. Screwing around with Time itself had its price; within the transports' little encased worlds, past and present became confused, impossible to sort out. Then there would be no forgetting; that saving mental grace, the only thing that made sanity possible, would be gone. Toxicity, madness, death. Better to sink the contaminated machinery into a dark, wet hole, the only place whose own temporal anomalies had a chance of matching these newly created ones . . .

"But I got out." Sarah spoke her thoughts aloud. She looked back over her shoulder at the two men. "Before it—the past—before it could contaminate me. Before it could kill me. I was only three years old when the *Salander 3* returned to Earth." That child, that long-vanished incarnation of herself, had been the only living thing aboard the transport when the autonomic piloting systems had brought it back to this world; when the *Salander 3*'s doors had been unsealed and the Tyrell Corporation's employees had gone in, they had found only the little girl named Sarah—and the corpses of her parents.

Family history, deep and dark as the currents of the ocean surrounding Scapa Flow. Little things that hadn't been in the old memoranda, the company's official archives, but that she had found out anyway as she had been growing up. The way children always find out things, by overhearing whispers . . . and even more tellingly, by hearing the silences that the adults clicked into when they knew she was in the room.

That was how she had found out what had happened to them. The faces she knew, recognized from the digitized press clippings in the company files. Anson and Ruth Tyrell; there had been a photo of the two of them with—an oddly human, sentimentalizing touch—a long-haired marmalade cat in the woman's arms, a pet that was going to accompany them on their exploratory voyage to the Proxima system. The two people in the photo had been smiling, full of an eager confidence—Sarah had calculated that her mother had become pregnant either shortly before the photograph had been taken or just after, when the interstellar transport had left Earth orbit. Her parents had been unaware of their fate, the fate of the *Salander 3.* The transport had turned back a sixth of the way to Proxima, the clever relays and circuits wired into its computers doing the best they could, ferrying back the dead and the living, two adult corpses and an infant tended by machines, nursed on synthesized breast milk. Her second birth had come three years later, when the Tyrell Corporation employees had unsealed the transport's main hatch and one of them had led her out by the hand—there was no way Sarah could remember that. Just more of what she had been told, and had overheard, and had dug out of the company archives.

And what happened to the cat? she wondered, not for the first time. The poor thing—Sarah gazed out at the uncommunicative water, feeling the chill seep closer to her core. She supposed that was another mystery, the answer to which was down there with all the others, in the hulk of the *Salander 3* itself.

"That's why you want me to go down there, isn't it?" She managed to bestow a bare fragment of a smile upon the two men. "To find out what happened to that silly cat."

They showed no sign of puzzlement at her words. "You have to go down there," said Wycliffe, "to save—to restore—the Tyrell Corporation."

"Something went wrong . . ." Zwingli gazed out across the Flow. "A long time ago . . ."

"At the beginning." Wycliffe nodded slowly. "It had to have been then. When Dr. Tyrell and his brother created the corporation. Somehow, everything that happened since then . . . including the destruction of the Tyrell Corporation . . . the seeds were planted right back at the start of it all."

She envied the dead—this also, not for the first time. *They've got it easy,* thought Sarah. The two Tyrell brothers and the wife of one of them—all the bad things that fate had had in store, they had already gotten through. And gone on to whatever place there was that had no time, neither past nor dreaded future. She knew she wasn't that lucky . . . or at least not yet. The past was waiting for her, just a few minutes ahead, when she would go down into the remains of the *Salander 3,* her first home. Which, in some way, she had never left.

"We can't go back to the very beginning—that's too far." Wycliffe's voice continued at the edge of her thoughts. "There's nothing left. It's lost. But this much we can do. We can go this far. To whatever happened . . . then. In there." He nodded toward the grey water and the vessels hidden beneath the surface. "But you're the only one who can go there and find out. The secrets, the mysteries. All that we need to know."

This is what I get—she supposed it served her right. She had envied the dead and had tried to become one of them. Deckard had loved—and still loved—the replicant with Sarah's face. Rachael had already become one of the dead, the termination of her four-year life span postponed just a little bit. Not that it mattered, finally. For either herself or Rachael. The dead were the only ones who escaped. For the living, there was only the past and the future, the same thing in either direction, and equally painful. *It was stupid of me to even try.*

Standing behind her, Wycliffe was still wrapped up in his explanations, the rationale behind their journey to this bleak spot. "We don't even know *why.*" His voice spoke in a child's baffled tone. "The Tyrell Corporation sunk an awful lot of its operating capital into the *Salander 3* expedition. And we don't even know what they were looking for out in the Proxima system. What they were trying to achieve, what they thought Anson Tyrell was going to find out there."

"Not in the files, was it?" Sarah knew; she'd looked herself. "That information was deleted; erased, extinguished. And you know, don't you, who must have done that."

Both men nodded. "Dr. Tyrell," Wycliffe morosely said. "Eldon Tyrell. Your uncle."

"Eldon Tyrell did a lot of things that you don't know about." She heard her own voice darken in tone. "Some of them . . . you don't want to know about." Sarah looked over her shoulder and saw the two die-hard loyalists appearing uncomfortable, exchanging glances from behind their square-framed lenses at each other.

"Those kinds of things . . ." Zwingli spoke up. "That might be personal information. Family secrets. That we don't need to know about. To bring the Tyrell Corporation back into existence."

"That's where you're wrong," said Sarah. "There's no such thing as *personal* with the Tyrell Corporation. There never was. Or to put it another way . . . *everything* is personal. When my uncle was alive, the company was just the contents of his head, made big."

"And then it was yours." A softly uttered reminder from Wycliffe. "Your company. And your . . . personal matters."

Head turned, Sarah regarded the man, seeking any clue as to just exactly and how much he and his partner were aware of. *Maybe I was wrong,* she mused. Maybe they weren't quite as stupid as they looked. She'd have to be careful—her own reminder, this time.

"But all that came later." Wycliffe spoke, letting his steady gaze meet hers. "We need to find out what happened a long time ago. On the *Salander 3.*"

"That was really the turning point," added Zwingli. "If you study the history of the Tyrell Corporation. What can be pieced together from the files and the other records. After the failure of the *Salander 3* mission, and the deaths of Anson and Ruth Tyrell—your parents' deaths—then things were never the same. That was when the company's Los Angeles headquarters became such a fortress. A fortress that your uncle retreated into. And the Tyrell Corporation grew both in power and secrecy."

"You're telling me things I already know." Sarah turned from the Flow's shore to face the two men. "I've gone over the files as well."

"Ah, but it's not just what's in the files—or what Dr. Tyrell left there." Wycliffe looked smug, pleased with the workings of his brain. "Some of the connections you need to make . . . those happened outside the company. In the rest of the world. The *Salander 3* expedition, that you were born during—that was the last exploratory voyage outside the solar system. After the *Salander 3* came back, without even having reached its destination, the U.N. launched its off-world colonization program. Within a couple of years, the U.N. was sending the first groups of human settlers out to the stars. *And* the Tyrell Corporation had the exclusive franchise on supplying replicants to the colonization program. That's when the money started to happen, in a big way." The man's eyes glittered behind the square glasses. "It's what enabled Dr. Tyrell to establish a monopoly on all aspects of replicant technology. With the money he was getting from the U.N., he was able to either buy up any patents that he didn't already own or drive the other companies out of business. For all intents and purposes, from that point on, Tyrell *was* the replicant business. The company had no competition, and the U.N. went along with whatever prices Dr. Tyrell decided to set. The Tyrell Corporation was the sole supplier for the one essential element to the colonization program."

"Bad move on the U.N.'s part." Sarah gave a shrug. "Just goes to show that those people don't know how businesses are run. You never let somebody get a hand on your throat that way."

"Perhaps." The smug look didn't vanish from Wycliffe's face. "Unless the U.N. didn't mind paying that price; they didn't mind giving the Tyrell Corporation such an expensive monopoly. That might all have been part of the deal that had been set up between the U.N. and Dr. Tyrell. The company gets the franchise on supplying replicants to the colonists . . . and the U.N. gets the colonization program. What Dr. Tyrell gave the U.N. as his part of the bargain made the program possible, so the U.N. could go ahead with it." The smugness shifted into a self-satisfied smile. "And that's where the *Salander 3* comes in."

"Really?" Sarah raised an eyebrow. "That's your theory? The *Salander 3* expedition—my father and my mother—found something out that the Tyrell Corporation sold to the U.N.—some information, perhaps, about what was out there in the stars. And that was worth enough to the U.N. for them to hand over the replicant monopoly. Interesting conjecture."

"Perhaps it wasn't information, Miss Tyrell. Perhaps it was something even more valuable to the U.N. and its program. Perhaps it was the *suppression* of information."

Silence, marred only by the passage of wind over Scapa Flow's waters, as she considered the other's words. *But that would mean . . .*

"Exactly," said Wycliffe, as though he had discerned the currents of her thinking. "It would mean that Dr. Tyrell did whatever was necessary to suppress the information that the *Salander 3* expedition had discovered. That the expedition had been aborted and brought back to Earth on his orders. And that those who possessed the information—your parents—were . . . shall we say? . . . suppressed as well."

"Murdered." A homicidal spark flared in Sarah's heart at hearing more of the man's dancing, evasive words. "That's what you mean."

“Of course it is.” Both of the men gazed owlishly back at her. “You’ll have to excuse our efforts at being diplomatic. But this is . . .” Wycliffe spread his hands apart. “A delicate subject. A not-very-pleasant possibility.”

“You should’ve thought of it yourself,” muttered Zwingli. “The fact you didn’t—that says a lot.”

“Precisely.” Lanky, black-sleeved arms folded themselves across Wycliffe’s chest. “This smacks of avoidance on your part. Which seems odd, given your rather obvious antipathy toward your uncle.”

“You know . . . you might be right.” Sarah slowly nodded. *It just goes to show,* she thought. *You can never hate some people enough.* There was always more.

She looked away from the two die-hard loyalists and back toward the dark waters mirroring the steel-clouded sky. The answers were there, beneath the small waves that lapped across the stones toward her feet.

Her uncle hadn’t been able to suppress everything. The past remained, captured and bottled and buried away from the light. Waiting for her.

“All right,” Sarah said aloud. “I’ll go down there. And see what I find.”

“Thank you, Miss Tyrell.” The voice came from behind her; she didn’t know which of them it was. “That’s all we’re asking of you.”

As if that weren’t enough. She tugged the fur-collared coat closer around herself, futilely trying to ward off the cold winds.

8

"I've seen you around here before," said the man inside the booth. The ramshackle stall, tucked into one of the darkest corners of the emigrant colony's convoluted marketplace, surrounded him like a scuttling sea creature's protective carapace. "Coming and going, on your little mundane, unimportant errands. The things that you thought were so important. But now you've seen the light."

There would have been a time for Deckard, back when he'd been a cop in L.A., when he would've reached across the space between this person and himself and grabbed the guy's throat and squeezed until veins had stood out like twisting blue snakes. Right now, he let it go.

"Kind of in a hurry," said Deckard. Behind him, he could feel the crush and push of the dense paths and de facto alleyways, the tight presence of other human bodies that always tripped a memory flash of that distant city. "Maybe you could just sell me what I need—what I came here for—and we could skip the conversation."

"You think it's as easy as that? Shows what you know." The man behind the counter had fierce eyes set in deep circles of black, as though his contemplation of the divine was slowly blinding him to any other world. "You come to your senses and decide to go looking for that which you should've sought all along—it's not going to be a 'kind of in a hurry' process. Narrow is the gate, and long and hard the road beyond it. You don't buy grace, you *earn* it."

The temptation of his old police ways tingled again in Deckard's hands. He glanced for a moment back over his shoulder; there were too many people here, too many watching eyes, for him to throttle the man into submission. He couldn't risk alerting the colony's authorities about what he was trying to do; the place was crawling with snitches and narks. He'd left the briefcase sitting on the kitchen-area table back at the hovel, there being no place to hide it that anyone else couldn't have found in five minutes' worth of tearing the flimsy structure to bits. The nagging voice, coming from the briefcase, had told him to fetch the necessary items as fast as possible; even the disembodied Batty felt the time pressure clamping down on them.

Just my luck, thought Deckard. This particular booth in the marketplace appeared to be the only one trafficking in dehydrated deities at the moment. Every other time he'd shoved his shoulder-first way through the crowd, there had seemed to be dozens of the technically illegal but officially tolerated outlets. Another glance around, to the limit of what could be seen under the banks of dead or jittering fluorescents, showed gaps in the merchant stalls, the tiny businesses shut down, eliminated, and not yet replaced by the next wave of hustling or evangelism. The emigrant colony's police force, or the larger and more efficient squads of the cable monopoly's rent-a-cops, must have swept through in the last couple of days—either to restore public decency or, more likely, to keep their captive audience hooked to the video wire rather than fuguing off into religious visionary trips.

Maybe this low-level entrepreneur had upped his *mordida,* his payoff bribe, before the hammer had come down. Or else he'd brewed up the contents of a packet from his stock and had been lights-out under the stall's counter, walking and talking with some Old Testament prophet or bo tree–sitting with a wide-faced Buddha, and had conveniently missed all the action.

"Look—" The cheap fiberboard flexed beneath Deckard's hands as he leaned toward the other man's face. "I really don't have a lot of time. Not in this world or the next." He kept his voice low, using a quick nod to indicate the packets fastened to the stall's interior. They were all the same small, flat rectangular shape as the one he'd found inside the talking briefcase; they varied in color, from monochrome to shimmering, eye-aching full-spectrum assaults. "But if you're selling, I'm buying. Got it?"

Before the merchant could reply—he'd backed up a step from Deckard on the other side of the counter, sensing at least the possibility of violence—another customer came up. A wraithlike figure, all starvation eyes and scab-picked shivering flesh, arose trembling at Deckard's elbow. "Do you . . ." A mouth studded with a few cracked and yellow teeth, beneath unattended running nostrils, quivered open. "Do you have any more of the . . . the New Orthodox West Coast Fundamentalists?" The emaciated figure struggled to bring his scattered thoughts to words. "Specifically . . . the Reformed Huffington Rite? The Santa Barbara branch?"

"Get out of here. You mooch." The stallkeeper glared at the creature. "This is a cash-only business. Nothing on credit. Not that I'd ever have given *you* any."

"I got money! Look!" A grubby fist unfolded, revealing wadded paper with pictures of famous dead people. "Not even scrip—real money!" The supplicant voice rose in pitch, a sympathetic vibration shivering the ragged man's body. "I can pay!"

Grumbling subaudibly, the stallkeeper turned, pawed through the thin packets stapled behind him, pulled one off, and slapped it on the counter. Distaste curled the corners of his mouth as he sorted out the grease-impregnated bills and octagonal coins. "You're a dollar short," announced the stallkeeper, as though that pleased him more than a simple sale would have. He snatched the packet away as the ragged man's shaking fingers reached for it.

"For Christ's sake—" Deckard reached into his own pocket and dug out a bill from his dwindling stash. He flicked it into the stallkeeper's hollow chest. "Give the guy what he wants, and let him get out of here." Worth it, just to get things moving.

A second later, the wraith had fled back into the churning crowd, the packet clutched to the visible bones beneath his throat. "All right," said the stallkeeper, turning his dark-ringed eyes back toward Deckard. All pretense of religious feeling had been stripped away, leaving the pure mercantile entity beneath. "What do you want? Buy it now and get what you can out of it, before you wind up like that asshole."

"It's not what I want." Deckard pulled out the rest of his money, enough to evoke a swift glance of interest from the other man. "It's what I need."

"Let me guess." In another life, another world, the person inside the stall could have been a tailor; the tape measure was at the center of his empty pupils. "Pentecostal? Got a wide selection here." He gestured at the packets surrounding him. "You'll have to supply your own snakes, or at least have 'em inside your brain, if you want to get into that Southern Degenerate thing." A shake of the stallkeeper's head. "Naw—you don't look the type to have even that much fun. Nothing Jewish line, either; you'd know how to deal with guilt, if that was the case. No . . . I'd say Heavy Calvinist. You look like you're into predestination. Badly so." The man gave an ugly, knowing smile. "Like Weber said: 'Forced to follow his path alone to meet a destiny which had been decreed for him from eternity.' "

Deckard knew the rest of the quote. " 'No one could help him.' " He nodded. "From *The Protestant Ethic and the Spirit of Capitalism.*"

"Good for you. I should give an educated man a discount, but . . . we've really got the spirit of capitalism here." The man fingered a couple of packets at the side of the stall. "How about Dutch Reformed? That should be a severe-enough God for you. Give you a good price—I'm trying to move this stock before it goes stale."

"No, thanks." Deckard shook his head. "I don't need anything like that." *Got enough of that kind of shit already,* he thought to himself, *without acquiring any more.* "No packets. I just need the supplies. Couple quarts colloidal suspension fluid, calibrated beaker, inert glass rod. That's all."

The stallkeeper gave him a hard look, eyes narrowed. "You got your deity already? The one you're going to use?" He didn't wait for an answer. "If you're going with some back-alley, home brew pile of dust, you're asking for trouble, man."

"Think so, huh?" Deckard let a partial smile show as he gazed around at the stall's wares. "This stuff you're peddling doesn't exactly look like it's FDA approved."

"Hey. There's standards in this business." The stallkeeper drew back, offended. "I'm here, and my competition's not, because I sell quality. I've got customers right up at the top, man, the very top. I go in the *front* door of the cable offices, I've got merchandise sticking out of my jacket pockets, and the guards don't even blink."

"I bet," said Deckard. It explained a lot. "Did you have a good time getting your competition cleared out of the marketplace?"

"Loved it, pal. Made my day." The stallkeeper's deep-set eyes glittered. "And just to show what a nice guy I am, I only jacked up my prices ten percent. But for you, because you're such an asshole, it's twenty." He reached beneath the stall's counter and fetched out a plastic gallon jug; the contents sloshed in a slow gelatinous wave as he set it down. The beaker and glass rod were slapped down beside the container. "There you go, sport. Knock yourself out. You want to see God on some low-rent basis, it's your head's funeral, not mine."

A minute later, his roll lighter—Deckard had never bought this kind of stuff before, so he didn't know whether he was getting absolutely screwed or not—he turned away from the stall, purchases hugged to his chest. Before he could bull his way into the crowd, the merchant called after him.

"Hey—" The man held up a creased, much-used paper bag. "Don't be an idiot and just go walking with it where everybody can see. The next millennium hasn't arrived yet, pal."

The briefcase harangued Deckard as soon as he walked in the door of the hovel. "Did you get it?" Batty's voice drilled insistent at his ear. "Did you get everything I told you to get?"

Deckard set the bag on the table next to the briefcase. "I'm not so screwed up I can't handle a three-item shopping list." He pulled out the plastic jug and the other objects. "This is what you asked for, this is what I got."

"Anybody see you?"

He laughed. "Hundreds. Thousands. Not exactly a depopulated zone around here."

"Come on." The briefcase sounded annoyed. "You know what I mean. Cops, the police, the authorities. People who *shouldn't* have seen you. Not if you want to take care of business without being interrupted."

"We're all right—for the time being." Deckard didn't know if that was true or not. And didn't care. In some ways, it would be a relief if the hovel's front door were suddenly broken down by jackbooted storm troopers from the deepest basements of either the cable monopoly or the U.N.'s diplomatic headquarters. Then he wouldn't have to go ahead with what he'd already told the briefcase he would. "Don't sweat it. You're not the one who has to worry about what happens."

"Only because the worst already has." Batty's voice prodded at him. "Let's get going."

He'd already gotten his instructions, the measuring and pouring and mixing involved in the process, from the briefcase. The colloidal suspension poured out like transparent molasses, heavy and glistening. He thinned it out with a half cup of water from the kitchen tap, stirring the results with the glass rod. A reddish tinge, rust from the emigrant colony's decaying pipes, mingled with the faint ionic discharge of the colloid's activation.

All through the back alleys and in the surrounding hovels, as well as in the crowded cities back on Earth, the same preparations were being made, all the differing communicants readying their sacraments, assembling the doorways through which they would pass to meet the God they had chosen. Back in L.A., Deckard had never been attracted to the whole dehydrated deity underground, or repelled by it, either; he'd developed enough cop glaze to favorably regard anything that kept the citizens off the streets, tucked away in their little rooms or dorm cribs, bodily inert while their central nervous systems were off in the ozone, walking with the King. Less trouble generated that way—usually; some of them came back with the light of fanaticism in their eyes, ready for a private *jihad* on anything that crossed their paths. Those types never got very far; religious obsessives—at least the murderous kind—did everything in public and found a snipered martyrdom preferable to reloading their own weapons. That was the kind of thing that made L.A. police work easy, even enjoyable at times.

Deckard tapped the glass rod on the rim of the calibrated beaker. Already, as the less-viscous fluid settled, the flakes of rust were precipitating out, drifting to the bottom of the container like some obscure precious metal.

From somewhere on the edge of his consciousness, Batty's voice intruded. "Nothing happens," the briefcase said dryly, "if you just sit there looking at it. The rest is in the little packet."

"Right." Deckard picked up the thin rectangular shape, the same as yet different from the ones at the marketplace stall. The one word, the name SEBASTIAN, in large block letters—*Not much of a clue there,* he thought again. Or even instructions. "What, do I just dump the whole thing in?"

"Christ, no." The briefcase emitted an exasperated sigh. "Not unless you're mixing for a party or something—and then you'd need a beaker a lot larger than that; maybe a bathtub or something. No—you throw the whole packet in what you got there, you'll be at a toxic level. It'd strip the catecholamines out of your brain so fast—burn out all the neural receptor sites along the way as well—you'd wind up a vegetable. At least in this world; no way of telling where you'd be on the other side."

"You sound like you believe in this kind of thing. Like it's true."

"I don't believe," replied Batty. "I know. At least enough not to screw around. The rep-symps back down on Earth, the same ones who scraped me off that freeway where you left me and put me in this box . . . those people know what they're doing. They may be visionaries, but they still know what's going on. They wouldn't have put that packet inside me, and told me to lay it on you, if there weren't some serious *force majeure* to it."

As with most things this version of Batty said, that one made sense as well. A lot of effort had been expended, with corpses attached, to get the briefcase and its contents here, in Deckard's hands. Even if his old partner, Dave Holden, hadn't gone through some big crisis of conscience, hadn't had the change of heart that would've put him working with the rep-symps—there wasn't any way that someone like that would have signed up on a pure chump mission. No matter what side he'd been on.

"You know . . ." Deckard reached over to the packet on the table and picked it up between thumb and forefinger. "I'm taking an awful lot here on trust."

"What choice do you have? It's like that old Chinese proverb: Safety is on the shore, but the pearl is in the ocean." A silent shrug. "You want answers, you have to go somewhere to find them. You're just lucky—you're holding that somewhere in your hand."

Deckard didn't feel lucky. He wasn't sure he'd recognize the sensation, if it ever happened to him. *You want answers?* That was what the briefcase had promised him; that had been the whole reason for his little shopping expedition out to the colony's illicit marketplace. So he could come back here to the hovel he called home—as much as he'd ever called any place home, even back in L.A.—and mix up a small batch of the dehydrated deity in the packet. The one with Sebastian's name on it.

He asked what he had asked Batty before. "Why would Sebastian—if it's really him inside here—why would he know the answers?" Deckard remembered the little wizened genetic engineer as a decrepit childlike creature with no more control over his destiny than he had over his own rapidly aging body. The last time he had seen Sebastian in the flesh, major parts of it had already been lost, limbs amputated in the attempt to keep the core functions going. *Too bad,* mused Deckard, *that he couldn't take the knife and cut the stupid bits out of his heart as well.* The poor little truncated bastard had been in love with Pris, or the remains of her, and hadn't even been aware that she wasn't a replicant, but a human the same as him, only crazier. Sebastian had set up housekeeping, out in the sideways zone at the edge of L.A., with the animated corpse he'd adored—and then he'd had even that much happiness taken away from him. A loser like that—a loser by fate, written right down into his own genetic code—didn't sound like a very promising candidate for deity status. "What the hell," asked Deckard aloud, "could somebody like that have figured out?"

"I don't know." Batty's reply was a flat, simple statement. "I've never been in there . . . where you're going. Those pocket universes, that whole dehydrated deity trip—I never did any of that, and now I can't. Not possible in my present condition. The activated colloidal suspensions only interface with organic human nervous systems. Leaves me out." The briefcase laughed. "Hey, I'd love to go in there myself, rather than counting on you. But as it is, you've got the only ticket."

"All right," said Deckard. "Whatever." Thinking about fate, whatever Sebastian's had been, left him resigned to his own. He might as well get this stage—even if it was the final one—over with. "Let's do it."

The Sebastian packet was still in Deckard's hand. He rapped the edge a couple of times against the table, to make sure the contents were all at the bottom, then tore the upper edge open.

Batty must have heard the sound of ripping paper. "About a teaspoonful should suffice."

Spoons he'd had already; Deckard rinsed one off in the kitchen sink and brought it back to the table. He measured out what the briefcase had instructed him to, then folded down the top of the packet.

The powder in the spoon smelled like yeast, though he knew it wasn't. When it hit the watered-down fluid in the beaker, the minute grains sparked off more luminous ions; the faint blue light tinged his hand as he picked up the glass rod and stirred.

"Bottoms up," said the briefcase.

The blue ionic discharge had died out, leaving clear liquid again; Deckard supposed that meant the colloidal activation was complete. A deity of some kind—hard to imagine it actually being that pathetic double amputee—existed in the beaker. Or so it was to be believed. Deckard picked up the container and took a sip.

Bitter on his tongue; he managed to swallow. In his throat, he felt nothing, as though the liquid had already seeped into his tissues, heading for the first connections with his spine and brain.

He drained the rest at one go, placing the empty beaker on the table. Then he leaned back in the chair and waited.

It didn't take long.

9

She opened the door, a metal door like others through which she had gone in her life . . .

And stepped into the past.

I've been here, thought Sarah Tyrell. The smell of ocean water, the salt of invisible tears, drifted through the canned atmosphere. A snake of water, a leak curling underneath one of the rubber-flanged seals, threaded down the corridor extending in front of her. The metal door closed behind her with a sigh, its security mechanisms sealing her with the interstellar ship's world. A world she didn't recognize from memory but from dreams. Long, slow, empty dreams, from which she had always awakened trembling, gazing up at the nightbound ceilings, blue light of moon and stars like ice upon the skin of a frightened child.

There were no stars here. No skies but the rust-streaked silver metal above, that could almost be touched by her fingertips if she reached as high as she could. If there was any memory of that, it would be as a child's remembering. *It must've looked like a real sky to me*—as far away as any of the Earth on which her parents had been born, cloudless and unmarked by time and the enveloping ocean's decay. Even when her father had carried her in his arms, taking his infant daughter from one part of the *Salander 3* to another—surely he had done that, he must have carried her; Sarah didn't remember, but she believed, or tried to—even then, what would that child of the past have known about any world, any sky, other than this one?

The real sky, that grey realm of storms and ice-honed winds, was far above her and the waves rolling over the *Salander 3*'s hull. Her faithful and demanding retinue, Wycliffe and Zwingli, were probably back on the shore of Scapa Flow by now, the deserted town and looming cathedral at their backs as they shared a thermos of coffee and waited for her to reemerge. Or if night came on—a relativistic darkening in a zone as northern as the Orkneys—without her returning back from underneath the waters, the two men would likely retreat to the warmth and safety of the interplanetary yacht in which they'd brought her to this place.

And what if I don't come back up? The thought had occurred to her, even as the two men had rowed her across the Flow in a tiny, primitive low-tech wooden boat, probably something they had found abandoned on the shore. Out to the triangular opening of the shaft by which she would descend to the *Salander 3* and the past—she had watched them inexpertly manning the oars, splashing more than actual rowing, yet still somehow managing to make progress against the wind feathering the tops of the low waves. The last she had seen of them—perhaps the last she would see—they had been bobbing in the little boat, looking down at her as the shaft's hatch had irised shut, sealing her in darkness until sensors had registered a human presence and flipped on a faint dotted line extending down toward the Flow's depths and the scuttled ships layered over the rocks. She supposed that if she didn't come back, bearing all the secrets of the past in her seaweed-festooned arms—if the past swallowed her whole, the way it had always threatened to, and didn't let her go—then the two die-hard loyalists would likely move on to Plan B for resurrecting the Tyrell Corporation. She could imagine them winging their way off-planet, a whole Mutt-and-Jeff routine in the cockpit area of the yacht: *Well, Mr. Wycliffe, going into the past didn't seem to accomplish much. No, Mr. Zwingli, it sure as hell didn't . . .*

Meanwhile, she'd be dead or worse, scuttled at the bottom of the Flow along with the Imperial German Navy from the end of the First World War. The little cage inside the shaft had gone on falling, through fathoms and decades, until it had hit the bottom with a soft thump, and the metal doors had opened to the interior of the *Salander 3*.

Sarah walked farther into the ship, toward the corridor's branching junction. At the limit of her hearing, the sound of motors switching on, somewhere deep in the craft's innards; air stirred and brushed against her face as the programmed ventilation systems came to life. The workings of her birthplace, the mechanical womb that had enclosed the softer one of her mother, switched on as she passed by the triggering sensors, each measuring and recording the blood warmth of her presence.

"Do we know you?" A voice spoke softly from above her.

She glanced up at a round speaker grille set between luminescent panels. She smiled, wondering where the optics were that focussed on the slight movement of her facial muscles. "I don't think so."

"It's very puzzling," continued the ship's autonomic computer. "I feel as though I should pick you up in my arms—if I had arms—and rock you to sleep."

"I'm sure that would be very pleasant." She wasn't being sarcastic; the desire rose in her to rest her head against the shining corridor wall and close her eyes, drifting to sleep.

"There's a genotype file on you in my data banks." The computer was still trying to puzzle it out. "That is, there's a file that you match." The ventilation flow in the corridor reversed for a second, as though the machinery behind the walls had taken another sniff at her. "But you don't match it somehow. You're too *big*."

The fussy, worrying voice reminded her of another one; it took a moment for Sarah to remember. *The calendar,* she thought; the one that had hung on the wall of the hovel, out on Mars, that she'd lived in with Deckard. Or existed, at least. It'd had the same solicitous manner programmed into its numbered pages. The ship's computer had the advantage of being effectively invisible; she didn't have to look at tacky postcard photos of rural Oregon.

"I'm all grown up," said Sarah. She gazed around the empty corridor. "Since you saw me last. That's why. That's why I'm different and the same."

"Oh no, child—that can't be." The voice softly chided her. "For you to be different . . . different from what you were . . . or are . . ." The computer displayed the same limited grasp of difficult concepts that she remembered the calendar struggling with. "That would mean that time had passed. Has passed. And that's just wrong, sweetheart. No time has passed. All my clocks and chronos, they all say the same thing, the same as they always have. Since we came back, I mean. No time, no time—nothing has passed. We don't do that here."

She felt sorry for the computer, and by extension, the whole ship. It was doing the best it could. If its maternal instincts were only electrons moving along wires and through silicon, they still exceeded what could be found in most humans.

"I wasn't here." Sarah tried to explain. It delayed having to go farther down the dimly lit corridor and finding . . . she didn't know what. "I went outside you. I was *taken* out. Don't you remember?" She had seen the photos in the company archives, and the ones that her uncle had kept in the bottom drawer of the intricately wrought table beside his canopied bed, so she could describe what had happened back then. "The men came, and the nurse, and they took me away. When you—when we—came back here to Earth. I was just a child then. That's how you remember me. That's the file you have."

"Oh, sweetheart—I don't think I would've forgotten that. You were such a pretty little thing." The ship's computer lapsed into its own fond reel of memories. "Both of you were . . ."

The last words puzzled Sarah. "What do you mean? Both what?"

No answer; silence rolled down the corridor, a wave upon an unseen ocean.

Yet not perfect. In the distance, somewhere inside the *Salander 3,* the sound of footsteps. Impact upon metal, then echoes, even softer. Someone walking; it felt as though it were along the knots of her spine, beneath her prickling flesh.

"Very funny," said Sarah. "That's a good joke. You don't have to try so hard to amuse me." No reply came from the speaker grille above her head. "I'm a big girl now."

The little noises had faded away. The recirculated air sighed through the vents.

"Maybe . . ." The voice of the ship's computer whispered, as though the round speaker grille had come up next to her ear in a cold metal kiss. "Maybe you should go home, little girl. You don't belong here. Not anymore. This isn't your home . . ."

"Yes, it is." Sarah's voice broke inside her throat. With something close to astonishment, she touched her face and found a tear rolling down her cheek, as though the surrounding salt ocean had broken through some seal within her. "It *is.*" The words sounded like a child's, scared and clinging. "I don't have anywhere else to go."

The footsteps sounded again, the soft echo floating by her ear. Closer, perhaps in the darkness at the end of the corridor.

"Go anywhere, child. Anywhere but here . . ."

The realization had welled up inside her from spaces just as dark, deep and hidden. The ocean rolled above, locking her tight within this little bubble at the center of the universe. *It is here,* thought Sarah. *It has to be.* If it wasn't, she was lost. More than she had ever dreamed or feared possible.

Now she knew why she had come here. Why she had let the two men with the eyes of her uncle talk her into it—if they had known, they wouldn't have even bothered to. No argument or attempt at convincing needed; all she'd had to do was realize what some part of her had always known, that the day was coming when she'd be here in this place, this little world, again. That part knew because it had never left.

"I won't go away," said Sarah. She looked upward, as though she could find the computer's face. It didn't have one; all she saw was the blank, curving metal that lined the ship's corridor. "You can't make me."

"No one can." The voice from the overhead speaker sounded mired in the awareness of grief. "It's too late. Even where there's no time, it's always too late." The voice shifted, as though becoming part of a machine again. "Very well. Suit yourself. I won't try to stop you."

Silence, as though the *Salander 3*'s computer had shut itself off, the circuitry going dead, the wires empty of whatever time-free consciousness had lived in them. Silence encased in silence; the approaching storm winds that stroked the waves of Scapa Flow had stilled themselves. That was what it felt like to Sarah, buried beneath the waters. The subtle motions of the currents had stopped rocking the ship's hull, leaving it without tremor on the decayed hulks beneath it.

In that tomb quiet, she knew she should have been able to hear the beat of her own heart, tapping under bone and flesh—but she couldn't. She laid a hand on her breast, fingers slipping below the edges of her coat. Nothing, even when her fingertips touched the bare skin at the base of her throat; nothing but the cold chill that her body temperature had been brought down to, as though seeking equilibrium with the ocean.

Sarah held out her hand, palm upward, far enough to expose her pale wrist. The thin blue snake of her pulse was motionless as well, stopped in the moment between one beat and the next.

Time; plenty of it, and none. That was what Wycliffe and Zwingli had told her she would find, and what she'd known she would. The toxicity of the depleted interstellar drives, the cumulative effects of the ship's journey to the stars, building up in the hull and everything it held even before the aborted expedition to the Proxima system; time had built up here and couldn't be dissipated.

And what, wondered Sarah, *is so toxic about that?* She stood in the *Salander 3*'s central corridor, the doorway to the surface of that other world, the one where things moved and happened in time, sealed behind her. The way they had talked about it, not just Wycliffe and Zwingli but everyone else, all the memos in the Tyrell Corporation files; toxic to lethal, poison to death. It had suddenly struck her that perhaps they were wrong, always had been. That here was eternal life, a resurrection that didn't even need to be disinterred from its grave. All you had to do to find it . . . was to die.

Another silence, another memory, rose inside her. Far from here: a cabin, not more than a falling-down shack, in a forest silvered by moonlight. With a black, glass-lidded coffin inside it, and inside that, a woman either sleeping or dying or both. A woman with Sarah's face. *That's why I envied her,* thought Sarah. Rachael had already died—the last little drawn-out fragments of her curtailed life hardly mattered—and had entered that world where there was no time, just memory. Deckard's memory, as he sat beside the black coffin and gazed upon that which he loved, that which he'd been fated to love, nailed down to that iron track of his desires. As long as he remembered Rachael—and that was all he'd had left to do then—she'd never die.

Another world, another time; Sarah tried to push it away from her thoughts. For a moment, she'd been there, the shadow of an owl passing across her face, masking the stars that had glittered hard in the cold night air. And another part of that same time, that memory: when she had told him to say to her what he had said to Rachael, long before.

Say that you want me . . .

The memory didn't fade so much as it dissipated, like a scrap of paper ignited and crumbling to black ash. Leaving her inside the *Salander 3* again, the cold metal walls close around her. The darkness at the end of the corridor still lay ahead.

She walked past where the last of the luminescent panels had flickered and gone out. How that could have happened, she wasn't sure of; a strict logic would have taken that to indicate the passage of time, the ship's component parts' aging and wearing out. A thin shard of plastic crackled beneath her footstep; she reached down and picked it up. Enough light filtered down the corridor from where she had entered to show that what she held was a fragment of the same translucent covering from the fixtures recessed overhead. She reached up, standing on tiptoe; her outstretched fingertips caught hold of a larger, sharper piece, one of several radiating from the plastic's center. The panel, and the rest extending down the corridor, had been shattered, rendered useless; as her vision adjusted to her dim surroundings, she could make out the repeated damage.

Somebody did that, Sarah told herself. *On purpose.* It had to have been done before the ship had landed back on Earth. The light behind her was a retrofit, something that had been installed when the shaft to the surface had been hooked up. From what Wycliffe and Zwingli had told her, that was as far as anyone had gone into the *Salander 3* since that long-ago day when the dead bodies of her parents had been carried out. She found it hard to believe that any of the Tyrell Corporation's employees had also had the time and inclination then for this kind of vandalism. *So it happened out there,* thought Sarah. *Way out there.* On the way to the Proxima system, or on the way back from the *Salander 3*'s aborted mission. Something had happened that was fit only for the dark. Somebody had wanted it that way, lights out, darkness within that greater darkness between the stars. There had only been two people, Ruth and Anson Tyrell, aboard the *Salander 3* when it had left Earth. And one human presence, Sarah herself, a child, when it had returned. That tended to reduce the number of possible suspects.

Unless the cat did it, she thought wryly. That furry creature in her mother's arms in the old newspaper photo. The notion produced a partial, humorless smile on her face. *When pets go bad . . .*

The protection of irony wore thin and vanished; she couldn't keep up that defense. Fear-driven nausea tightened her gut, dizzying her. She had to lean her shoulder against the corridor's wall to keep from falling.

Something wet seeped through the sleeve of her coat,

touching her arm inside. She barely felt it. Something as soft as the touch of another person's fingertip, even the same temperature, warm as the substance within her own veins. Sarah pushed herself back from the wall, her palm miring in the fluid thick upon it.

She looked at her hand. And saw blood.

Ink-black in the corridor's partial light; knowing what it was filled in the redness. Her thumb smeared it across her fingertips; spreading them apart revealed the larger, irregular blot filling her palm. For a moment, she wondered if it might be her own blood, if she had cut herself accidentally on the broken plastic she had picked up, the sharp-edged fragment from the smashed overhead lights. She could have wounded herself and not even known it; she would've preferred that to any other possibility.

Not wanting to, she turned slowly to one side. Dreading, Sarah forced herself to look at the corridor's wall, to try to see what was there.

Words, a message. Big red letters, black . . . in the darkness, she could no longer tell the difference. Enough light trickled down the corridor, slid beneath her flinching eyelids and back to the farthest spaces inside her skull—enough to make out the ragged shapes of the letters, the scrawl reaching up higher than her own hand could reach, to the angle of metal above.

This is craziness. Her own words, unspoken voice, to herself. She knew that; everyone did. You found words written in blood, in big smeary letters on the wall, when there were crazy people around. Bad crazy people, the kind that hurt other people. And worse. Sometimes it was the crazy people's own blood—another memory trip flashed through her head in a millisecond, a buried one that kept coming back into the light where she didn't want it, a memory that ended with her watching herself, standing just outside in true schizoid fashion, as she had written her name in red exactly like this on the mirror over a green-veined marble bathroom sink with golden faucets, her wrists dripping into pinkly darkening water. That memory ended in blackout, as that other Sarah she'd watched had fallen, hand smearing across the bloodied mirror, as her uncle's doctors and security guards had been breaking down the door. *Crazy.* But she still knew that most times, the blood had been inside those other people, the ones who got hurt, cut instead of cutting, the ones who weren't alive anymore. *Crazy . . .*

She stood back from the wall, as far away from it as possible, in the middle of the lightless corridor. Far enough away that she could read what it said, the edge of the distant glow picking out the wet letters, the one word, the name, as a slow line trickled from the bottom curve of the *S* to the floor.

SARAH

Her own name. As big and crazy as possible; not in a bathroom mirror this time—in this time—but filling a whole wall, each letter standing higher than herself. Written a long time ago, by the measurement of the world outside, up above, where the grey waves rolled beneath the mounting storm clouds. Written just now, in the now that never ended, could never end, inside the *Salander 3.*

The voice of the ship's computer whispered inside her head, a tape loop of what it had told her, warned her about, as she had walked away from the light. *Maybe you should go home, little girl. You don't belong here . . .*

She should have taken the computer's advice. It had only been trying to protect her, just as it always had. *I should've listened*; too late now, Sarah knew. She had come this far; there could be no leaving until she had gone all the way to the end.

With a shudder arcing down her spine, she turned away from the red-scrawled name on the wall. As she looked down the corridor again, a light appeared, a tiny, flickering thing. Not at the height of her gaze, but lower; she had to shield her eyes for a moment from what might have been a flashlight beam turned straight at her.

The beam shifted away, toward the floor; Sarah lowered her hand. Light shimmered on liquid. The thought came to her that the ship was slowly flooding with water; the sealing mechanisms had broken loose, jarred by nothing but her footsteps, or the hatch to the shaft behind her hadn't closed properly, letting the Flow's waters seep in. A dark expanse stretched in front of her, covering the floor; the breath of the ship's ventilation system stirred a shimmering ripple across the surface.

But it wasn't seawater; she had known that as well, and couldn't deny it to herself, when the red trickle from the word on the wall reached the bottom of the wall. The red line, running down from the big smeared *S* of her name, merged with the dark pool and was the same color, the same substance, black in darkness, red in her knowing.

The glow from the flashlight, or the lantern or whatever it was, reflected from the small lake of blood, faintly illuminating the figure on the other side. She could see the person now.

"Hello," spoke the child, in a child's unafraid, curious voice. "Did you just get here?"

Sarah said nothing, then slowly shook her head. "No," she managed to say. "Perhaps. I don't know."

"I don't know, either."

The light wavered across the surface of the blood, sending the child's shadow fluttering behind her. Sarah's eyes made their final adjustment to the dark, revealing a little more of the image across from her. A little girl, perhaps ten years old, no more than that; dark hair falling to her thin shoulders, dark, serious eyes. A beautiful child who would grow more beautiful. *No,* Sarah reminded herself. *Would have grown.* Someplace where time moved.

"But . . ." The girl looked up shyly, through her long black lashes. "You can stay here if you want to. I don't mind."

Sarah felt her heart tightening under her breast; a pulse would have shattered it to pieces. *Not real,* thought Sarah. She closed her eyes, taking the child from her vision for a moment. *She's a ghost.* That was the toxic effect of this place. The past didn't die and go away, as it should. *You see things.* That didn't exist, except in memory and the past.

"I'll stay," said Sarah. "For a little while, at least."

The little girl couldn't keep from smiling. "What's your name?"

"It's Sarah. That's all."

A puzzled look shaded the girl's eyes. "Like that?"

She glanced over her shoulder to the bloodied wall, then back to the girl. "That's right." She nodded. "What's yours?"

The same shy smile appeared. "It's Rachael," said the image of the little girl. "My name's Rachael."

A Spanish-language double bill was playing at the Million Dollar Theater. The same movies had been playing there forever, or seemingly so; the management never changed the plastic letters on the marquee. They just let the red plastic letters fall off one by one, hitting the rain-soaked sidewalk and lying there like cryptic messages underneath the sizzling broken neon. The hot blue colors ran crazy on the wet street, reflected in every puddle and gutter, upside down and backwards—who could tell?—and legible as the fire-tinged storm clouds rolling across the L.A. night sky.

Christ, thought Rick Deckard. *This is a fake.* A real good fake, better than the sets and stages and all the other phony rigging at the Outer Hollywood studios. As real-looking as it'd ever gotten there—with accurate rain piped over and drizzling down on walkable streets colored with the same intricate lights and electricity—still, all you'd had to do was look past the camera lenses and the show was over, illusion shattered. This false Los Angeles was a better job—dehydrated deities lived up to their advance billing, as far as he was concerned; no wonder people got into them—but it was still just as much a fake as any other. Perhaps even as much as the real one back on Earth.

He looked up at the garish marquee as he walked down the center of the empty street. The effects of downing the beaker loaded with the colloidal suspension, activated by a spoonful of the Sebastian packet's contents, were still setting in on him. For a few minutes—though it was hard to gauge the passage of time in a place that didn't exist—he had been able to see both the hovel's interior, with the tap still dripping into the kitchen-area sink and the briefcase with Batty's voice lying on the table, and the lineaments of this pocket universe, like two photo transparencies laid on top of each other. He'd even been able to see himself, his legs sprawled out, his hand resting on the table beside the empty beaker he'd just slapped down, as another perception of his body, standing not sitting, wearing the long pseudo-trenchcoat he'd always affected in L.A., had disorientingly faded into his consciousness. The Deckard body sitting in the hovel on Mars had faded out, the first thing in that other universe to go. The one in the pocket universe had tilted his head back, getting the grey-tinged rain in his face and seeing past the roiling clouds to sectors of hard-edged needle-tip stars, with gouts of flame bursting beneath them. Deckard figured the stars were as fixed in place as the heavy, dark clouds, indicators of this L.A.'s eternal night.

Dicking around with time like that was the main indicator of the pocket universe's fake status. A night that never ended—though the real L.A. had often felt like that to him—and little anachronisms. Right down to the Million Dollar's marquee above his head; that was a fragment from the past, something vanished from the real world. This whole ten-block sector of the city's decaying downtown had been levelled by urban-renewal terrorists to drive out the last squatter tribes some time after Deckard and Sarah had gone off-planet; news footage of the mini-nuked buildings had shown up on the Martian cable's nightly clown-wrap. Even on the tiny video screen in the hovel, he'd been able to recognize the old movie palace's curling ornaments, lifeless and unlit in the rubble.

The news clip hadn't shown the old Bradbury Building, across from the transplanted theater, or what had been left of it—Deckard had assumed that even if there'd been no explosive charges planted there, the concussion from the surrounding blasts would've knocked the structure over; the place had been falling into plaster dust and splintering support beams when he'd been inside it. All the old intricate wrought-iron balustrades and open stairwells, the clanking antique of an elevator and its cage, the grand fabric of early twentieth-century business enterprise fallen on hard times—the building had looked like some kind of vertical mausoleum when he'd tracked the last of his quarry in there, the replicant Batty and the psychotic would-be replicant Pris. He'd gotten the shit kicked out of himself there as well, by Pris and the nonhuman Batty in turn. But as somebody else had said an even longer time ago, the race wasn't always to the swift; they had died and he was still alive, both in this world and the other one, the real one.

Though he didn't feel too swift at the moment; a wave of nausea rolled up in his throat, the hallucinated city street blurring and thinning to insubstantiality for a few seconds. The colloidal suspension, the deity stirred from a dry powder to a potentiated liquid, was still asserting its hold on his central nervous system. His perceptions, what his flesh and mortal eyes were gazing upon inside the hovel, were being overridden by . . . what Sebastian saw. *After all,* thought Deckard. *It's his world.* Whatever he was now.

Deckard turned away from the movie theater and toward the building directly across the street. It looked the same as when he'd seen it last, in the real world, in the real L.A. Complete with the fat-bellied swirling columns that had been grafted onto the original structure in an ill-advised attempt to evoke some kind of pseudo-Arabic multiculturalism, and that had only resulted in the same kind of bastard kitsch the city had always been known for. The other added ornamentation was the wadded-up trash in the entranceway, the same rain-soaked pile of unidentifiable rubbish that the wet winds stacked up against every Angeleno doorway. He picked his way through the mess, greasy food wrappers tangling against his ankles, then drifting away to the empty, glistening street.

That was the other fake thing. Even more so than the sets up in the Outer Hollywood station; at least there, extras had crowded the action, simulating the restless urban population. Here, in Sebastian's pocket universe, the streets were devoid of any human, or close-to-human, activity. As depopulated as this zone had been in the real L.A., there had still been some life stirring about, even if only dwarf scavengers climbing over his police spinner, trying to unbolt the roof-mounted air filters. If this place was Sebastian's show, he'd made it a private one. *Believers only,* thought Deckard. *Or at least just communicants.* The little guy had obviously never had much use for other people, or at least not for anything other than the autonomic toy friends he'd manufactured for himself. And Pris; but that'd been true love.

Deckard shoved the building's front door with the flat of his hand; it swung into darkness. The colored light from the movie theater marquee seeped past him, picking out small details—brass handrails still recognizable under layers of dirt and tarnish, rain puddling and spilling from one open floor to the next—in the cavernous space. He stepped inside, letting the door fall shut behind him, sealing out the street sector of the hallucinated world.

He stood in the middle of the space looking upward. What he saw produced a partial smile, one constructed of both irony and grudging admiration. *Too perfect,* thought Deckard. Through the building's broken roof, past the levels of iron-grilled walkways, beams of shifting light penetrated the darkness like the radiance of magnified stars falling from the fixed spheres in which this little world was enclosed. The lights came from the blimp, the old U.N. advertising vessel with its billboard viewscreen and spiky antennae, looking as though it were some kind of sea creature that had inflated itself enough to rise up in the air.

Squinting against the slants of light, Deckard could just barely see the blimp's shape cruising in absurd majesty above the building and the surrounding streets, the Eurohybrid *geisha* face on the viewscreen smiling with a mute guardian angel's uncommunicable wisdom. Sebastian had brought that back as well, another fixture for his pocket universe; in the real world, the real L.A., the blimp was gone, taken out by a mortar round from rep-symp fringe terrorists. Deckard himself had seen the blimp go down in flames, a latter-day *Hindenburg*, something even the most blasé or stoned L.A. citizens had had their attention caught by. A nonevent for Sebastian, though; he'd already been living out in the sideways zone's wasteland, with his patched-together Pris, so he'd missed all that. This urban concoction was the L.A. that Sebastian had known before he'd left.

Rain from the building's leaking roof sluiced down the brass handrail that Deckard grasped. As he looked up the flight of stairs, their treads rotted to creaking sponges, his other hand moved inside his coat. From force of habit, old ingrained cop ways, as well as from the memory of when he'd been here in long-ago reality. His fingers were searching for his gun, that great black metal weight, a hammer as big and effective as a cannon; they found nothing but lint and a rip in his shirt, through which his sweat-moist flesh could be felt. He drew his hand back out, empty. He would've felt better with even a hallucinated weapon in his grasp, but he wasn't surprised that such things had been edited out of Sebastian's universe.

The last traces of the other world, the hovel where his real body was sitting without consciousness, blindly watched over by the talking briefcase, had faded away. This world had locked in tight; he could feel the wet steps yielding beneath, the rail's cold metal chill against his palm. The smell of rust and crumbling plaster, the stink of decades-old pigeon shit, mired in his breathing. A mist-smeared shaft of light from the blimp above the building crossed over his face, then cut a diagonal through the empty lobby he'd left behind.

"Sebastian!" He called out, voice loud in the building's silence, as he mounted to the floor where the genetic engineer had kept his suite of rooms. Deckard looked down the open walkway to the tall double doors, one of them pushed slightly ajar. No answering voice came. From somewhere past the doors, a wavering light fell, as though from a lit candelabra. "Anybody there?"

He knew there had to be. As empty as the building felt, with its vacant spaces and nailed-down shadows, there was still another human presence inside it. Or something slightly different from human, something imbedded in the walls and pockmarked floor tiles. *You're walking around in his head,* Deckard told himself. *Or as good as. Remember that.*

At the double doors, halfway down the walkway, the silence was broken by a drip of rain into the puddle that had formed in front of the sill. The water rippled like a softly broken mirror as Deckard stepped into its center and pushed one of the doors all the way open. Flickering candlelight brushed against his face as he gazed across the high-ceilinged room within.

Toys; he remembered them from that time when he had tracked Pris and the replicant Batty to this spot. There had been a pocket universe for Sebastian even then, a little world that he had created for himself, and this place was it. His refuge, a child's refuge, from the hurtful, bustling world of grown-ups, everybody bigger than him, everybody who wasn't dying from a galloping progeria, the accelerated decrepitude that had turned him into a wrinkled, fading nonadult. L.A. wasn't a city for children; no wonder Sebastian had been dying in it. If he hadn't built this hiding place for himself, his small corpse would have been trampled in the streets.

Past the candles guttering in their branched silver settings, Deckard saw torn, gauzy curtains drifting in an unfelt breeze, their ragged ends trailing across the nearest mannequins and stuffed animals. Whatever contents of Sebastian's head hadn't spilled out to reenvision the L.A. street and the decaying building were exposed here, like some soft, babyish army. Glass eyes stared at nothing or were reflected in gilt mirrors with ornate frames, the inert photo-receptors switched off or robbed of batteries. When Pris, on the run with the escaped replicants she had thought she was one of, had disguised herself as one of Sebastian's mechanical creations, a leotarded bridal doll with a veil draped over her strawlike hair, she had finally achieved the nonhuman apotheosis her cracked brain had been seeking all along. To be a thing, a killing thing or a loved one; it didn't matter.

One of the mannequins stirred, fat clown of ambiguous gender; it croaked out a woman's laugh as the rubbery wattled neck shook, white-painted face tilting back. Stubby fingers pawed the air like pale anemones brought up from ocean shallows.

Deckard halted in the center of the room, forcing his breath to a measured pace, pushing back an emergent claustrophobia. The place would've seemed uncomfortably close, crammed with too much junk—disassembled tube radios and thrift shop antiques and patzer chess pieces, all the hobby collectibles of a perpetually dying, too-clever child—even if there hadn't been unpleasant memories filling up the unoccupied areas. He'd come close to getting killed here, twice in rapid succession, first by crazy Pris, then by the even loonier replicant Batty; the human original he'd met up with later, the one whose cerebral contents were stored in the talking briefcase, had been a piece of cake by comparison.

His fingers ached, not just for the want of a soothing gun—not that the real weapon had been much use here, the real here—but from old wounds; the replicant Batty had broken fingers as easily as snapping twigs. The fingers had healed badly, aching when provoked by shifts in weather or the pressure of memory.

The laughing clown's barking noise suddenly shrilled up another octave, the rubber hands jerking even more spasmodically above the fright-wigged head. Deckard stepped away from the device, watching as a shudder of ill-meshed gearing ran through its frame. The clown suddenly froze, the garish face paralyzed in a rictus of manic hilarity; the room's silence congealed once more as a wisp of black, burnt-rubber smoke trailed out of the parted mouth.

Another face appeared, popping up from behind the stricken clown. "Oh . . . hi." The black cloth covering the device's workings was draped over Sebastian's shoulders; his moist-eyed gaze, still set in the wrinkled flesh of his aging disease, blinked at Deckard. "I didn't hear you come in. I was busy working on this old thing, trying to get it running again." He laid a wrinkled, protective hand on the clown's shoulder. "It's a real keeper; used to be in an old amusement park and stuff."

"No, it didn't." Deckard shook his head. "It's not even real. Nothing here is."

"Well . . . yes and no." Grease marked Sebastian's hands; he rubbed them against his trousers. "Real in the what's-it, uh, Platonic sense." With an extended forefinger, he poked at one of the clown's eyes, getting its line of vision to match the other. "This is the *idea* of the physical manifestation, of what came from the amusement park. Ideas are real things, too." Sebastian's voice went on the defensive. "Just as much as all that stuff . . . you know . . . out there." He nodded toward the room's high, arched window, but it was clear that he meant someplace farther away than the visible street. "Where you just came from."

"That's why it's called the real world," said Deckard. "And this isn't." He gestured toward the other man. "In the real world, you didn't have legs. Not anymore."

"Yeah." Sebastian nodded slowly. "I had to get rid of them . . . out there." His expression brightened. "But here—'cause this is *my* world—I figured I should have 'em again. And I was right! They come in real handy."

"Should've given yourself a second pair of arms. Be even more convenient."

"Oh, they told me I could do that if I wanted—"

"Who's 'they'?" Deckard peered closer at the short-statured image.

A matter-of-fact response came from Sebastian. "The rep-symps. When they did this for me. You know, what they call 'dehydrated'? Only it's not dehydrated at all; that's just a slang term. Same way with being a deity; I don't *feel* like one." He smiled shyly. "I just feel like myself. The fact that they were able to do me over, to take what was left of me and turn it into a polymerized sensorial override encapsulate—that's the technical term for the process—it doesn't change anything. Real or not."

Deckard gazed around the overstuffed room, then back to his host. "There's one big difference here," he said quietly. "You don't have to die here. The way you were on the outside."

"Well, I could if I wanted to. Anything's possible." Sebastian placed a hand against the front of his coveralls. "I could make this whole body go away. I mean, it could just crumple up and blow out the window like dust. But . . ." He looked across the silent dolls and toys. "There's enough of me left in all this—it's all me, actually—so I guess I'd still be here. In spirit, kinda." Sebastian frowned, as though trying to puzzle the situation out. "Like that old bit—did you ever hear about it when you were a kid?—about splitting an apple and finding God in the seed. So maybe I am some kind of deity, like all those genuine name-brand ones that you get in those little packets. Huh."

Deckard felt sorry for him, the same as he had long ago, in the real world. "Yeah, maybe you are."

"You shoulda seen it, though, when I first got here and I was joking around and stuff." The moist eyes glittered with excitement. "I made myself ten feet tall! Always wanted to be." A forefinger pointed up. "Hit my head on the ceiling, though, so it wasn't really practical. Guess I coulda made the room bigger, though—but then it wouldn't have been the same as before. And that was the way I wanted it. Just the same. And with my little friends, too." He shouted past Deckard. "Hey, Colonel! And Squeaker—come on out here. We've got company."

A glance over his shoulder, and Deckard saw two even smaller figures, an ornately uniformed teddy bear and a long-nosed toy soldier, waddle-marching from one of the other rooms. The bear's button eyes fixed on Deckard with evident suspicion; the soldier's spine went rigid, as though the automaton was considering its courses of action.

"Now, come on, fellas. Be nice." Sebastian waggled his finger, stained with black grease, at them. "Mr. Decker isn't going to do anything to hurt us. He can't, anyway, even if he wanted to. Least, I don't think he can." The watery eyes peered at him. "Can you?"

Deckard shook his head. "No. Not anymore."

The toy companions weren't convinced; the bear emitted a soft growl. "Foo," said the soldier. "He's not a nice man."

"I'm sure, Colonel, he's as nice as he can be. Mr. Decker hasn't had as easy a life as we have. As *I* have." Tilting his head to one side, Sebastian regarded his guest thoughtfully. "He doesn't have real good friends like I do. He's all alone. Aren't you?"

"Not alone enough." Time might not be ticking along in this room—like everything else, that might have been left outside in the real world—but Deckard knew that there was at least one other person waiting for him somewhere. Unfinished business, his mutual fate with Sarah Tyrell still to be worked out. "But I can deal with it."

A shrug from Sebastian. "Suit yourself. That's *your* pocket universe. The one inside your head."

"What about you?" The other's low-rent holiness had irritated Deckard, bringing out a mean streak he didn't feel like concealing. "Your little buddies really enough company for you?"

"Sure—" Sebastian looked suddenly nervous, picking up on the edge of hostility in the dust-moted air. "They always were. They had to be."

"What about Pris?" Deckard felt his own thin smile appear. "Where's she?"

The childlike innocence flashed out of Sebastian's face, as though the switch on one of his mechanical toys had been thrown. Replaced by something both hotter and darker, that could be seen like black-enameled metal at the center of the man's eyes. "That's not any of your business, Mr. Decker." His hard, annihilating stare could have bored holes through real-world skin and flesh. "You don't have any right to ask about that."

"Just a simple question." Deckard's turn to give a shrug. "You don't have to answer. It's *your* world, remember."

That world trembled in sympathetic connection to its creator. Plaster dust sifted from a network of cracks that suddenly shot like negative lightning across the water-stained ceiling. The crystal attachments to the candelabra and unlit chandeliers rattled, as though the fault lines beneath the real L.A. had been duplicated here.

"Stop!" Another voice shrilled from the opposite side of the room. "Stop that!" The toy soldier shook his tiny fists in the air, as high as the point on his spiked helmet. "Let him alone!" Beside the soldier, the uniformed teddy bear stamped its feet, anger sufficient to have caused this earth's tremors. "Wicked, wicked, wicked!"

"No, fellas . . . don't . . ." Face wet with tears, Sebastian held one palm outward as he sank into a carved wooden chair. "It's all right . . ."

The teddy bear attacked first, the tassels of its epaulets shaking as it locked stubby arms around Deckard's leg, the round face nuzzling a muffled growl against the long coat's lower edge. Deckard peeled the animated creature from himself, hoisting it up just long enough to pitch it against the approaching toy soldier. Both of Sebastian's automatons sprawled into a corner; the soldier burst into whimpers of frustration.

"Don't hurt them . . ." Leaning forward, Sebastian grabbed hold of Deckard's sleeve. "It's not their fault. They're just doing what I programmed them to do. They're just trying to protect me . . ."

Deckard looked down at the weeping man. "From what?" An old, deeply buried cop circuit linked inside Deckard's brain, producing the almost shamefully cruel satisfaction that came with doing the job well. This might have been Sebastian's world, his little private pocket universe, but Sebastian didn't control it any longer. *I do,* thought Deckard. Things had to be broken before the things they concealed could be seen, out in the open. Now he could find out what he needed to know. "Protecting you from what?"

Sebastian took a deep, shuddering breath, drawing himself upright. "Oh . . . everything, I guess. I don't know." He made a visible effort to calm himself down, the fragile body parts drawn together by an invisible string. "Nothing, really." His trembling fingers wiped the last tears from his eyes. He looked up at Deckard. "I mean that. From *nothing*. She's not here."

"Pris? Why not?"

"I just don't know . . ." Sebastian morosely shook his head. "I tried to make her be here—you know, the way I made Colonel Fuzzy and Squeaker Hussar just be the way they were before." He pointed to the bear and the toy soldier, who had sullenly withdrawn into a corner of the room. "I *should've* been able to do that. This is my world, isn't it? The rep-symps put me here, they made me a dehydrated deity, they gave me all this . . . I should be able to have what I want, shouldn't I?"

"I suppose so." Deckard nodded. "Whatever you want."

"But I just couldn't make it *be* that way. I tried and tried, but it just wouldn't happen. That's really why I didn't change anything, why I kept it all the way it was before. Look—" Sebastian jumped up from the chair, ran to one of the tall windows and yanked its gauzy curtain to one side. "I got that right, didn't I?" His finger stabbed toward the dark, rain-drizzled urban landscape below. "That's the street, isn't it? Just the way it was."

Another slow nod from Deckard.

"And all this. The building and everything." The small man turned around in the center of the room, hands upraised to indicate all its contents and the spaces beyond. "I *know* I got all this right. I lived here so long, not here but out there, out in the real world—this was my world. I just had to make it all over again. And I did."

Deckard watched him and listened. He felt even sorrier for the poor little bastard. *He's finding out.* The same things that Deckard had found out, had learned and written on the charred scroll of his heart. There were some things you couldn't bring back. You could grieve for them, and that was all.

"But Pris . . ." Sebastian looked puzzled, as if he was about to start crying again. "When I got done, she still wasn't here. She was supposed to be—I made it that way—but she wasn't."

Deckard knew why Sebastian, the deity of this pocket universe, had failed. He wondered if he should tell him.

"I tried and tried—"

"Look," said Deckard. "It's not going to happen. Why don't you just give up on that? You've got your memories. Those'll have to do."

A big sigh from Sebastian rendered him even smaller and more fragile. "I know. I know you're right." His shoulders slumped in desolation. He looked hollowed out, insubstantial, as though the contents of his skin had been converted to loose atoms and exhaled; another night breeze coming through the windows might have blown him away entirely. "There's a reason for it. Why she's not here."

"You don't have to talk about this if you don't want to. That's not why I came here."

"Of course not. You've got important business to take care of. Still . . ." Sebastian turned back to the silent and motionless clown mannequin. He lifted the black cloth covering its mechanical innards; from one of his coverall pockets, he took a yellow-handled screwdriver and poked at the meshing gears. "Like I said, I *know* why. Or to put it another way, kinda, it's because of what I don't know. About Pris." He extracted some small part from the workings and studied it between his thumb and forefinger. "I mean, I know all about something like this. And all the other stuff I got." Still holding the metal piece, Sebastian gestured toward the room's contents. "And the building, and the street outside, and the whole city even . . . I know what those *are.* So I've got 'em the right way inside my head, and so I could make 'em be here, the way they were before, out there. You know, in the real world. But with Pris . . ." He leaned close to the clown's workings, screwing the little part back into place. "I thought I knew what she was. But maybe I was wrong."

Deckard said nothing. For a moment, the room and all the empty spaces around it were silent, except for the touch of rain upon the window glass and the corridors' pools of dark water.

"Do you think, Mr. Decker, that that's possible?" Sebastian's gaze, sharper beneath the constant moistness, like a knife under blurry water, fastened onto him. "You think I could've got it all wrong?"

"I'm glad you're here," said the little girl. She reached up and took Sarah's hand, and gave her a shy, pretty smile. "I was getting kind of lonely. All by myself . . ."

Poor little thing, thought Sarah. *She's not even real.* The notion of ghosts and shadows, and all other unreal things, suffering from loneliness, the same way she always had, now weighted her down with an inescapable sadness. If this little girl—or the little girl that she saw, a temporary incarnation of memory and the past that was all jumbled up inside the *Salander 3*—if she could feel lonely, then loneliness was some sort of universal constant, like gravity or the speed of light. Everything in the world, this one or any other, was made, at least in part, of it.

The little girl's dark hair, dark as Sarah's own, was pulled back into a long braid tied with a red ribbon at the end. The girl—the image, the ghost, the hallucination—didn't draw away as Sarah felt the ribbon's thin substance between her fingertips. The ribbon felt real enough, and even touched by the passage of time; it looked old, faded and frayed, the gossamer threads coming loose at the edges.

"Did you do that?" Sarah spoke gently to the little girl, as though any harsh word might have dispersed her from even this illusory existence, like a hand brushed through a curl of smoke. "Or did somebody here fix your hair for you?"

"I can do it." The girl spoke with affronted dignity. "If I want to. But usually I let the nanny do it."

"The nanny? What nanny?"

"You know." The girl, still holding Sarah's hand, used a nod of her head to indicate the corridor walls and hidden machinery of the ship. "The things that take care of you. That's their *job.* But they don't have to do so much for me anymore—I'm not a baby now. But it makes them happy if they can do things, so sometimes I let them."

Sarah knew what the girl was talking about. The *Salander 3*'s computer was still silent, as though they had left its voice behind them as they had walked farther through the ship's interior. But she could sense the pseudo-life imbedded in the structure of the vessel, the flow of electrons, the activation of solenoids, the meshing of gears; all the tiny functions that had been programmed into the lifeless metal and silicon. That had, she knew, kept her alive as well; that had been her nursemaid all the way back to Earth, so many years ago. When the *Salander 3* had turned back from its voyage to the Proxima system, and had returned with two human corpses and one living child as its only passengers—the computer and its most delicate manipulators hadn't tied any red ribbons, but it had done everything necessary to preserve the real life that had been left in its charge.

Their steps, hers and the little girl's, had led them farther into the *Salander 3*; Sarah had wanted to get away from the pool of blood near which she had found her illusory companion. The girl had seemed to pick up on Sarah's queasiness; she had led the way, her hand in Sarah's hand, past the entrances of other corridor branches, down which had been visible other scrawled markings on the walls in the same wet red that looked black in the overhead fluorescents' partial spectrum. Only when they reached a section of the ship that had escaped whatever violence had rolled through the other enclosed spaces—it seemed to be some kind of storage area; crates and boxes with stenciled lettering lined the sides—had Sarah been able to draw her breath and speak again.

She halted, turning the little girl to face her. "Tell me," said Sarah. "And you have to tell me the truth, the real truth." She knelt down, so that her gaze was on the same level as the girl's. "Is your name really Rachael?"

"Of course." The girl gazed back at her, somber and unblinking. "What else would it be?"

Sarah didn't answer. The girl's image stepped from a mere optical perception to something else, which moved through other dark corridors, the ones inside her own memories. She knew what the girl reminded her of: one of the photographs that had been inside her uncle's desk, the ornately carved and gilded *bureau plat* in his vast and lofty-ceilinged office suite in L.A., that she had inherited along with every other object belonging to the Tyrell Corporation. The photograph had been of herself, taken when she had been about the same age, ten years old or so, as the girl who stood before her now. She couldn't remember when the photo had been taken, though she supposed it had been in Zurich, in the expensive, conventlike boarding school where her uncle had lodged his orphan niece as soon as she'd been old enough for it; the girl in the picture had been wearing the stiff-collared uniform that had itched so badly through her thin white stockings.

There had been something else in that old photograph. Her hair had been pulled back, the same as this little girl's, but without a ribbon of any color, or else it just hadn't been caught by the camera. *And bangs,* thought Sarah; she'd had bangs when she'd been ten years old, combed down to a half inch above her eyebrows. Whereas this little girl had hers parted at one temple, then brushed slanting across her forehead. That was different; but the face . . . the face was the same. Sarah could see that, calling up the photograph in her memory and comparing it with the child in front of her. The same dark eyes, the same incipient beauty, the fragile paleness. And something else, deeper and more hidden, yet obvious to see. That sadness, even when the little girl smiled, even when that vanished Sarah in the old photograph had smiled, shy and hesitant. Exactly the same.

That proves it, thought Sarah. It didn't make her any happier to know that the little girl she knelt before and in whose dark eyes she saw her own grown-up face mirrored was a ghost, a hallucination, a temporal anomaly. Something that the toxic effects of the *Salander 3*'s depleted interstellar drives had conjured up out of the jumbled past held inside the curved metal. *Or out of my head*—that must be what the little girl's name meant. *Rachael.* Where else would she have gotten it? Straight out of Sarah's own memories and desires; Sarah had even called herself Rachael, had tried to *be* Rachael, back when she had thought she could replace, the original for the copy, the replicant that Deckard had loved. *I'm going crazy down here,* thought Sarah. *Or crazier.* Wycliffe and Zwingli had told her it was a poisonous environment; they hadn't been lying. She had the proof of that in front of her eyes, or in the trenches of her misfiring central nervous system, wherever a hallucination like this could be said to exist at all.

Sarah stood up. "Your name's not Rachael," she said coldly.

The little girl frowned. "Yes, it is. I know my own name."

"Your name is . . ." She took a deep breath, fighting against a wave of fatigue that had suddenly risen inside her. "Nothing. Nothing at all."

"That's silly. How can somebody be called *nothing*?"

"It's easy. If she doesn't exist."

"Speak for yourself," the child said with an adult's dignity. "I know *I* exist. What's *your* problem?"

"Let's not go into that now." She rubbed the corner of her brow. "Your name's Sarah. Just the same as mine."

The girl laughed scornfully. "That's just stupid. How can we both have the same name?"

"Because you and I are the same person." She wondered why she was trying to explain this to an illusion. "In a way, that is. You're part of me. You're just something that came out of my head. You're not real, except to the degree you're something that my subconscious put together out of my memories."

"*You're* the one who's not real." The child's mood had quickly changed to sullen. "I never saw you before. I've been here a long, *long* time, all by myself. Then you show up and you start saying awful things." She glared darkly at Sarah. "Where did you come from anyhow?"

"From far, far away." One of Sarah's hands made a vague gesture toward the ship's walls and everything that lay beyond. "From someplace where there's light and time and . . . all sorts of useful things."

"No . . ." The girl studied Sarah, then reached out and grabbed her hand, more roughly than she had taken it before. She peered intently at Sarah's palm, the veins and sinews of her wrist. The girl shook her head, the braid brushing against her shoulders. "You came from *here.*" She sounded puzzled. "I can tell. You're made of the same stuff. As me." The sharp gaze moved up to Sarah's face. "But you weren't here before. I don't get it."

She's right, mused Sarah. *I am from here.* This had been where she had been born, though then it had been out among the stars instead of at the bottom of Scapa Flow. *Not that it makes any difference*—Sarah looked around at the stacked crates and the silvery walls behind them. The ventilation's breeze carried scrubbed and filtered molecules to her lungs, the same canned air she had been born breathing. *Like coming home,* she thought.

"Maybe that's what I should do." Sarah spoke aloud, almost forgetting the other perceived presence standing next to her. "I should just forget about all that other stuff—"

"What other stuff?" The child had noticed the drift of attention, and tugged on Sarah's hand.

"Everything else. Up there." She gestured with a toss of her head. "Out in that other world, the one you don't know anything about." *How could she?* Sarah reminded herself. *She doesn't even exist.* "Perhaps it'd be a good idea to just forget about that world."

"You made it sound kind of nice." Puzzled again, the girl stared at her. "Light and stuff. It's dark a lot here."

"It's dark a lot up there, too." Sarah couldn't keep a trace of bitterness from filtering into her voice. "Believe me; I'd know." A long hallway lined with doors ran down the length of her memories to that vanishing point beyond which it was useless to go. She kept all the doors carefully locked, though she knew exactly what was behind each one of them. And sometimes the locks didn't work, and the doors opened, whether she wanted them to or not. "And . . . you've got enough here. To see your way." She wondered whether the *Salander 3*'s batteries would ever run down, or whether the ship was sufficiently mired in time that the lights would stay on forever, whether the ventilation system would go on sighing through the corridors. Maybe not; there were probably some laws of physics that would be contravened thereby. She didn't care; she wouldn't even mind living in the dark down here, breathing whatever stale air remained, over and over again. Perhaps this was what she had been looking for, why she had let Wycliffe and Zwingli convince her to come down here. A return to the womb . . . or to the grave. She didn't care which. "You've got plenty," she whispered, eyes closed. "More than enough of what you need . . ."

"Well . . . *I* don't want to stay here." The voice of the little girl made a sour announcement. "It sucks."

"Why do you say that?" Sarah opened her eyes. "Wouldn't you like to stay here forever? As long as I did, too?" She tried to give the child a friendly smile. "We could have little tea parties, just the two of us. And we could sleep in the same bed, if you wanted. All warm." The ocean could cradle them to their dreams, supposed Sarah. If there were any need for dreams in a place like this. "Wouldn't that be nice?"

"No." The little girl scowled, face darkening as though the shadows had crept out from behind the boxes on either side. "It's creepy and scary down here. I've been scared the whole time I can remember. Which is *always*."

"Why? What's to be scared of?"

"There's others down here." The Rachael child's voice dropped to a whisper. "Others who aren't nice."

"I thought you were the only one—until I came here." The

way the little girl spoke had raised chill, prickling flesh on Sarah's arms. "That's why you were so lonely."

"You sure don't know very much." The brooding, apprehensive look hadn't vanished from the girl's face. "Don't you know? That you can be alone even when there's other *things* around you?"

The emphasized word made Sarah wonder. She had said *things,* not *people*—what did that mean?

"Look. I don't need to be lectured by some piece of my own subconscious. Especially about the nature of being alone—"

"Shh! Be quiet!" The Rachael child grabbed Sarah's arm with both hands, squeezing tight. "There they are! Don't you hear them?"

"Who? What?" The child's evident terror jolted Sarah's spine rigid. She looked over her shoulder, in the direction from which she and the Rachael child had come. "I don't—"

Then she did. The sounds of footsteps, not the little girl's, as she heard when she had first entered the ship. But louder and heavier, echoing from the distance and down the *Salander 3*'s metal corridors; what she would have thought to be a man's, except for the slowly ominous pace, as though lumbering under some heavy and unnatural burden.

The child had pressed herself against Sarah, arms wrapped around her waist and hugging tight. Sarah grasped the thin shoulders and drew her even closer, as much for her own comfort as the child's. "Who is it?" She managed to pull her gaze away from the dark recesses of the corridor and down to the little girl. "Who's coming here?"

"We better go. Come on—" The Rachael child had peeled herself away and was now tugging at Sarah's hand.

"Wait—" The footsteps had grown louder. If that was what they were: the noises had turned to impacts upon the ship's metal decking sufficient to tremble the walls, the stacked boxes and crates shifting with each blow. Even the lights flickered, as though the hidden wiring were being jostled loose from its connections; her shadow and the child's jittered nervously, as ancient dust sifted down from the joints between the overhead panels. "I have to *see.*"

"No! You don't want to!" The illusion's tugging hand became more insistent, pulling Sarah back a few steps. "Come *on*."

It's nothing, she told herself. *It can't be anything at all.* Her own voice, strident inside her head, insisted upon that. Whatever was in the darkness at the other end of the corridor was nothing, a ghost or hallucination, a cobbled-together fragment of the dead past, as insubstantial as the image of the little girl yanking at her hand. What was there to be afraid of? *This is what I came down here to find out,* she told herself, her voice shouting above both the thunderous footsteps and the trembling of the blood in her veins. All the pleasant notions of childlike tea parties, of curling asleep and dreamless beneath the ocean waves, had vanished, scoured clear by the rush of adrenaline through her body.

"Let's go!" screamed the child.

Sarah angrily jerked her hand free from the image's grasp. "Go on, then!" Her shout tightened the cords in her throat. "Get out of here—I don't care. You want to leave, go ahead—you're not even real!"

Tears coursed down from the girl's dark eyes. "I won't go without you . . ." The voice, the audible hallucination, could barely be heard against the other, greater one pounding through the *Salander 3*'s corridors. It sounded now as if some unseen force was driving a sledgehammer into the walls, the metal deforming and shimmering from the distant and approaching violence. "I found you!" howled the Rachael child. "You were lost *and I found you*! I'm not going to let you go—"

Face reddened with weeping, the child tried to grab Sarah's hand again. Sarah snatched it back, raising the hand almost to shoulder height, as though she were about to slap the image and drive it away from her. "Go away! I don't need you! Don't you understand? *You don't exist—*"

The child had cowered away from the undelivered blow, her own arm brought up to her face to protect herself. She lost her balance as another impact, louder and more violent than all the ones before, shuddered through the space, rippling the floor beneath them. The child's image landed on its side, skidding a few feet before its neck and one shoulder twisted against the nearest stack of boxes. The back of the Rachael child's head snapped against the container, hard enough to daze her, her eyelids fluttering at the point of losing consciousness.

Sarah came close to falling, staying upright only by catching and bracing herself against the wall. The vibration of another impact travelled through her flesh and into the center of her bones. For a moment, the thought came to her that the *Salander 3* might be shaken apart, seams tearing loose from one another, letting the Flow's icy waters come pouring in. Even if she could make her way back to where she'd entered the ship, it might do no good; a picture flashed through her mind of the shaft from the water's surface having been snapped loose from the sunken hull, drifting out of her reach. Wycliffe and Zwingli, bobbing around in their little boat, would look at each other through their square-rimmed glasses and know that something had gone wrong . . .

Silence, broken only by her own panting and the softer breath of the Rachael child, filled the corridor. Sarah's stilled heartbeat was useless as a chronometer of perceived time; seconds or minutes, measured by the outside world, could have crawled by as she watched for whatever approached in the darkness before her.

Something touched her, though not her skin; she sensed the presence rather than felt it. Sarah looked down and saw that the flooring on which she stood had changed, become glistening and wet. She saw her face in a red mirror, a thin film of blood that had seeped out of the dark, a soft, inexorable tide that mired around her shoes. Nausea welled inside her as she stepped back from the pool, leaving two red footprints that the larger redness swallowed, one after another.

When another footstep sounded, just marring the corridor's breathing silence, Sarah looked up. A hand, clenched into a white-knuckled fist, left its shadow on the glistening floor. A man's fist, scarred and cut, as though breaking glass had chewed raw the skin over the bones. The small wounds oozed red, trickling one drop after another, or the same one over and over, that fell and broke the pooled blood into a rippled shimmer. Sarah's reflection shattered and recoalesced, as though there were no escape for it, either.

The fist struck the wall across from Sarah, hard enough to dent the metal around it, straining the welds on all four sides of the panel. But she heard nothing; the impact took place in silence, the air seemingly unable to carry any more shock waves to her ears. *Or else*—the random thought tumbled inside her skull—*my hallucinations have a limit. They know how much I can take.*

That limit, if there was one, shattered when the man's image stepped forward from the darkness into the light. His face was still shadowed, as boots that were already bloodied up to the knees stepped into the thin puddle that reached to the point where Sarah had retreated.

She looked up into the man's face. Saw him, and recognized him from the overlapping layers of her own memory, at its farthest recesses, and from images that weren't memory but things on paper, scraps of the long-buried past. Sarah looked into the image's eyes and saw her mirror reflection there, two bright points locked in darkness into which the flickering glow of the ship's overhead panels could never extend; the reflections held fast, not scattering into fragments the way her face in the pool of blood had gone.

Taking another slow step backward, Sarah watched as the man stepped forward, as though his motion was locked to hers, inseparable. Her gaze was held as well; from both his face, that she saw even clearer now that he had come full underneath the overhead panel's radiance, and her own doubled image. He took his fist away from the wall, its imprint left beneath a smear of red. Something as bright and wet glistened on his face. She saw now the stripes of blood and torn flesh, three vertical, parallel rows on each side, just below his eyes; the wounds might have been from someone else's nails, someone struggling futilely against the figure's advance and the closing of his hands upon a throat and the breath within.

For a moment, the man's brow creased, a flicker of puzzlement passing across his sight. His upraised fist opened, the fingers pulling from the blood at the center of his palm. "Who are you?" His voice was a harsh, grating sound, a part of him that had become unused to speech. "You can't be . . . you're already dead. I already took care of you . . ."

You're the one that's dead—Sarah wanted to shout out the words, but her own voice wouldn't move. She backed away from the figure—the man seemed to tower above her, his black hair scraping against the light panels so that he had to lower his head to the level of his shoulders to come any nearer.

Her heel caught on something behind her; she was barely able to keep from falling. Her hand caught on one of the stacked boxes as she looked over her shoulder. The Rachael child lay on the corridor's flooring, back partway raised against one of the bottom crates. Her eyes drifted open, looking first up at Sarah, then widening in terror as she caught sight of the figure looming at the other end of the narrow space.

Sarah's own will broke; the figure had come close enough that his red hand had started to reach for her, broad fingertips inches from the tangle of hair that had come loose and fallen across her neck. The face that looked back at her from the dark mirrors of his eyes had paled with the same fear that had wrapped around the child cringing behind her. If the image wasn't real, it was real enough. *Enough to kill,* the voice inside Sarah whispered.

She turned to run, to escape from the space's narrowing confines, to get anywhere that blood, hallucinated or real, was not seeping tidelike toward her feet. Another hand caught hers; the child had reached up and caught hold, clinging to Sarah's wrist.

The child wasn't real, either; she knew that. But she didn't shake the illusory grasp from herself. She swiftly knelt down and gathered the child under the arms, pulling her upright. With her own arm pressing the small form tightly against her side, Sarah hurried for the doorway at the opposite end of the corridor, away from the man standing in the middle of the expanding pool of blood.

A glance over her shoulder; Sarah glimpsed the red hand

closing on nothing, on the empty space where she had been standing. She had recognized the face, though she had seen it before only when she had been an infant; she had brought it back from that past almost beyond memory, and from the old photographs in the Tyrell Corporation's archives—

The face was that of her father. The features darkened with rage, as red and trembling as the image's clenched fist.

Pushing the child in front of herself, Sarah ran into the darkness, toward any dark but the one in which she had seen her own face reflected.

"Anything's possible." Deckard shrugged, feeling uncomfortable. The other man—or whatever Sebastian was now—had figured it out, at least partway, but there was no need to confirm his suspicions. If Sebastian's beloved Pris had been replicant or human, what did it matter? "I've been fooled by things. And people. I thought they were one way, and they turned out to be something else. It happens."

"I suppose so." Sebastian made a few more tinkering adjustments to the clown's gears. "You're probably right," he said, nodding slowly. "You've got more experience along those lines than I do. 'Cause of your being a cop, a blade runner, and everything. That's your job, isn't it? To go around and find things that are pretending to be one way—like human—and they're really just replicants. And then you—what was the word?—you eliminate 'em or something."

"Retire." Deckard glanced over his shoulder at the teddy bear and toy soldier, who were still huddling sullenly in the corner. "I don't do that anymore."

"But still . . . it must've done things to your head. Changed it. Permanently. So that's how you see things. Nothing is what it seems to be. Everything's lying." Sebastian's voice turned bitter. "Everyone . . ."

"Maybe so. But that's my problem. Doesn't have to be yours."

"Sure." Bitterness shifted to self-laceration. "I could just go on being a fool. An idiot. That's what everybody thinks of me anyway. Even the rep-symps, when they put me in this place. They just figured I could do a job for them. Same as when I was working for Dr. Tyrell. You just do what you're told, and maybe they'll let you alone for a little while. With your silly little toys and shit."

"Take it easy," said Deckard. He'd seen processes like this before. The small man, or the image or perceptual incarnation or whatever he'd become, was undergoing a complete collapse. Which didn't fit into his own plans. "It's not that bad—"

"Yeah, that's easy for you to say. You don't care." Sebastian gave him a venomous look. "You're trained not to, aren't you? Like all cops. That's just the world you live in. Not that this one's any different." He pulled out the screwdriver and tucked it back into his coveralls. His eyes had become rimmed with red, as though blood were leaking into the perpetual tears. Letting the black cloth drape over the clown mannequin's workings again, Sebastian flipped some hidden switch. The device came to pseudo-life again, the head tilting back and the pudgy arms rising.

The clown's high-pitched mechanical laugh grated on Deckard's nerves. "Shut that thing off."

"Why? Is it bothering you, Mr. Decker?" A vindictive gleam showed in Sebastian's glare. "But you've got ways of taking care of things that you don't like. Why don't you just blow it away, like you used to? Oops, sorry; I forgot. You don't have your gun with you—I didn't give you one when you showed up here. Well, it's too late now." Sebastian's voice had risen in pitch, competing with the noise from the mannequin shaking back and forth with its own laughter. "Maybe you can toss it out the window—that should do it, I imagine. Or you can tear it apart with your bare hands. You'd like that, wouldn't you?"

From the corner of his eye, Deckard saw other motion in the room. The clown's laughter, growing louder and more abrasive, seemed to have set off the rest of Sebastian's collection of toys. Things haltingly stirred to life, a ballerina with empty eye sockets elevating itself *en pointe,* a sawn-off *commedia dell'arte* Punchinello grinning with malice and shaking a bell-cuffed fist at unseen enemies. The ornate howdah on the back of a miniature elephant collided with the chessboard's corner, scattering the white and black pieces across the floor. In an ornate Victorian birdcage, a mechanical nightingale trilled, its wire-and-silk feathers moulting onto layers of age-yellowed antimacassars and cracked circuit boards.

The touch of claustrophobia that Deckard had fought off before now reasserted itself, stronger and tighter; he could feel the cold sweat of panic encasing his skin. Too many things, both dead and animated, pressing around him; with his forearm, he shoved away a tottering, slack-limbed Oz scarecrow that had thrust its idiot smile into his face. The rag-garbed creature fell onto its back, waving its arms around and shedding plastic straw. Deckard edged away from it and the other toys, his cop instincts driving him toward anyplace where he could see what was coming toward him.

"All right—" He held up his hands, palms outward, as though trying to ward off the chaos welling up in the room. "Okay, just settle down." His words were directed at Sebastian. *The little bastard's doing all this.* They were Sebastian's toys, his creations. "Just shut 'em off."

"Why? Don't you want to have any fun?" A malevolent delight suffused Sebastian's face. He no longer appeared child-like, a decrepit infant; his withered skin was that of an old man, a sexless, ageless being. "You're my guest. You should enjoy yourself."

For a second, Deckard had a flash of another wrinkled visage, another cruel, time-scorched entity. One that had gazed upon him from behind square-rimmed glasses, an owlish regard that had weighed and judged more keenly than any Voigt-Kampff machine. That had been in another high-ceilinged room, even emptier of any human presence . . .

The image of Eldon Tyrell's face vanished as Deckard forcibly pushed it out of his head. "That's it." The miniature elephant bumped against his shin, and he angrily kicked it away. "You can stop all this crap now. I've had enough."

"Oh, I don't think so. Not yet. We're just starting."

"Just! Starting!" Behind Deckard, the toy soldier had scrambled to its feet and marched out of the corner, followed by the uniformed teddy bear. The soldier's elongated nose quivered with a feverish excitement. "Fun!"

A sudden gust of wind blew out the nearest row of tall windows, scattering crystals of glass through the room; Deckard raised his arm, protecting his eyes from the razor-edged shards, blue-tinted in the luminous night that flooded past the tattered curtains. The candelabras and other wavering lights were extinguished, collapsing all the room's shadows into darkness.

The floor buckled, gaps splitting between the scarred wooden planks, carpets sliding into rumpled corrugations beneath the sideboards and high-backed chairs. Paintings framed in tarnished gilt fell from the walls, canvases ripped through as they were impaled upon the stiff-fingered hands of mannequins undergoing spasticlike seizures. A pegboard the length of an entire wall section, covered with soldering irons and needle-nose pliers, folded and tore loose from its mounting bolts. It toppled across a banquet table like a two-dimensional bat feasting on the silver bowls filled with dusty wax fruit.

Deckard stumbled back against the smallest table, feeling the chessboard skid beneath his hand, a knight piece digging into the palm; the room tilted as another seismic convulsion rocked the building. For a moment, as he was thrown toward the wall, he had a glimpse through a window ringed with broken-glass knives of the street below and the gaping chasm that had jagged down its center. The theater marquee burst into sparks, the neon curlicues snapping loose, raking blue tendrils across the sidewalk.

"Isn't this fun?" Sebastian's face had reddened into fury; he'd braced himself spread-legged in the middle of the room, riding out the successive impacts of the quake. "Come on—you got to admit it is!"

With the teddy bear wrapped around his leg, Deckard pushed himself away from the wall. He dove toward Sebastian as the bear's toothless mouth managed to chew a dry hole through the fabric of his trousers. The impact knocked Sebastian off his feet, sending him and Deckard skidding through the rubble of chess pieces and hand tools. Still-warm candle wax smeared across Deckard's cheek as he trapped Sebastian's arms against his chest. The smaller man grimaced and spat, writhing futilely.

Outside, the U.N. blimp had floated lower, the light beams from among the spiked antennae slashing through the broken windows, pulling sections of the room into bright illumination, then back to hard-edged shade. Deckard got his knee onto the other man's chest, pinning him to the floor.

Another light seeped through the room's walls. Enough plaster had fallen to reveal the skeletal understructure of the building; beyond the broken laths and support beams, the image of a smaller area, the confines of a hovel on Mars, began filtering into Deckard's perception. For a few disorienting seconds, he could see himself—his other self, the real one—sitting at the rickety table in the hovel's kitchen area, head nodding with eyes closed as though in sleep or drug stupor, the briefcase silent now, waiting for him to come back from wherever he had gone . . .

More than vision: the quake rolling through the fabric of Sebastian's private universe seemed to shake the dim outlines of the hovel on Mars. The empty beaker rolled from the table and shattered on the floor; shards of glass nicked across the back of Deckard's hand. Blood welled between his fingers and onto the shoulder of the figure struggling beneath him.

The distraction had been enough for Sebastian to work one arm free; the butt of his palm shoved up against Deckard's chin with a hysteric's strength. Head pushed back, Deckard could just glimpse the infused life draining out of the toys and mannequins. The clown froze, paralyzed, laughter choked in its rubber-swaddled throat; the ballerina doll collapsed, the sequins across its meager breasts dulling to flakes of lead. Into the floor's dark lightning cracks, the chess pieces rolled and disappeared, like crumbs swept from one of the overturned tables.

"Don't fade out on me, you little sonuvabitch—" Deckard knocked Sebastian's hand away from his face; with the same fist, he clouted the smaller man on the side of the head. "I'm not done . . . with you yet." His own breath came panting with exertion; around him, he could feel the planes and corners of the room growing even less substantial, the illusion of their existence dissipating along with Sebastian's will to maintain them. "Came here . . . to find out something . . ." Deckard gritted his teeth, aiming another blow with the flat of his hand. "Not leaving . . . until I do . . ."

"I don't care," sobbed the other man. Sebastian's eyes squeezed shut, his wrinkled face looking even more like an aging infant's. "Go ahead and kill me—I don't care."

"If I could, I would. Don't tempt me into trying, though." The uniformed teddy bear had let go of Deckard's leg, toppling onto its back, button eyes staring lifelessly up at what remained of the ceiling. A few yards away, the bear's comrade-in-arms had fallen face-downward, long nose skewed to one side, the point of its helmet broken off. "Just shut up and listen." His brain raced in desperation, trying to figure out what to tell the weeping figure. "Look. Just because Pris isn't here . . . that doesn't mean she isn't anywhere at all. Maybe you just haven't looked for her in the right places."

"Huh?" Sebastian rubbed his wet face with his free hand. As Deckard let go of him, he scooted back and sat up. "What do you mean?"

"Come on. Figure it out." Deckard knew he was talking crap, but managed to conceal it. "This is where she was killed, right? I mean, right here in this building. I should know; I'm the one who did it, who blew her away. Out in the real world. You think if you put this place back together here, she's going to want to hang around it? Get real."

"Huh." With his sleeve, Sebastian wiped his reddened nose. "Never thought of that."

"Only natural." Deckard wasn't sure if that word applied in a private universe like this. Raising his knees, he rested his forearms on them. From the corner of his eye, he could see that the room's accelerating dissolve had been halted, perhaps even reversed; the walls, while still cracked and flaking plaster, appeared less nebulous. He could no longer see the other room, the one where his real body was sitting at a table with a briefcase on it. "Maybe you haven't put the place back together yet where Pris would be." He gestured toward one of the broken windows and the night sky beyond. "How far does this go?"

"How far . . . you mean the city? L.A.?"

Deckard nodded. "Everything. All the stuff you put together for yourself here. Did you just do the street outside this building, or does it go beyond that?"

"Gosh. I don't really know." Sebastian gazed up to the cracked ceiling, sorting through his thoughts. "I never really go outside anymore. Not since the rep-symps put me here. It's not like I go out walking around or anything. I just made the stuff come back that I could see from the windows—you know, what I saw when I was back in the real world and I looked out and there was the street and everything." He got up and walked over to the nearest window. With one hand, Sebastian pushed away the rags of the curtain. "Well . . . it's hard to tell from here. I mean, just how far things go. All the other buildings on this street are so much taller. There's just kind of one angle over there where you can see some more of the city." He pointed out to the night. "Doesn't look too . . . you know, real or anything. Kinda fakey." Sebastian shrugged in embarrassment. "Guess I sorta skimped on that part. I wasn't really paying attention."

"You ought to get out more," said Deckard dryly. "Do you good."

The room looked as if a storm had passed through it, scattering the contents. Deckard stood up, then reached down to set upright one of the little tables and the candelabra that had been on it. In the rubble on the floor was a scuffed Second World War–vintage Zippo lighter; he flicked on its thin flame and lit the half-burnt candles. The wavering light drove the shadows back to the corners.

"Maybe . . . maybe you're right." Still standing at the window, Sebastian leaned toward the darkness, gaze searching across the close urban vista. "About Pris. You're right, she *wouldn't* be here!" His voice grew more excited; he turned back toward Deckard. "If she came back—and she must've; I wanted her to—she would've run away from someplace like this. Where she got hurt so bad and all. She might've gotten away before I even got a chance to see her again."

Deckard kept his silence. There was nothing more to be said to the little man, to sell the point to him. He'd lied to Sebastian, raised his hopes, just to keep him from totally dissolving his private universe. *There's no Pris out there,* thought Deckard. *There's not even an out there.*

Beyond the building's walls, the U.N. blimp drifted slowly overhead. The enormous viewscreen on the blimp's side was reflected in the rows of intact window glass across the empty street. Deckard saw a fragmented image of the screen's *geisha* face, the smile replaced by a somber, knowing pity.

"I've got to go looking for her!" Sebastian appeared ready to immediately rush out of the building and onto the street below. "Maybe she's waiting for me—" His manner became even more frantic and agitated. "She might be all alone somewhere, and wondering why I haven't come to be with her—"

"Hold on." Deckard grabbed hold of the other man's shoulder as he started for the door. "Wait a minute. We've still got things to talk about."

The room and the surrounding building, the fabric of the pocket universe, had resolidified. Or the illusion of it had—Deckard had to remind himself that the place wasn't real. He wondered how much time he had left here; at some point the effects of the activated colloidal suspension would wear off, flushed out of his percept system by the constant, slow percolation of his own biochemistry. For all he knew, the spoonful of the Sebastian packet that he'd ingested had already worked its way through his kidneys and was, along with its various breakdown components, ready to be pissed out. At some other time, the notion that one deity or another could reside in his bladder might have wryly amused him; right now, he was in a hurry.

"Let's go! Let's go!" The toy soldier, its nose still bent at an angle, tugged at Sebastian's coveralls. "Right now!" At the other side of the room, the reanimated teddy bear had started rooting through the objects that had been knocked loose and scattered during the quake, as though it were assembling provisions for the journey. "Come on!"

"No, no, Squeaker—Mr. Decker's right." Sebastian patted the soldier on the top of its helmet. "He came all this way to talk with me; he's our guest, so we should treat him right." He glanced up with an embarrassed smile. "I'm real sorry for what happened just now. I got kinda carried away."

"That's all right. I understand." The twinge of guilt sharpened underneath Deckard's breastbone, though he was careful not to let any sign show on his face. *Maybe*—a small trace of hope moved inside his thoughts—*maybe he will find Pris out there. Or something like her.* "I know what it's like."

"Well, yeah . . . I suppose so." Sebastian tilted his head, his wet gaze narrowing as he studied the figure in front of him. "You know, though . . . maybe it wasn't Pris I got all wrong. Maybe it's you."

"What's that supposed to mean?"

"You shouldn't have been able to just come in here and push me around like that." Sebastian spoke without rancor—he had obviously gotten used to being pushed around, one way or another. "This is my world, remember; my little private universe. I'm supposed to be the deity here. If I'd wanted to bring the whole thing crashing down, I shoulda been able to do that. And you wouldn't have been able to stop me. At least, that's the way it's supposed to work. No . . . something funny's going on." He raised an eyebrow. "When we were wrassling around and all, I was trying to make you disappear—well, I was losing, wasn't I?—and you just wouldn't. You're still here. That's really strange, don't you think?"

Deckard shrugged. "I'm not an expert on these places. This is the first time I've even been in one."

"Yeah, well, I *live* here now. This is the only place I exist. So I should know what the deal is on 'em." He slowly shook his head. "I don't get it. What *are* you, Deckard?"

"I don't know." *What the hell's that supposed to mean?* The question didn't even make sense. "Is it important?"

"Maybe not." Sebastian brushed his hands off on the front of his coveralls. "Whatever." All around him, the cracks in the walls' plaster were slowly disappearing, the edges stitching themselves back together. He leaned down and pulled the ballerina doll clear of the crevice in the floor before it could close up on her leg. "So . . . what is it you came here for? What'd you want to find out?"

"You tell me. I was sent here. To see you."

Sebastian nodded. "Yeah, like I said . . . I knew you were coming. The rep-symps told me you'd show up eventually. That was all part of the plan. With the Batty box and all."

"The briefcase," said Deckard. "If that's what you mean."

"That's the one. You know that's Batty in there, don't you? Of course you do—it's not like he's ever exactly quiet about it. Not the one I first met—the replicant who came here—but the other one. The original, the human templant."

"He was the one who told me to come here. He gave me the packet with your name on it; it was inside him, inside the briefcase." Deckard glanced toward one of the windows as though some change in the night's darkness might have indicated the passage of time. "And to get the stuff to mix it up. He had all the instructions. They must have briefed him pretty well."

"In a lot of ways," agreed Sebastian. "Those rep-symp guys . . . they're pretty sharp. Psychologically, I mean. They knew you'd take some convincing."

"I still do."

"They thought you'd trust me." Sebastian's guileless, ingratiating smile appeared again. "Do you?"

Deckard shrugged. "I don't know that, either. Depends on what you tell me."

"All I can do is tell you the truth. Or at least as much of it as I know about."

"That'd be a novelty." Deckard didn't bother to smile. "The truth, I mean."

"Well . . ." Sebastian fiddled nervously with one of the screwdrivers he took from his coveralls pocket. "You can start with this. Batty wasn't lying—the Batty box, I mean; the briefcase—when he was telling you what the deal is. Whatever he told you about . . . what was the fella's name? Something Holder?"

"Holden. Dave Holden."

"Yeah, that's the guy. He's probably dead now, huh?"

Deckard gave a short nod. "Pretty much."

"It was kind of a risky job they stuck him with. Taking the Batty box out to you. He must've known what the chances were." A troubled expression shaded Sebastian's face. "I don't think the rep-symps would've lied to him about that."

"If that's who he was working for."

"Oh, no . . ." The teary eyes went round. "You don't need to have any doubts about *that.* That's one of the true things I'm supposed to tell you about. Convince you and everything. That's what you came here for, isn't it? For me to tell you that, so you'd know it's true—you believe me, don't you?"

"I'm not sure." He wasn't going to admit any more than that. "You could be telling the truth. I just don't know."

"But you've *got* to believe me!" Sebastian's voice went up in both pitch and anxious trembling. "Your old partner, that Mr. Holden—he'd gone over to the side of the rep-symps, and the insurgents out in the colonies, and all those people. He'd decided that was the right thing to do. Just like you did, when you quit the police department. When you stopped being a blade runner."

Deckard barked a quick laugh. "When I quit the department, I didn't exactly go out and sign up with a bunch of psychotics and traitors who're all out looking to get themselves iced by the U.N. security squads."

"Maybe you would've, if you had the chance then."

A shrug. "I'm past caring about that. So what about Batty?"

"What about him?" Sebastian looked puzzled.

"He's with the rep-symps as well, I take it."

"Well, yeah, obviously. I mean, we all are. Your old partner David Holden certainly was—and that's the truth." Both of Sebastian's hands rose in an appeal. "Why would I lie to you about something like that? Jeez, Mr. Decker, I'm way out of the loop now. I don't even exist anymore, at least not in the world you do. So it's not like I've got something at stake in getting you to believe this. I'm, like, a disinterested party. Sort of, anyway. I mean, I care what happens and all. So you could say I'm on the rep-symp side, too."

"You know . . ." Deckard laughed again, softer and more ruefully. "The funny thing is, I'd really like to believe you."

"You should! I'm telling you the truth!" Sebastian's hands quivered. "Look, you did me a favor just now. When you told me about why Pris wasn't here, and about where she might be. That . . . that gives me hope, Mr. Decker. That I didn't have before. I was going to give up, just let this whole place disappear. And me with it—I can do that if I want to. I don't *have* to exist. Here or anywhere else. But I've decided to stick around—because of what you told me." He stepped forward and grasped Deckard's arm. "So I owe you one. I do, really. I wouldn't lie to you, especially not about the stuff you came here to find out. David Holden brought the Batty box out to you because he believed in the rep-symps' cause; he died for it. Now it's up to you—it's your decision—about whether you should find a way to get the briefcase, and the information that's inside it, to the replicant insurgents out in the colonies."

Deckard regarded the other man. "What do you know about the data in the briefcase?"

"Not much. Just that it's important that the insurgents get it. If they're going to have a chance of winning and being free and all. Or even being allowed to live."

"The U.N. would wipe them out? Exterminate them?"

Sebastian nodded vigorously. "You bet. In a second, if they

could. And they might be able to—things really aren't going that well for the insurgents. At least, that's what I picked up from the rep-symps. So there's a lot at stake in getting you to carry that briefcase out to the replicants. In some ways . . ." He let go of Deckard's arm at the same time his voice dropped. "There's a *lot more* at stake than just the fate of the replicants out in the colonies and their rebellion. That's just . . . just the least little bit of it!" A fervent gleam appeared in Sebastian's eyes. "It's not just the replicants; it's humans . . . it's everybody . . ."

The sudden intensity of the other's voice pushed Deckard back. "What're you talking about?"

"They told me you weren't supposed to know . . ." Sebastian squeezed his pale hands together. "I wasn't supposed to tell you . . ."

"About what?"

"I promised them I wouldn't tell . . . but . . ." The little man was growing more visibly agitated by the second. "Like I said, I owe you one. I owe you everything . . ." Sebastian's voice suddenly began to grow fainter and fainter. "It's like this. The stuff the rep-symps didn't want me to tell you—it's all about the difference between humans and replicants. If there is any—remember what Dr. Tyrell used to say?" The voice had diminished to the level of a whisper. "The Tyrell Corporation motto? 'More human than human.' He didn't know how true that was . . ."

"Hey—what're you doing?" Deckard had leaned closer to the other man, trying to hear the words being spoken. "Sebastian—" He realized that he could see through the other's image; the details of the scattered toys and dolls, even the cracked plaster of the far wall, had begun to show. Layers of transparency: each object, Sebastian object, seemed to be turning to clouded glass, or mist contained in the outlines of what had been solid. "You're fading out on me—"

"Huh?" Sebastian's gaze refocussed as he pulled himself from his monologue. His partial image looked as though he was shouting, but the sound that emerged was barely audible. "Mr. Decker—where are you going? You can't go now—"

Deckard reached for the other's arm, as though he could drag Sebastian back into perceived reality. His fist closed on nothing. Sebastian's image wavered and grew fainter.

"It's not me, Mr. Decker—it's you!" Sebastian's faraway voice became more frantic. "The stuff you took, that activated colloidal suspension stuff—it's wearing off. It's going out of your system; you're not here anymore—"

"Goddamn—" A wave of vertigo rolled over him. The indistinct walls and ceiling had exchanged places.

From somewhere above him, Sebastian's voice called out. "Wait! There's still things I gotta tell you!" The ghostly form grabbed an object from the table and hurriedly thrust it toward Deckard's hands. "Here—take this—"

A small metal box; it felt light and hollow, but real, against Deckard's palms as the rest of Sebastian's pocket universe lost its substance. He suddenly found himself toppling backward, balance lost as the floor beneath him thinned out of existence.

Distance and direction vanished with all the other aspects of that world. He fell into the rapidly enfolding dark.

"Miss Tyrell! Over here!" A voice came out of the darkness, the words barely distinguishable against the howl of the wind and the lashing of the rain. "We're coming—"

The water, salt of the Flow mixed with ice crystals driven from the dark roil of clouds above, stung beneath Sarah's eyelids. She shielded her face with one hand, holding on to the edge of the shaft's doorway with the other. The triangular structure bucked on the surface of the water, storm waves lifting and dropping the platform beneath her feet. The shaft itself, leading down to the *Salander 3,* strained with the violent motion as though it might snap free, like a rope stretched to its breaking point. All the way up from the sea-buried ship, as the tiny elevator had carried her toward light and air, she had wondered if that would happen. *If it does,* she had told herself, *I'll drown like a bug in a soda straw.*

That some kind of atmospheric turbulence was pounding Scapa Flow had been no surprise to her. The clouds had been gathering, growing more ominous and heavy-laden, when she had first stepped onto the Orkney mainland, in sight of the old stone cathedral stuffed with its bogus monitoring equipment. And if the storm's fury had been unleashed while she was locked away in a little bubble of stilled time, that made sense as well. Given what Sarah had witnessed, the things she had seen, the past made visible and tangible—given all that, it would have been little wonder to her if this world's sun and moon had crashed together, with wormwood and the stars tumbling into the ocean like hot coals.

"Just hold on!" The call came from the boat careening on the Flow's dark, churning surface. She could just barely make out the silhouette of Wycliffe standing braced at the prow, while Zwingli behind him manned the oars. "We'll be there in a second!" A wave mounting as high as Wycliffe's chest slammed into the boat, nearly toppling him overboard. Zwingli's frantic rowing clawed helplessly at the raucous water.

Just my luck, thought Sarah; the phrase had become the obvious refrain to the events around her. *I would've been safer back down below.* She knew that wasn't strictly true; as it was, she had barely escaped from the *Salander 3* with her sanity intact. There was no way she wanted to see those things again; once had been more than enough.

The foam-crested waves struck the platform, a hammer seemingly more solid than liquid. Her fingers gripped tighter to the doorway as the impact tore at her, then passed, the shaft's tension snapping it down into the trough that came after.

"Here! Catch this!" Wycliffe had mounted into the boat's prow again, a heavy rope coiled around his arm, one end of the rope fastened near Zwingli. He managed to synchronize his throw with the Flow's swell; a knot and loop sailed through the rain.

Sarah took one hand away from the shaft's entrance; her hand missed the rope, but she pinned it against her side with her arm. It slithered like a coarse, wet snake, but she hung on to it, gripping and maintaining her balance as the platform rolled and tilted beneath her. She looped the rope over the projection of the doorway's broad hinge, just above her shoulder, then used her weight to draw the line taut to the boat.

"That's it—" A crevice had opened up in the storm clouds overhead, enough to let a thin sliver of moonlight onto Wycliffe's face. Rain coursed across his brow and eye sockets, then into his open mouth as his chest labored with the unfamiliar exertion. His fanatic loyalty to the Tyrell Corporation and its human emblem was all that kept him standing in the small boat, his hands tugging at the rope. Behind him, Zwingli had pulled the oars alongside himself, turning where he knelt and grasping his partner around the waist, securing him against the next wave to hit.

The boat swung around and hit the edge of the platform broadside. Wycliffe leaned down and forward, catching the raised metal lip with his fingers, straining to hold the boat tight against the force of the water drawing it back. "Miss Tyrell—" His drenched face looked up at her. "You must—" The words came out as gasps. "Jump—"

She let go of the rope, getting to her knees and then half falling, half scrambling into the boat. A smaller wave tilted it; her back struck the other side, sending a quick stab of pain up her spine.

"Are you all right?" Zwingli had grabbed her forearm and pulled her next to him.

Sarah nodded. "I'm fine." She pushed her sodden hair away from her face. "Let's go—"

"Wait a minute—" Kneeling at the prow, Wycliffe still grasped the rope in one hand; the knot at the far end had snagged against the hinge of the shaft's doorway. "There's somebody else there. Look!"

A glance over her shoulder, and through the sheets of rain Sarah was able to make out the small figure standing just inside the entrance to the shaft, clinging to the edge. The little girl's face was filled with both awe and terror at her glimpse of the outside world's unlimited size and violence.

"Who's that?" Wycliffe looked back at Sarah. "Who came up with you?"

"Wait a minute." She turned her gaze from the child to the

man at the boat's prow. "What are you talking about? Are you trying to tell me . . . that you see her, too?"

"Right there." A puzzled expression crossed Wycliffe's face before he pointed to the doorway. "Of course I see her; she's right there."

"So do I," piped up Zwingli. He leaned forward, from where he crouched beside Sarah. "I can see her. Who is she?"

Sarah laughed, head thrown back, throat exposed to the rain. Even after all that had happened down in the *Salander 3,* the things she had seen both before and after her father's murderous apparition had shown itself to her, it still struck that this was a weird place to be having a conversation like this. *Stuck out on a boat,* she thought, *in the middle of a storm that's going to drown us all. And these two idiots want to debate the existence of an unreal thing, a total hallucination.* The laugh died when another realization struck her; she gazed slit-eyed at the man beside her, then at the other one. She wondered what they were trying to pull, what scheme was being forwarded by their claim of seeing the little girl. *She's my hallucination*—they had no claim on the child.

"All right; that's it." Sarah made a cutoff gesture with one hand. "I've really had enough of this." The boat pitched in the water, rising to the crest of another wave and dropping again, banging against the edge of the platform. She had to raise her voice even louder to make her words audible against the rush of the wind. "I don't know if this is part of some little plan of yours, or what. But I'm not in the mood for it. You want to claim that you see a little girl there, fine; go ahead. But you're not convincing me that you see her. Because I know she's not real—"

"But, Miss Tyrell . . ." Wycliffe gestured toward the shaft's doorway. "She's right there!"

She looked where he pointed and saw the Rachael child, just as she had known she would. The child's image—and the sound of her breathing, even the scent of her dark hair, everything that worked to make the hallucination seem real—had come up with Sarah from the *Salander 3,* all the way along the storm-buffeted shaft to the surface of Scapa

Flow. The child had said nothing, but had gazed up at Sarah with her big and sad dark eyes, seemingly aware that some change was coming in her existence. Or nonexistence, as Sarah had had to remind herself. Whatever part of her subconscious was responsible, in league with the influx of material from the ship's bottled-up past, it was certainly doing a thorough job. The illusory child hadn't remained as Sarah had perceived her down below, but had taken on the aspect of being caught out in a gale from the North Atlantic: her clothes, soaked through, clung to her small body as her wet hair tangled across her brow, the braid even heavier and darker against her neck. The water that had trickled down her legs and from her ankles had collected in a pool around her feet, shimmered by the gusts of wind.

"Look. Just drop it, all right?" Sarah spoke fiercely, drawing her arms tight around her body. "I'm cold and wet and tired. And believe me, I've seen enough of things that don't exist. Including this little girl—which you *can't* see, unless you're as crazy as I am. All right? So let's get back to shore. Immediately."

"We're not going to leave her here." An obstinate expression formed on Wycliffe's face. "We can't."

"I'm *ordering* you to. How's that?" Sarah shook her head in exasperation. "We can play whatever games you want to later on."

Wycliffe made no reply. The waves had slackened a bit, enough for him to loosen one hand's grip on the platform's edge and extend it toward the image of the little girl. "Come on," he said to the nonexistent child. "I've got you . . ."

A few seconds later, the apparition who called herself Rachael was in the boat, next to Sarah. A few feet away, Wycliffe stationed himself in the prow, watching as the wind and rain whipped into his face, as though he was concerned that Sarah might do some impossible harm to the child. The boat moved away from the triangular platform as Zwingli applied himself to the oars.

"Some loyalists," she said darkly. "I thought you were supposed to do what I told you to. Both of you."

"I'm sure that . . ." Wycliffe shrugged uncomfortably.

"That you'll agree that this was the right thing to do. When you've had a chance to reconsider."

"I doubt it." Beside her, the Rachael child pressed closer, trying to get warm; she tucked Sarah's hand into both of hers, snuggling into the woman's ribs. "Well. I hope you're satisfied." Sarah looked down at the image. The child ignored the acid comment, rubbing the side of her face against Sarah's sleeve. "You're not even really here, and you pulled this one off."

Once ashore, Wycliffe and Zwingli skipped the cathedral, even though it was closer. With the rain lashing at their backs, they led Sarah and the Rachael child back to the shadow corporation's interplanetary yacht. The breaks in the storm clouds let the stars' cold light through, enough to pick out the rocky edges of the trail. Ahead of them, the running lights and docking signals of the yacht glinted and blinked in sequence along the ovoid shape's circumference.

Thank God, thought Sarah as the gangway irised open. All she wanted now was another shower and a change of clothes. She had glanced down at herself as she and the others had trudged away from the little boat pulled up on the Flow's pebbly shore. The palms of her hands were still stained with blood from when she had tripped and fallen, running from all that she had seen and feared inside the *Salander 3*; the rain hadn't managed to wash it away. Nor had it taken the blood from the patch along one leg or the side where she had landed hard against her rib cage; there had been so much blood inside the ship that it had seemed to imbed itself in every fabric of her being, like the canned and recirculated air drawn into her lungs.

A half hour later, Sarah found herself wondering how many of the black undertaker suits Wycliffe and Zwingli had aboard the shadow corporation craft. While she had been in the master suite's facilities, looking down through billows of gratefully received steam at the trickles of red sluicing off her body, thinning pink as they ran down the drain near her bare feet, the two men had managed to transform themselves back into the muted—and dry—personae in which she had first seen them. With the thick bathrobe pulled around herself, the Tyrell Corporation logo monogrammed over her breast, she sat down in the ship's central lounge, taking the largest and plushest of the chairs available. The two men had remained standing—she wondered how long they had been waiting for her to reappear—but one other figure was already there, sitting with her legs tucked up under her in one of the lesser wing chairs. With large grave eyes, the image of the little girl watched and waited.

"You're still here?" Sarah had extracted a cigarette from the enameled case on the nearest small table. She lit the cigarette, inhaled, then let the grey smoke be carried away by the yacht's ventilation, so much quieter and unobtrusive than the ancient system she'd encountered at the bottom of Scapa Flow. "I thought—well, perhaps I hoped—that you'd have gone away by now." The hot shower, taking away the chill that the storm winds had driven into her bones, had seemed so therapeutic that a diminishing of hallucinations had not seemed entirely unlikely. "You know . . . this could become quite tiresome. You're not really needed anymore."

"I'm not going away." The little girl's face darkened with her stubborn defiance. "And you can't make me."

"We'll see about that." Sarah regarded the glowing tip of the cigarette. "There are ways. These things can always be accomplished. One way or another." She'd have to look into it—when there was time. Or if. A fatalistic calm had settled over her, part fatigue, part resigned acknowledgment of the meshing of the universe's gears. "Even if, say, psychotherapy didn't work. Drugs might. Or surgery, perhaps." She nodded slowly, as though contemplating the possibility. Though it was technically easier to get material in and out of the brains of replicants—the whole system of control through implantation of false memories was a Tyrell Corporation development—it could be done, to a limited degree, with humans as well. Sarah imagined that a sufficiently skilled neurosurgeon could root around inside her skull with his microscalpels and tiny electrified probes and root out whatever lump of grey matter contained the little girl's image.

Or there might be even simpler ways. The ultimate surgery: "I could just kill myself." Sarah enunciated the words clearly, with no hesitation attached to them. She had considered the option enough times to render it free of pain. "Then you *would* disappear, wouldn't you? If I blew a hole in the side of my head, you could just flutter out and be gone."

"Miss Tyrell . . . for heaven's sake." Wycliffe had turned pale. "Don't say things like that."

"Why? Will it blow up the franchise or something?" When all else had failed, there was still some sadistic pleasure to be gotten out of needling the die-hard loyalists. "I nearly forgot. Without me, your chances of resurrecting the Tyrell Corporation are just about zero. A suicide would ball up your plans, wouldn't it? All this work for nothing."

"It's more than that," insisted Wycliffe. "There's a certain matter of . . . personal loyalty."

"He's right." Zwingli added his voice to the statement. "Since there really is no difference between you and the corporation. That makes it sort of a liege-vassal relationship."

"It didn't sound like that out there on the Flow." Sarah nodded toward one of the viewports, through which the storm-lashed waters could be seen. "You weren't exactly taking orders from me when I told you to leave behind this . . ." She gestured in the direction of Rachael. "Child . . . apparition, or whatever . . . that you claim to see."

"I'm not," announced Rachael sullenly, "an apparition. I know what that word means."

"Miss Tyrell. If it would do any good—" Wycliffe sounded desperate. "We'd be happy to pretend we don't see any child sitting here with us. You could *order* us to do that."

"What child?" asked Zwingli helpfully. He watched Sarah for an approving reaction.

"But it really wouldn't change anything." Hands spread apart, Wycliffe hunched up his shoulders. "We'd still *see* her. And since she did come with you out of the *Salander 3,* it's vitally important that we get whatever information we can from her. Whether she's an apparition or not."

"You people must be crazy." The Rachael child turned a withering look on all of them. Sitting back in the wing chair, she folded her arms across her chest. "An apparition is something that doesn't exist. The nanny told me all about it. Because there were plenty of apparitions down there. I was told to be *very careful* about them. Because even if they don't exist, they can still hurt you."

"Truer words," said Sarah dryly, "were never spoken." She flicked grey ash onto the lounge's carpet. "Though in this case, I'm not much worried."

"Perhaps we could settle this later." Wycliffe looked both fretful and conciliatory. "When you're not quite so worn out from your efforts, Miss Tyrell—"

"You mean, when I'm not feeling cranky. About you two claiming you can see my hallucinations." She was still wondering—or worse, coming to conclusions—about what they were trying to accomplish with that bit.

"Whatever. But there really is some time pressure here, Miss Tyrell. We'd like to debrief you about what you encountered down in the *Salander 3* while the memories are still fresh—"

She laughed, holding the half-drawn cigarette off to one side. "They're not exactly the kind that fade. Believe me."

"Every detail," persisted Wycliffe, "might be important. If the Tyrell Corporation is to be brought back to what it was before. We need to know."

"Sometimes . . . I think I must be working for you. Instead of the other way around."

Wycliffe stiffened to his full funereal height. "We are all in the service of the Tyrell Corporation."

"Really." She smiled as she regarded him. *Pompous twit*—though she supposed it was ever thus with religious fanatics. *No sense of humor at all.* A good thing for him that he hadn't been the one to enter the scuttled *Salander 3.* He wouldn't have made it back out alive, or with even as much sanity as she'd retained intact. Because that moment had come, while she had been down there, with all the mass of the ocean on top of her and the even more crushing and airless weight of the past sealed around, that it had seemed at last like a joke, a hard and cruel one, but a joke nevertheless. That she had gone all that way, a complete round-trip to the place and frozen time of her infancy, just so the one who would have killed her so long ago could have another chance at her . . .

It must've seemed so very accommodating of me, thought Sarah. She breathed out smoke, tilting her head back and watching the insubstantial, disappearing shape it made. All the murderous ghosts of the past; if they dreamed, it would have to be of death. They couldn't die themselves, not while the past endured unbroken, sealed tight within its bottle, away from the real world and real time. But as the little girl had said: *Even if they don't exist, they can still hurt you.*

"Miss Tyrell?" Wycliffe's voice poked at the edge of her awareness.

She brought herself the rest of the way back from the *Salander 3*'s world, the replica of it inside her head. "Very well." Sarah ground out the cigarette stub in the green-veined malachite bowl beside her. "What do you want to know?" A smile below half-lidded eyes, directed in turn at Zwingli and Wycliffe. "What do you want me to tell you?"

"You don't have to tell us anything other than the truth." Wycliffe appeared as if he had won some obscure debating point. "What you saw. What happened to you. Everything that happened down there."

Kill them all, thought Sarah. Her eyelids went all the way closed. *And let God sort them out.*

She heard the child's voice, piping up: "There were bad things. The ones that're always there. That's what she saw."

"Yes," said Sarah, nodding. She opened her eyes and gazed at the two men watching her. "That's what I saw. The things that are always there." Her thin smile became laughter that she couldn't help from tearing her throat. "Excuse me. But it's really very funny."

"Are you all right?" Zwingli spoke, sounding genuinely concerned. "Can I get you something?"

"No, no; it's all right." Sarah gestured with one hand. "It just struck me that I solved the mystery . . ."

"Mystery?" From inside his jacket, Wycliffe had taken out a small notepad. He glanced up from the few words he had scribbled. "What mystery is that?"

"Is there more than one?" She brushed a tear away from

the corner of her eye. "The cat, of course. I found out what happened to the cat."

"Cat?" The stylus remained poised on the notes.

"The one that my parents took with them. The official pet of the *Salander 3* expedition. You must've seen it, in the old news photos, in the company files. A big, fluffy marmalade cat."

"Ginjer," said the image of the little girl, sitting forward in the wing chair. "That's what it's name was. That was what my mother called it. The nanny told me so."

"Miss Tyrell . . . when I said that everything could be important, I might have misspoken." Wycliffe tapped the stylus on the notepad. "The cat—and yes, I do remember seeing it in the old photos—that actually might not be critical to our mission. If the cat is alive and well down there, that's wonderful, but really—"

"Hardly alive." Sarah glared at the man. "And it probably wasn't too well when it died. Though that probably didn't take too long, from the looks of what I found." Her voice turned flat and grim. "It wasn't that big a cat when it was alive. When Anson and Ruth Tyrell took it aboard, and they all went sailing off toward the Proxima system. But it's amazing how large an area an ordinary domestic house cat can cover . . . when somebody puts their mind to it." She looked down at her hands, which she had spent so much time scrubbing clean in the shower, long after the red marks had swirled down the drain. "And somebody did."

"Miss Tyrell . . ."

"Be quiet," she snapped. "You wanted to know everything. You don't get to pick and choose now." Sarah let her voice drop to a whisper. "We were running . . . the little girl and I. Because we were scared. Because we had seen the bad things; they had come right out and spoken to us, they had told us what they wanted to do. That's why we were scared. And it was dark—there are some very dark places down there—and I tripped and fell. I had Rachael by the hand; she was running to keep up with me, and then she almost fell, too."

"But I didn't," said the girl.

"That's right. You didn't." Sarah nodded. "Because you knew." For a moment, she wondered how a piece of her own subconscious could know something that she herself wouldn't have been able to know. But she let the thought pass away. "You knew your way around; you knew what else was down there. I didn't; that's why I fell. On the cat. Or what was left of it."

She paused, looking from one man's face to the other's, gauging their reactions. Why they should be so queasy about the death of a cat that had happened over two decades ago—she supposed their reaction was due to the closeness of detail. The deaths of so many people in the apocalypse of the Tyrell Corporation's L.A. headquarters—hundreds? Thousands? She had never bothered to find out the exact number—they didn't matter.

"The person who did it," continued Sarah, "must have been very thorough. From the evidence. It's one thing to just make a mess—anyone can do that—but to have a certain artistic sense . . . that's almost as admirable as it is evil." Under her breastbone was a cold, hard stone where her heart should be; Sarah knew that she wouldn't be able to speak like this, otherwise. *I wouldn't even be able to live. Not anymore.* "I don't suppose the cat would have suffered too long—it wouldn't have been able to. It would have to have died at some point early on in the process. So it wasn't done for the cat's sake . . . or at least no more so than was necessary."

"For whom, then?" Wycliffe's voice was nearly as soft as hers. "And who did it?"

"Who did it? My father, of course. Anson Tyrell." A shake of her head, as though chiding the one who had spoken. "And don't pretend that comes as so much of a shock to you. I have a feeling that you both knew—perhaps the whole shadow corporation knows—just what happened aboard the *Salander 3.* About my father's insanity and his homicidal rampage. You all knew; perhaps you were the ones who erased any mention of it from the company files. So that I wouldn't know."

Wycliffe and Zwingli exchanged glances with each other, but said nothing.

That was enough for Sarah to know that she had surmised correctly. "Don't worry about it," she said, amused by the flicker of panic she had seen in the men's eyes. "I'm sure you and the others did it for the absolute highest of reasons."

"It was . . . to protect you." Zwingli blurted out the words. "Really."

"Of course it was. If I didn't know what had happened when I was just an infant in my mother's arms—all those things of which I was supposedly too young to have formed memories—then I wouldn't have bad dreams, would I? How thoughtful of you. And naturally, I wouldn't be quite so resistant to your plans for resurrecting the Tyrell Corporation as I might have been if I already knew what was in the *Salander 3*. You might not have been able to talk me into going down there."

"That's not quite fair," said Wycliffe. "As you've said before, without you there is no Tyrell Corporation. The opposite can be said as well: *you* don't exist, or you can't for much longer, unless the corporation comes back from the shadows. Any subterfuge was as much for your benefit as ours. And as it happens, there are only the slightest, fragmentary records of what might have happened during the *Salander 3*'s final expedition. A few transcripts of statements made by the company employees who went aboard the ship after it had returned to Earth—and most of those had been severely edited or destroyed before anyone from the shadow corporation would have had a chance to access them."

"You have to give my uncle credit for his thoroughness, all right." Sarah felt her face hardening. "God forbid anything should besmirch the Tyrell Corporation's public image."

"Eldon Tyrell might have had motivations beyond that." Wycliffe shrugged and spread his large-jointed hands apart. "If things are as you found them inside the *Salander 3*—and we have no reason to doubt you on that score—then it might not have been for the company's sake that Dr. Tyrell acted as he did in suppressing this information. It might have been for the family name."

"Oh? And there's a difference?" Sarah raised one eyebrow. "Between the family and the corporation?"

"Not much, admittedly. Let us say, then, for your father's sake. And the way he was remembered. Anson Tyrell wasn't a psychotic murderer when he left on the *Salander 3*'s expedition; whatever happened to him aboard the ship, it happened *out there.*" One of Wycliffe's bony fingers pointed upward, to the night sky beyond the yacht's contained spaces. "Something happened that made him do what he did."

"You said 'murderer.' That was the word you used." Sarah's narrowed gaze fastened onto the man. "People don't say 'murderer' when they're talking about a cat getting eviscerated and hung around a room like a Christmas garland." One of her hands balled into a fist, knuckles as white as those she had seen through the blood smeared on her father's hand. "Perhaps 'psychotic'—that's easy enough. But not the other."

Wycliffe's mouth opened, but snapped shut again before any words came out.

"I caught you out on that one," said Sarah with grim satisfaction. "I haven't told you yet about the other things I saw down there—"

"The *really* bad things," chimed in the little girl sitting in the wing chair. "Not just some stupid old cat."

"Ah. Yes . . . exactly so." Wycliffe attempted a feeble smile. "I must have been . . . anticipating what you were about to tell us."

"I don't think so." She lifted the lid of the ornate box on the small table beside the chair, and watched her hand run a fingertip across the cigarettes' silky paper, before turning her gaze back to the two men. "I think you knew very well that my father didn't stop with the cat. When he had his psychotic breakdown, somewhere between here and the Proxima system—he didn't go just a little bit crazy. He went all the way."

"There were . . . some indications . . . about that."

Sarah slapped the box lid down. "Gentlemen—I found more than indications. I found my mother's body. Or what was left of it. Perhaps, for my father, the cat had just been a little warm-up, a practice session to get ready for the main event. Which was my mother." One fingertip ticked against the box lid. "And myself."

"That would seem to be . . . consistent." Wycliffe's hands folded around each other. "With the fragmentary reports of those who went aboard the *Salander 3* when it returned to Earth." He gave a single nod. "It's fortunate, of course, that Anson Tyrell didn't manage to fulfill his deranged agenda."

"Oh, I agree." She made no attempt to disguise her sarcasm. "I doubt that even when I was an infant I would have enjoyed those particular attentions of my father. You see, I've been inside his head; that's what the *Salander 3* is now. With all that toxic past locked up and unchanging inside it—it's like that Jungian definition of the psychotic condition as that state when no new thing ever enters into a person's thoughts. Just the same thing over and over again, like an endless tape loop. And that thing in my father's case was murder. And blood, lots of it; more than what's inside a cat, or what was inside my mother." Sarah's voice grated rawer and tighter. "An ocean of it. That must've been what the inside of his head looked like before he died. Just big hollow spaces like the ones inside the *Salander 3,* washed with blood."

"Was . . . was your mother . . ." Zwingli's words came out in a stammer. "Had he done the same thing to her? Like he did to the cat?"

"No." A shake of the head. "That didn't happen. From what I could tell . . . he slashed her throat. And then . . ." Her own words came slower and slower, close to halting. "He stopped there."

"That's not the whole story." The Rachael child spoke up, her voice hard with scorn. "She's not telling it right!" Gripping the arms of the wing chair, the little girl looked around at Wycliffe and Zwingli in turn. "And she even saw what happened. She *saw* it!"

Wycliffe turned from the child back toward Sarah. "Miss Tyrell . . . what did you see? What happened?"

The tape loop inside her head, that segment of the long-buried past that had wormed its way into her own memories, became visible once more as she closed her eyes. It would never go away. Once seen, it was as unending as it had been in the hulk of the *Salander 3.*

"What happened." She spoke without raising her eyelids to admit the lounge's softly filtered light; even that was too much for her now. "I saw her—my mother; Ruth Tyrell, whatever you want to call her. It doesn't matter. She was running, too; she was running with the baby in her arms. Because she knew what he wanted to do."

"That's the real story." From somewhere outside Sarah, the little girl's voice spoke again, approvingly this time. "That's what really happened. I know, because the nanny told me. Because when I saw those things happening over and over again, they scared me. I wanted to know, so I wouldn't be scared anymore. So the nanny told me who they were."

Sarah waited until the child was finished speaking, without even wondering if the two men could hear those words or not. "The infant . . . that was me." She spoke slowly, trying to get everything exactly right, as if that could help somehow. "And then . . . and then he caught her. He caught up with my mother. His wife. Ruth and Anson . . ." Her voice trailed away.

"Go on, Miss Tyrell. We have to know everything."

"There's not much more, is there?" She sighed and shook her head, opening her eyes to look up at the radiant ceiling. "My father knew his way around the *Salander 3* better than my mother did, so there was really no place for her to hide. Plus she had the baby—she had me—with her. Plus . . . you can't ever get away from the really bad things. Whether they exist or not. Eventually, they catch up with you. The way my father caught up with her."

Nothing but silence surrounded her. They were all waiting for her to go on.

Those poor ghosts, thought Sarah. For a few seconds, she wasn't sure who she meant. The people here, in the richly appointed lounge of the shadow corporation's interplanetary yacht—they didn't seem any more real to her than the figures she had seen down at the bottom of Scapa Flow, acting out their endless time-stilled rituals of fear and madness and death. *They might not even know they're dead.* She supposed that statement might apply to the ones here as well. In a way, the only one that did appear real to her was the hallucinated Rachael child. At least that one had come out of her head, up from her unlit subconscious, the same way Sarah herself had come up from the sunken ship. *So she's at least as real as I am.* That wasn't saying much. *Maybe just a little bit real, perhaps.*

As if on cue, the child spoke again. "He cut her throat." A simple announcement. "That's what he did. He had a knife and he cut her throat. Just like *that.*" The girl made a quick swooping gesture, one hand holding an invisible blade. "And she died."

Sarah didn't wait for the two men to ask what happened next. "And then," she said, "so did he. My father died." The tape loop inside her head had run to its end and started over, one moment of the past welded inexorably to its antecedent. "He had his dead wife at his feet and a wailing infant lying in the pool of blood on the floor." She had watched all that, with the hallucinated Rachael child close beside her, the two of them pulled back into the shadows of one of the ship's unlit corridors, as the ghosts locked in time had gone through their rituals in the light, as though they were the ones who existed outside of memory. There was something else that she didn't speak of, not because she didn't want Wycliffe and Zwingli to know; it was just too painful to try to find the words. That her mother had died shielding her, protecting the infant in her arms. Even when the crazed figure with the knife had taken her mother down to her knees, his other hand twisting her hair tight into his fist, drawing her throat taut and vulnerable; even then, Ruth Tyrell hadn't screamed, but had gasped out a plea, not for her own life but for the smaller one she'd held desperately against her breast.

Desperate because Ruth had known—as her daughter, Sarah, had known, when she had seen the madness in her long-dead father's eyes—that the child, the infant in her mother's arms, had been the true target of his wrath. He'd murdered his wife, drawn the knife across her white throat, only to get at his own child . . .

"But he didn't." Sarah spoke her thoughts aloud. She didn't care whether anyone else heard them. "For a moment . . . he wasn't crazy. And that was all it took. He must have heard what she said to him, what Ruth had said." Sarah, watching from the dark corridor, hadn't been able to make out the words her mother had spoken. Words in a ghost's mouth; perhaps they hadn't even been words at all but just some inarticulate cry. Or articulate enough. For that brief section of the past, the past that had happened so long ago and so far from Earth, one sixth of the way to the Proxima system; for just that long, a matter of a few seconds, Anson Tyrell had been sane again; whatever gripped him had relaxed its hold, letting a horrified rationality possess him once more.

He had his dead wife at his feet, the blood still running from her opened throat and pooling around the two of them, forming a redly shining mirror in which he looked down and saw his own unrecognizable face. And saw the knife in his upraised hand, which he might not even have known was there, he'd been that crazy. And saw his face in that smaller red mirror, the one smeared on the blade's bright metal; and recognized.

That was how it had appeared to Sarah, watching the ghosts. Who were so locked into the past that she would have seemed like a ghost to them if she had stepped out of the dark corridor. If they had been able to see her at all. Sarah's time, that she was locked into and that she carried around with her as though it were some invisible diving bell, had separated out from the time held in the *Salander 3,* like the markings of trace elements divided by their specific gravity. Those elements, her time and the ghosts' time, had been swirled together for a little while, when she had first descended and entered the transport. So that the elements had bumped up against each other, become visible to each other, the dead looking at the living, or at least the not-so-dead. Her dead father had been able to see her, had probably thought she was one more part of the craziness sparking away inside his head. Would he have been able to do more than just look at her and say crazy, murderous things? She didn't know;

that had been when she had turned and ran, snatching up the Rachael child by the hand and pulling her along after herself, not caring that the child was even less real than her dead father.

"And then your father killed himself."

She didn't know which of the men had spoken. "That's right." She supposed that was something else of which they had been aware all along, another little fragment left in the company records, transcribed from one of the employees who had gone aboard the returned *Salander 3.* What else they found: the two corpses with slashed throats, the knife still in Anson Tyrell's hand. "When he was sane again, and he could see what he had done. He used the same knife on himself." That kind of grief, she knew, being another sort of insanity. Or else it was being really, truly sane at last. It all had the same results. "He didn't worry about the infant lying in the pool of blood, wailing away and kicking its little feet. He knew that the *Salander 3*'s computer and all its built-in autonomic machinery would take care of me. Better than he would be able to; that's what it was designed for. Especially since he had no way of knowing how long he would stay sane. The craziness had come over him like a storm, and it had passed, but it might come again. Better to let the ship bathe and feed and comfort his child."

"And bring it back to Earth," said Wycliffe. "Bring you back. The *Salander 3*'s return program wouldn't have kicked in while your father was still alive. The computer only went into autopilot when it could no longer detect any adult human presences aboard."

There was some small comfort to be had from that. Sarah felt cold and empty, the hard bravado she had been displaying now worn thin, as though the warmth of the yacht's lounge had failed to reach the bones chilled by the ocean's storm. *Still,* she thought as she gazed at the elaborate marquetry of the cigarette box's lid and did not see it. *Still . . . he was trying to protect me the only way he could. From all the bad, crazy things. From himself.*

"But . . . we don't know why he did it. What could have caused Anson Tyrell to go mad."

Sarah looked up and saw the two men in conference, heads leaning toward each other, voices lowered but not to whispers, as though they had simply put her presence out of their minds for a moment. Between them, seated in the wing chair, her hallucination of the Rachael child looked up at them, following their conversation like a tennis spectator.

"That's true," replied Zwingli. He nodded thoughtfully. "We have more details . . . but not really any more information. Not that we can use."

"That's a problem." Behind the square-rimmed glasses, Wycliffe's eyes seemed to focus on his own deep considerations. "To have come all this way . . ."

"Yes . . ." As though in a slightly distorted mirror, Zwingli's gaze looked the same, complete to the spectacles exactly like those of the late Eldon Tyrell. "It seems a shame . . ."

Wycliffe remained silent, lips pursed in thought.

"Do you really suppose we could? I mean, ask her to do that . . ."

"Ask me to do what?" Sarah heard her own voice cut across the yacht's lounge. "What are you two talking about?"

"We wouldn't ask it of you, Miss Tyrell . . ." Wycliffe raised and spread his hands. "If it weren't so absolutely critical to our mission . . ."

"That's right." Zwingli nodded vigorously. "We're really only thinking about the ultimate fate of the Tyrell Corporation."

"I bet." A bitter taste formed on Sarah's tongue. "You want me to go back down there. Back down to the *Salander 3.* I didn't bring back enough information with me on that last trip. Not enough to suit you, at any rate."

"As I said." Wycliffe made an attempt at looking apologetic. "Only because it's so crucial. That's the only reason. You understand that, don't you?"

"Oh, I understand all right." Sarah stood up from the chair. She pulled the robe tighter around herself, grabbing the dangling ends of the belt and cinching it hard at her waist. "And as you also said—" She could feel the stiffer embroidery of the company logo against her skin, just above her heartbeat. "Without the Tyrell Corporation, I'm nothing. So I really don't have much choice in the matter."

"That's rather a . . . *harsh* way of looking at it—"

"Stuff it. You're supposed to be working for me. And I don't need your lectures." Sarah held out her hand, palm upward. "You promised me something. Back on Mars. And I haven't gotten it yet."

Wycliffe looked puzzled. "Promised you what?"

"A gun. Another one, to replace the one I had."

The two men exchanged nervous glances.

"Don't worry about it, for Christ's sake." Sarah shook her head in disgust. "It'll be all right—"

"Miss Tyrell . . . that might not be such a good idea. Not right now . . ."

She glared at Wycliffe. "You mean, not after I've been talking about killing myself."

"Well . . ."

"Look, you want me to go back down there? Then give me the gun. Because I'm not going to go down there without it."

A faint smile showed on Zwingli's face. "A gun wouldn't help you. Not there. Not with those kinds of things."

"I don't care about that." Sarah kept her hand extended in the same position. "Give me the gun. Or you can kiss off getting anything more from the *Salander 3*."

Wycliffe's owlish gaze regarded her for a few moments longer. Then he turned and walked over to the cabinets at the far end of the lounge, extracting a ring of keys from his pocket as he went. He came back with a large black object in one hand. "Here you are," he said stiffly. "As you requested."

She examined the gun, turning it from side to side. It was bigger and heavier than the one she'd had back on Mars. *That should do.* "How do I know that it's loaded?" Sarah held it at arm's length, sighting along her wrist and down the weapon's massive barrel. "Or that it works at all? Maybe it's a dummy, just some prop you got ready for me."

A sigh from Wycliffe. "It's loaded. We keep them that way."

"I need to test it. Before I go back down there."

He glanced toward one of the lounge's dark-filled

viewports. "Perhaps when the storm is over. In the morning; then you could go outside with it—"

"No." Sarah shook her head. "I don't have to go outside." Arm still extended, she swiveled the gun around. "Not at all."

The bullet caught Wycliffe in his chest, sending him aloft, arms spread wide, as though he were falling back onto some invisible bed just behind him. He landed in a crumpled mass at Zwingli's feet. The other man looked down at his partner's corpse, then back up at Sarah, eyes wider behind the square glasses than they had ever been before.

This is too easy. The echo from the first shot was still rolling around the space as she pulled the trigger once more. *They must have wanted it this way.* She didn't care whether they had or not.

"Gosh." The Rachael child had gotten out of the wing chair and had gone over to look at the two bodies, one lying on top of the other. The Eldon Tyrell memorial glasses gazed blankly at the lounge's ceiling. "What's going to happen now?" Unfazed, the child looked over at Sarah.

She set the gun down on the small table, then extracted a cigarette from the ornate box. "I've got other business to take care of." Sarah slipped the lighter into the robe's pocket. "Far from here." Tilting her head back, she exhaled smoke. "Unfinished business."

"Can I come with you?"

A shrug. It didn't matter to her. The little girl didn't really exist, and, for all practical purposes, the two die-hard loyalists had stopped existing as well. She was alone.

"Sure." She turned and started back to the master suite, to finish dressing before going up and setting the yacht's course. Back to Mars. And Deckard. She wondered idly how he'd react when he saw her again. *I'll know soon enough.* "Don't fade away on my account." Sarah glanced over her shoulder at the image of the little girl. "Stick around as long as you like . . ."

14

He woke up and wondered where the hell he was.

For a moment, Deckard thought he was back in L.A. Or that he'd never left it and that everything that had happened anywhere else had been a dream, the kind you snap out of like falling off a cliff or the edge of one of the tallest buildings. Covered in night sweat, heart pounding inside your chest, fingers scrabbling at anything that would provide a second's hold.

An alley; he could tell that much, as full consciousness seeped back into his head. Narrow, cramped, and dark, at the bottom of thickly grimed and graffiti-scrawled walls with no windows. A damp cushion of rubble beneath him, moldering urban decay that had been swept or pushed or just blown by the wind into these forgotten dead-end niches; the sweet, rank smell of garbage and other human castoffs filled Deckard's nostrils. His own stink as well, as though he had been lying there for some undetermined amount of time; he ran a hand across his chin and found the stiff, short bristles of a two-day beard.

There had been an alley like this back in L.A., lots of them, most of which he'd been in during his blade runner days. Often with an escaped replicant at the terminus, at that point where there was no place left to run to. Where all they had left was to press their spines against the buildings' steaming bricks and retrofitted exhaust shafts and wait for the shadowed figure to approach and lift the big black gun in his hand, aim, and fire, that roar of light the last thing their manufactured eyes would ever see. Deckard knew he didn't have a gun on him—he couldn't sense that weight tugging anywhere in his begrimed clothes—so he felt sure he hadn't fallen back into that soul-killing time.

The Outer Hollywood studios? He pushed himself up into a sitting position, scanning the area for more clues. Maybe he'd found himself in that perfectly reconstructed L.A., the *faux* cityscape orbiting above Earth's brown atmosphere. A few seconds was enough to convince him otherwise. *No extras,* thought Deckard, looking out to the alley's mouth. So it couldn't be Outer Hollywood—the money had always been spent there on a crowd of pedestrians, expertly gotten up like the real L.A.'s packed and cultish street life. The area he could see now, out beyond this alley, was empty, at least for the time being.

"Hey. Hey, buddy . . . let me help you with that . . ."

Deckard heard the voice at his ear, a ragged, whispering sound. And felt the other's presence, whoever it was, close enough to touch. *My cop skills must be all shot to hell,* he couldn't help thinking ruefully. He'd let somebody get right next to him without any instinctive defenses' being triggered.

A hand fumbled at the place where Deckard's own hands were crossed over the front of his jacket, holding on to some light object like a souvenir from his forgotten dreaming. It felt like thin metal, a box of some kind, light enough to be empty; his thumbs felt the ridge where the lid snapped tight. The other person's hands tugged at the little box, trying to slip it out from under Deckard's grasp. That pushed him to full awake; his eyes snapped all the way open, catching sight of a grizzled, cadaverous face close to his. One hand left the box and backhanded the stranger, knuckles spattering blood out of the gap-toothed mouth.

"Jeez . . . you didn't have to do that . . ." The other man scuttled a few feet away and then crouched, wiping the red from his face, yellowed eyes sulkily watching Deckard. "You want to be left alone, just *say* so . . ."

The alley had to be on Mars, in the back reaches of the emigrant colony; the ineffectual roller had the twitching, jittery look of someone just starting to fall under the effects of acute stimulus deprivation. The skin under the rags and dirt seeped raw from the man's broken fingernails' plucking at his own flesh. Deckard drew himself up farther, leaning his back against the wall behind him. He looked down at the box in his hands—chipped white enamel on thin metal, with a faded red cross in the lid's center—and tried to remember what it signified. Inside his head, the blurred components of a dream moved toward each other, linking up one by one.

Now I got it—a picture had formed, a little wrinkled face with weepy eyes. It grew clearer; Deckard saw the rest, not a dream but memory. Not entirely real, but real enough; something that had actually happened. A room with earthquake cracks running through the plaster, even across the high ceiling, the white dust sifting over toys and dolls, big ones, a frozen ballerina and a fat, silently laughing clown. The face of an aging child wasn't one of those, but a human's face; or what had been a human, Deckard corrected himself. Now a deity in his own little pocket universe. Which is where he'd just been, and from which he'd fallen out of . . . how long ago?

Deckard reached over and grabbed the quivering man's thin wrist, pulling him closer. "How long have I been here?"

"Huh?" The yellow eyes stared at him. Stringy muscles jumped beneath the man's hollow cheeks. "What're you talkin' about?"

His temper flared higher as he yanked the man right into his own face. "How long have I been lying here in this alley?"

"Huh-how should I know? C'mon, fella—uh!" The pawlike hands shoved futilely at Deckard's chest. "I don't—"

"When did you first see me here? How long ago?"

"Maybe . . . maybe yesterday. Yeah—" The man gave a nod vigorous enough to rattle his whole body. "Yeah, there was a pile of stuff here when I went by, and that was yesterday, and then I came back to check it out . . . and it was you. Okay? So that's how long you been here. Since yesterday. Let go of me, willya?"

Deckard released him with a hard thrust of his arm. "Take a hike." The man scurried out toward the street, twitching slightly less from the input to his nervous system.

A day at least, lying in this alley—Deckard shook his head, trying to clear out the last of the fog. Even without having been unconscious, his time sense was screwed up, an aftereffect of being in Sebastian's private universe. That was one of the well-known problems with getting involved with any of that dehydrated deity stuff: a true Rip van Winkle syndrome, only in reverse. He had probably spent less than an hour of perceived time in there, and years could've gone by out here in the real world; no way of telling how much time had elapsed before he'd fallen into the alley's muck and trash.

The rest of his memories coalesced, sharper than the indistinct images and forms left by dreams. He could recall everything that had happened, from the moment he'd found himself walking along Sebastian's re-created L.A. street, with the Million Dollar Theater's neon glimmering off the rain-soaked pavement, all through the seismic fragility of the toy-stocked hideaway at the top of the Bradbury Building. *I lied to the poor bastard,* thought Deckard. He was in no condition to start feeling guilty about it. All he'd been trying to do was buy a little more of that false world's time, enough for Sebastian to tell him the big secrets. So he'd conned the genetic engineer turned small-scale god, handed him that line about Pris's being somewhere else at the fringes of that patched-together L.A., waiting for Sebastian to come find her. *What a shuck*—maybe it was just as well that he'd dropped out of the pocket universe and back into this larger one before Sebastian had found out he'd been given the shaft again. The guy might have really gone to pieces, worse than just the building shaking into plaster atoms.

Something else had been there, that Deckard remembered: the little box, battered white metal with a red cross on the lid. Sebastian had forced it into Deckard's hands, pressing it on him, excitedly going on about how important it was . . .

Deckard looked down at the object in his hands, the exact same one as he'd seen and held in the dehydrated deity's pocket universe. *Makes no sense,* he thought. The box looked like the container for some sort of regulation first aid kit; it even had clips on the back for mounting on a wall or in a cabinet—ordinary enough, but it didn't belong here. It'd been part of that other, smaller universe, the one that the transmogrified Sebastian had pulled together from the contents of his head. Everything Deckard had perceived there, from the snakelike glow of the theater marquee's neon shimmering on the empty wet sidewalk to the maniacal laughter of the clown mannequin, had its existence in that world, not this one. Even the feel of the box's lid, both enamel smooth and rougher where the rusted metal was exposed; by rights, it should have stayed back there in Sebastian's illusory hideout. Deckard knew he should have woken up with hands empty, no matter what some tiny withered god had tried to put in them.

The temptation to throw the metal box away—just another encumbrance, when Deckard had enough on his mind already—rose in him. He could just pitch it onto the rest of the trash and junk that formed the alley's bottom strata, and not miss it. The box, first aid kit or whatever it was, or had been, felt virtually weightless—he gave it an experimental shake and heard some even smaller objects rattling around inside. Prying the lid open, Deckard found a couple of small brown vials, antiseptic liquids that had dried up despite their seals; a plastic bottle of aspirin with nothing but white dust inside; a few once-sterile bandages, now suspiciously stained with age. A paper label had been inexpertly glued to the inside of the lid; if it had had instructions or words of medical advice, they had long since faded away.

I should've let the guy have it, thought Deckard. Instead of getting into a hassle with the twitchy stim-deprived case who'd been trying to lift the little metal box from him. Then it would have been *his* problem, about what to do with it.

Deckard cocked his wrist, preparing to flip the ancient first aid kit into the farther reaches of the alley, then hesitated. For some reason, Sebastian had wanted him to have it, had hurried to shove it into his hands when the pocket universe had started to fade away. And the box had come with him when Deckard had fallen back into this world. If nothing else, it made for a strange, sad remembrance of the age-wrinkled figure and his retinue of somber toys.

He tucked the box into his jacket pocket and stood up. The empty vials rattled against the metal, an erratic, hollow rhythm as Deckard headed for the colony's streets that had people in them. Cop instincts shifting to criminal: if anybody was looking for him, it would be easier to hide in a crowd than out in the open.

The door of the hovel was unlocked; the knob turned in his hand without resistance. It had taken him another half hour, pushing and shoving his way, head down, through the thickest part of the milling pack, to get to the Niemand residence; the last dozen or so yards, where there had been no one about except for a few total burnouts rooting blindly through the accumulated debris, had been the most nervous-making for him. He knew that if any kind of trap had been laid, it would be right here on his own front step. The old instincts, hard to root out as the sinews along his bones, had again moved his fingers under his jacket, searching for the gun he'd carried in his other life; his hand came out as empty as it had on the neon-lit street of Sebastian's private universe.

Darkness inside; he pushed the door open, enough to reach in and flip the switch on the wall. In the hovel's cramped spaces, everything looked as it had before he'd left, minus himself sitting at the table, slumped unconscious. The briefcase was still there, handle turned toward the door; he could see his initials on the small metal plate beneath. And the various paraphernalia, the graduated beaker and glass rod, the packet torn open with a few granules of the white powder spilled out, the spoon from the kitchen area . . . a tableau that might have been of more interest to a drug enforcement agency, if any had stuck their heads inside the hovel.

He shut the door behind himself. As soon as he had, he knew there was someone else there with him; he could sense the minute disturbance in the trapped air, different from the leakage through the ceilings' and walls' multiple patches and caulking. Deckard halted, listening, hearing nothing; then stepped quickly around the table, taking the couple of paces to the bedroom door and shoving it open.

"Mr. Niemand—thank goodness you're home!" The calendar on the wall spoke in its flutey, overexcited voice. "Terrible things have happened while you were away! Murder and ruin!"

Deckard ignored the calendar. In the fall of light from the room behind him, he saw a figure lying on the bed. Smoke from a strong tobacco, more expensive than anything available in the colony's black market, drifted as a thin grey wraith to his nostrils. The figure on the bed brought the cigarette to her lips and inhaled; the small glow of fire drew the familiar angles and shadows of Sarah Tyrell's face. She didn't even bother to look at him, but went on gazing abstractedly up at the water-stained ceiling, her dark hair unbound and spread across the pillow.

"You're home," said Deckard. He sat down on the edge of the bed. "Where'd you go?"

"Far, far away . . ." Ash drifted, unnoticed by her, across the back of her hand and onto the blanket. "You'd be amazed, probably, if you knew."

"Probably so." He let his shoulders slump forward, his forearms against his knees, tiredness stepping along the chain of his bowed spine. The clock on the little bedside table was gone, its metal and plastic bits scattered outside. No great loss; he'd hated the clock and its idiot chatter as much as Sarah had.

Clockless and shadowed, the room seemed to exist outside of time. From the corner of his eye, he could see her without effort. Overlays of memory slid beneath the thinning smoke. They looked so much alike, this face and that other; identical, as Eldon Tyrell had meant for them to be. He had no need to close his eyes in this darkness; he could see the other one, the one he'd loved, the dead one. Deckard had to make a dead thing out of himself, something without desire, to keep from lying down beside her. Taking her in his arms, bringing his face to hers, smoke and kiss and the presence of her body, alive and real and an illusion. He wouldn't have cared . . .

The calendar on the wall sensed the deep reverie into which he had fallen. "Mr. Niemand," it whispered, as though fearful of intruding. "There's something you should know."

He didn't look up from his own hands dangling empty before him. A slow nod and sigh. "What's that?"

"There's somebody else here. I mean, besides you and Mrs. Niemand."

Deckard raised his head, taking a slow scan across the room. He stopped when he encountered another pair of eyes gazing back at him. "Who are you?"

A little girl, with dark hair drawn back into a braid, regarded him somberly. "Don't you know?" She sat on one of the chairs from the kitchen area table that had been dragged into the bedroom's corner. The girl tossed her head so that the braid fell across one shoulder. "*She* knows."

He looked over at Sarah, lying on the bed. "What the hell's going on? Who's this?"

"Oh, for Christ's sake." Sarah emitted a groan of disgust. She kneaded her brow with one hand. "Don't you start with that." Pushing herself up against the wall behind the bed, she fixed an angry glare upon him. "You *know* there isn't anyone there. Don't pretend you see someone."

For a moment longer, Deckard gazed into the dark centers of the woman's eyes, then turned back toward the presence in the room.

The girl shrugged and shook her head. "That's the way she's been talking. She didn't believe those other two men, either, when they said they saw me." The girl lifted her chin in obstinate defiance. "*She* doesn't think I'm real. But I am."

Deckard nodded. "She has her little ways." He looked back

at Sarah. "Where'd she come from? Why did you bring her here?"

"Now I'm really pissed off." In swift, angry motion, Sarah swung her legs over the side of the bed; she jabbed her cigarette out against the table as if she could drive it through the imitation wood like a nail. "You know goddamn well where she comes from. She comes from whatever weird little scheme you and those die-hard Tyrell Corporation loyalists must have cooked up together. I don't know what kind of twisted gaslight agenda you people thought you could get rolling." She turned a fierce, annihilating glare upon him. "Maybe you wanted to drive me even crazier than I already am. Though why you'd want to bother is beyond me. I'm already at the limit." Her words came through gritted teeth. "*I* can see her, but I'm *supposed* to; she's my hallucination."

He resisted the temptation to go over and grab Sarah by both shoulders and rock some sense into her. "Look," said Deckard, setting a hand flat on the bed. "I'm not going to go into details now, but I just came from someplace that doesn't exist. Not the way that real things exist. So I know the difference. There's a girl sitting in this room with us, and I want to know what she's doing here. That's all."

The radiation that lasered out from beneath Sarah's eyelids went up another notch in lethality. "Fuck you, Deckard." She stood up and strode past him, out to the front part of the hovel.

"All right." Every encounter with Sarah Tyrell left him feeling exhausted, not the least of which came from the cognitive warpage of seeing the face of the woman he'd loved looking back at him with utter contempt and hatred. He leaned forward and placed his hand gently on top of the little girl's. "So you'll have to tell me. What's your name?"

"You know . . ."

"No, I don't." Deckard tried to smile as gently as possible. "I really don't."

"I'm Rachael." She looked straight back into his eyes. "My name's Rachael."

He felt the room go still around him, around the two of them, himself and the grave, dark-haired little girl. A moment of stopped time, as though the world itself had held its breath, caught the way his was, next to his heart.

"Is this some kind of a joke?" He spoke without anger, all harshness filtered out of his voice. The child's hand, a thing of warmth and flesh and skin, was tangible beneath his palm. "I won't be mad—I won't be mad at you—if it is. Did somebody tell you to say that?"

"Of course not." She looked offended. "It's my name. It's my real, real name." A pitying expression came into her eyes. "I don't have any other."

The calendar on the wall rustled its pages. "I don't think she's lying, Mr. Niemand."

"No . . . I don't think she is, either." He didn't look up at the calendar and its photogenic scene of a vanished wilderness. "That's not the problem." Deckard's gaze was still held by the unblinking regard of the child. Sometimes people lied and sometimes they didn't; sometimes they simply believed things that weren't true. "What's your last name?"

She shook her head, the thick dark braid swinging behind her. "I don't know. Nobody ever told me that."

"Who are your parents?"

A cloud passed behind her eyes. "They're dead. They've been dead a long, long time."

Around them, in the silent room and the world outside the hovel's thinly fabricated walls, time had started up again; Deckard could feel his heart once more moving through its paces. Something had happened, he knew; a door had opened to some other time, and this child had stepped through. *It's her,* thought Deckard. *She's not lying. Rachael . . .*

He could see it in the child's face. In the darkness of her hair, bound behind her; in the open, unashamed eyes; in the calm self-possession that radiated through every posture and motion of the small frame. He had loved, kissed and held in his embrace, slept with an adult Rachael, if a replicant that would live only four years total could be called an adult; she had been created that way, her childhood a false memory stolen from the human woman Sarah Tyrell and implanted inside her head. He had never seen Rachael as a child, except for a moment, a dehydrated slice of time; in the photos that she had brought to his apartment, that she had shown to him in a futile attempt to prove that she was human. Those had been photos of Sarah, he knew, or else total fabrications, bad-faith evidence concocted in Eldon Tyrell's workshops, as phony as the ones that the replicant Kowalski had been obsessed with. There was no need for Deckard to have seen those old photographs, the ones that the adult Rachael's trembling hand had thrust toward him, to recognize the child now sitting a few feet away. He could have closed his eyes, or kept the room in absolute darkness, not even seen the child's eyes and face, and he would have known that Rachael—not the woman he'd loved, as a woman, but some aspect of her—was there with him.

From his own memory, Deckard pulled up another question to ask the child. Something that he'd been told, reminded of, in the Van Nuys Pet Hospital, that sanctuary for escaped replicants where Isidore busied himself converting them into creatures that could pass for fully human. There had been another photo there, an old news clipping on the wall of Isidore's office that he had looked at and wondered about. Because the woman in that ancient photo had looked so much like Rachael.

"Tell me something." He leaned forward, bringing his gaze level and just inches away from the little girl's eyes. "Was your mother's name Ruth?"

The girl's face lit up. "Yes! It was!" She did a quick, excited bounce in the chair. "That's what the nanny told me her name was. It was Ruth."

He angled his head to one side. "What nanny?"

"Well . . . not like a proper nanny. Like in the storybooks and the videos." The child named Rachael gave an embarrassed shrug. "That wasn't real; not like me and you. It was just the computer, and the machines and stuff, that took care of me. 'Cause there weren't any real people . . . at least until *she* came along." The child gestured toward the door—and Sarah, in the hovel's other room. "There were just ghosts and things that looked like people—they were all dead, though. So the nanny had to tell me all about stuff." She looked closer at him. "Do you understand?"

"Sure." Deckard nodded. He had an idea of what she was talking about. "This place, with the nanny and the ghosts—did it have a name? Was it called the *Salander 3*?"

"That's it!" The little girl looked excited and pleased, as though finding herself on another human being's wavelength. She suddenly looked puzzled, forehead creasing. "How do you know that? You weren't there."

"Oh . . . I know all sorts of things." More flashes from the time he'd spent with Isidore, and even before that, rummaging through what was left of the LAPD's ancient files on the Tyrell Corporation. There had been all sorts of fragmentary data, bits and pieces transferred one way or another into the personal memory bank he carried around inside his head. *The problem isn't in knowing things,* mused Deckard. *It's understanding them.*

Like how did this little girl come to be here? She didn't look to be more than ten years old, if that—the mix of a somber adult quality, a wary regard of the things happening around her, and those kid reactions, when he'd guessed her mother's name, made it hard to precisely fix her age. Deckard suspected that if he asked her that simple question, the reply would be that she didn't know. How could she? Something had gone wrong with the flow of time itself for the girl to exist at all. If she really was the daughter of Ruth Tyrell—he tried to remember the father's name, having to concentrate on the memory of the old newspaper clipping, before coming up with the name Anson, the brother of Eldon Tyrell—if that was true, and right now he felt sure it was, then it meant that the girl had somehow been born after her parents had died on the *Salander 3*'s aborted mission to the Proxima system.

And what did all the rest of it mean? Deckard tried to sort through the pieces as he studied the girl's face. He could see the other Rachael, the one she would grow up to be, already present there, as though an embryo, or more accurately, a flower that had only begun to show the color of its petals. No sexual feeling was triggered in him by the girl, though everything about her—the color of her eyes, the lift of chin and shape of cheekbone, even the barely perceptible fragrance of her dark hair—reminded him of the adult Rachael who had slept in his arms. A sadness-tinged wonder, rather, at the girl's appearance; she could have been the child that Rachael and he would have had together, if replicants could bear children. One more thing of which Eldon Tyrell had deprived them. But that was what the girl looked like; a convoluted genetic inheritance, yet breeding true, from the smiling beauty of Ruth caught in the old news clipping photo . . . and how much farther back? Perhaps the woman that Anson Tyrell had married, had tried to take with him to the stars, had been part of a long line of heartbreakers, not so much beautiful—though Rachael had been that, and Sarah Tyrell was, even now—as some other quality, almost invisible but still real, that laid a fingertip on men's hearts, stilling the pulse like a soft, effective bullet.

She'll also be that way, thought Deckard as he looked at the child sitting in front of him, waiting for him to speak again. *Not for me.* For him, there would only be Rachael, the one he'd loved and had taken from him. *For someone else . . .*

"What's going to happen now?" With the slightest tilt of her head, the Rachael child indicated the bedroom's doorway. A shadow passed through the light from the other part of the hovel. "She doesn't seem to like me very much." A note of worry sounded in the girl's voice. "And I don't have anywhere else to go. I don't know my way around here, like I did back home."

"Well . . . it'll be all right." Deckard squeezed the girl's hand. "Nothing bad will happen to you. I promise."

"What a performance." The air temperature in the hovel seemed to drop several degrees as a bitterness-laden voice spoke from the doorway. Deckard looked up and saw Sarah standing there, leaning against the plastic door frame, arms folded across her breasts. "I really have to hand it to you." She slowly shook her head, her glare daggering straight into his eyes. "Who would have thought you were such a consummate performer? I should've learned by now not to put anything past you."

"Oh, oh." The calendar, sensing trouble to come, whispered from behind its image of snow and trees. "I don't think—"

"Be quiet." Deckard hadn't taken his own gaze away from Sarah. "What're you talking about?"

"Your little show here." With a sharp flick of one hand, she gestured toward him and the girl. "I could almost believe that you really do see her. The same as I can."

He didn't feel like arguing the point with her any further. "You went off-planet—didn't you? You must have." That had to be the case, though Deckard had no idea yet of how it could have been accomplished. But the *Salander 3,* the interstellar transport upon which Ruth and Anson Tyrell had headed for the Prox system, wasn't here on Mars. If it existed anywhere, it would have to be back on Earth, sandbagged somewhere to keep the notoriously toxic effects of the old-style propulsion units from leaking out. "Where did you go? Who took you?"

"You sound like a cop," said Sarah disgustedly. "Always ready for the interrogation, aren't you? Maybe you'd like to take me down to the station and slap me around a while. That'd probably seem like old times, wouldn't it? Oops, sorry—" She held one hand up. "I forgot. With blade runners, it's shoot first and don't even bother asking questions later. Right?"

"Knock it off." The needle of her words had gotten under his skin, as intended. "Look. I went away, I came back, and you're not here. I go away again—" That was what he figured his time in Sebastian's pocket universe amounted to. "I come back, you're here. Great; whatever. But things have changed. There's a kid sitting right here—" He pointed to the Rachael child. "I see her, you see her . . . she's real. I don't want to hear any crap about hallucinations. I just want to know how you got to Earth, how you got into the *Salander 3,* wherever the hell it is now, and why you brought this girl back with you." His voice had hardened with his growing anger. "How about that for right?"

"Don't try to bully me, Deckard." With one hand, Sarah pushed herself away from the door frame. She stood looking at him with her hands planted on her hips. "I don't even want to *talk* to you, let alone listen to you. You're just making it easier for me to go through with what I've already decided to do. Not that I was going to find it hard to do it."

A great weariness settled on Deckard's shoulders, his own fatigue meeting all the sense of lost hope and futility that Sarah Tyrell's mere presence evoked in him. *A bad marriage,* he thought, just as if the aliases of Mr. and Mrs. Niemand had been the names of real people. There had been a time, when he had first taken Sarah from Earth, when he had believed he could accomplish something by welding his fate to hers. Even if it had been no more than moving her so far away from any sources of power that she could wreak no more harm to humans or replicants. *But you can't fight crazy people*—he told himself that once more, something he had known from the beginning. *They're always crazier than you are sane.* When he looked into Sarah's eyes, past the memory image of the Rachael he'd loved, he saw the black hole of madness that could consume all reason and desire and life itself, a place that could give nothing back to the living, imploding as it were with the dense gravity of its own obsessions. He should have known—he had known—that it was hopeless to fight against something like that.

"All right," he said, pulling his bent spine upright. "Whatever it is you've set your mind on, go ahead. I've got other business to take care of." There was still the briefcase sitting on the hovel's table, the one that spoke with the voice of Roy Batty and that had Isidore's list of disguised replicants encoded somewhere inside. Whatever else had happened in Sebastian's pocket universe, he'd at least been convinced of that much. Both Batty and the rep-symps who'd put the dehydrated deity packet inside the briefcase had been right: he would believe Sebastian when he would believe no one else. Not because of the little genetic engineer's transmogrification, his new enhanced status as a small-scale god, but simply because Sebastian was incapable of lying. A nature as simple as his didn't change, from this world to any other. Deckard looked up at the woman in the doorway. "I've got things to do."

Sarah laughed. "Like what?"

"You don't need to know." Somehow, he had to find a way to carry the briefcase to the replicant insurgents, out in the stars. Belief in the briefcase's contents and the acceptance of his mission were locked together for him now; he had no choice.

The mission would have been hard enough to pull off even if the U.N. were still sending new emigrants to its far colonies . . . but possible. The shutdown of the emigration program, the absolute bottleneck here on Mars, was compounded for him. *They're looking for me,* thought Deckard glumly. The people who'd already killed Dave Holden, the first courier attached to the briefcase, they might be right outside the hovel, right now, watching and waiting, the only mystery being why they didn't just move in and ice him immediately. Maybe they were showboats, the breed of cops who liked to kill in public, where everybody could see; that was the kind of display that could get someone promoted to the blade runner unit. He supposed that some grunt climbing to the ranks of the elite over his ventilated corpse would be an ironic justice. *But one I want to avoid,* Deckard reminded himself.

"What about me?" The Rachael child spoke up, as though she had been able to read his milling thoughts. "You said . . . you promised . . ."

"That's right, sweetheart. I promised." And now this complication. Whatever he had to pull off to ferry the briefcase and Isidore's data to the insurgents, it would have to be done with the little girl in tow. *And I don't even know where she came from or how she got here.* Still—"I'm not leaving you behind."

"True," said Sarah from the room's doorway. "That's because you're not going anywhere, Deckard. That's what I came back here to tell you."

He looked back around at her, but another voice broke in before he could speak.

"Mr. Niemand—be careful," said the wall calendar. "She's got a gun. A new one."

The calendar was telling the truth. The evidence was in Sarah's hand, pulled from her coat pocket. The black metal hung suspended a short distance from Deckard's face; the muzzle's hole looked as deep and dark and fatal as the centers of the woman's eyes.

He allowed one eyebrow to rise. "That's what it's come to?" Deckard was really only surprised that it had taken this long.

"Oh . . . it's always been this way." Sarah's gun hand displayed no wavering. "I just didn't know it until recently."

"Well, it's always good to know what you want." Right now, he wanted to keep her talking while he figured out what to do. She knew how to use the gun; he was aware that she could pull the trigger without flinching. No chance of making a sudden grab for the weapon; Sarah stood a carefully judged distance from him, just far enough away that a quick lunge was out of the question, especially from his sitting position. And just close enough that she could unload the gun's clip right into his chest, grouping the entrance holes into a pattern tight as her fist. "So . . ." A trickle of sweat ran down one side of his neck. "What finally decided you?"

Sarah tilted her head back, keeping her narrowed gaze and the gun aimed at him. "This little act of yours, this thing you've cooked up with the shadow corporation, the die-hard Tyrell Corporation loyalists—"

"I don't know what you're talking about. What shadow corporation?"

"That's good, Deckard. That's real good." One corner of her mouth lifted in a humorless smile. "You're a real professional. An actor—you're going to keep your part rolling right up to the very end."

"I'm not acting." He gave a shrug. "I just don't know what the hell you're going on about."

"Deckard . . . there was probably a time when I would've believed you about that." A slow shake of the head; her expression changed to one of sad regret. "I would've *liked* to have believed you. It might have made things easier in some ways. But it's too late for that." A twitch of the gun's muzzle indicated the little girl across from him. "This business—this performance—of sitting here and talking and acting as if you can see somebody else here with us. A child who says her name is Rachael." She took a deep breath and expelled it through clenched teeth, an audible hiss. "Those other two—Wycliffe and Zwingli; I bet you know their names—that was how they were going on as well. Before I took care of them. Trying to make me think they could see my hallucinations; trying to make me think what I saw was real. You sonsabitches must've thought you were really being clever."

"Never heard of anybody named that. At least not outside the history books." Deckard spread his hands apart. "Besides—even if these people, whoever they are, and I were in on some big conspiracy against you, what would we accomplish by pretending we could see things that don't exist? I don't get it."

"Why should I try to figure it out? Perhaps you're just sick individuals." Sarah's face darkened with anger. "Sicker when you put your heads together. Perhaps you're all just crazy." The same thin, ugly nonsmile appeared. "Perhaps even as crazy as I am."

He saw an opening. "You think so? I'm not joking around now." Deckard kept his voice low and serious. "But did you ever really consider that possibility? You know, that I might be as crazy as you are. And not just that. But crazy in the same way."

Without saying anything, Sarah regarded him over the top of the gun. The muzzle dropped a quarter inch, no more.

"Think about it." Deckard pressed on, trying to expand the tiny fracture he'd created. "Wouldn't I have to be? You know how contagious insanity is; it spreads from person to person. From you to me. After the things we've been through together, how could it be any other way?"

"Shut up." The gun jerked back into position as Sarah visibly tensed. "I don't want to listen to you. It's just another one of your con jobs, the stuff cops will say to get themselves out of a tight place. I just didn't think you'd be quite so good at it anymore."

He decided to backtrack, to come at her from another angle. *Work fast,* he told himself. Even without a clock in the room, he knew that time was running out, the moment approaching when she would realize she had been stalled, the moment when she'd pull the gun's trigger.

"Tell me something," said Deckard. "After you kill me . . . what're you going to do with her?" He nodded toward the little girl across from himself. "Anything?"

Sarah gave a noncommittal shrug. "Hadn't thought about it. Perhaps I'll try shooting her as well."

The Rachael child shrank back in the chair, her eyes wide and apprehensive.

"Doesn't seem like that would accomplish much. If she's not even real."

"True," admitted Sarah. "But it might get her out of my head. It doesn't matter, anyway, if it works or not. Since I'm already planning on killing myself. That should do the trick."

The hovel's bedroom had become a little world of madness, with Sarah as the gatekeeper, the black staff of her office weighing in one hand. For a moment, Deckard considered whether he might have spoken more truly than he'd intended. *Maybe I am as crazy as her.* A sure sign of that condition, when you could talk calmly about death, about desiring and willing it, in a strange parody of rationality.

"What if I'm not conning you, though?" Deckard kept himself still, unthreatening. "I'm not in any conspiracy against you; I don't know these two men you've been talking about. And I can prove it."

"Really?" A sneer passed across Sarah's face. "How?"

"You say I don't see her." He pointed a thumb toward the Rachael child. "That I can't; she's a hallucination. *Your* hallucination. So ask her to tell you something."

Sarah eyed him with suspicion for a moment, then glanced over at the girl. "When we were inside the *Salander 3* . . . when I found you there . . . what was on the floor between us?"

"That's easy," said the girl. "There was a big pool of blood. It was so big you could see yourself in it, like a mirror. That's what you said."

" 'A big pool of blood,' " repeated Deckard. He looked up and caught Sarah's gaze, fastening tight upon it. " 'It was so big you could see yourself in it, like a mirror.' " He spoke the words dryly, in a matter-of-fact tone. " 'That's what you said.' That's what the girl here just said."

"Impossible . . ." Sarah's expression changed to one of puzzlement. "You shouldn't have been able to hear her say that. She doesn't exist. Except in my head . . ."

"But I did hear her. So she's in my head, too. Isn't she?"

The gun dropped lower as Sarah tried to figure out the puzzle. "She's not real . . . she isn't really here . . . but you heard her . . ."

He was aware of the child watching them both. *Maybe she's the only sane one here,* thought Deckard.

A genuine smile, one of realization, appeared on Sarah's face. "Then you're right," she said. "You *are* crazy. Just like me."

"Just like you."

With her free hand, Sarah rubbed one corner of her brow. "That's so strange. You know . . . it comes as rather a relief. It's like when I went into the *Salander 3.* And I found her." She nodded toward the girl. "I didn't feel quite so alone. It didn't matter whether she was real or not."

"You're not alone." *Make her believe it*—Deckard softened his voice, the way one would speak to a lover. "You and I—we really are in this together. Whether we wanted it to be that way or not."

"Is that true, Deckard?" She gazed at him in wonder. "Is it?"

He pulled something up from memory, his memory and hers. "Do you know what you had me say, a long time ago? Do you remember that? It was what you knew I'd said to her, that other Rachael . . ."

A slow nod as that tiny fragment of the past became clear to her once more. "I wanted you to say those things to me. The way you'd said them to her."

The past that had been his and Rachael's, that had become his and Sarah's. He spoke the words again. "Do you trust me?"

Gun in hand, Sarah closed her eyes, hearing him this

time, and in that other time, and in that time stolen from the woman he'd loved. "I trust you," she said softly.

Deckard knew he had her now. The gun still hung in the air between them, her finger on the black trigger's curve, but not for much longer. "Say . . . I want you." More words from the past. "Say it."

"I want you . . ."

He stood up and reached toward her, not to take the gun out of her trembling hand but to take her in his arms, press her close to himself. The way he had taken Rachael and brought her lips to his, felt her heartbeat trip and accelerate, in sync with his own. In this time, the gun was caught between them, her hand trapped against his chest, the black metal like a second shared heart, one with no pulse, no time, nothing but the death they had both raced toward. Deckard kissed her, and for that moment she wasn't Sarah, she was Rachael. Memory, the past, madness—all folded around him and he didn't care.

He would have given anything, everything, for that moment to last.

The woman in his arms—Sarah, Rachael; he wasn't sure which—yielded to him. Perhaps she didn't know which one she was, the living or the dead. *Madness,* thought Deckard as he drew her to the bed, his arm around her shoulders, sitting her down beside him at the mattress's edge. He brushed her dark, tousled hair away from her brow; her face burned feverish as she leaned it into the cup of his palm.

For a few seconds they were alone in the room; the other, the child, forgotten.

"You're right," whispered Sarah. "You're as crazy as I am. You poor bastard . . ."

He nodded. "There's not much we can do about it."

"Nothing . . . except . . ." She looked down at her hand, still gripping the gun resting in her lap. "Except what I'd already decided to do." Her unmasked, desperate gaze searched for some sign in his eyes. "That's right, isn't it? That's what you want, don't you?"

Deckard could almost feel sorry for her. "Sure." When he

looked back at her now, he saw only Sarah Tyrell. The woman he'd loved was dead. A long time ago. "That's what I want."

"I knew it." An odd, broken happiness sounded in her voice. "I should've known it."

"Tell you what." He squeezed her shoulder, bringing her closer into his side. "I'll do it. It's easy for me; you know that it is. I'll kill you, and then I'll kill myself." He brought his head down to look straight into her eyes. "That'll work."

A coy smile appeared; she looked up through her eyelashes at him. "I trust you, Deckard . . . but not that much. Besides . . . if I went first, then I wouldn't get to see you dead. And I wanted that, too."

"You can have whatever you want." Deckard brought his face closer to hers again. "You deserve it." As he kissed her, he brought his free hand between them, onto hers holding the gun. Her fingers had relaxed, loosening their grip on the cold metal. As he had hoped, known, they would.

In one swift arc, he grabbed the gun and pulled it away, sealing it in his own fist. The arc was completed when he leaned back from her, the gun's black weight swinging up and smashing across the angle of her chin. The impact rocked Sarah's head back, lifting her partway and throwing her back onto the bed, one empty hand reaching futilely toward him.

"Come on—" Deckard stood up and grabbed the Rachael child's hand, yanking her to her feet. He shoved the gun inside his jacket; it produced a hollow clank of metal against metal, the blunt muzzle rapping on the ancient first aid kit that he had brought back with him from Sebastian's pocket universe. Ignoring the sound, he pulled the girl toward the door. "We're getting out of here."

"Mr. Niemand!" A voice shrilled from the wall. "Now's your chance!" The calendar's pages fluttered. "Don't just leave her—kill her! Shoot her! She's a wicked person—she blew away the clock!"

He was already reaching inside his jacket, his hand closing around the gun, as he looked back toward the figure on the bed. *It's right,* his thoughts ran, *don't be a fool, do it—*

All he saw was the woman's tangle of dark hair, an angle of her face shadowed both by darkness and the overlay of his own memory.

"Goddamn." He shoved the gun deeper into his jacket. The chances were more than good, they were certain, that he'd regret this. "Let's go."

In the front part of the hovel, Deckard let go of the Rachael child's hand long enough to pop open the lid of the briefcase on the table. "What's going on?" asked Batty's voice. "I could hear you people talking—"

"Later." Deckard swept the Sebastian paraphernalia, the packet and other bits and pieces, into the briefcase, then snapped it closed. "Just shut up for now."

Briefcase in one hand, leading the Rachael child with the other, he emerged from the hovel. No hail of gunfire met him. *That's a good sign,* thought Deckard wryly. He set off at a fast pace, carrying his burdens with him.

"That sonuvabitch." She splashed cold water onto the bruise that had begun forming along one side of her jaw. Small, but darkly colorful; it looked like a smoky-red L.A. sunset as viewed from the top levels of the no-longer-existent Tyrell Corporation headquarters. "I knew I shouldn't have trusted him."

Sarah fixed her angry glare at her own reflection in the hovel's bathroom mirror. Angrier at herself than Deckard; she had known what kind of a schmuck he was, and she had still let herself be conned by him. *I want you . . .* The memory of those words in her mouth pooled salt on her tongue, tasting like the blood from the cut lip Deckard's blow had given her. The perfect image of a woman wronged; she looked at herself with contempt. *I trust you . . .* Typical, she knew. *They'll say anything, get you to say anything, and then they're gone.* Right after the fist is applied.

She emerged from the hovel's tiny bathroom, toweling her

face, punishing herself with the wincing pain from the bruise. At least the chair near the bed was empty, the hallucination of the Rachael child vanished for the time being. Deckard, for whatever twisted reasons were in his head, had kept up the act of pretending that the little girl was real right up to the moment he was beyond the hovel's front door and out of earshot; she didn't even want to speculate why. *Probably just to drive me crazier.* As if that were possible.

"Mrs. Niemand . . . you know, it's not too late." The calendar on the wall had spotted her; the hectoring voice had taken on an irritatingly superior tone. "There are still viable options."

"What?" She scowled at the calendar and its too-perfect scene of trees and distant mountains. "What're you talking about?"

"You can still kill yourself. These things can always be arranged. Just because Deckard is gone, that doesn't mean you have to change your own personal plans."

"Oh, I like that." Sarah shook her head in amazement. "Suicide as a viable option—that's good."

"Well, or therapy perhaps," the calendar said helpfully. "Some other kind of therapy, I mean. You were talking about that, remember? In regard to these hallucinations you feel you're suffering from. Now, in my opinion—and you can certainly take it for what it's worth—I feel that surgery would be your last option. That's a little extreme—"

"Just shut up." She reached over and ripped the calendar off the wall. "You traitorous bastard. Telling Deckard to go ahead and shoot me." She flung the calendar into the corner of the bedroom, where it landed with a fluttering squawk. "You're lucky I don't have a gun right now."

That was the problem. Out in the hovel's kitchen area, as she rummaged through the cupboard over the sink looking for the meager stash of coffee substitute, Sarah weighed her options. *If I had the gun,* she thought grimly, *I probably would.* Kill herself; she hadn't changed her mind about that. There was just no way that appealed to her as much as the finality of a bullet through the head. After being so tritely humiliated by Deckard, she didn't want to employ any less violent method, anything—like a drug overdose or a Plathian head-in-the-oven genuflection—that smacked of feminine frailty. After all this time, she had to admit that she was of the blood of Eldon Tyrell in more ways than one. If she could crack her own head open like an egg, she would have.

She brushed away a trace of white dust on the sink counter and spooned the ersatz coffee into a chipped-edge cup. Her jaw still ached, reminding her—as if she could forget—of Deckard. *He probably enjoyed that.* Even more than the hit, the mind trip, the getting her to believe that he was ready to die with her. Turning on the tap, she held her hand in the thin stream of rust-tinged water, waiting for it to heat up. *Well,* she thought, her Tyrell blood bringing her own decisions back into focus, *if he doesn't want to go voluntarily, that's all right.* She held the cup under the tap and watched it slowly fill. *There are other ways.*

Pulling a chair out from the table, she sat down with the fake coffee in front of her. It tasted like brackish plastic. *I should've brought some real stuff back here from the yacht.* There had been every indication that it'd been stuffed with the expensive pleasures of life, as one would expect from a part of the late Eldon Tyrell's private fleet. However bleak her situation might be otherwise, she wasn't without resources; she supposed she could find a way of unloading the yacht's contents—and the yacht itself—on the emigrant colony's black market. Perhaps she could track down some high-up exec in the Martian cable monopoly who'd give her a package deal for the whole thing, rather than having to dispose of it piece by piece; either way, it'd come to a good deal of operating capital, more than enough with which to buy Deckard's murder.

She took another sip of the repellent black liquid, holding the cup between both hands. She didn't need to; the muscular tremors of her rage had died down, replaced by cold, nerveless calculation. And regret: she wished now that she hadn't gotten rid of Wycliffe and Zwingli. She could have used them. If nothing else, they had been her only means of getting in touch with the rest of the shadow corporation; she imagined that there were others dedicated to the Tyrell resurrection. And among those, former members of the security department, hard men and deadly. Those were the ones she really needed now. She didn't feel like waiting for them to show up at her doorstep, the way the first two die-hard loyalists had appeared. Another slow, meditative sip, her tongue almost numb to the taste; she'd have to think of some way of contacting the shadow corporation . . .

A sharp, quick sound came from behind her. Someone had knocked on the hovel's front door.

That's too good, thought Sarah. She carefully set the cup down on the table. Either the universe, in its mysterious and infinite workings, had learned to read her mind, or her hallucinations had become even more convenient. All she had to do was ask for something and it would be provided. With only one catch to it . . .

She turned around in the chair, facing the door. "If you don't exist," she called out, "then go away. I don't need you."

A muffled response came through the thin fiberboard. "Hello?" The knob rattled, as though the person on the other side had tried it and found it locked. "Is there anybody home?"

If it were a hallucination, considered Sarah, *I would've given it a key.* She got up and went to the door, pulling it open.

The man on the hovel's doorstep was shorter than her, running to fat, as if compressed from a taller size. "You must be Sarah—" He smiled, blinking at her from behind ordinary-seeming lenses. If he was part of the shadow corporation, he hadn't adopted the same square black rims as the late Wycliffe and Zwingli had. "Sarah Tyrell? Am I right?"

It struck her that hallucinations shouldn't need introductions. *Maybe he's real.* "You could be." She put her hand against the door frame. "Depends on who you are."

"Miss Tyrell, my name is Urbenton. That's all I go by." His smile broadened, creating more elaborate details in his rounded cheeks. From his breast pocket, he extracted a business card and offered it to her. "That's how people know me."

She looked at the card, holding it by one corner. The man's name appeared beneath larger letters spelling out SPEED DEATH PRODUCTIONS, with a company logo of a stylized, sharp-edged skull with wings. "Charming." She tried to hand it back to him, but he refused it with an upraised palm.

"Keep it." The man radiated an oily unctuousness, as though his excess body fat were percolating into the air around him. "Just in case we can't come to an agreement right now, Miss Tyrell—"

"How do you know my name?" Sarah tilted her head, eyeing him with increasing suspicion. "My real name."

"I've got a lot of contacts," said Urbenton with a wink. "Contacts are important in my line of business. I'm a video director. Producer, too. I do it all."

A memory fragment drifted through Sarah's head. The names, of both the man and his company, sounded vaguely familiar to her. Deckard had said something about them, a long time ago. Before he had left the planet the first time. Something about going to do a job for them. *That's how he knows my name,* she thought. *Because of Deckard.* She tucked the business card in her neckline. "What's that got to do with me?"

Urbenton glanced around the narrow, shadowed streets of the emigrant colony, then back to Sarah. "May I come in? So we can talk?"

"We're talking now." She folded her arms across her breasts. "As I said—what's that got to do with me?"

His smile appeared more forced. "Let's just say . . . that maybe we can do business together. You and me."

"Oh?" She raised a skeptical eyebrow. "Such as?"

"I have good reason to believe, Miss Tyrell, that you'd like to have a certain Rick Deckard taken care of. Murdered, as it were." The smile disappeared, replaced by a hard glitter in the man's eyes. "How would you like it if I made that possible for you?"

Sarah regarded the man for a few seconds, then stepped

back, clearing the doorway. "Perhaps," she said, "you'd better come inside."

"This'll do. For now." He steered the child toward an opening beneath words outlined in flickering lightbulbs, half of which had gone permanently dead. "Let's go in here."

Behind the bar, an unshaven figure swabbing out glasses with a dirty towel; he spotted Deckard and the Rachael child as soon as they stepped into the dimly lit interior. "Hey—" The bartender pointed a black-nailed finger toward the little girl. "No minors."

Deckard left the girl a few steps away from him. With the briefcase dangling from one hand, he leaned an elbow on the bar. "Let me tell you something." He kept his voice low, face close to the bartender's. "I was just talking with somebody who claimed that there's no little girl at all. She's a hallucination."

An ugly smirk curdled the other man's lip. "Yeah, right. Now get her out of here."

Opening his jacket partway, Deckard displayed the black metal of the gun he'd taken from Sarah. "About that hallucination. Some very influential people think the same way."

The bartender's eyes shifted from the gun back up to Deckard's face. "There's a real nice booth in the back. Suitable for a party of one." He tried to smile. "Like yourself."

"Thanks." Deckard peeled a bill from the rapidly dimishing roll in his pocket and laid it on the bar. "I really value my privacy."

The establishment was dark enough, and so sparsely inhabited that he was able to steer the Rachael child to the back with little fear of being spotted. Once away from the bar and its pallid fluorescents behind the ranks of bottles, the only illumination came from the video screens hanging at strategic intervals from the ceiling. A flickering wash of blue tinted the isolated faces gazing up, their hands cradling the carefully nursed drinks that kept the patrons from being eighty-sixed out of the place. None of them looked around at

Deckard and the girl slipping into the farthest booth; eyes remained on their stimulus fix from the cable monopoly. He stashed the briefcase beneath the table.

"Won't he call us in? That guy?" The Rachael child had easily figured out that Deckard was trying to keep them from being spotted by the emigrant colony's police. The evasive route that he had taken them on this far left little doubt. "You don't trust him, do you?"

"Of course not." Deckard didn't look at her, tucked into the darkest part of the booth and shielded by his own body. Eyes adjusting, he scanned the bar's interior for any suspicious indicators. He was grateful that Batty, the part of him imbedded in the briefcase, had heeded his warning about staying quiet in public. "But we don't need to worry just yet. The bartender'll keep a lid on it for a little while, just on the hope that I'll feed him some more money."

"Is a little while all we need?"

The child's voice was capable of unnerving him; she sounded on occasion like an adult asking questions with a child's sharpness. Deckard supposed that came from her unusual upbringing, whatever it had been, on the *Salander 3.* "I just need time to think," he said, glancing over at her. "If I get that, maybe we have a chance."

"Oh." The Rachael child mulled over his words, forehead creasing. "What're you going to do?"

"I said, time to *think.* Not talk."

He was rewarded with silence. Spreading his hands flat on the table, he leaned his head back against the booth's padded leatherette and closed his eyes.

"Not interested in the show, huh?"

Deckard's eyes snapped open at hearing, not the child's voice, but a man's. Even before he focussed on the figure that had slid in on the table's other side, his hand had darted inside his jacket and fastened onto the gun.

He wasn't quick enough. The other man was quicker, reaching across and seizing Deckard's wrist, pinning his hand beneath the jacket. "You don't have to do that." The other man smiled. "Think of all the commotion it'd make in here. Nice quiet place like this." He squeezed the wrist tighter, numbing the fingertips on the gun's cold metal. "Perfect for a little conversation."

The Rachael child had shrunk back in the booth, watching the two men to either side of her.

"Yeah. It's lovely." The speed of the other man's movement indicated some kind of professional status; if not cop, then something equally deadly. Deckard nodded slowly. "Very intimate."

"I knew you'd agree." The thin smile had remained on the other man's face. "Now . . . I'm going to let go of you, and then we can just sit here politely looking at each other without things getting all ugly between us. I'm going to do that, Deckard, because I know you really do want to talk to me. The bit with the gun . . . I'll just chalk that up as a nervous reaction on your part."

The other's hand still hadn't let go of Deckard's wrist. "I don't go in much for conversation."

"You will." The man loosened his grip slightly. "Because you either talk to me or you can forget about going much farther than this bar. Your ass is in the proverbial sling, Deckard. I can get it out."

Deckard was silent for a few moments, then nodded. "All right. Let's talk."

"You're a smart man, Deckard." He let go and sat back in the booth, folding his arms on the table. "Or smart enough."

"Who *is* this?" The Rachael child sounded annoyed as she scowled at the broad-shouldered figure.

Deckard didn't answer her, but looked closer at the other man, letting the angles of the face assemble and connect with one in his memory.

"I know you," said Deckard. "You were there at the Outer Hollywood station. I remember now—" The whole scene flashed through Deckard's mind, including the corpse of David Holden, laid out in a reproduction of the interview room at what had been the Tyrell Corporation headquarters in L.A. "You were the one who killed that Kowalski replicant right in front of me."

"That's right." The man looked pleased with himself, as though flattered by Deckard's recall. "There really wasn't time for proper introductions. The name's Marley." He extended his hand across the table again, as though to shake Deckard's. "Or at least that'll do for now."

Deckard looked at the hand in distaste. "You must be joking."

"Not about this." The man shrugged and pulled his hand back. "You're a tenderhearted soul, aren't you? It's not as if you hadn't ever killed any replicants."

"I never went around bragging about it."

"Ah . . . I see. The money was enough for you." Marley appeared even more amused. "Well, Deckard, you don't have to like me. You just have to . . . shall we say? . . . do business with me."

The constant, self-assured smile irritated Deckard. "What kind of business?"

Marley didn't answer; he looked up to the nearest video screen. "You're right, you know; this isn't too interesting." Some kind of sporting event that involved oxygen masks and a medical triage staff at each end of the playing field was on. "That's all right, though." He turned the smile back toward Deckard. "There's something better coming on in a few minutes."

"I'm not interested in the cable schedule," grated Deckard. "Just tell me what you want from me."

"You've got it all wrong, pal. It's what you want from me. I spent a great deal of time and effort tracking you down, just so I could offer you my help."

Deckard didn't return the man's smile. "I don't need it."

"Oh, I think you might," said Marley. "You've got a big job ahead of you."

"What do you know about that?"

The other man shrugged. "Bits and pieces. Or maybe the whole thing. You're trying to put together some travel plans, aren't you? For you and the little girl here. And someone else. Or should I say some *thing*? I guess it depends on how you regard that briefcase you've been toting around. Is it human enough for you to think of it as a person?"

"Hey!" Batty's voice sounded from beneath the table. "Fuck you, pal!"

Deckard gave the briefcase a kick. "Shut up. Let me handle this."

"You tell him," said Marley. "That old bastard's out of the loop now. He's luggage. Too bad you can't just wrap him up, stick the postage on, and mail him out to the far colonies."

"Who says that's where we're going?" Deckard wondered just how much the man sitting across from him was clued in on. "I could be taking him and the little girl anywhere. Maybe back to Earth, for all you know."

"But you're not." Marley's smile broadened. "And I *do* know. I know all about the job you've undertaken. I know that's what you're racking your brains over, trying to figure out how you're going to get off-planet with that thing, how you're going to deliver it to the replicant insurgents . . . the whole bit."

Deckard coldly regarded the other man. "You know an awful lot."

"More than you do. I know what's really in that briefcase." The smile faded, the man's face turning hard and serious. "And I know who the little girl really is."

"Somebody who knows things like that . . . or somebody who even claims to . . ." Deckard looked straight back into the other man's eyes. "Chances are good it means that person's a cop. So who are you working for? U.N. security? LAPD?"

"I'm not with anybody like that." Marley glanced up at the video screen. "You should think of me as your friend. Like I said, I'm here to help you."

"And like I said, I don't want—"

"Hey, just hold on a bit." Marley held up his hand, palm outward. "We can talk some more in a little while. But this—" He pointed at the video screen a couple of yards away. "*This* is going to be a good program. I really want you to take a look at it. I think it's something you'll get a bang out of."

Beside him, the Rachael child had sat forward, trying to get a better viewing angle. Deckard looked over at the screen. The sports event, whatever it'd been, had apparently ended; the cable monopoly's logo, all swirling colors and state-of-the-art abstract graphics, danced and shivered its pixels. He knew it wasn't going to be a news show; there weren't any. The cable's feeds were all entertainment, or what passed for it in this captive market.

"You know," said Deckard, "I'm not really interested in whatever soap opera you might be addicted to. Maybe you should watch this on your own time. I've got more important business to take care of right now."

"Not any more important than this. Trust me." Marley gave a nod toward the screen. "This is just about the most important thing in the universe for you. Just sit back and watch, all right?"

The cable logo faded out and was replaced by another one, a stark black-and-white graphic of a stylized skull with wings. Deckard recognized it even before the words SPEED DEATH PRODUCTIONS pulsed into view; the skull image and the video company name had been on the advance check he'd received from that sweating, pudgy director he'd walked out on back at the Outer Hollywood station. It took a moment longer to remember the guy's name. *Urbenton*—the recall prompted a slow nod from Deckard. That was it.

In the bar's muffled quiet, the sound of a cheaply synthesized sound track, all throbbing bass and disembodied string choirs, oozed out of the video monitors' tiny speakers. Deckard found himself watching intently, leaning forward across the table, despite his earlier scorn. On the screen, a black night vista was suddenly broken by a leaping gout of fire.

"That looks good." Marley nodded admiringly. "Real spooky and dramatic."

The title appeared on the screen, blanking out everything but the darkness behind it. Two words: *Blade Runner.*

"What the hell . . ." A surmise weighted with dread started to form inside Deckard.

A crawl of other words, smaller than the video's title, moved upward across the screen. Broken phrases lodged in Deckard's head—*based on a true story . . . from actual LAPD case records*—with their meanings slowly adding up to the realization of what he was seeing. The final piece locked in when he saw his own name listed in the opening credits as technical adviser.

Marley pointed to the words. "That was nice of that Urbenton fellow, don't you think? Considering that you voided your contract with him—he didn't have to leave your name on there."

"This . . . this is the video he was making." With a sick feeling, Deckard gazed at the screen. "That he hired me to go out there and help him with."

"Come on—he hired you for more than that," chided Marley. "Urbenton bought your life story—or at least that part of it that went down in L.A., when you were tracking that last bunch of escaped replicants. Well, here it is." He made a sweeping gesture toward the nearest monitor and all the other identical screens mounted in the bar. "This is the premiere showing. Right now, on the entire Martian cable network." Another smile. "See? I knew you'd dig it."

"Shit—" Deckard stared at the video monitor in dismay. The fury of his own thoughts drowned out anything coming from the audio track. "Everybody's going to see this. Everybody on this entire planet."

"That's right, pal." Marley's hands made an expansive gesture, as though in congratulation. "There's only one channel, and you're the star. It's your fifteen minutes, Deckard; enjoy it."

Deckard didn't have time to respond to the other man's sarcasm. This was something he hadn't counted on. *Now I'm really screwed,* he thought. In a few minutes, once the video got past its opening sequence, with all the artsy Los Angeles location shots that Urbenton had faked from the Outer Hollywood street sets—once the story got rolling, Deckard's own story—then it would be his own face up on the video screens. Not just here in this bar, but everywhere. Nice, big close-ups, all zoomed-in and personal; he had watched Urbenton directing the cameras during the video shoot, bringing them in tight on the actor in the distinctive long coat carrying the police-issue gun through the city's dark and rain-soaked streets. There had been some full-on shots that would very likely fill the monitor screens. *And it'll be my face,* he thought. *Not the face of the actor playing me. But my face.* That had been the other thing that he'd sold the rights to, that Urbenton and his Speed Death Productions had bought. Spelled out in precise contractual language: . . . *the undersigned contracting party, in consideration of the financial remuneration specified above, grants as well the right to use a full and accurate facial depiction of self, along with any associated physical mannerisms consistent with an identification of the portrayed individual as the former Los Angeles Police Department special agent known as Rick Deckard . . .*

That was what he'd agreed to, the contract he'd signed, back when he'd still been under the impression that the money from Urbenton would be enough to get him and Sarah Tyrell off Mars and heading out to the U.N.'s colonies in the stars. Deckard hadn't anticipated being on the run, with Christ only knew what kind of police agencies breathing down his neck. It was a wonder he hadn't been nabbed already; the suspicion had started to grow in him that the cops were giving him a long rope, seeing if there was anybody else he'd entangle before they picked him up. Eventually, they'd tire of that game, get tired of waiting for him to contact his nonexistent accomplices, and then Deckard would find the rope around his neck, where it'd always been.

It was going to be a lot easier to tighten that noose now, or as soon as this video had finished airing over every cable-linked monitor in the emigrant colony. When Deckard had been there, at the Outer Hollywood station, orbiting above Earth, Urbenton had even shown him how the special-effects people were going to digitize his face, from the bones up through the web of muscles, to the skin and every whisker stubble and freckle on it, every little detail that made up the world-weary, tired-of-killing but still deadly gestalt that Deckard saw when he looked in a mirror. Standard practice in the modern video business: in postproduction, once the principal photography was done, the techs would lay the digital face over that of the actor who had gone through the paces on the set, who'd hit the marks and had the prop guns fired at him, taken the hits from the other actors, done all the hard stuff . . . and what the audience would see, when the video was broadcast, would be a reconstituted Rick Deckard walking those garish, milling, neon-streaked L.A. streets again, just as the real one had, gun in hand, eyes scanning for his prey.

That's what they're going to see, thought Deckard, *right now.* The only chance he'd had was based on anonymity, on being able to move through the emigrant colony's crowds without being spotted, on hiding out in the open, his face hidden in the torrent of other faces. And now that was going to be taken away from him. *They're going to see me. My face.*

On the monitor screens, the video's opening credits had ended; the camera angle had dropped from the fire-laced night skies above L.A., crossed by the screaming flares of the police spinners, to street level; the reflection of a neon dragon, red tongue darting through a crudely animated sequence, shimmered on the wet asphalt. A figure in a long coat, shoulders hunched with fatigue, was seen from the back. As the real Deckard watched from the booth, the video's all-seeing eye moved in on his taped double.

Then a quick cut, the shot going to a front angle, tight on the Deckard figure's shirt beneath the open coat's lapels, buttoned to the top with a costume department duplicate of the rough-woven tie he'd always affected back then. The shot moved up to the image's face, a close-up in good lighting, a noodle bar's bright fluorescents driving away any concealing shadows; the real Deckard winced, anticipating what he was about to see—

He didn't. In the booth, in a cheap dive somewhere in the Martian emigrant colony, Deckard stared in amazement—and with an uncomprehending sense of relief—at what he saw on the monitor, echoed simultaneously on the screens throughout the bar.

"That's not you," said a small voice behind him. The Rachael child looked past Deckard and Marley, on either side of her, toward the nearest screen. "I thought this was going to be about you and everything, about stuff that happened to you before. But that doesn't look anything like you."

"No . . ." Deckard continued to watch the video image. The Deckard there, the figure reenacting the story of those nights in L.A., had moved away from the camera and into a medium shot; the face was still visible, though. "It's not my face."

"Now that *is* interesting." No surprise registered in Marley's voice. "You weren't expecting that, were you, Deckard? I was getting kind of a kick out of watching you. Really thought your cover was about to be blown, huh?"

Deckard said nothing, but just nodded slowly, still watching the image on the screen, the Deckard that didn't look like him.

"Something must have happened," continued Marley. "For that Urbenton fellow to change his plans like that. I know that wasn't the original deal. They were going to ceegee your face on top of that actor's; all he had to do was go through the motions and it would wind up looking like you were doing all that stuff all over again. Hunting down those replicants like the bad ol' blade runner you used to be."

"I know." Deckard felt a measure of tension easing out of his spine. The dismaying prospect that every other face in the bar would turn toward him, connecting him with the image on the video monitors, had vanished. If the police agencies were going to put out the net for him, they would have to do it without the advantage of having every person with eyes doing their spotting for them. "That's a break."

"You figure it's just luck? The director Urbenton just happened to change his mind?"

He looked over at the other man. "No—" Deckard shook his head. "I don't have that kind of luck. If I ever did. Nothing happens without a reason."

"For anybody not in the kind of position you are, that would be considered paranoia. For you, Deckard, it's the beginning of wisdom."

Whatever relief he had felt over the broadcast of the video, and the absence of his face from it, was replaced by the suspicions he had for this character. "I don't have to be real wise, buddy, to wonder what it is you want from me."

"What do I want?" Marley looked back at him with wide-eyed, feigned innocence. "Like I said, I want to help you. And the way I do that is by stopping you."

"Stopping me from what?"

"Come on, Deckard. I'm way ahead of you." The naive mask had dropped from Marley's face. "I know what you're up to. You've accepted a little job, haven't you? The fact that you're carrying around that talking briefcase only goes to prove it. If you had any sense—if all you were interested in was saving your own skin—you would've ditched it by now." Marley tilted his head toward the other occupant of the booth. "Same with the little girl. Nice kid, but she's only going to slow you down."

"That's my problem," said Deckard.

"Oh, exactly." Marley's thin smile returned. "It's your problem because it's your job. The job you've taken on for the rep-symps of getting that briefcase and its data contents out to the insurgent replicants."

Deckard stiffened. "If you know all that . . . and you want to stop me . . . then you must be some kind of cop. You'd have to be working for the authorities."

"Not at all." The smile grew wider. "I'm with the rep-symps."

For a few seconds, Deckard thought that one over, then slowly nodded. "Sure you are. You blow away that Kowalski replicant right in front of me, and then you come and tell me that you're working on behalf of the replicants. You really think I'm going to believe that one?"

"Shooting the Kowalski replicant . . ." Marley shrugged. "Regrettable, but it had to be done. And not even all that much to be sorry about—he was pretty much at the end of the four-year life span that the Tyrell Corporation had built into that model. So he didn't really lose that much. And besides, there are other Kowalski replicants."

"That's a pretty cold attitude." Deckard studied the other man. "At least I had the grace to develop a guilty conscience over what I'd done."

"Good for you." Deckard's words had left Marley unfazed. "That must be why you got picked for this job you're doing. Guilty consciences screw up people's heads, make 'em easy to manipulate. Like you. Otherwise, if you were thinking straight, you would've been able to figure out a few things about the situation you're in."

"Yeah? Like what?"

"Work on it, Deckard." The other man leaned closer across the table. "You think because I've said I want to stop you—to make sure you *don't* get that briefcase and its data out to the insurgents—you think that must mean I'm with the authorities. Have you ever thought that it's exactly the authorities—the police, the U.N., whatever—who want you to get that briefcase out to where you've been told it's supposed to be delivered?"

"Hey!" The voice of Roy Batty piped up from beneath the table. "Don't listen to this guy! He's trouble!"

Deckard glanced over to the monitor screen, where the Deckard of the video, still wearing the actor's face, was talking to somebody in a set that was supposed to be the LAPD's high-ceilinged main headquarters. He didn't hear the characters' words, concentrating instead on what the figure across from him had just said.

"Look at it this way," continued Marley. "The cable monopoly here does whatever the authorities tell it to do—that's why it gets to remain a monopoly. If U.N. security tells the monopoly to run this video or that one, or *that* one"—he pointed to the screen—"then it gets broadcast all over the colony. Same way with Urbenton and his little Speed Death Productions company; if he wasn't in tight with the police before, it wouldn't take much pressure, if any, before he'd do whatever they tell him to. Especially since he doesn't owe you any favors. If they told him to cut the computer graphic effects, the dubbing in of your face over the actor who was playing you—he'd do it in a second. Urbenton wouldn't care if it helped you or hurt you; just the kind of guy he is."

Deckard had to admit that Marley was right, at least as far as that part of the analysis went. "I think I'm starting to see what you mean . . ."

"I bet you are. You're not totally stupid, Deckard. If the police and the U.N. security forces and everybody else who should be after you, if all those people wanted to find you and stop you from carrying that briefcase out to the insurgents, they wouldn't have let that actor's face stay in the video that's being broadcast. They would've told Urbenton to go ahead with his original production plans and dub your face in there. So that everybody in the emigrant colony would know what you look like; so they could put out a bulletin, offer a little reward, and there would've been no place you could hide. We wouldn't be sitting in this cozy little hole having this conversation; the police would've hauled your ass away by now."

It made sense; or put another way, the video broadcast didn't. *This was their chance,* thought Deckard, *to make sure everybody knows what I look like.* And it hadn't happened. The corollary of the principle that, for him, everything happened for a reason—not paranoia but wisdom, a survivor's assessment of how the universe worked—was that when things didn't happen, that was also because somebody wanted it that way.

"Then that would mean . . ." Deckard slowly picked through his own words. "It would mean the authorities don't want to stop me. They don't want to catch me . . ."

"They *want* you to get away." On the other side of the table, Marley regarded him with evident satisfaction, pleased with the impact his arguments had made. "So the question you have to ask yourself now is . . . why?"

"Why do they want me to get away . . ." Deckard rubbed his mouth with a knuckle. "They must have a reason . . ."

"It's not you, pal." Marley seemed to be taking pity on him. "If it's any comfort to you—nobody's ever considered you to be that important. So you needn't bother building up your ego now. It's what you're carrying. The job you've undertaken. Got it?" He smiled. "It's the briefcase. They want you to deliver it. Not the rep-symps, but the authorities. The police, the U.N. . . . all of them. The bad guys."

"I told you!" Batty's voice shouted louder from beneath the table. The briefcase vibrated against Deckard's shin. "I told you this guy was trouble. He's messing with your mind. Don't listen to him!"

The Rachael child leaned to one side in order to talk to the briefcase. "It's okay," she said in a soothing tone. "Nothing bad's going to happen to you—"

"Christ," spoke Batty disgustedly. "I don't need this. You

people are all screwing up big-time. Man, I wish I still had legs. I'd walk out of here right now and take my chances on my own. I'd let you all just sit here until you rotted away."

"Shut up." Deckard resisted the impulse to give the briefcase another kick. "Problem is, the guy's making sense."

"That's not a problem." A smile and a shake of Marley's head. "It's your salvation, Deckard."

"Goddamn it, don't listen—"

Batty's voice had gone up enough in volume to require action. Angrily, Deckard reached down and grabbed the handle, pulling the briefcase up and slamming it down hard on the table. He looked around to see if anyone in the place had noticed; as far as he could discern, the bartender and the patrons scattered among the tables were still watching the dimly lit adventures of the re-created Deckard in the video.

"Listen up," said Deckard, laying his hand on top of the briefcase's lid. "You're getting on my nerves. You keep yelling and carrying on, somebody's bound to think that's a little unusual. And I don't really feel like attracting attention right now. Understand?"

"You're the one who doesn't understand." Batty's voice had turned sulky. "You got a job to do, and this asshole is getting in the way."

"I don't care what I agreed to do." He pulled his hand back. "Just shut up and let me work this out, or so help me, I'll leave you at the nearest pawnshop and I'll take the two bucks I'll get for you and spend it on aspirin. I'm not joking."

The briefcase said nothing. It radiated a silent, sullen fury.

"Good call." Marley nodded approvingly. "You're the one in charge. Remember that—"

"Fine." The anger boiling up in Deckard hadn't abated. "I'm in charge? Then I want answers. I want to know what's going on. Right now, without any more cute shit from you."

"All right." Marley laid both his large-boned hands on the table. "I'll give you the short-and-sweet version, if you think your little mind can handle it. The briefcase here"—he tapped on it with one fingernail—"it's not what you think it is. It's not what you've been told."

"Yeah? So what is it, then?"

Marley smiled coldly at him. "You're carrying a bomb."

Deckard sighed wearily. "The hell I am." He had been hoping for something more plausible than that. "The authorities supposedly want me to carry this briefcase out to the replicant insurgents—because it's some kind of bomb? Get real."

"I *am* real." Marley's smile didn't change. "This is as real as it gets."

"Come on." Deckard pointed to the briefcase. "How much damage could be accomplished with something this size? And it came to me virtually empty; even if it were packed with high explosives—Christ, even if it'd been shoved full of fissionable materials—how much of a bang do you think that would amount to? Not enough to destroy a rebellion that's spread across all the U.N. colonies out in the stars. You're talking some big distances there, and a *lot* of replicants. If this so-called bomb killed thousands of them—even hundreds of thousands—that wouldn't change anything." He shook his head in disgust. "How about you figuring something out? Tell me—why would the authorities go to this much trouble just to enable me to carry one piddly bomb out there? Doesn't make sense."

"Oh . . . it might." Marley shrugged. "Depends on what kind of bomb it is, doesn't it? Problem with you cop types, all you can ever think of are things that go boom. Little boom, you kill one person; big boom, and you kill lots. But that's as far as your imagination goes. There are some things that don't go boom at all, and they kill all the people you need to."

"For Christ's sake." Batty's voice came from the briefcase. "The guy's a liar, and he's not even a good one."

Deckard ignored the disembodied words. "So you'd like me to believe that there's some kind of biological agent in this thing. A virus, a bacterium . . . some kind of disease vector. And my taking it out to the insurgents would somehow introduce that disease into their population and wipe them out. Is that it?" He felt even more disgusted, considering the shallowness of the concocted story. "It doesn't wash. That makes even less sense. One, replicant genetics are based upon their human originals, like the way the replicant Roy Batty was based upon the human Batty who got stuck in this box. So the replicant population is as genetically diverse as the human population, so the chance of coming up with a disease that would cut a wide enough swath through the insurgents is just about zero. And second, even if you could come up with a disease like that, some kind of superbug, it would almost certainly be just as deadly for the humans out there in the colonies. The U.N. authorities aren't going to wipe out all their emigrants in order to take care of the insurgents—what would be the point?"

"You know, Deckard, you're kind of a wordy bastard. For a cop, that is."

"I get inspired," he replied sourly, "when I think somebody's trying to bullshit me. You want a third? I'll give it to you for free. Replicants have four-year life spans. You don't have to do *anything* to kill them off, let alone introduce some bio-engineered disease. If all the U.N. wanted to do was to eliminate them en masse, it would just have to outwait them, let 'em come to the ends of their own built-in ropes."

"Very good." Marley smiled and nodded in admiration.

"Not bad arguments for somebody who's under the kind of pressure you are. You make some big assumptions, though. You're underestimating both how scared and how ruthless the U.N. can be. The insurgents have them in a panic; they'd happily kill off the entire human emigrant population if that's what it took to knock the replicants down. They can always get more emigrants; how much rottener does life have to get on Earth before everybody's lined up to go? There's already a nice little bottleneck full of 'em right here on Mars, just waiting for their tickets out. And as for the business about the replicants and their four-year life spans . . ." Marley shook his head. "Maybe that's not quite the issue that you think it is. But the main thing is that you're just wrong. You're wrong about what you think I'm trying to tell you. I never said the briefcase had some kind of disease agent inside it. You're just jumping to your own conclusions way too fast, Deckard. Maybe you should learn to just sit back and listen for a change."

"All right." Deckard leaned his shoulder blades into the booth's padding. "I'm listening."

"When I said you were carrying a bomb, I didn't mean the kind that goes boom, or something full of nasty little bacteria and viruses." The smile had evaporated from Marley's face. "I'm talking a *memetic* bomb. Pure information that changes what people do—in this case, what replicants do. When you were told that there was important data imbedded in the briefcase, that wasn't a lie. That's all there is inside it. And that's enough. Enough to take care of the insurgent replicants."

" 'Memetic bomb'? What's that supposed to mean?" Deckard gazed at the other man in disbelief. "You're talking about a meme? Just some kind of idea, and that's all? I suppose it's some really bad one—something like 'Why don't we all just commit suicide? It's fun and it's easy.' And that bad idea is just somehow going to infect the replicant insurgents, they'll kill themselves, and the U.N.'s troubles will be over. You must be joking. You have to be."

"No . . ." Marley actually looked sad. "I wish I were."

The shift in the other man's attitude made Deckard uneasy. "What is it, then? What good is a meme as a weapon if the replicants could just come up with a countermeme for it? Because that's all it would take. Any idea, bad or good, isn't something that people have to obey without even thinking about it. It's not like a bullet—or a real bomb. You don't get to argue about those."

"Guns have triggers," said Marley. "So do bombs; the things that make them go off. That's what you don't argue with. When the triggers get pulled, things happen. Real bad things. When the meme is the trigger—a trigger for something that already exists inside the target—then that completes the bomb as soon as you bring the two together. And that's what you'd be doing by taking that briefcase out to the insurgents. The bomb that would go off isn't some bad idea, some little self-destructive notion, that they'd be able to argue with. It's something that's built into them, just like those false memories that the Tyrell Corporation implanted into them. It's already in their heads, Deckard, where they can't get at it. They don't even know it's there. But they would as soon as you showed up with that briefcase and the data inside it. What the insurgents out there believe would be a list of the disguised replicants on Earth, their fifth column that they could contact and bring in on their side—they'd have a big surprise coming. It wouldn't be any list. It'd be their death warrants that you'd delivered to them. And they'd take care of the killing by themselves." The smile, when it appeared this time, was a mordant twist in one corner of his mouth. "That's a pretty good bomb, wouldn't you say?"

More than one change; the other man's voice had gone deadly cold as well. "How does it work?" Deckard was almost ready to believe. "What is it inside the replicants' heads?"

"Remember what I said about the four-year life span's not being an issue anymore? That's got a lot to do with it." Marley leaned across the table. "The replicants have changed. Because of being out there. Out in the stars, so far away from Earth. That's what the Tyrell Corporation was afraid would happen, and what the U.N. authorities have found out to be true. That's what started up the rebellion, made the replicants think they had something worth fighting for. Their own lives. And not just some crummy little scrap with a built-in cutoff date. In the outer colonies, that's what started happening: the replicants began spontaneously living longer than the four years they were intended to live. They changed. They're still changing."

"If that's true," said Deckard slowly, "then it means . . . everything. Everything would be different. And not just for the replicants."

"You got it, pal. That last batch of replicants that escaped and came to Earth—the ones you hunted down—they weren't part of the insurgents. The Batty replicant and the others—they didn't know what was going on. The rebellion hadn't gotten hold of them yet. And they missed it." Marley shrugged. "Kind of ironic, don't you think? Cruelly so. The Batty replicant and the other ones with him—they all wanted more life. To live longer than four measly years. And they could've had that if they'd just stayed where they were. Out in the stars. Instead of coming to Earth. That's where their death was waiting for them all along. And it didn't even have anything to do with you."

"What do you mean?" Deckard looked harder at the other man, trying to figure out the words.

"The spontaneous life extension—it's only happening out there." Marley pointed up to the bar's ceiling. "In the outer colonies, where the insurgents are. It doesn't happen anywhere near Earth. Actually, there are some indications that replicants who've changed, who've acquired a life span longer than four years, will revert if they get within range of their home planet, the place where the Tyrell Corporation put them together. Earth is toxic to them; the planet itself is the trigger for that life span bomb that Tyrell wired into each one of them."

"You said they were still changing. The ones out there . . ."

"That's right," said Marley. "Because there's more to life, isn't there? More than just extending your own. There's the cycle, the way one generation gives birth to another. That's a big part."

He could already see where Marley was going. "But that's

something replicants can't do. Give birth. Have children. Replicants are sterile; they can't reproduce. They were designed to be that way. That's how the Tyrell Corporation built them. The only way you could get another replicant would be to have Tyrell build it for you." Deckard regarded his own hands for a moment, then looked back up to the other man. "That's the way it's always been . . ."

"But that's not the way it is now. Now, things have changed. *The replicants have started to reproduce.* On their own, without the Tyrell Corporation; there are replicant mothers and fathers, and replicant children." Marley tilted his head toward the Rachael child sitting next to him. "And guess what? They look just like human children, the way replicants look like adult humans. And they grow up and become like their parents, just the same as human children do."

"Then what's the difference?" It was the Rachael child who spoke, peering at Marley. "What's the difference between them? Between humans and those other people?"

"Ah." Marley nodded. "That's a good question. A real good question."

"Then answer it," said Deckard. "I'd like to know."

"All right. Here's an answer for you." Marley regarded the girl for a moment, then looked back up at Deckard. "The replicants aren't the only ones changing out there. So are the humans. Or what used to be the humans. This is what the U.N. doesn't want people back on Earth to hear about; it would put a real crimp in the emigration program if it got out that going to the stars has some real hairy effects on the human species."

"Like what?"

"Sterility, for one. The colonists are in danger of dying out just from lack of reproduction. There hasn't been a human infant born in the outer colonies for a nearly a decade." With his thumb and forefinger, Marley made a zero. "*Nada.* No kids; the end of the line, unless the U.N. starts sending out more colonists. Who will in turn go sterile, from all indications; nobody's found a cure for what's happening. But that's not the only change. The mass reproductive failure is just the most obvious sign that something is going wrong, at least for the humans out there. There's other changes, which are a little more subtle but just as bad."

"And you're going to tell me about them." Deckard felt a wave of foreboding pass through him. "I'm beginning to be sorry that I asked."

"Too late for that," replied Marley. "It's why I'm here. To clue you in. Here's the deal on what else is happening with the emigrants in the outer colonies. Psychological changes; a decrease in that faculty usually known as *empathy.* You remember that one, don't you, from your blade runner days—the ability to feel what another living creature is feeling: its pain, its suffering, its joy. Well, the colonists are showing lower and lower marks on the standardized tests that measure that sort of thing. To the point where, if they were administered empathy tests with a Voigt-Kampff machine, they'd flunk. Some of them have already been given the V-K tests, and they didn't make it; the machine registered them as being below the cutoff point for the empathic response that characterizes human beings."

"Then they're not human." Deckard saw the cold logic of what he was being told. "They're not human any longer."

"Well, there you go." Hands grasping the edge of the table, Marley sat back in the booth. "Life's a bitch, isn't it? Things just happen, and then you have to deal with them." He shook his head as though in wry amusement. "Of course, the U.N. authorities have their own way of dealing with the situation." One hand patted the briefcase's lid. "Thus, you and this bomb you were told to carry out to the replicant insurgents."

"But if what you're saying is true . . ." Deckard no longer doubted it. "Then they're not replicants anymore. They're the human ones out there."

"Matter of semantics, isn't it? It's all in how you define the word." Marley's hand gestured lazily toward Deckard. "Now you, given your background—being a blade runner and all that—you just naturally tend to think that anything that passes a Voigt-Kampff test is human, and anything that doesn't isn't. And maybe you're right. But what it means is that the U.N. emigration program has been successful, but not in the way they intended. There is a human presence in the outer colonies, way out there in the stars, but it's not us; it's not the things that used to be human beings. It's those other ones, that were the replicants. They're the humans now."

"Why . . . why is it happening?"

"There's different explanations." Marley shrugged. "Little hard to get a definitive answer right now; the U.N. authorities want to keep a lid on what's going on, and the replicants are busy fighting for their lives and their freedom. All that sort of thing. But there's basically two schools of thought on the issue. One is more or less scientific, having to do with a hypothesized morphogenetic field centered on Earth itself, a field that determines, in addition to the genetic code carried in our DNA, the essential characteristics of the human species. The outer colonies are beyond the range of that morphogenetic field. Once that happens, there's slippage for both humans and replicants. Their outward physical appearance might not change, but other things will happen, like the shift in fertility and the empathic faculty." Another shrug. "As good a theory as any."

Cold, abandoned vistas opened inside Deckard's thoughts. "I knew," he murmured to himself, "we should never have left home." He found himself inside a seedy bar in the Martian emigrant colony, wrapped in darkness, an image with his name but not his face on the scattered video monitors, an image in a long coat like the one he used to wear, moving through neon-laced streets and endlessly deep shadows, none of which were real but all a simulation, far from home, far from L.A. *And this isn't even as far as those other ones went,* he mused. They went so far, and got so lost, that they even lost themselves.

He wondered what they were like now, those things with human faces that used to be human. A bleak memory came to him of riding back into the colony on the shuttle filled with the native mine workers, the grown-up children that had been born here on Mars. And of feeling alone among them, more alone than he had ever felt, even in L.A., where aloneness had pretty much defined the human condition in the thickest of crowds. The stage beyond alone, that of disconnected; he had looked around the shuttle and seen faces like his, human faces, but had felt no kinship with them. In turn, their unfathomable gazes had swept past him with no spark of recognition. They'd changed just by coming this far. Not so much evolved, which implied some better state, but at least adapted. They'd shed their skins, all the excess baggage that came with being human; they didn't need that stuff anymore. "Maybe nobody does . . ."

"What was that?" Marley leaned toward him, trying to catch his whisper.

"Nothing. Just thinking." He let the uncheering vision drain away, like water poured on the red desert sands. "You said there was some other explanation. What's that one?"

"Simple enough. There are some more mystical types who believe that being human isn't an inherent, genetically based condition at all. Humans don't decide who's human and who's not; that's taken care of by something outside them. Way outside." Marley looked uncomfortable, as though he were speaking of things not meant to be revealed. "There's supposedly an aspect of God that's called the Eye of Compassion . . . and it can only see suffering; it's blind to everything else. And those things that it sees, the suffering ones, those are what are fully human. Anything else is . . . something less. So there may have been a time when the things that we consider to be human may actually have been that way . . . but not anymore. The Eye doesn't see us; you and I, Deckard, we're part of that which *causes* suffering. The ones who used to be the replicants—the ones we made—they suffer at our hands. They suffer, and the Eye of Compassion sees them and judges them to be human. They become human. It's the gaze of the Eye—its ability to empathize with other creatures—that determines who's human. It's nothing we do. There's nothing we can do about it." He gave a nervous shrug. "Anyway . . . that's what some people think."

" 'More human than human . . .' "

"What was that?" Marley peered at him. "What did you say?"

Deckard had closed his eyes while listening to the other man. He opened them, then slowly shook his head. "Nothing. Nothing important. I was just thinking of that slogan that the Tyrell Corporation had. 'More human than human.' " A grim half smile appeared on Deckard's face. "Eldon Tyrell didn't know how true that would be."

For a few moments of silence, Marley studied him. "You know, though. You know it's true, don't you?"

He made no reply. He looked at the image of himself on the nearest monitor; that Deckard had a gun raised in one hand and was picking his way carefully over a field of shattered glass. "I don't care," he said at last. He looked back around to the other man. "Human is as human does, I suppose. It doesn't make all that much difference to me. There was a replicant that I fell in love with, and it didn't matter to me if she was human or not. Like you said—I'm not the one who decides about that sort of thing."

"That might be, Deckard. But there are still other things that you do have to decide about. That nobody but you can decide." Marley tapped a finger against the briefcase. "Like what you're going to do with this thing. Whether you're going to go ahead and try to carry it out to the replicant insurgents. Or whether you're going to bag that whole notion, because you know what kind of a weapon it is."

"But I don't know." He looked hard at the man across from him. "I've heard a lot of talk from you about what's happened to the humans and the replicants out in the stars. And maybe I even believe some of it. But even if it's true that the replicants have started becoming human—that they live as long as humans, and they have children like humans—that doesn't tell me anything about what's inside this box. And about why it should be so deadly to the replicants."

"That's right." Batty's voice broke into the conversation, coming from the briefcase. "Remember that, Deckard. This guy hasn't proven anything. All you know for sure is that he wants to stop you. Just like the U.N. security forces and all the other cops in the universe would like to stop you. He's just got a fancier line."

"Yeah," agreed Deckard, "he does talk a good line. Which makes him a funny kind of cop. I'm used to the kind that solves problems with a bullet." He studied the other man, looking for the clue he needed. "That was the kind of cop I was. And let's face it, Marley—you're not exactly squeamish about that sort of thing yourself. You didn't have any trouble over killing that Kowalski replicant when you thought you had to. So why are you being so careful with me?"

"I'm not being careful at all." Marley smiled at him. "I don't *care* about you at all. I'm just thorough, that's all. I've got a job to take care of, same as you. So I've got my orders, and they specifically said to leave you alive. Since I'm working for the rep-symps—the real rep-symps, not the phony-ass U.N. collaborators who set you up—I figure they must know what they want. Otherwise, I would've taken care of this whole problem my own way. The same way I took care of that Kowalski replicant back at Outer Hollywood." The smile became wider and meaner. "You know, you cop types are right: a bullet really *is* the best way. Simple and effective. If I weren't operating under restrictions, you would never even have seen what hit you, and that briefcase would be dismantled to atoms. And I'd be long gone from here."

"Hey! Screw you, pal!" Batty's miffed voice sounded again. "I'd kick your ass—if I could get to it."

Both men ignored the angry words. "So what is the deal?" Deckard pointed to the briefcase. "All that stuff you were talking about a memetic bomb. Some kind of data, pure information. That the U.N. security forces want to get piped to the insurgents. What kind of data would cause that much damage, to make all this worthwhile?"

"You got to remember," said Marley. "The Tyrell Corporation had all sorts of clever ideas. Eldon Tyrell had a knack for looking ahead and imagining the worst possibilities. Like the replicants' getting out from under his and the U.N.'s control. So they built in things like the four-year life span. But that wasn't the only fail-safe mechanism that Tyrell designed into the replicants. There's another one that's specifically related to the whole reproductive issue. The only reason it works is that it's a variation on a deeply buried mammalian instinct, some dark coding that's in the primitive layers of the human nervous system. Which is, after all, the basis for the replicant nervous system, so it's in there as well. All that Eldon Tyrell did was to invert part of it, design his own little twist into the replicants." Marley took a deep breath before going on. "The original instinctive behavior is the one by which adult male animals are driven to kill the offspring of other adult males of the same species, thus increasing the ratio of their own offspring in the breeding group; it's sometimes called the 'stepfather syndrome.' Just one of those ugly parts of genetically directed behavior where the gene's own survival and propagation are the only things important to it. Morality doesn't enter into the equation. What Eldon Tyrell did with the replicants he designed was to program in a pair of aberrations to that basic, primitive instinct. The first was to make it much stronger, to the point of being a homicidal obsession; the child-murdering behavior takes over the entire organism, overriding even its own instincts for self-preservation. The other aberration on the basic instinct directs the behavior *toward the organism's own offspring.* You following me? The organism—the replicant—murders his own children. It's like a breakdown in an extended immune system, one that extends beyond the replicant's own skin. The primitive drive is inverted, so that the individual attacks and destroys the very thing it's supposed to protect."

"I don't get it," said Deckard. "If that's the behavior that's programmed into the replicants, then there's no contest. There's no way that they can win any kind of struggle against the U.N.'s colonists. Because they'll destroy themselves; they'll reproduce, but they'll murder their own children. It's all over for them. They're a biological dead end."

"Not quite. The 'stepfather syndrome' behavior is built into them, but it's buried. It's not activated unless it's triggered. That's where you come in, Deckard. You and the little job you agreed to undertake for the cops and the U.N. security forces that had managed to infiltrate the rep-symp underground. You're carrying the trigger right here in this briefcase. The data that's been imbedded in it isn't any list of disguised replicants on Earth; that was just the cover story to get you to agree to the job. What the people who put this together did was encode the memetic bomb, the trigger to activate the buried behavior pattern, and stick it in here, in this box. Then they wrapped it up, like putting a bow on a birthday present, by imbedding Roy Batty's cerebral contents in there—more to goad you into taking on the delivery job than to actually help you get there. Because in reality, you don't need any help; there's no real effort being made by the authorities to stop you. The U.N. and the police, all of them—they want you to get there. You delivering that briefcase to the replicant insurgents is what their big plan is all about. You'd be showing up on the replicants' doorstep with the trigger to the bomb that's already wired into them. The buried behavior pattern would be activated, and there'd be nothing they could do to stop it. And that'd be the end of the replicants. When they die, there'd be no replicant children to replace them."

"This is crap," growled Batty's voice. "Don't listen to this jerk. He's just playing with your mind, Deckard. He's the one who's working for the authorities."

"I'm afraid our friend here protests too much." Marley rapped his knuckles on the briefcase's lid. "He's hardly a disinterested party in this whole affair, is he? Since his whole existence is bound up with what the two of you have been told about his contents. And why you should go ahead and deliver them."

"There's someone else," said Deckard. "Batty's not the only one. There was someone else who convinced me I should do it."

"Ah, yes. Our transcendent authority in these matters." Marley nodded. "The good Sebastian, who's gone from this mortal realm to a higher if slightly smaller one. It only goes to show that even a deity, albeit a dehydrated one, can be wrong."

"You knew I went to see him? In his little pocket universe?"

"Of course." Marley gave a casual shrug. "The people I'm working for—the real rep-symps—know all kinds of things. The other rep-symps may have been infiltrated and taken over by the police, but it doesn't end there. My bunch has its contacts and moles on the other side. They know what kind of data was imbedded in the briefcase, and what else they put in it. And what they instructed Batty to tell you so you'd go off and get convinced by Sebastian about your holy mission. Your delivery job. The problem is, Sebastian can tell you only what he himself believes to be true; he's not omniscient, at least as far as this world goes."

If he couldn't believe Sebastian—and Deckard had to admit that could be the case, that the little genetic engineer, even in his new transfigured incarnation, could've been lied to and misled—the question became, once more, a matter of trusting anyone at all. This Marley character had at least the advantage of a certain cold logic on his side to carry his arguments. *They've made it easy for me,* thought Deckard. He glanced over at the video monitor. All it would have taken, a simple thing, was to have let the director Urbenton go ahead and dub Deckard's face onto the actor playing him. A standard production technique. *And then I would've been a marked man.* Anybody in the emigrant colony could have recognized him and turned him in, if the authorities had, in fact, been hunting him down. But instead . . .

"You're asking me to believe a lot," said Deckard. "Not that everybody I run into hasn't been doing the same. But this 'stepfather syndrome' business—this memetic bomb that I'm supposed to be carrying—that seems pretty extreme. Why should I believe you on this one? Got any proof?"

"Mere evidence isn't enough for you." The smile appeared on Marley's face again. "Or logic, what you can figure out about what's happening around you—"

"It's not that." Deckard didn't bother with a smile. "I just don't trust murderers."

One of Marley's eyebrows rose. "So not even yourself?"

"Especially not myself."

"All right," said Marley, exuding an affable calm. "You

want proof? Or at least as much as can be gotten in this fallible universe. Fine—you've been carrying it around with you."

"The briefcase?" Deckard laid his hand on it. "I thought that was the whole problem, not the answer."

"Well, maybe you've packed a few extra things inside. Things that might sort out the situation a little bit." Marley pulled the briefcase out from beneath Deckard's palm and turned it around toward himself.

"Get your hands off me—"

Marley ignored the protest that came in Batty's voice. His thumbs pushed back the latch buttons on either side of the handle; a second later, he had thrown the lid back, exposing the lined interior.

"Not a lot in here." He glanced up at Deckard. "You could've made better use of it, you know. Thrown in a change of clothes or something. No matter—there's enough. At least for right now."

Leaning back against the booth's padding, Deckard watched as the other man examined the briefcase. A rectangular packet, one end torn off and then folded down to preserve the contents, was held up before him.

"You held on to this?" Marley looked at the name SEBASTIAN on the packet. "Thought it might come in handy, I guess. Just in case you wanted to talk to him again. Though what more he could tell you, I have no idea. Still, maybe you could just keep it as a little souvenir of your travels." He laid the packet down on the booth's table. The briefcase's lid blocked Deckard's view of the other man's hands rummaging inside. "Or perhaps you just wanted to keep the original package all together, with all the bits and pieces—since the collaborator rep-symps, the ones the cops have taken over, put this in here, you might as well keep it the way it came to you. But this is something new." Marley held up another object. "I know what was in here originally, and this wasn't part of it. You just put this in here since you got back from Sebastian's pocket universe."

Deckard looked across the table and saw a square of white-enameled metal in Marley's hand. The other man turned it slightly, revealing the broad red cross on the small box's lid. The old first aid kit—ancient, perhaps, considering how battered and scuffed it appeared. He had almost forgotten about it; when he had left the hovel, tugging the Rachael child along with him by one hand, the briefcase in the other, he had stopped when he had felt the little metal box slipping out of his jacket. He had popped open the briefcase and thrown the box in there for safekeeping, not even trying to figure out why he was hanging on to it at all instead of pitching it away as a worthless piece of junk.

"You do remember, don't you? Where you got this?" Marley held the white metal box up in front of his smile. "It wasn't that long ago."

"What do you know about that?" The question of just how extensive the other man's sources of information were troubled Deckard again. "You weren't there when it happened."

"No," admitted Marley. "But I knew Sebastian had this. It's a pretty important little item, even if it doesn't look it. So it's worth keeping track of. If Sebastian had it, and now you do, chances are good that you got it from him. Logical, huh? And I'm right, aren't I?"

A nod from Deckard. "So what's so important about it?"

"Well, why don't we take a look?" Marley gave a playful wink. "Shouldn't be too hard for a couple of geniuses like us to figure out. Let's see . . ." With his thumb, he pried open the lid; rust in the hinge joint creaked as the flat metal was prodded back by one fingertip. "Not too promising, if you're looking for the secrets of the universe." He glanced up at Deckard. "Old bandages and dried-up disinfectant." The fingertip now pushed around the box's antique-looking contents. "How about these aspirin?" When he pried the lid off one of the tiny bottles, the decayed vinegar smell wafted through the booth. "Hm, I think the expiration date might've gone by already—"

"Cut the crap." Deckard scowled in irritation. "Get on with it."

Marley ignored him, continuing with the routine. "Not

much else in here. Hardly seems worth the trouble, does it? You'd have to wonder why anybody would make a fuss over something like this."

"*I* know what that is." At the back of the booth, the Rachael child had pushed herself forward, hands flat on the table so she could see better. "There were things like that where I came from. Like that box and all that stuff in it."

"Of course there were." Marley turned his smile toward the girl. "You're absolutely right, sweetheart." He glanced over at Deckard. "She knows what the score is—or at least part of it. Because this is a standard-issue item, something that was stocked in all transports going outside Earth orbit. No big deal, just your basic little kit for small emergencies, incidents you didn't need to bother going to the infirmary for. There were probably dozens just like this aboard the *Salander 3.* But this particular one . . . it's very special. Not because of the bandages and the dead aspirin. But something else."

"It's all old." The Rachael child's brow creased as she studied the box in Marley's hands. "The ones we had, they were new. I mean, they weren't all beat up like that one."

"Sure—" Marley nodded. "That's because those other first aid kits were still there with you, where there wasn't any time. This one fell out—well, it was taken out. Somebody carried it out of the *Salander 3.* Because they had found out how important it was. So it's been out here, in real time. And that's where things get old and beat-up. Like this." He turned back toward Deckard. "You don't know yet what I'm talking about. But you will."

"I don't know if I want to."

"You don't have a choice, Deckard. Not anymore. Not that you ever did." Marley set the first aid kit down on the table. "If it's not the contents—all this old crap—then maybe it's the box itself. Think that could be?" He didn't wait for an answer. "See the inside of the lid here? What's it look like to you?"

"Paper." Mottled and browned by the same passing of time that had marked the small box's exterior; Deckard didn't see anything remarkable in the thin lining. "That's all. Probably it was some instructions, or a list of supplies." The paper was blank, whatever words that had been on it long since faded. "Standard issue, like you said."

"Wrong on that one, pal." Marley watched as one of his fingernails picked at the edge of the paper. "What was standard on these kits was to have the contents list printed right on the metal. See? Like that." One corner had been peeled away enough to reveal the black lettering beneath. "So somebody must've stuck this in here. For a reason." He grasped the wrinkled paper between thumb and forefinger and tore it away. "Which you shall see."

Something else was behind the paper, a rectangle just as thin but stiffer. Marley pulled it from the hiding place and looked at it for a few seconds before handing it across the table.

A photograph. Deckard held it by the edge, looking into the frozen section of the past that had been caught there.

He was still looking at it and listening to Marley explain what it meant, what it showed—listening and understanding at last—when the first bullet hit.

For a moment, Deckard thought it was something from the video monitor, something that was happening to that other Deckard, the actor playing him in the reenacted past. The noise of the shot was so loud that it pulled his gaze away from the ancient, long-hidden photograph and toward the monitor. That Deckard, with his long coat but without his face, was backed up against a motorized urban trash-retrieval unit; the gun was a gleam of black metal spinning away, knocked out of his hand by the taller figure looming above him . . .

A quick scream of fright from the Rachael child, and he realized that the shot had been in this world and not in the one held by the monitor. The bullet had torn into the fiberboard ceiling above the booth, gouging out a ragged trench from which a loop of electrical conduit dangled like a silvery intestine.

The second bullet took out the video monitor a few feet away, sending bright specks of glass across the floor and the table, as though that other Deckard and his small world had been further reduced to their component atoms, a furious energy propelling them from one reality to a larger one.

Deckard's hand, guided by its own instincts, was already pulling the gun from his jacket as his gaze snapped toward the doorway. Black-uniformed figures stood between the bar's darkness and the light outside, their weapons raised and aimed straight toward him.

She saw everything that happened.

They had told Sarah to stay back, out of danger; they would take care of the situation. Right now, she didn't have to do anything except watch.

"These guys are professionals," said Urbenton, standing beside her on the street outside the bar. The area hadn't been cordoned off—no need; the operation wouldn't take more than a few minutes—so a small crowd from the emigrant colony's surrounding alleys and warrens had formed, attracted by the audible stimulus of the gunshots and raised voices. "I wanted to use some of my video crew—I figured they're good enough at faking this kind of thing, they should be able to pull something off in reality, with real guns and stuff. But I got overruled on that account. So we got the heavy hitters on our side."

A glance over her shoulder, and she saw a few more of the uniformed men keeping the gawkers back with well-directed blows of their rifle butts. She looked back toward the doorway of the seedy bar, where all the rest of the U.N.-provided storm troopers had blitzed a few seconds ago. "I'm going in there," she said, walking without haste toward the scene.

"Hey!" The short, round video director grabbed at her arm, trying to pull her back. "You can't do that—"

She shook Urbenton off and kept walking.

The predictions had been right; the extraction procedure was happening so fast that Sarah managed to see only the last bit of action. She had no qualms about being around the U.N.'s elite squad members; they reminded her, in their wordless, cold-eyed efficiency, of some of the men who had worked for her when she took over the Tyrell Corporation.

They set about their jobs, and did them, and then melted back into the shadows, minus whichever of their number had crossed over and become corpses.

Standing in the bar's doorway, looking down the short flight of steps that led in, Sarah could see overturned tables and chairs, the few unnecessary figures of the other patrons shoved up and huddling against the walls, the ceiling-mounted video screens either smashed or still displaying the end sequence of Deckard's reenacted travails in Los Angeles. And at the far end of the space, the targets, the whole reason for her bargain with Urbenton and his backers.

A last flurry, which she was able to witness over the dark-uniformed shoulders. Deckard, sitting at one side of a booth, had pulled a gun out of his jacket, the same weapon he had taken from her back at the hovel. Before he could level it and fire, the other man—she had been told he would be there, and for whom he was working—reached over and wrested the gun away from Deckard. The other man had a more urgent agenda, one that he had a chance of accomplishing; he emptied the gun's clip into the briefcase lying on the table. At that close range, the elongated bursts from the gun's muzzle touched the briefcase's imitation leather like quick tongues of fire; the heavy slugs ripped the briefcase into tattered shreds, suspended for a moment in the air beyond the table's edges. A cry, not of pain but furious rage, sounded from the fragments before they fell in twisting, charred scraps across the glass-littered floor.

That was all that the man sitting across from Deckard accomplished. The U.N. troopers had their orders; the man was driven backward by the assault rifles' bullets, his chest shattered to the spine. Deckard had scrambled from the booth, reaching to grab the barrel of the nearest gun. The trooper expertly turned the rifle around, catching Deckard across the angle of the jaw, the hard blow sending him sprawling and unconscious. Another storm trooper reached into the booth and grasped the wrist of the little girl cowering there, then yanked her out into the open.

The operation was over, silence filling the debris-strewn bar. "Let's go," said Urbenton, taking Sarah by the elbow and drawing her back from the doorway. "Nothing else is going to happen here." The troopers behind them swung their rifles, clearing a path to the ground vehicle that would take them out to the emigrant colony's landing field.

"You should have killed him," Sarah said when she and the video director were back aboard the shadow corporation's yacht. She had kept her silence until then. "When you had the chance."

"But that wasn't the deal we made." Urbenton glanced up at her, then returned to fussing with the intercom buttons on the lounge's desk. "You accepted my help—all the assistance we needed to pull this off—but you knew there were conditions attached. You should just be grateful that the authorities owed me a favor for going along with them on that video they just broadcast here."

She sat back in the wing chair, her favorite one. "You sound like you're not even interested in having Deckard killed."

"I'm not, particularly. I just think it'll make a great tape when it happens. A really neat show, even better than this last one I did." His broad fingertip jabbed at another button. "And I just want to rev up the image, that's all. The right set, the right feel . . . it'll be wonderful." Another voice spoke up, unprompted by any of Urbenton's poking at the intercom controls. When it finished and clicked off, he turned toward Sarah. "That's it," he announced. "They've got the little girl aboard. We're ready to go."

Finally, she thought. She could feel it deep inside herself, the end time coming at last. She didn't care if Urbenton and all the rest of them went on acting and talking as if they could also perceive her hallucinations; it didn't matter.

She didn't even care which L.A. they were heading toward. Just as long as she knew that—soon enough—Deckard would be there as well.

He took the gun with him even though he knew that Marley had fired off every round that had been loaded inside it. The weapon might still come in handy, despite feeling so much lighter.

"You're back here?" The man on the other side of the counter sneered at Deckard. "I thought you didn't care for our services. Figured we'd pretty much lost you as a customer."

Deckard didn't feel like getting into another argument with the man; the last one, when he'd brought the skiff back to the rental yard upon his return from the Outer Hollywood station, had been pointless enough. He dug into his pocket and brought out all the cash he had, a hot sweaty clump of scrip, and dumped it on the counter. "Just give me the same one I had before," he said. "If it's fueled up and ready to go."

Leaning his weight against the counter's front, Deckard didn't bother watching as the other man sorted through the bills. He felt tired and bruised, the physical aftermath of the attack on the bar where he'd been sitting and listening to the late Marley. The front of his jacket was still spotted with Marley's blood, memorial evidence of the assault rifle bullets that had poured into the booth. *I got off light,* thought Deckard as he looked down at himself. His jaw ached from the rifle butt blow he'd taken from the U.N. storm trooper; when he'd come to on the floor of the bar, it'd taken a few minutes for a spell of blurred double vision to clear, at least enough for him to stumble out onto the emigrant colony's streets.

"You're short," announced the man behind the rental yard's counter. He stirred the bills about with his greasy forefinger. "There's not enough here for the deposit."

Deckard brought himself up from his bleak thoughts and levelled his gaze at the man. "Then I'll take it on credit."

The man's laugh barked out. "We don't do that."

Wearily, Deckard sighed and reached inside his jacket. "Yes, you do." He placed the cold muzzle end of the gun against the man's forehead.

A few minutes later, as the skiff was passing through the orbits of Phobos and Deimos—the rental yard man had told him to just keep the little craft, to not even bother returning—Deckard pressed his aching body back into the cockpit seat and assessed his situation. *There's a limit to what you can do with an empty gun,* he told himself. Especially since, where he was going, they would likely know that it was empty, that he was essentially unarmed. In some ways, it didn't even matter; he wasn't sure why he was going at all.

Just to get killed—that was the likeliest answer to come to him. Could there be a better reason? Before he had lost consciousness, lying on the floor of the bar, Deckard had caught a glimpse of the figure standing in the doorway, past the U.N. storm troopers taking care of business. Even without that sighting, he would have known that Sarah Tyrell was the prime motivator of all that happened. A dramatic touch, typical of her; she might have arranged for the lighting to be as perfect as that, spilling past her into the bar's darkness, silhouetting her like some shadowed angel, merciless and unavoidable.

One other glimpse, sighted as he had rolled onto his back, the last of his awareness pouring out through the hole that the rifle butt blow had knocked in his world—he had even reached up, a futile hand swamped by the black wave engulfing him. Reached up to stop the men pulling the Rachael child out of the booth, taking her away . . .

That was all he had seen. The memory of it rushed through his aching skull as soon as he had been able to lift his head from the bar's floor. Deckard had brushed bits of glass from his face as he'd worked himself into a sitting position and looked around the empty space. He'd been alone, patrons and bartender having wisely fled. The presence of the dead had been with him, both in Marley's corpse, slumped across the blood-mired table, and the briefcase, torn to mute fragments. Deckard had prodded the largest remaining piece, a corner with one lid-hinge still attached, and had gotten no response. Whatever part of Roy Batty, the human original, had been imbedded in the briefcase was gone now, dispersed to atoms as cold and fine as the white powder scattered irretrievably from the empty Sebastian packet. The walls of the bar had seemed to recede as Deckard had dropped the dead rubbish from his hands, as though the dimly lit space had grown as hollow as the one inside his chest.

Before he had gotten to his feet, balancing himself with one hand against the booth's table, he had found one other thing in the wreckage. Obviously left for him, placed right at his fingertips—Deckard had reached down and picked up the white rectangle of a business card, flipping it over to see the words SPEED DEATH PRODUCTIONS and Urbenton's name below that.

I'm doing just what they want me to, thought Deckard as he gazed out the skiff's cockpit at the stars wheeling by. The gears meshing around him were pushed by both the living and the dead, with no great distinction made between those categories. Even the dead Marley had conspired, in his way, to limit all possibilities for action to one inevitable line. Quick thinking on Marley's part: when the U.N. storm troopers had burst into the bar, he had used the gun to eliminate the briefcase itself, and thus any chance of Deckard's accomplishing the job he'd accepted. There'd be no carrying of Batty and whatever other information had been encoded into the box—Isidore's list of disguised replicants or memetic bomb; no telling now—to the insurgents in the outer colonies. Before he'd died, Marley might have had the comfort of knowing that his own job, the one of stopping Deckard's delivery of the briefcase, had been pulled off.

Which left the teeth of the other gears. Sarah Tyrell and Urbenton, and the forces aligned with them, had correctly read Deckard's mind, had predicted what he would do when he regained consciousness and found both the Rachael child missing and the simple card indicating where she had gone. Urbenton's card; the only address on it was a contact point in care of the studios at the Outer Hollywood station. That was Urbenton's world, the one in which he comfortably operated. That was the destination to which Deckard had programmed the skiff, as inevitably as the tape unrolling on some distant video monitor.

They knew he would come there, gun loaded or not, whether his chances of survival were at zero or any point above. Not just for the little girl, the child named Rachael, but for Sarah as well. Wherever she went, he would have to go there, inevitably. Her destiny had become so intertwined with his that there was no escaping. *I should've killed her when I had the chance*—Deckard gazed out of the cockpit without even seeing the stars. Too late for regrets now; he had waited too long, his hand stayed by memory of another woman's face, the one he had loved, identical in every aspect to Sarah. The great plan that he'd had, that he'd conceived all the way back on Earth so long ago, had been the excuse for not putting the muzzle of a gun against her temple and pulling the trigger. Deckard knew that now. *I should've killed her, but I couldn't have.*

Things had changed, though; he wondered if they had changed enough. Maybe he could do it now, despite her mirror resemblance to the dead Rachael. *If I have to,* he decided at last. If that was what Sarah was counting on, his inability to kill anything that looked so much like the woman who had slept in a glass-lidded coffin and who now slept and woke only in the sealed chambers of his remembering, then she might have a surprise coming to her.

They all might. In his hand, when he'd come to, had been the last thing that Marley had given him, the ancient photo that had been hidden inside the lid of the *Salander 3* first aid kit. That photograph was now safely tucked inside his jacket. And in another compartment of his memory were Marley's words, explaining what the photograph showed, what the image meant . . . everything. As much as the others knew, the strings that Sarah and Urbenton and the ones behind them could pull, there were still some things that they didn't know. And that he did.

Deckard laid his fingertips against the lapel of his jacket, feeling underneath the thin, still substance of the photo, warmed by his skin and pulse. He figured the time was coming, and soon enough; at the front of the cockpit, the miniature lunar sphere of the Outer Hollywood station was rapidly approaching. A ripple passed across the stars as the skiff's drive units modulated down into uncompressed space.

The hissing of snakes was merely the station's docking gates sealing behind the skiff, followed by the cockpit unlatching. Deckard emerged from the craft into near-total darkness; a few LEDs glimmered on the control panel mounted on a nearby bulkhead, and the skiff's own running lights sent his blue-edged shadow merging with the empty space.

His footsteps rang against the metal flooring as he headed toward a faintly recalled passageway. No point in trying to conceal his presence or his movement toward the station's center; they knew he was here. Or not, depending upon whether anyone else was; the last time he'd been at Outer Hollywood, the girdered substructure had vibrated with the activity going on in the various soundstages and studios; the recirculated air had carried the subliminal molecules of the techs' and extras' sweat and exhaled breath. This time, as soon as Deckard had stepped down from the skiff, he'd perceived the station as empty and dead, as though abandoned by all the human and close-to-human forms that had been here before.

He resisted the urge to call out, to attempt provoking a response. No need; reaching the limits of the station's landing dock, he laid his hand on the rim of the barely perceived doorway, and pseudo-life creaked into action. A beam of light flared on and swung toward him, striking him full in the face. Even as Deckard winced and shielded his eyes, another section of machinery stirred at his presence. He saw the glistening eye of a camera lens, suspended a few meters above, as it tracked and focussed upon him. The device's aperture irised farther open, then narrowed, as though the overlapping blades were biting down upon his curved reflection.

A few more lights came on ahead of him, not enough to dispel the darkness, but sufficient to divide it into crescent shadows and blind corners. In the metal struts above, cameras flexed and shifted like roosting birds, control cables and video mix-down feeds looped like the tendrils of a black neoprene jungle. All the blank, glassy optics turned toward him, some drawing back for wide-angle shots, others zooming in close upon his face. In the closest ones, Deckard could see himself, his own eyes turned into yet smaller mirrors in which the station's tracking network could be discerned.

Nothing human behind the lenses; he could sense that they were on automatic, programmed to find and lock upon him, recording every step he took. With idiot concentration, they performed their appointed task, their wide, obsessive eyes staring at Deckard in perfect, rapt silence.

As he stepped onto the outskirts of the *faux* L.A. sets, picking his way over the tangles of cables and massive, banyanlike tripod legs, a rumbling sound came from the unlit reaches above his head. He looked up and saw neither stars nor clouds; the video cameras swiveled beneath an interlinked net of white PVC piping. The first drops of water struck Deckard's brow; within seconds, a monsoon torrent swept over him and along the empty, simulated street, as the rainstorm from the metal disperser heads was whipped horizontal by the silvery rotating blades stationed around the set's edges.

"That's good!" He couldn't keep himself from shouting, from tilting his head back so that the artificial rain—warm as his own blood, as though it had rolled all the way across deserts to the east—trickled under his collar and down his chest. "That's really good! I like that!" Deckard's voice boomed against unseen walls, beyond the false-fronted buildings next to him. The rain plastered his hair against his brow, pooled in the palms of his hands, dripped from the hem of his jacket. The wet skin of pavement shivered around him as the neon tubing at the corners and above the vacant shops' doorways sparked and flickered into blue and red life. One more switch had been thrown, a circuit completed, somewhere in this world's artificial heavens. "Bring it on!"

As though in reply, the wind edged up to storm level, the puddled water at his feet driven into a sea of miniature waves before it was sucked away by the plumbing system hidden in the gutters. Deckard came close to being knocked off his balance, staying upright only by grabbing a lamppost wrapped with sodden *kanji* posters; the paper's heavy ink smeared across his hands and the point of his shoulder. Above his head, a dragon's red tongue flickered, the serpentine grace of its illuminated coils an icy electric blue.

She's here, thought Deckard. He scanned across the drenched cityscape to the enclosing reality of cameras and shuttered lights beyond. Everyone else—Urbenton and his crew—might have left Outer Hollywood, but Sarah Tyrell was still here. Deckard felt sure of her presence, as though some part of her had seeped into the fabric of the irreal Los Angeles. The lenses that watched him might as well have been her eyes, the steaming rain the fury of her kiss. He had wanted to confront her—he had been fated to—and now found himself embraced by her in a zone of no escaping.

The rain slackened a bit; it could almost have been an invitation to him. Deckard pushed himself away from the lamppost and walked, with the false storm in his face, deeper into the city's artificial heart.

"Wake up! Time to die . . ."

He heard the voice before he saw the figures before him. Two men, or what could have been men; Deckard saw one of them only from the back, as the long-coated figure was lifted nearly off its feet by the other's fist bunched at the throat. Deckard recognized one of the Kowalski replicants, but couldn't tell which it was, or what segment of repeated time he had stumbled into. *Then that must be me,* thought Deckard; his gaze shifted to the one the replicant's fierce smile burned toward. A burst of visual static rolled across the images. Deckard reached out his hand; his palm and fingertips touched the smooth, cold glass of a high-rez viewscreen, billboard size, taller than himself. The Kowalski and Deckard inside the screen's illusion of depth were as big as in life, as in the reality on the other side. One world enfolded the other, each equally false; Deckard looked away from the image before him and saw the walls of the same alley, the high metal flank of the autonomic trash-collection vehicle against which he had been trapped by the first Kowalski, the one back in the real L.A. on Earth, all the details that had been re-created on the Outer Hollywood set. He looked back again at the giant viewscreen and saw, only slightly blurred by the magnified pixel lines, the same alley's confines, like a photocopy one generation further on.

The camera angle shifted, cutting to one directly over the Kowalski replicant's shoulder. Deckard saw his own face struggling for breath against the massive knot of the white-knuckled fist under his chin. *They dubbed it in,* he realized. The video unreeling on the screen was what Urbenton had originally intended, the computer-generated simulation of Deckard's face over that of the actor playing him.

Time to die . . .

Kowalski's line, the echo from real time and Deckard's memory, had already been spoken. On the other side of the viewscreen, he watched as the replicant's blunt fingers rose toward his double's eye sockets. He braced himself for the sound of the gunshot, the bullet that would shatter Kowalski's forehead from behind, dropping the dead replicant to the ground . . .

There was no shot. No gun roared from the mouth of that other alley, the one inside the viewscreen's doubly false world. The scene played on to the end that left its Deckard a bloody-faced corpse sprawled at Kowalski's feet. From outside that world, Deckard had watched his own death with a mixture of fear and awe. For a moment, he wondered which side of the viewscreen was real, whether the dead thing with his face was the one who'd lived and died in L.A., and the one watching was its substanceless ghost. He looked down at his own hands, almost expecting to see the alley's rubbish-strewn ground through them, as though they were made of mist and rain.

He heard the gunshot then, not at the mouth of the viewscreen's alley but the narrow space in which he stood. It shouted from behind him, the muzzle blast tinging his shadow with fire. At the same moment, the viewscreen shattered with the bullet's impact. The other alley, with its Deckard corpse and blood-handed Kowalski, broke into darkness and shards of whirling glass. He flinched, turning his shoulder against the razor-edged storm, shielding his face with his upraised hands as the fragments bit at his wrists.

In a few seconds, the shards had finished tumbling to the ground with the quick, high-pitched notes of breaking ice. Deckard lowered his hands; in front of him was the metal frame of the viewscreen, bent and twisted by the bullet's explosion. Scattered around it were the cables and debris of the workings, now reduced to dull, unrecognizable scraps of silicon and unlit phosphors. The world that had been contained in the screen was gone, replaced by the one in which Deckard stood, the simulation of an alley in Los Angeles. No corpse, his own or Kowalski's, lay on the rain-soaked concrete this time.

He turned, knowing what he would see behind him. Standing there, as Rachael had stood so long ago, her coat's high collar brushing against her bound hair—Sarah Tyrell lowered the gun she held in both hands. The neon of the empty cityscape silhouetted her form, enough light leaking past to show the coldness of her gaze, the slight lift to one corner of her mouth.

"That's not right," said Deckard. "If you want to get it just the way it was. Rachael didn't smile after she shot Kowalski. It wasn't so easy for her."

Sarah let the gun dangle at her side. "We don't need an exact re-creation." She regarded him through half-lidded eyes. "Why don't we just say that . . . we're rewriting history. Changing things to the way they should have been." With the gun, she gestured down the alley's length, as if the other figures were still visible there. "After all—consider how much simpler things would've been, for so many people, if Rachael hadn't come out and found you, and saved you. Then . . ." Her gaze shifted back to him. "Whatever else happened . . . you would've been dead before I'd ever had a chance to meet you." An undertone of regret sounded in her voice. "Simpler . . . but I wouldn't have wanted it that way . . ."

From the front of his shirt, Deckard brushed away a few more bits of glass. "Where's the girl?" That was his most important business. "Where did you take her?"

"The girl?" Sarah looked puzzled for a moment, then nodded. "Now I remember . . . they left her with me. Urbenton and the others; they thought you wouldn't come otherwise. But that's not true, is it?" She smiled knowingly. "You would've come here . . . just for me."

"That's true." The backs of Deckard's hands were spotted with blood where the shards of the viewscreen had struck him. "I wouldn't have missed it. For anything." He watched a red drop fall from the tip of his little finger, then looked back up at Sarah. "But I just want to know that she's safe. Where is she?"

"Oh . . . she's safe enough." Sarah looked unconcerned. "As safe as anything can be in this world." She raised the gun, bringing it up at the end of her straightened arm. "You should be more worried about yourself." The black muzzle pointed directly at him. "You're the one who's not quite safe."

He didn't bother taking the unloaded gun from inside his jacket; he knew she couldn't be bluffed by it. Instead, Deckard looked up at the video cameras mounted in the rigging overhead. "What about all those?" Some of the lenses were focussed on him, others on Sarah, with a few drawn back to take in the whole scene. "You must have cut some kind of deal with Urbenton. To provide him with the kind of footage he likes." He pointed to the gun levelled at himself. "Is this going to do it?"

"You're good, Deckard." She nodded in appreciation. The fur of her coat's collar was spiked with raindrops, like miniature jewels. "That's the cop in you—always analyzing the situation." The gun lowered in her hand. "You're right, though. They wanted more—Urbenton and the rest of them. They set this all up . . ." She gestured toward the lights and the tracking video cameras. "Just for the two of us. There's just some things that special effects and computer-generated images can't really do." A shrug. "No substitute for live action, is there?"

Deckard shook his head. "No—there isn't."

"Or death, either. It's so unsatisfying when that's faked. It's like . . . what was it the replicant said to you? I read it in the script. 'Like an itch you can never scratch.' " Sarah smiled at him. "That's why I'm so glad you could make it here, Deckard. We've been through so much together—it would be a shame not to do it right when we're just about at the end."

"Oh . . . I agree." He wondered how he was going to get the gun away from her. If she had been crazy before, she was worse now. But not stupid—Sarah had carefully kept enough distance between them so that he didn't have a chance of suddenly lunging toward her, grabbing her arm and twisting it behind her until she dropped the weapon. She'd drill him before he got halfway to her, and he'd land at her feet with the back of his skull at the closed end of the alley. "Maybe we should go somewhere and talk about it."

"We'll talk, all right. But not just now." Sarah turned away from him, then coyly glanced over her shoulder. "I think you'll know where to find me."

He watched her walking away, out into the empty street, the pools of rain reflecting her image like polished obsidian.

A bank of video cameras watched as well, the glistening lenses turning on their pivot mounts to follow her, until she had disappeared from view.

His guess was right. Even before Deckard got to the entryway of the set's replica of the Bradbury Building, he saw the footprints shining wetly in the protected space between the ornate columns; small, a woman's, with no attempt having been made to erase them. It had to be Sarah; no one else was aboard the station, Outer Hollywood having been vacated by the watchers of his progress. He supposed that Urbenton was safely tucked inside some transport in the same orbit, viewing at long distance the results of his production arrangements. As Deckard had sloshed from one rainy zone of the L.A. set to the next, the certainty of being isolated in this small world had increased, as though the city itself had been emptied of every face except his own.

Behind him, the artificial rains lashed the street, the marquee of the Million Dollar Theater shedding its plastic letters one by one, the winds spelling out some obscure noun in the pooling waters. Deckard pushed the creaking door into a cathedrallike dark, then stepped after it. The cameras focussed on his back went dead, like birds in winter, as the ones inside the building were roused by his presence.

Shafts of clouded light swerved through the elaborate set's interior as he gripped the stair rail and looked upward. No U.N. blimp moved outside—there wouldn't have been clearance for even a simulation beneath the rigging's pipes and struts—but a carefully synchronized array of lights achieved the same effect. *It's not even as real,* thought Deckard, *as Sebastian's world.* In that little pocket universe, at least, there had been something like a sky and distance between one point and any other; there would have been miles for the genetic engineer turned deity to have travelled before he found his heart's desire. But here, in this false L.A., everything had been compressed and squeezed down to its essentials, the way the insane obliterated all but the pieces of their obsessions. As Deckard mounted the steps, cold wrought iron sliding under his palm, he wondered if it was his head or Sarah's that he had entered, the thin trails of light revealing the wreckage of her hopes or his own.

At the end of the encircling corridor, with rain trickling down through the rafters and decaying plaster above him, with the unlit empty space traversed by the elevator's elongated vertical cage to one side, Deckard pushed open the door. The same door that he had opened in the past, in memory, in a real L.A., and in dreams and a pocket universe—it swung away from his hand, revealing the high-ceilinged room beyond. He almost expected the same things to happen as the first time, the two sawn-off friends of Sebastian's—the animated teddy bear and the spike-helmeted toy soldier—to march out and greet him.

Instead, Deckard saw the Rachael child sitting at the massive claw-footed table, her legs dangling at the front of the chair, its carved dark-oak back extending above her head. She didn't notice him when he first stepped inside the room; the braid of her dark hair draped over her shoulder as she bent her head over the sepia-toned illustrations in a Victorian gardener's manual. Between the pages a single rose had been pressed; she lifted the brown, ancient flower to her nose, trying to catch whatever scent still remained. That was when she spotted Deckard silently watching her.

"You're here." The Rachael child spoke calmly, flipping her ribbon-tied braid behind her back. She carefully laid the papery rose inside the book and closed the stiff leather covers. "I knew you would be. Eventually."

"Are you all right?" Cautiously, Deckard scanned the room as he stepped forward. It looked as it had when he'd been in Sebastian's private world, dusty and stuffed with wind-up dolls and mannequins. The laughing clown figure towered over one end of the table, its manic smile frozen on the stark white face. "Did anything happen to you?"

"I'm fine," announced the child. "Well . . . I'm *bored.* This is a stupid place. Everything's broken, or it doesn't work." She poked the bride doll standing next to her chair; the organza veil fluttered as the doll fell over, its arms and delicately poised hands sticking up in the air. "But those people, the ones who brought me here . . . they didn't hurt me or anything. They were nice enough, I suppose."

"All right . . ." Deckard barely listened to what the girl said. The crash of the bride doll had echoed through the room, stirring the white powdery plaster that had settled on the toys and overstuffed furniture. As the dust settled, he tried to hear anything else moving nearby. Lenses glinted as the video cameras, more carefully hidden in this set than outside, swiveled silently on their mounts, tracking the slow turn of his head. "Is there anybody else here with you?" He glanced at the child from the corner of his eye. "Anyone at all?"

"That woman." The Rachael child laid her hands flat on the book. "You know, the one that looks like me. The one you call Sarah." An annoyed expression crossed the girl's face. "The one who didn't think I was real. She's here."

"Where?"

"Up there." She gave a single nod to indicate the room's ceiling and what lay above. "That's what she told me. She'd just gotten back here a little while ago; she'd been out in the rain and stuff, like you. See?" The girl pointed to one of the other chairs, where Sarah's high-collared coat had been tossed across the scrolled arms; the floor beneath was spotted with the raindrops shed by the fur. "She said she was going up there to wait for you."

"I bet." Deckard realized he was being a fool. He knew what he should do; he should just gather up the Rachael child and lead her out of the building and off the *faux* L.A. set entirely. The skiff was waiting at the station's loading dock, and it could carry both him and the little girl away from here. What was the point in going up and confronting Sarah, with her loaded gun and equally lethal madness? She was primed to blow him away, only delaying the moment for the perfect camera opportunity. Up on the building's roof—the set that had been put together by Urbenton's techs, the detailed reproduction of the one in L.A.—the two of them would again be under the multilensed eye of the video cameras and lights in the overhead rigging; much better, cinematically, than the relatively constricted setup here in the rooms beneath. *That must've been part of the agreement,* thought Deckard. *To get me out where the best camera angles are.* Completing the arc, a nice sense of structure on the director's part: to die where he hadn't died before, where he'd been saved from dying by the replicant with Roy Batty's face. "I'll just bet she wants me to go up there."

"That's what she *said.*" The Rachael child gave a shrug. And a sharp-eyed gaze at Deckard. "You don't have to do it if you don't want to."

The little girl was eerily smart—for reasons that Deckard knew something of; back in the Martian emigrant colony, Marley had told him about the child's lonely, eccentric growing-up aboard the scuttled *Salander 3,* and more than that—but she was wrong now. He did have to do it, to go and meet Sarah on the rain-swept roof beneath the watching cameras.

"We could never get away," he said to the girl sitting at the table. "There'd be no place we could go . . . that I could take you to. Not Earth, not Mars, not anywhere. No place that she wouldn't find us again. So I'd just have to do it eventually. And get it over with. Here or there; now or some other time. But it has to happen."

"I don't know about any of that." The Rachael child looked guilelessly at him. "That's not any of my business. But you have to do what you think is best."

"All right." Deckard nodded slowly. "That's just what I'll do." He took the gun out of his jacket and laid it on the table. "This isn't any good—it's not loaded. So forget about it; I just don't want to carry it around with me anymore. If anything happens . . . if I don't come back down, or if Sarah comes down without me, or if those other people come here . . ." He shrugged. "There's not really anything you can do. And you shouldn't have to."

"Should I go hide? If that's what happens?"

Deckard smiled at the girl. "Where do you think you'd go?"

"I don't know." The Rachael child gave another shrug. "Somewhere. There's a whole city out there." She pointed to one of the arched windows. "With people and stuff. I could find someplace where nobody would know where to look for me."

He glanced over his shoulder at the window, with the artificial rain beating against the glass, the gauzy curtain stirred by the drafts that had penetrated the meticulously constructed decay of the interior set. *She believes it's real,* thought Deckard. The ones who had brought her here—Urbenton and the others—had let the child go on with the notion that they had left her in the middle of a real city, the real Los Angeles. He didn't know if that had been cruel or kind on their parts, or whether it made any difference. The way the girl had been brought up, by the autonomic machinery of the *Salander 3,* the city outside these windows, such as it was, probably seemed as real as any other could have.

"No," said Deckard. "That's not a good idea. Don't try to hide. I don't think they'll hurt you. If I don't come back . . . then just let them take you to where they want to. Maybe they'll take you back home. You know, where you came from. You could stay there a long time, and you'd be all right."

"But I don't want to." A tear had welled up and trembled at the Rachael child's dark lashes. "I don't want to go there. I'd rather stay with you." The high-backed chair toppled over with a crash as the girl pushed herself away from the table; she ran to him and hugged him around the waist, the side of her face against his jacket. "I'm going with you."

"No, you're not. You can't." The same protective, almost paternal feeling as before passed silently through Deckard's thoughts. The girl looked so much like Rachael, the woman he'd loved; she could have been their daughter, a child that could never have happened. *Not here,* he mused. *Maybe out there, in the stars.* Perhaps Rachael would have been one of those that changed, became human; they could have had a life together . . .

Too late for that, he knew. Now there were only the bits and pieces of his own life to pick up and sort out, make something of. Something other than killing. That was why he'd quit being a blade runner a long time ago—but that hadn't been enough. That was why he'd agreed to take on the other job presented to him, the business of delivering the briefcase with Batty's voice and Isidore's list inside it; too late for that as well. Whether it had been salvation or death for the insurgent replicants—it didn't matter now.

The only things left to him were the little girl . . . and what Marley had told him about her. About who she really was. And the slim proof—not even that; evidence that had to be taken on faith as to what it meant—that Marley, two minutes away from death, had given him. Deckard touched the front of his jacket, a finger's width away from where he had been carrying the empty gun, and felt the thin stiff rectangle of the ancient photograph, the one that had been hidden in the *Salander 3*'s first aid kit. That was all he had with which to confront Sarah; one way or another, it would be enough.

"Look—" With difficulty, he managed to push the child away from him. "You stay down here, and everything will be all right. I promise." He wondered for a moment why she had formed such a sudden, dramatic attachment to him. *There's no one else,* thought Deckard. The child was all alone in this universe, or in any other. Plus—it was impossible to tell—she might have sensed the fragments of his past, the memories of someone else named Rachael that the girl's dark eyes and grave manner conjured up so painfully in him. Even if she didn't understand yet how those things had come to be. Maybe she just felt sorry for him. "All right?" Deckard put his hands on her shoulders and leaned down to look straight into her eyes; the glimpse of them ran through his own heart like a dagger of silver and ice. "The bad things have already happened," he told the girl. "Nothing else can go wrong," he lied. "So don't worry about me."

He left her sitting at the table again, surrounded by the mutely uncomforting dolls. The Rachael child folded her arms across the thick, leather-bound book and laid her head down, concealing her face from him. Deckard stepped out to the open corridor beyond and quietly pulled the door shut behind himself.

18

The last time—the first time Deckard had been in this building, in its original form back in L.A.—he'd had to climb laboriously to its roof, his scrabbling progress through the crumbling, waterlogged plaster and sagging beams impeded by a hastily bandaged hand, the fingers that the Batty replicant had broken aching and useless. Fear had driven him then; he'd been trying to escape death. This time, he was walking toward it. *I'll take the stairs,* he thought wryly.

A shaft of utility stairs at the back of the building—it was undoubtedly the same route that Sarah had already taken. In the damp air, as Deckard craned his neck to look upward, he caught a trace of perfume, one of the opiated floral scents that his mind and senses had learned to associate first with Rachael, then with Sarah. The invisible molecules were tinged with something more acrid but just as distinctive and evocative: cigarette smoke, something dark and expensive, suited to the taste of a Tyrell heir. He looked down and spotted, on the landing's rough concrete, silken white paper and brown shreds of tobacco ground out cold by her shoe.

The metal steps echoed in the narrow space, loud enough to evoke a shiver in the video camera lenses that peeked out at him from their clefts in the unfinished walls. Up ahead, above him, Deckard saw a rust-mottled door left open, creaking on its hinges as the fan-driven storm winds swung it back and forth. He stopped, rain spattering in his face as he tried to catch sight of anyone waiting in the darkness. Nothing; he grasped the cold pipe rail and continued climbing.

"Sarah?" He pushed the door all the way back—the metal clanged against the side of the hatchway structure—and stepped out onto the roof. Warm rivulets trickled down his throat as he called out again. "Where are you?"

No answer came. Deckard walked farther from the door, leaving the stairs and his escape behind him. Looking up, he saw no stars but the broader points of the lights in the studio's truss-work rigging; only a few meters away, as though—in a child's notion of the world—he had climbed all the way to the dark heavens, the universe's weld-stitched limit. The lights' spectra had been shifted down to an icy blue, colder than the streets' veins of neon; shadows fluttered across him like the wings of unseen, untouched birds as staggered ranks of archaic wind turbines, blades long and scimitar-curved, rotated in the damp breeze coming from the edges of the set.

He worked his way through the windmills, avoiding the scything arms, coming at last to the roof's raised parapet. His hands, grasping the crumbled brick and thick tatters of asphalt sheeting, looked as bloodless as a corpse's flesh. They hardly seemed to belong to him at all; the uncanny sensation passed through him as though he were looking at someone else, someone who had slid inside his body and face. The hands, and the body that leaned its insubstantial weight into them, might have been those of the actor who had played him in the video he had seen; the disoriented feeling increased, setting him even farther away. For a dizzying moment, Deckard wondered if he were still watching the video, the artificial world into which his own life had been transformed.

Squeezing his eyes shut, his hands gripping even tighter on the fragile stone, he tried to make himself feel real again. Or as real as possible. *I've become my own ghost,* thought Deckard. A dead thing that watches and mourns the past; he'd felt that way before, when he'd sat beside a glass-lidded coffin, leaning forward with his chin on his doubled fists, looking at the sleeping, dying woman he'd loved. Keeping his vigil through one sleepless night after another, time seeping away beneath the real stars, the rain swallowed by earth and the dead leaves beneath the trees. It might as well have been his own face he'd seen beneath the glass, in a video monitor rather than a coffin. He had died, or as good as, even before Rachael had; he'd just had the privilege of witnessing his own death, over and over, in one cold world after another.

The bleak meditation didn't end, but became familiar enough, an old wound, that he could function once more. Deckard opened his eyes and looked over his shoulder at the elaborate rooftop set. *They did a good job,* he had to admit. Urbenton and his crew of technicians, the people who had constructed the set—in the thin, fragmented light, he could see how close they had come to the original, how much the fake was indistinguishable from the genuine. The turbines spun in place, like idiot dervishes on edge, over a buckling field speckled with pigeon shit—had they scraped up the droppings from an actual L.A. building roof and shipped them here, or was there a flock of birds kept on hand in some remote aviary zone of the station? It all smelled real enough, a blending of monsoon steam and guanoid archaeology, that at least some of Deckard's senses were fooled.

He looked back over the parapet at the imitation city that surrounded the building. All the little tricks of the video trade had been used, from foreshortened perspectives to banks of fiber optics for a vista of pinpoint lights stretching to an imaginary horizon; other whole sections were blank or covered with chroma-key backdrops, for digitized mattes to be ceegeed in during postproduction. The miniature city seemed caught between different levels of reality, at some muddled point halfway on the line from dream to something that could be touched. In some way, that made the dark nocturnal city he saw now as real as the L.A. he remembered on Earth. *Realer than real,* thought Deckard. A night made of the same stuff as the replicants, dreams and fears and a desperate longing to exist. He had lived in that inchoate city, had been part of it, but—he knew now—hadn't belonged in it. *It's their world.* He nodded slowly, rain trickling across the backs of his hands. Their night as well, in which he was just a shadow, a thing that wouldn't even be remembered when the sun came up.

"Hello, Deckard." The voice—the one that he'd known he would hear—came from behind him. "I was waiting for you."

From over his shoulder, he looked and saw Sarah standing a few yards from him, in the center of the roof's area, the wind turbines spinning and stretching away into darkness. He turned and leaned back against the parapet, hands gripping its edge on either side. "I had some business to take care of first. With the little girl. I had a talk with her."

"How sweet." Sarah stepped forward into the partial light filtering down from above. The skin of her face and throat looked cold, bloodless. "I suppose that was a good thing for you to do. Whether she's real or not. Actually . . . I don't care anymore." The gun in her hand glinted as though a piece of the dark had frozen. "It's not important, is it?"

"Maybe not." His heart had ticked faster for a moment at seeing a weapon in someone else's hand, knowing that he didn't have one. "It all depends. On what you want."

"Ah." She nodded and smiled. "That's true. I used to want things. Different things." With cruel playfulness, Sarah raised the gun to eye level, arm straight, and looked down the barrel at him. "And now . . . just one thing. Guess what it is."

"I've got a pretty good idea." Inside him, his pulse had slowed back down as a resigned calm moved through his blood. Whatever was going to happen, he had prepared himself for it. "I wouldn't have come here if I didn't know."

The face of the woman he loved studied him over the gun's

black metal. "You're not really human, are you, Deckard?" Rachael's face, Sarah wearing it like a mask, though it had been hers to begin with. "If you ever were, you've managed to get over it. Like I have. So it's not just a cop thing, having ice water going in and out of your heart. It's just something that happens to people like us."

He nodded in agreement. "The Eye of Compassion . . ."

"What was that?"

"Nothing," answered Deckard. "Something . . . somebody told me about. We're not the ones who decide who's human and who's not." He looked over to the faked skyline surrounding the building, then back to her. "There's nothing we can do about it."

"Yes, there is. There always is." No trace of irony or sarcasm sounded in the woman's voice. "You shouldn't give up hope like that." Her hand squeezed the gun, tight and trembling. "You can always kill. That works. Especially if you do it to the things you love. Then . . . then you have a chance."

"A chance of what? Of being human?"

"No . . ." Sarah gave a shake of her head. "Of not caring anymore. So when you die—when you take care of yourself finally—it's not so hard."

The voice of madness, speaking the same words inside his head—Deckard listened to her and knew that it would be easy to agree. Or to go even further, deeper into one's own madness; the temptation always existed in him to accept only what he saw, what part of him wanted to see and believe. That it really was Rachael standing in front of him, alive again, unchanged. That the other woman with the same face, the one named Sarah, was as irreal as she had thought the child waiting downstairs inside the building was. A memory, a bad dream, a hallucination. If that were the case, he wouldn't have any problem with her pointing a gun at him and pulling the trigger. That was a small price to pay for seeing Rachael again, if only for the moment between the firing of the bullet and its entry into his deluded heart.

He had closed his eyes, though he could still see her—remembering was enough for that. Easier as well, to mentally edit out the infinitesimal differences—the coldness at the dark centers of her eyes, a hard curl at one corner of her mouth—that made her Sarah instead of Rachael. It didn't help much; when Deckard opened his eyes again, the sight of the woman sent a sharp-pointed blow through him, more painful than if she had actually squeezed the trigger of the gun.

"Is that what you're going to do?" He'd watched as the momentary tremor left her upraised hand. "Kill yourself, too?"

"Why not . . ." Sarah's eyes almost seemed to be looking for sympathy from him. "Why should you be the only one to get lucky?"

Deckard continued to watch as she strode forward, all the way to the building's edge. She turned and leaned back against the parapet a carefully judged distance away from him, just far enough that there was no chance of his being able to grab the gun before she fired.

"You know . . ." Sarah mused aloud. "The illusion kind of breaks down here." She glanced over her shoulder, toward the street below. "It's not really very high up at all, is it?" Her gaze turned to him. "Not like the real one, back in Los Angeles. I've seen that one; I've been there." Head cocked to one side, she smiled coyly at him. "When I was first finding out all about you, Deckard; I went and looked at the places you'd been, where things happened to you." She nodded toward the drop on the parapet's other side. "You must've been pretty scared, back then; if you'd fallen from the real one, they would've had to have picked you up from the pavement with a sponge. Whereas here . . ." Sarah gave an unimpressed shrug. "Hardly enough to kill someone. You might actually even survive."

"Maybe." Deckard looked over the edge behind him. She was right; the illusion of the city's reality was dispelled from this angle. The machinery and interlaced cables of the set were detectable, like the secret workings of the world revealed by a paranoid vision come true. "Is that the deal you made with Urbenton? He always wants the best footage he can get. So a shot of me falling . . . I imagine that would be just about perfect. He could re-edit the video he did about me, put in a new ending, one where I die. Maybe that would suit both him and the people he's working for."

"Oh, it would. You're exactly right on that one." Sarah nodded, as though admiring his take on the situation. "That's pretty much the U.N.'s little agenda. The first version of the video—the one you saw—that was only shown in the Martian emigrant colony." She pointed toward him with the gun. "They'd love to do another version for broadcast on Earth that would really prove just how dangerous escaped replicants are. In case there might be anyone starting to feel sorry for them. Urbenton could always fake your getting killed, do it with special effects, all the different tricks they have for that sort of thing—but there's nothing quite as convincing as reality, is there? No matter how much you have to fake it. Plus, this way, there's no living blade runner named Rick Deckard turning up later to embarrass everyone. The little details . . . like your not being killed by the fall but from a bullet . . ." Sarah gave another shrug. "Urbenton can fix that up in postproduction. Or not. That's his business, not mine." She studied the gun in her own hand for a moment, then looked at Deckard again. "I'll have kept my part of the bargain."

"You're a person of your word. In your own way."

"I try to be." Sarah spoke with no more irony than before. "I've only lied when I had to. When there was something I had to have. And what did it get me?" She shook her head. "Nothing. I learned my lesson." Her voice turned bitter. "I should've just stayed what I was. Not tried to be something else. Like your precious Rachael. It's just no good—the dead get all the breaks in this world."

The artificial rain had lessened a bit. Deckard looked up to where the clouds and stars should have been, letting the drops wash down his face and throat. "But do you know?" The words were soft, almost a whisper. "Do you know who you are?"

"Come on." Her response was sour, irritated. "I'm not in the mood for the usual mind games, Deckard. I'm tired of playing even my own. So it's not likely I'm going to fall for yours. If that's what you're going to try, then I'll just stop wasting time and kill you now. There's a limit to how sentimental I get."

He said nothing. Instead, he reached inside his jacket and took out the thin, flat rectangle of the photograph, the one that had been given to him by the dead man back on Mars. Deckard held it by one corner and gazed at the long-past scene it revealed. Then he held the photo out to Sarah.

"What's that supposed to be?" She leaned back, regarding the object with suspicion. "Something you and your rep-symp friends faked up?"

"No—" He shook his head. "This is the real thing. Go on, take it."

Keeping the gun levelled at him, Sarah reached out and grasped the photograph between her own thumb and forefinger. She turned it around and studied it. "I don't get it," she announced after a few seconds. Her brow creased. "Who is it?"

"Come on, Sarah. You know." He tried to make his words as gentle as possible. "You've seen them before. You've seen other pictures. They're your parents."

She said nothing. Deckard watched her staring at the photo. The image it contained was in his head as well, engraved there from the moment he had first seen it. And Marley's voice, telling him what it meant; those were fused together, insoluble. He knew what Sarah was looking at: a photo of a bed, the sheets and covers all white, a woman sitting up with the pillows mounded behind her; the woman was smiling, as was the man standing beside the bed, leaning down to get his face close to hers, the two of them looking into the lens of the camera. It must have been mounted on a tripod or a high shelf; the remote control was just visible in the man's grasp, his thumb pressing down the button that had flicked the camera's shutter.

The two people were Ruth and Anson Tyrell—the same two people, the couple, that Deckard had seen in another old photograph, a newspaper clipping on the wall of a cramped, cluttered office at the Van Nuys Pet Hospital, back in the real L.A. on Earth. A moment of the past, a frozen section of time, caught and preserved; those people had been alive once, and then they had become memories.

"When . . ." The expression on Sarah's face grew more troubled. "When was this taken?"

"You can figure it out," said Deckard. He made no move from the parapet he leaned against, but pointed to the photo in the woman's hand. "Look at what he's wearing." That was also the same as it had been in the clipping on Isidore's office wall. "Look at the emblem on the breast pocket. That's the jumpsuit from the expedition. The picture was taken on board the *Salander 3.*"

He could tell, just from watching, that the meaning of the photograph was becoming clear for her. Bit by bit, as though the image was gradually moving into focus, the past it held becoming real once again.

"This wasn't on Earth." Sarah raised the photograph higher, a few drops of rain spattering against its empty white backing. "This must have been when they were still on their way to the Proxima system . . ."

"That's right." Deckard nodded. "Before . . . those other things happened."

In the artificial night, the glow from the lights suspended above was enough for her to make out all the details of the old photograph. There were more than just the two people, the adults, Ruth and Anson Tyrell, held in the image.

"If that's my parents . . ." Sarah spoke slowly, wonderingly. "Then . . . that must be me." She used the tip of the gun's muzzle to point. "One of those . . ."

That was what he had wanted her to see. What she needed to see. The photo's image was just as clear in Deckard's thoughts, as clear as it had been when Marley had taken it from the hiding place in the *Salander 3*'s first aid kit and had shown it to him.

There were two infants cradled against the new mother's breast, one nestled in the crook of each arm. "Your mother had twins," said Deckard simply. In that faraway time, on board the galleon, somewhere between Earth and the stars, Ruth Tyrell had looked exhausted but happy, smiling at the camera. In the photograph, Anson Tyrell had the traditional dazed grin. "Your father delivered them with the help of the *Salander 3*'s built-in medical circuits."

"Twins . . ." Sarah's voice was a murmur. "There were two of us . . ."

Deckard didn't stir from his position at the building's edge. "Twin female infants." He repeated verbatim what Marley had told him. "Two healthy baby girls. You and your sister. Sarah . . . and Rachael."

She looked up at Deckard when he spoke the second name. "My sister?" Sarah shook her head in disbelief. "That's impossible."

"It's true," said Deckard. "And there's proof. The little girl downstairs, inside this building—her name really is Rachael. She's not a hallucination. She's your twin sister."

"Oh, of course." Sarah gave a quick, sharp laugh. "Even though she's—what?—ten years old? There's a problem with that, Deckard. I'm sure you can see it."

"There's no problem. You and the little girl were born at the same time . . . or a few minutes apart. You're twins. But you know that bad things happened aboard the *Salander 3*; you know because you saw them when you went there again. After you and Rachael were born, something happened. To your father. And then a lot of bad things happened. Your mother managed to save not only you but your twin sister, Rachael, as well. But your mother died in the process—she was killed by the man who loved her. Insane when he killed her; sane—or close enough—when he killed himself."

"Still a problem, Deckard. Even if everything you say is true—" Sarah held the photo in one hand and the gun, still trained on him, in the other. "There was only one child taken off the *Salander 3* when it returned to Earth. And that was me."

"That's right." He returned her level gaze, straight into Sarah's eyes. "Your sister was left on board the *Salander 3*. In the sleep transport chamber that was part of the ship's equipment." When Marley had told him, he'd had a vision of the infant, a small, helpless thing inside the glass-lidded coffin, another of the suspended-animation devices like the one his own Rachael had slept and died in. "That was where your mother hid her to save her from your father. You were still in your mother's arms when your father killed her. Then the ship's autonomic circuits took care of you on the voyage back to Earth. And all the while, your twin sister, Rachael, slept on inside the transport chamber. Slept and didn't age—even after the *Salander 3* had returned home and you were taken from it. You're right; only one child was taken from the ship. Your twin sister, Rachael, was either overlooked where she was sleeping inside the transport chamber—the Tyrell Corporation employees who went aboard might not have searched very thoroughly, given the things they found when they went in—or she might've been deliberately left there. Either on Eldon Tyrell's orders or someone else's; I don't know. That part's still a mystery. Just like it's a mystery as to who took your sister, Rachael, out of the transport chamber ten years ago and left her there for the *Salander 3*'s autonomic circuits to rear. That might've been done on your uncle's orders as well." Deckard could hear a grating edge in his own voice. "He'd already started to let some of his—shall we say?—*personal* obsessions take over his thinking. That's what led him to have another Rachael created, a replicant based on you." An invisible knife carved away another section of Deckard's heart as he found himself speaking so coldly of the origins of the woman with whom he'd fallen in love. "Maybe Eldon Tyrell was too impatient to wait for the real Rachael, the child still inside the *Salander 3,* to grow up. So he found another way to get what he wanted."

"Don't be too hard on him." Sarah looked at the photo again. "I hated him and I wasn't sorry to hear that he was dead—but I've got a right to feel that way. You don't. My uncle was just another poor bastard who loved something too much. He must've loved Ruth . . . a great deal." Her voice went softer. "But he couldn't have her. Because she loved his brother, Anson, my father. And she went off with him. Far, far away . . ." Sarah slowly shook her head. "And that's what made him do the things he did, with me and with Rachael, the replicant he created. Because he loved *her.* He loved Ruth."

"Pygmalion." One word was all that Deckard spoke.

"What do you mean?"

There were still things that she needed to know. And that he had to tell her. "An old, old story," said Deckard. "About someone who fell in love with his own creation."

Sarah's gaze narrowed above the gun. "I don't know what you're talking about."

"It's simple." With one hand, Deckard brushed rain from the side of his face. "When the *Salander 3* left Earth, heading out on its mission to the Proxima system . . . *there were no humans aboard it.* Ruth and Anson Tyrell—the parents of you and your twin sister, Rachael—they weren't humans. They were replicants."

A look of panic flitted behind Sarah's widened eyes. "That's . . . that's impossible."

"Nothing is impossible." Deckard gazed at her sadly, as though regretting the need to speak of these things. "Especially not when it's part of the Tyrell Corporation's secret history. There's stuff you just don't know about. Eldon Tyrell did have a brother . . . but that brother died when he was a child. The Anson Tyrell that headed out to the Proxima system aboard the *Salander 3* was a replicant, created in the Tyrell Corporation's labs as a special, top-secret project. As was the female replicant they named Ruth. Neither one of them knew that they were replicants; like the adult Rachael—when I first met her at the Tyrell Corporation headquarters—they thought they were human. And they went on the *Salander 3* still believing that. They were misled about their own nature, what kind of creatures they were, so it's no surprise that they didn't know the actual reason for the *Salander 3*'s so-called mission to the Proxima system."

"Which was? According to you, I mean."

He shook his head. "It's not just according to me. I didn't figure out all this stuff—I wouldn't have been able to."

"Somebody told you this?" A cold fury narrowed Sarah's gaze. "Who?"

"Nobody you can touch. He's dead now." Deckard could still hear the other man's voice inside his head, the secrets that Marley had imparted to him. All the secrets of the world that Sarah Tyrell lived in, the world that she could never escape, no matter how she tried. The secrets that she had never known, that her uncle had never told her, that Eldon Tyrell had done his best to make certain she never found out. Deckard could see Marley leaning across the table in the bar's little booth, looking straight into his eyes . . . and seeing reality there. That all the words Marley spoke, all the connected bits of what had been purged from the Tyrell Corporation archives, were true. Eldon Tyrell had tried to murder the past, to make it cease to be . . . but he'd failed.

The past still existed. The record of it, the history of the *Salander 3* expedition—Eldon Tyrell had been able to do whatever he wanted with his corporation's archives, but even he hadn't been able to touch the U.N.'s top-secret databases. The rep-symps that Marley had worked for had managed to infiltrate the U.N.'s emigration agency, and they had found the truth, the evidence of that which they had already come to suspect.

Marley had told him . . . and now Deckard spoke the same words to the woman standing in front of him.

"The *Salander 3* was never meant to reach the Prox system." He watched Sarah's reaction to what he told her. "It didn't need to for Eldon Tyrell to find out what he wanted to know." The things that Marley had told him back in the bar in the Martian emigrant colony—Deckard recited them now, a well-memorized lesson. "All that the mission needed to accomplish was to get beyond the reach of the Earth's morphogenetic field. That's what keeps humans—and replicants—the way they are. On Earth, replicants don't reproduce; they don't have children. They can't; it's physiologically impossible. But what the *Salander 3*'s mission showed was that all that changes out in the stars. There had been indications of this before, but Eldon Tyrell required proof. And he got it." Deckard nodded toward the figure before him. "You're the proof that the *Salander 3* returned with. You and your twin sister, Rachael. The little girl down below us. The ship came back with the first two replicant children. The children born to the replicants that Eldon Tyrell had sent out there."

Rain had darkened Sarah's hair, a shining black curve

having come loose from where it'd been bound and now trailing alongside her throat. "That can't be . . ." The gun in her hand was studded with drops of water, like domed black sequins. "You're lying . . ."

He pointed to the photograph in her other hand. "There's the proof. That what I'm saying is true."

Her dark eyes flared in anger. "This is nothing!" Sarah flung the picture away; it landed facedown on the wet roof. "I don't know where you got that thing, and I don't care—"

"I got it," said Deckard, "from your mother. From the replicant Ruth Tyrell. In a way, that is; she had hidden it back aboard the *Salander 3.* Inside one of the first aid kits on the ship; she just had time to do that before she was hunted down and killed by your father."

"Really?" Sarah looked scornful. "And why would she want to do that?"

"I don't know." He gazed down at his own rain-wet hands for a moment. "Maybe she had found out something. Maybe . . . she suspected the truth about herself and about her children. There might have been a slip, something in the *Salander 3*'s computers that had been inadvertently left there by Eldon Tyrell, some little clue about the ship's mission." Deckard shrugged. "Or maybe not. Maybe it was just something that Ruth knew . . . inside herself. And she knew she had to leave a message, some kind of proof. So that people would know what had happened. And they did. They found the photograph, then hid it again, even better. It became a little sacred object, a relic. A holy thing. But it wasn't really for them; that wasn't why Ruth hid it there. It was for you." He brought his gaze back to Sarah's eyes. "So *you* would know. Her daughters."

The scornful expression had changed to one of desperation. "I still don't believe it. That photograph could've been faked—"

"Maybe so. But the things that happened aboard the *Salander 3*—the things you saw when you went there again, when you saw the past—those things couldn't have been faked. It really happened—that your father killed Ruth, that he would have killed you and your sister, Rachael, as well, if she hadn't managed to protect you." Deckard folded his arms across his chest. "There's only one possible explanation for all of that. The replicant named Anson Tyrell wouldn't have gone insane—murderously insane—for no reason. But the reason he did had been programmed inside him. By Eldon Tyrell. As a fail-safe protection in case it turned out that replicants could be made capable of reproducing themselves. He wanted to make sure that that knowledge was suppressed, so he built into Anson's brain a whole destructive sequence, a 'stepfather syndrome' based on primitive behavior patterns. And it worked; your father would've killed both you and your sister, Rachael, if he had been able to get to you. As it turned out, it was still enough to destroy both your mother and your father. That was enough; Eldon Tyrell could cover up or get rid of the other evidence about what had happened out there, what it meant. The only thing he didn't do was go ahead and have the two children destroyed, the daughters of the replicants he'd sent out on the *Salander 3*. Maybe it was guilt, maybe it was something else . . . but he let you live. Rachael went on sleeping in the transit chamber on board the ship, and you became his niece. Even you believed it—and why shouldn't you have? You thought you were human; you thought you were the original, the template, for the replicant Rachael that Eldon Tyrell created later." Deckard tilted his head back, letting the rain strike his eyelids, then looked over at Sarah again. "You just didn't know that that Rachael, the adult one, was a copy of a copy. A replicant of a replicant. Just because she wasn't a human . . . that doesn't mean you're one."

Sarah's gaze had fastened upon her hand, the one holding the gun, as though she were seeing it for the first time. "Who . . ." She spoke falteringly. "Who told you . . . all this . . ."

"Does it matter?"

"Whoever it was . . ." Her teeth clenched with anger. "They were lying."

"Sarah . . ." Her name, his voice low, the syllables as kindly said as possible. "You know it's true. You might not have known all the details, but the truth . . . you knew that all along. At least from the time you went back to the *Salander 3.* And you found her. The little girl; your sister. The first Rachael. She was real, and you knew it. You knew you weren't crazy; you knew you weren't suffering from some hallucination. Yet you kept on saying that you were, saying that she wasn't real, she didn't exist. Even though you knew she did." He drew a deep breath, the damp air filling his lungs. "You wouldn't have done that if you hadn't realized what it meant that that child should be there at all. And you knew somehow—you felt it—that she was your sister. That she was the same as you."

The words had had an impact on Sarah. She closed her eyes, swaying slightly where she stood, the gun's weight trembling in her hand. After a moment, she nodded slowly. "Yes . . ." Her voice was a whisper, barely audible. "I knew . . ."

"You knew," said Deckard. "But you did not believe. Because you didn't want to."

She said nothing. There was nothing more for her to say.

"Now what do you want?" He watched, pitying her now.

"I don't know." Sarah looked at the gun in her hand. "I suppose I could just go ahead and kill you." She sounded close to crying, a broken thing. "Since you don't love me. You never did."

"I never did. I never could."

She looked at him, eyes pleading. "Is that what I should do?"

"Maybe." Deckard shrugged. He felt tired, at the end of his own words. "But if you do that . . . remember . . ." He looked up at the video cameras watching them. "That's what they wanted you to do."

"You're right." Sarah nodded, her gaze focussed on some deep interior vista. "That's what I've always done. I've never even known what I wanted." She looked up at him. "But now I do."

He knew what she meant. He knew what would happen next. "Are you sure?"

Sarah nodded. "It was always going to come to this. You win, Deckard."

"No . . ." He shook his head. "You do. Because now you get what you want."

"I suppose you're right." Exhaustion sounded in her voice, as though from the long journey it had taken to reach this place. She managed a smile, a fragile turn of her mouth. "Could you . . ." She lowered her hand, letting the gun drop to her side. "Could you kiss me? The way you kissed her?"

No words. Deckard took her in his arms, feeling the warmth of her body through his own rain-soaked clothes. She turned her face, eyes closed, up to his.

Time stopped. Memory took its place. But even that had to end.

She was kind to him. She took care of herself.

The gun fell to the rooftop, a black shape surrounded by a thin, rippling mirror. Even as the echo of the shot rolled against the studio walls, the night city's false horizon. She fell then, and was still beautiful. He looked down at the crumpled form, something that might have once been human. The blood from her shattered temple flowed and mingled with the pooled rain.

Deckard looked up at the cameras. "How about that?" His furious shout battered the empty lenses. "Was that good enough? Did you get what you wanted?"

As though in answer, the observing spark died inside all the video cameras. The artificial rain had already stopped; now the lights came up, dispelling the false night. The taping was over. Deckard stood in the center of the building set's roof, a dead woman at his feet, one that had the face of someone he'd loved, now wrapped in the same sleep, the one from which there was no waking. The one he envied.

He still had a job to do. He left the gun where it lay, a few inches from Sarah Tyrell's hand, and walked back toward the stairs.

The Rachael child had fallen asleep at the table, her head upon the old leather-bound book. Deckard touched her shoulder; she sat up, blinking and frowning. She rubbed her eyes with her knuckles. "I'm kind of hungry," she announced.

"That's all right." Deckard took the child's hand and helped her from the high-backed chair. "We're going home."

The girl looked up at him as he led her toward the door, past the silent toys. "Where's that?"

"I don't know," said Deckard. "I guess we'll find out."

After

"Mr. Niemand—your papers are a mess." The U.N. bureaucrat looked at the documents spread across his desk and shook his head. "Do you really think you can get off this planet with your affairs in this condition?"

"I don't know," said Deckard. He leaned back in the uncomfortable chair that had been provided to him. "I don't much care, either."

The bureaucrat glanced up at him with small eyes filled by officious hatred. "You have an attitude problem as well." All the authority of the U.N.'s emigration program sounded in the man's voice. "Don't you?"

Deckard made no reply. The office, a tiny cubicle in the central administration building of the Martian emigrant colony, smelled like photocopy toner and the adrenaline of small-fry bullies. Deckard had no particular wish to be here at all; they had sent for him. The announcement of the resumption of travel to the far colonies had gone out a couple of weeks ago, but he hadn't bothered to make an application. *Let them come find me,* he'd decided.

And they had. The uniformed security men had shown up at the hovel, asking for him by pseudonym. He'd told the Rachael child to wait for him, that he'd be back before too long; then he'd pulled the door shut and had gone off with the grim-faced men on either side of him.

"Your original entry visa—" The bureaucrat flipped through a passport. "Shows that you came here with your wife." The mean little eyes raised from the leatherette-bound booklet. "Where's Mrs. Niemand?"

Deckard didn't even bother to shrug. "Why don't we just say . . . that she and I had domestic troubles."

The bureaucrat laid down the passport. "There's also nothing in the Niemand family documents about having a little girl with you. When you came to Mars, you were childless."

This time, he shrugged. "The domestic troubles didn't start right away."

"Obviously. From what our sources tell us, this child . . ." The small eyes glanced at another sheet of paper. "Reportedly named Rachael . . . is ten years old."

"That sounds about right."

"Mr. Niemand." The bureaucrat touched his fingertips together in a cage. "You haven't been on Mars for ten years."

"Then it's a mystery, isn't it"—Deckard looked straight back into the man's eyes—"how these things come about."

"No, it's not." Through his steepled hands, the bureaucrat regarded the figure on the other side of him. "Why don't we just cut the crap? We know who you really are."

Another shrug. "Good for you."

"We've gotten our orders . . . Mr. Niemand." The bureaucrat's lip curled as he spoke the alias. "From the top levels. We're to put you and the little girl on the next transport heading to the outer colonies. You wanted to emigrate?" He gathered the passport and other documents into a pile. "Then you're ready to go. Cleared, approved, expedited—you're out of here."

Deckard picked up the booklet on top of the rest, opened it, and looked at the rubber-stamped markings on the pages. "What if I don't want to go now? What if I've changed my mind?"

The eyes narrowed down to pinpricks. "It's not up to you."

He regarded his own hologram photo at the front of the passport, then laid it down. "You say you know who I am." Deckard kept his voice level, emotionless. "But what about you? Who are you?"

The bureaucrat's gaze shifted uneasily. "That doesn't matter. Mr. Niemand."

"It matters to me." Deckard leaned forward. "I don't know who the hell you are. You could be anybody." His voice grated harder. "You could be the U.N. You could be the cops; maybe you're really working for the LAPD. You could be the rep-symps; I don't know how far they've infiltrated the authorities. Maybe . . ." He studied the other man's round, insignificant face. "Maybe you're the Tyrell Corporation . . . that shadow of it. I just don't know."

"Let's face it." The bureaucrat showed an unpleasant smile. "Your track record on this sort of thing isn't the greatest. You can't even tell if I'm human or not."

"You're right. I can't even tell about myself anymore." Deckard slowly shook his head. "And I don't know why you want me to go out there. To the stars."

"You're not important," said the bureaucrat. Or whatever he was. "You don't matter at all. It's the girl. You know that much, don't you?"

Deckard kept his silence. The other man was right again. That was about all he knew for certain. He'd known it since he'd come back with the child from the Outer Hollywood station. She'd been born out there. *Far away,* he mused. *And strange.* The first replicant child, the beginning of that other species' inheritance. Of all that had once been considered the exclusive province of human beings.

There had been other things he'd agreed to carry to that place he'd never seen. And he'd lost them. For good or ill, he didn't know. But he still had the child with him. A child bearing his dead love's name, and her face with those dark, quietly watching eyes. *Rachael . . .*

That much he had also known. That whatever else happened—whatever he had to do, however it was made possible; whatever would come about when they reached that destination—he would take her there. That was the job he had, the job that he'd accepted.

"All right," said Deckard. He gathered up the other documents and held them with the passport in his hands. "I'll go." He pushed the chair back and stood up. "How much time do I have?"

The bureaucrat looked up at him. "The transport leaves in twelve hours." The small eyes were almost kind. "You're doing the right thing, Mr. Niemand."

"I don't know that." Deckard tucked the documents inside his jacket. He turned and grasped the knob of the office's thin door, then glanced over his shoulder at the other man. "And neither do you."

"It's not up to us, Mr. Niemand."

"Probably not." He pulled open the door. "Maybe out there I'll find out who does decide. And then I'll know."

The bureaucrat nodded. "Perhaps."

Deckard shut the door behind himself and headed down the narrow corridor. There was no hurry; the few things he had to pack for himself and the little girl wouldn't take long.

Whatever else they might need, he supposed, would be waiting for them at their journey's end.

About the Author

K. W. Jeter is one of the most respected sf writers working today. His first novel, *Dr. Adder,* was described by Philip K. Dick as "a stunning novel . . . it destroys once and for all your conception of the limitations of science fiction." Jeter's other books have been described as having a "brain-burning intensity" *(The Village Voice),* as being "hard-edged and believable" *(Locus)* and "a joy from first word to last" *(San Francisco Chronicle).* He is the author of thirteen novels, including *Farewell Horizontal, Wolf Flow,* and *Blade Runner 2: The Edge of Human.*